C. J. Grayson

CW00408538

DI Orion Tanzy Thriller
Book 3

C. J. GRAYSON

No One's Safe

C. J. Grayson

ISBN: 9798720534134
Print Edition August 2021
Version: First Edition

No One's Safe

Books by C. J. Grayson

Standalones –
Someone's There

DI Max Byrd & DI Orion Tanzy –
That Night (book 1)
Never Came Home (book 2)
No One's Safe (book 3)

'Many of life's failures are people who did not realize how close they were to success when they gave up.' - Thomas A Edison

1

Monday Evening
Napier Street, Darlington

Danny Walters finished the washing up, put the tea towel over the sink, and sighed. He was glad to be home with his family. After they had eaten, he'd put Mark and Peter to bed, kissed them both good night, then started his chores. They always demanded a bedtime story which, although was sometimes the last thing he wanted to do after a long, hard day, he relished it, as he too loved books.

He heard someone shout something from upstairs. It sounded like Peter, his youngest son, aged seven. He had been having bad dreams over the past year but recently had become worse. More graphic. More real. Danny had lost count of how many times he'd woke suddenly, discovering Peter standing by the side of the bed virtually camouflaged in darkness, staring at him.

'Just coming,' he said towards the dining room, hoping the sound would travel up the stairs to Peter's room.

His eldest son, Mark, had just turned eleven. He was in his bedroom playing on his Nintendo switch, no doubt with his headset on, so Walters knew he wouldn't be the one shouting; the game console was all he needed.

Danny's wife, Jessica, was out with her friends. Late night shopping or something. Said she'd be back in a few hours.

Walters left the narrow kitchen, made his way through the dining room, feeling the heat coming from the gas fire to the left and, although it wasn't cold outside, the boiler had broken for the second time in three months. Had no choice to hang the clothes neatly on an airer, place it a safe

ʻdistance from the fire, and hope the gas man would turn up tomorrow, as promised.

After he reached the top of the stairs, he looked along the narrow landing. Mark's door, the nearest on the left, was closed. The door beyond that was his and Jessica's room. The door straight ahead of him was Peter's, open a fraction.

'You okay, Peter?' Walters said, approaching the door, his footsteps creaking on the old floorboards below.

'Dad...' a soft voice said from inside the room.

Walters opened the door and stepped into the darkness. The light from the lamp at the end of the landing softly illuminated the room, allowing him to see Peter down in his single bed, his covers held tightly up to his chin.

'What's the matter, dude?' Walters asked, lowering to the bed.

'Dad, I'm scared,' he confessed.

'What you scared about, son?'

'I keep hearing noises. All the time.'

Walters could see the fear in his bright blue eyes, even in the dim conditions that surrounded them. He placed a palm on the side of Peter's face, stroked his cheek with his thumb.

'Don't worry about a thing. You're safe here.'

Peter looked away from him for a moment, unsure.

'What happened in the last house will never happen again, especially not here.' He fell silent, continued stroking his cheek. 'Go to sleep, okay?'

Peter managed a nod, turned onto his side, and closed his eyes.

'Good boy.' Walters stood up. 'I'll see you in the morning. Good night.'

'Good night, Dad.'

Walters edged Peter's door closed, padded along the landing, and opened Mark's door. He was hunched over on his bed, his attention on the Nintendo down in his hands.

'You okay, Mark?'

Mark glanced his way, nodded, and smiled. 'Yeah, Dad.' Then he focused back on his gaming.

'Ten more minutes on there, then shower, okay?'

Mark nodded again.

Walters closed the door and made his way downstairs. The dark feelings he thought he had control over slipped back into his mind as he entered the narrow kitchen. Shaking them away, he went over to the kettle, turned it on, then took a seat on one of the stools at the breakfast bar.

In silence, he slowly ran his fingers over the burns on his left forearm. An ugly reminder of what happened to them, what the monster did three years ago: set fire to their home.

Walters clamped his eyes shut, reliving the horrific moments in his head. He remembered he kissed Jessica goodnight and turned over to go to sleep. Shortly after, the fire alarm downstairs went off, a searing noise ripping through the house waking Walters up. The smoke drifted in through the bottom of the door. Then he'd heard his sons coughing and shouting in their rooms, followed by them banging urgently on the wall.

After he had woken Jessica, they stepped out onto the landing, grabbed Peter and Mark, and stood at the top of the stairs, staring down into the black smoke and dancing orange flames. There was no way out. It would only be a matter of time before the flames consumed the whole house.

They had returned to Peter's room and ran over to the window. Walters had elbowed the glass hard, causing it to explode outwards onto the roof of the kitchen below. He'd grabbed a t-shirt, wrapped it around his knuckles, and punched the remaining shards that were dangerously protruding around the edge of it.

He had helped Jessica through, who turned, waiting with open arms for Peter and Mark. One by one, she carefully helped them down before they made their way along the pitched roof away from the flames.

As Walters looked back at the landing from the window, he'd noticed the smoke was thick and black. The carpet on the landing had started to go up in flames; it wouldn't be long before Peter's bedroom went up too.

As he turned to the window towards his wife and the helpless faces of his two sons, that's when the explosion happened. It threw him forward through the window onto the kitchen roof with an unexplainable force, bending his arm the wrong way and breaking his ankle. His family, although lucky to be seven metres from the window, were thrown off the roof into the alley below, suffering several broken bones. The fire brigade had climbed onto the roof and saved his life. The family then spent five days in the hospital to recover, but Walters spent most of his time in the burns unit for the damage to his back and left arm.

After investigators checked the house, they couldn't work out the cause of the fire. Had it been a gas leak? Loose wiring? No one was sure.

Walters blinked himself to the present and made a cup of coffee. He sat back down on the stool, checked his phone. There was a message sent from one of his friends, Mick, which he opened and read, but apart from that, the usual rubbish on social media, people who he had as friends but weren't really friends, updating everyone on trivial things like what they'd made for dinner or checking themselves in somewhere, showing off they were getting out the house and lived exciting lives.

Moments later, the front door opened. Jessica, with several bags in her hand, walked into the kitchen, smiling.

'Hey,' Walters said. His eyes fell on her purchases below. 'Spend much?'

Her smile faded fast. 'Listen, it's on my card. I'll pay it all back next month.'

Walters half smiled and gazed back down at his phone. Something he had heard all before. Ever since they almost died, she decided to live life to the fullest. And that included buying unnecessary clothes, handbags, and God knows whatever else.

'It's just clothes. I even got us a nice new clock for in here.'

He looked beyond her to the clock that she had bought only two months ago and sighed. 'There's nothing wrong with that one.'

As she unpacked her bags and showed him her purchases, he smiled when she held up a black shirt she'd bought him for the weekend. She leaned in to kiss him but when he didn't fully commit to the kiss, she asked what was wrong.

'It's nothing…' he replied.

'We've been married for six years. Together for twelve. I know you. What's the matter?'

'Peter said he was scared earlier. He's okay.'

She smiled sadly. 'Is Mark on his Nintendo?'

He nodded. 'He'll be coming off in a minute.'

'Have you found your key yet?'

Walters shook his head. 'God knows where that is. It must have unclipped itself when I was out earlier. Good job you were in and we have spares. I'll get more cut tomorrow.'

They chatted for a while about their day then she told him she was going upstairs to kiss them goodnight. At their bedroom doors, she watched them for a long time. Their little sweet faces, the way the landing light gently illuminated their innocence.

Walters came upstairs, passed her, then went into their bedroom. 'You coming to bed?'

'In a minute,' she whispered. She eventually edged their doors closed and entered the bedroom, slipped off her clothes, and put her nightie on.

'Everything locked up?' she asked, climbing into bed.

Walters nodded and picked up a book from his bedside table. He read four chapters before his eyes got heavy, and placed it back, then succumbed to sleep.

Something woke him.

The bedroom would have been in total darkness if it wasn't for a slither of light on the landing. Something was different.

He turned over, looked at the door.

There was something blocking the light.

He rubbed his eyes, sat up, and swivelled his legs off the bed. Behind him, Jessica was sleeping soundly. Standing, he opened the door fully, and stepped out onto the landing.

'Peter?'

Peter was standing in the middle of the landing facing away from him. 'Peter, what are you doing?'

Peter stayed perfectly still.

'Peter?' Walters said, slowly approaching him, in case he was sleepwalking, which he'd done on several occasions over the past few months. He made his way towards him, feeling something wet on the floor under his bare feet. It wasn't the first time Peter had wet himself. One time, they had woken up and found him standing at the wardrobe with the door open, urinating all over their clothes.

'Peter, are you okay?' Walters asked him.

Peter, standing there in only his pants, didn't reply.

Walters placed a soft hand on his shoulder, feeling his son's warm skin. 'Peter, are you awake?'

'Yes, Dad,' he whispered suddenly.

The carpet was saturated, but Walters knew it would clean. It always did. It was just a shame they were cleaned the day before.

'Come on, Son. Let's get you back to bed.'

Walters slowly turned Peter around, guided him back to his bedroom. He changed his pants, put him back into bed, then smiled, knowing one day, he'd grow out of it.

Back on the landing, he frowned down at the carpet. It seemed too wet for one of Peter's occasional accidents. He padded along the landing, observing the wet carpet which seemed to reach the stairs.

The carpet was drenched, which was strange because two days ago, a cleaner had professionally done them and he was sure they'd almost dried. The chemicals that he'd used had left a slight odour, but the guy who'd done them said not to worry about that, and that it would go in a day or two.

But the smell was something stronger. 'This makes no sense.'

At the end of the landing, he leaned around the top of the stairs and looked down into the dark hallway below. The carpet on the stairs was also soaked. He glanced back along the landing towards his bedroom, thinking hard.

'It doesn't make sense, at all.'

His focus returned to the stairs but, this time, he saw someone standing at the base of them, looking up with a smile on their face.

'You?' Walter said. 'Wha…'

In the man's hand was a lit match. Then it dawned on him it wasn't Peter's urine on the stairs, it was petrol. The whole staircase and landing carpets were doused in flammable petrol.

Walters gasped and froze, feeling a sheet of heat envelope his whole body; every hair stood on end when he realised what was happening.

The man at the bottom of the stairs didn't say a word. He simply smiled, dropped the match on the bottom step, and laughed as the flames raced up the stairs.

Walters frantically dashed along the landing but, before he reached the first bedroom door, he felt his skin already burning.

2

Tuesday Early Morning
Napier Street, Darlington

DI Orion Tanzy turned off the engine, yawned, and looked through the windscreen at the house. Outside of it, an ambulance, a fire engine, and three police cars were parked. Officers nearby spoke with each other. A perimeter had been set up on either side, spanning the width of the narrow terraced street, preventing public access from both sides.

He stepped out, locked the Golf, and made his way towards the crime scene tape where people were standing, watching what was happening. On his approach Tanzy heard a lady in her mid-twenties, dressed in a white dressing gown and slippers that looked like they needed throwing out, asking PC Josh Andrews what was going on. Andrews, a tall, good looking Police Constable holding a clipboard, told her that information couldn't be given out just yet. Tanzy stepped around the small cluster of people and smiled at PC Andrews.

'Morning, boss,' Andrews said, turning away from the woman.

'Hey, Josh.' Tanzy, wearing a thin black jacket, black jeans, and black shoes, ducked under the tape. 'Is Max here yet?'

'Yeah, he's inside. Arrived about five minutes ago. He's beat you again.'

Tanzy smiled. 'Thanks.'

Outside the front door, the senior forensic officers, Jacob Tallow and Emily Hope were there, wearing their standard white paper overalls, their masks pulled down under their chin. Near them, were a few PCs who Tanzy knew, and, beyond them, at the other end of the street, standing behind the tape, were more people being held back by PC Amy Weaver.

Tallow and Hope glanced Tanzy's way as he approached.

'Morning, you two.'

'Morning, Orion,' Tallow said, nodding. Tallow was tall and thin, just over six foot four. He made Tanzy, who was six foot two, seem small. He had short black hair and hadn't shaved for over a week, which was unusual for Tallow. In his hand, there was a small clear plastic bag with something black inside. Whatever it was, Tanzy didn't know.

'Hey, Ori,' Hope said, half smiling. She was thin, held the qualities and curves of what some men, would call, the perfect woman. Her short blonde hair and excessive tattoos gave her an aura that she didn't give a shit, took none of it, and got on with things.

'What's happening?' Tanzy asked.

Tallow sighed heavily.

'That bad?'

Hope nodded. 'It's tragic, Ori. We've come out. We needed a breather.'

'God's sake.' Tanzy looked beyond them at the small crowds and vehicles parked in the centre of the road. People who lived across the road were looking out their windows at the commotion as if they had nothing better to do. 'Where's Max?'

'He's upstairs, Ori.'

'Who was the first responder?'

Tallow turned, pointed a few houses down. DC Anne Tiffin was speaking with a man Tanzy didn't know, probably a neighbour. Everything he said seemed to be noted on the pad in Tiffin's hand. Moments later, she smiled and nodded at him, then made her way towards Tanzy.

'Hey, boss.'

Tanzy smiled. 'First here?'

She nodded.

'That was quick.'

She explained to him she'd just started her shift and was heading over to Stanhope Road to speak with a resident who'd had her car stolen, so was nearby. 'I'll sign you in, Orion.' She pulled a sheet from behind her notepad and jotted something down.

'Here,' Hope said to him from his left, bending down to her bag. She handed Tanzy some overshoes. He put them on. She bent down again and grabbed something else.

Through the front door a thick-set fireman stepped down onto the path and smiled at Tanzy, then passed him, going over to the fire truck.

'You'll need this too,' Hope added. 'The smell is horrendous in there.'

He took the facemask and hooked it around his ears. 'I'll see you in there,' he said, stepping up into the house.

3

Tuesday Early Morning
Napier Street, Darlington

Tanzy could smell it inside the hall. He couldn't describe it but gagged in his mask. He moved forward, his feet slowly crunching on the black, crispy floor below, then glanced along towards the stairs that had been scorched to charcoal.

Upstairs, he heard voices, and immediately recognised Byrd and the crime scene manager, Tony McCabe. He moved closer to the base of the stairs and, to his right, stopped at the living room. The fire had barely touched it. The leather sofa against the wall looked new, the carpet, albeit a small area near the door, was untouched. Moving on, the next room was the dining room. He popped his head in to have a look. Everything a foot below the ceiling was as it should be. Two chairs positioned near the wall to the right, a desk housing a flat-screen monitor and computer in the right alcove, and a rectangular dining table with six chairs neatly tucked in around it. Everything within a foot of the ceiling was black. The flames must have burnt the ceiling and protruded through but spread no further.

There was a crunch to his left. He looked to see a fireman walking in from a door on the other side, presumably from a kitchen, judging by the house's layout.

'Hello,' the fireman said with a coarse voice, which Tanzy guessed was either from smoking or entering countless burning buildings. He stood short and stocky, had a thick moustache. Even though the fire station was situated next to the police station, Tanzy didn't recognise him. Not that they mingled with the fire department much.

'Hey,' said Tanzy. 'Bad one, eh.'

'No kidding.'

The fireman stopped and looked up at the ceiling for a moment, analysing something only he understood.

'I'm DI Tanzy.'

'Roger Carlton,' he replied, extending his hand.

'What are you looking for?'

'Just damage really.'

'Did it make it through there?' Tanzy asked, pointing behind him to the kitchen.

He continued to stare at the ceiling but knew where Tanzy meant, and said, 'No.'

Tanzy wasn't an expert on fires, and wasn't qualified enough to investigate one, but he understood the basics. 'Where was the origin?'

The fireman looked at him. 'The stairs. I'll show you.' Tanzy stepped back into the hallway, allowing him to pass through the door.

'The stairs is where it started,' he began, then lowered a little, pointing to the third step. 'See this.'

Tanzy leaned forward. The step was jet black and brittle.

'I believe this is our point of origin. I don't know if you can smell it but petrol has been used here. See how the third one differs from the second? And how it almost trails up the stairs in a kind of snake motion. The burning is different on the walls compared to the carpet, and that's not just because of the difference in materials either.'

Tanzy nodded. 'Okay.'

'Nasty work,' Roger said. He stood up and returned to the dining room.

'Thanks for the help.'

Tanzy very slowly moved up the stairs, one at a time. The paint on the walls and skirting boards had been fiercely stripped, leaving ashy plasterboard, crispy flaking paint, and exposed shrunken wood.

The higher he went, the smell worsened. It was a mixture of burnt wood, paint, used petrol, and human flesh. He'd smelled burnt skin before; it was one of the worst things he'd ever smelt.

When he reached the top, he turned right, stepping up a couple of steps until he reached the landing. It was a different scene. The carpet up here had vanished, leaving exposed wooden floorboards with holes dotted around where the petrol had helped the fire burn. The walls had been stripped of plasterboard, exposing singed brickwork, copper pipes, and curled up electrical wiring. The house, Tanzy guessed was probably built in the 1930s. The solid structure no doubt would have acted as a barrier against the fire compared to modern-day stud walls, but evidently, it hadn't been enough.

Up ahead, there were three rooms. All doors were open.

He moved along the landing and stopped at the first door on the left. Inside, the smell was horrendous. A few feet from the door, inside the room, stood Tony McCabe and DI Max Byrd, pointing to various parts of it. They seemed to have become accustomed to the smell, their face masks lowered under their chin.

'Hey,' said Tanzy, standing at the burnt doorframe.

Byrd glanced his way. 'Hey, Ori.'

Tanzy absorbed the room, which was black from floor to ceiling. Everything inside had been burnt, including the large body of a male lying in the middle of the floor and a smaller body curled up below the window at the far end of it. The sun shining through the window showed them how the flames had heavily scorched the window too.

'They had no chance, did they?' Tanzy noted.

Byrd looked his way and shook his head sadly. 'No.'

Tanzy stepped inside further. 'Father and son?'

'Looks that way,' McCabe replied, then he looked over to the boy in the corner. 'He's probably no older than ten. Imagine the pain they endured.'

'Unimaginable.' Tanzy exhaled heavily, gazing around at the sea of ash-coated items: single bed, table, chair, television, games console. If not for the shape, they'd be unrecognisable. 'Just the father and son?'

Byrd looked his way. 'No. Come this way.' He stepped around Tanzy out onto the landing, then took a left into the front bedroom. In the corner, were two figures crouching down holding each other. They resembled black mannequins you'd see in a shop window, apart from the skin being shiny and smooth, it was crispy and rough.

'Jesus. The whole family gone like that.' Tanzy looked down for a moment. 'Who the hell did this to them?'

McCabe walked in. He was short but stocky, had shoulders like boulders. His younger years spent boxing hadn't helped his looks but certainly had given him that rough, don't-take-shit-from-anyone attitude. 'Some evil bastards. I heard the origin was at the bottom of the stairs. My guess is that the father heard something and went out onto the landing. Then someone lit the stairs and he went into his son's room. The other child came out of his room and came in here with mum. Judging by their windows, it would have been impossible to get out. Same story in there, the only way to get out would be to break the windows.'

The windows looked like they only opened from a small area at the top. There'd be no way to climb up and safely get down.

'Why didn't they try?'

McCabe shrugged. 'Maybe they didn't have time. We'll leave that up to the investigator to determine the spread of the fire.'

'Do we know who the family are?'

Byrd nodded. 'Yeah. According to a neighbour, the husband was Danny Walters. The wife was called Jessica. And their two sons were Mark and Peter. They were eleven and seven.'

Tanzy didn't say anything, instead looked down sadly at Jessica and one of the boys.

They spent a few minutes in the room, then turned, and made their way downstairs. Coming through the door was the familiar face of Harry Law, the senior fire investigator.

They shook hands, a professional courtesy. Byrd and Tanzy had worked with him on previous occasions, but unfortunately, it was under similar circumstances.

'Apparently, the origin was right here,' Tanzy said, pointing to the third step behind him.

Law frowned and looked past him to the step. 'It is. How do you know that?'

'One of your men told me before I went upstairs. The guy with the moustache. Carlton.'

'Carlton?' Law asked.

'Roger Carlton. He was showing me before.'

'We don't have anyone here named Roger Carlton.'

It was Tanzy's turn to frown. 'If he's not in here, then he's outside. He was here only minutes ago.'

They checked the dining room and the kitchen and found both of them empty.

'I've been outside talking with forensics,' Law said. 'No one has come out.'

'If he didn't go out the front, then he's gone out that way,' Byrd said, pointing through the French doors that led into the small, narrow yard.

Tanzy and Law came back from the kitchen and looked out the window. At the end of the yard, the back gate was wide open.

4

Tuesday Early Morning
Napier Street, Darlington

The man who called himself Roger had seen what he wanted to: what he was looking for wasn't there.

He'd heard someone walk through the door and stop at the base of the stairs. He thought it would be better to leave the kitchen, pretend he was looking at something on the dining room ceiling.

Good job he did.

A detective by the name of Tanzy had started speaking with him, asking him about the fire. If he hadn't been responsible for pouring petrol on the stairs and landing, then igniting them, he wouldn't have been able to tell him where the point of origin was. He didn't know as much as a fire investigator, but he believed the detective bought the story.

He left the alley behind Napier Street and took a right - still dressed in the uniform he'd found on eBay and walked towards Duke Street. He crossed the road and glanced behind him.

No one was running out of the alley frantically looking for him. He was safe, for now.

He took a left into East Raby Street and saw his car parked up ahead. The street was quiet. It was before eight. He imagined the people inside the houses as he passed them, just waking up to another normal day, the kids off to school, the parents off to work, all eating their cereal around the table with their heads over their iPads, not knowing what had happened last night only a few streets away. They may have heard the fire engine late last night, but people only care about that for a moment, until the lights pass and the sounds fade away before it returns to normal. The media would be there, with their eager reporters and happy snappy photographers. He couldn't wait to see it on the news later.

He used a fob from his pocket to open the car and got inside. Once there, he took off his helmet, placed it on the seat next to him. He then carefully took the fake moustache off his upper lip and dropped it in the passenger footwell.

He started the car, put the gear in first, and edged out, making his way to the bottom of the street, where he took a left and went back up Duke Street. At Larchfield Street, he went right, idling along until he reached Napier Street and slowed to a crawl, looking down at the sea of police and firemen beyond the small crowds of people. Amongst the people standing near the door, he spotted the detective who he'd spoken to in the dining room, looking confused.

He smiled, looked forward, and whispered, 'Fire, fire, fire,' over and over again until he arrived home.

5

Tuesday Early Morning
Napier Street, Darlington

Outside the house, Tanzy and Byrd asked DC Tiffin, the first one on the scene and first responder, if anyone with the name 'Roger Carlton' was on her list.

She frowned, looked down at the paperwork.

'No, he's not here.'

The fire superintendent, Harry Law, walked out of the house a moment later.

'No, he's not on the list. He didn't come in the front way,' Byrd said to him.

'Why was he in there?' Tanzy said to no one in particular.

A few moments later, they heard footsteps behind them. They turned to see Emily Hope and Jacob Tallow, the two senior forensics, dressed in their white disposable coveralls and face masks. They both took off their masks, relieved to finally breathe some clean air.

'How's it going?' Byrd asked them.

Harry Law, a tall, overweight man, with a goatee - the kind you would see standing outside of a pub as a bouncer you wouldn't want to mess with – turned towards the senior forensic officers, interested in their answer. From the years he had been doing it, he had seen his fair share of fires and the damage they had caused. Seldom had he walked into something like this: a family of four burnt to a crisp. It was tragic, to say the least.

Hope sighed, looked towards Tallow, who met her gaze then looked back at Law and the detectives. Tallow knew Hope didn't want to discuss it with Byrd and Tanzy.

'I think you know roughly what happened,' Tallow started, 'but from what we've seen so far'—-he looked towards Law—'I'm hoping you guys can tell us, that Danny Walters was affected first, probably on the landing, judging by his position in the back bedroom. I think he spotted the fire and went in to save his son, then died halfway across the bedroom from the pain, more so that his body giving up.'

It was a known fact that when the body endures something excruciatingly painful, it shuts down. In medical terms, it's called Vasovagal Syncope. The brain tells the body it can't cope with it, momentarily shutting down. In this case, the smoke would have helped quicken the process.

'The fire took the whole room and got to his son who'd hid in the corner. I noticed scratches on the window where he'd clawed at it. He probably wasn't strong enough to break the glass.'

Byrd winced, imagining the scene in his head.

'The mother and other son found in the front bedroom tried to stay out of it, but I think, judging by the markings on the floor, that both bedrooms had been covered in petrol beforehand.'

'How can you be sure?' Tanzy asked.

'I'm not one hundred percent, and I'm no fire expert, but the carpet in the smaller front bedroom is different. You see, a material burns differently when there is something flammable on it. If this is the case, and both rooms were doused in petrol, they didn't stand a chance.'

Byrd looked towards Law. 'Does that sound right? Would you also say that the bedrooms had been covered in petrol?'

Law nodded. 'I agree with your colleague here.'

'So, so-called Roger Carlton walked into the house,' Byrd said, 'went into their bedroom, covered the carpets in petrol without waking anyone up?'

Law and Hope and Tallow all shrugged, not sure if that would be possible.

Byrd looked at the floor, then back to Tallow. 'Are there signs of a break-in?'

'We haven't got around to that yet,' he explained. 'We need to check the windows and the doors.'

'Guys, have a look out the back,' a voice said behind them.

They turned and standing in the hallway was DC Leonard.

'When did you get here?' Tanzy asked him.

'Minutes after you did,' Leonard said.

'What have you found, James?'

'Come and have a look.'

6

Tuesday Early Morning
Napier Street, Darlington

DC Leonard led them down the hall, through the dining room, into the kitchen, then through the back door into the narrow yard. It was a nice little space, with plant pots along the wall to the right and a trellis on the wall half-covered with a green plant growing through it. The sun was rising strongly from the east, hitting the yard from the left, brightening it up.

He walked halfway down the yard and stopped.

Byrd, Tanzy, Hope, Tallow, and Harry Law stopped behind him, wondering what he'd found that was so important to show them.

'What is it?' Byrd asked, unsure what he was about to be shown.

Leonard pointed at the far corner of the yard. Everyone looked. There were three bikes locked up under a slanted roof which had been built purposefully to keep them dry during wet weather.

'What are we supposed to be looking at?' Tanzy asked him.

'You see it?'

Tallow nodded. 'I can. The camera just under the roof?'

Leonard nodded. 'Yes.'

Tanzy stepped forward looking around for the wire coming out of it. It didn't take him long to see it trail across the wall at the back until it hit the brickwork and went through into the house.

'We'll be able to see Roger Carlton leaving if it still works,' Tanzy noted, remembering the back gate open earlier.

'Good spot,' Byrd praised him.

Byrd and Tanzy stepped back into the kitchen and looked down, trying to spot a wire coming in a similar height. The further they went, the more their frowns deepened.

'Where is it?'

Tanzy shrugged.

At the end of the kitchen, there was a closed door. Tanzy opened it, revealing a small bathroom that made him feel claustrophobic. You couldn't even swing a cat. The toilet was on the right, a small basin opposite, and a narrow, short bath against the far wall, with minimal floor space. Up on the wall to the right, he saw a wire enter through the plasterboard. It had been painted over with the same colour as the walls.

'There.'

They followed it along the wall's width until it dropped vertically, then a metre off the floor, it went through to the kitchen. Tanzy backed out and looked in the corner of the worktop. There was a small black electronic box, roughly the same size of a wireless router. It was plugged in but there was no power.

'It's dead,' Byrd said, noticing the plug was on but the green light wasn't.

'The DB is probably under the stairs. Will have been destroyed in the fire.'

Byrd's brows furrowed to the centre of his forehead. 'The DB?'

'Distribution board. The main electrical box.'

'If we took it, we could give it to Mac. He'd be able to get it going or at least find out what happened before the fire.'

Tanzy nodded and met with Leonard and the forensics. 'We're gonna head back, see what's on here. If Roger Carlton or whoever he is, left through that gate, then we need to get a better look at him. See if we can identify him.' He looked at Tallow. 'You guys be okay?'

Tallow nodded. 'We'll be here most of the day. There's loads to do.'

Byrd and Tanzy both knew what was involved in forensic work and would catch up with them later back at the station. As they left through the front door, DC Tiffin signed them out. Byrd took off his mask and held it in his hand.

'Where you parked?'

Tanzy pointed along the street at his Golf.

They walked side by side back to their cars. 'How's Claire doing?'

Byrd nodded. 'She's good. She's getting really big.'

'Must be coming up six months soon, is it?'

'She calls it weeks. Twenty-five weeks. Roughly six months.'

'See you back at the station. I can't wait to tell Fuller all about this one.'

Byrd smiled and got into his car.

7

Byrd and Tanzy hung their coats on the back of their chairs at the rear of the long, rectangular office. The six rows of desks were split by a walkway down the middle, leaving two desks on either side of each row. Tanzy and Byrd were seated at the back on the left-hand side. Directly behind them was DCI Martin Fuller's office.

No doubt he'd heard what had happened early this morning and would be expecting both Byrd and Tanzy to inform him as soon as they returned.

Byrd knocked on his door, waited for the usual 'Come in', and opened it. Tanzy followed. At the desk, they both took a seat on the empty chairs opposite to Fuller.

'Morning,' Fuller said.

He was a thick-set man with short dark hair and possessed a look of impatience about him. He wasted no time getting to the point and didn't care if his peers liked him or not. Being a DCI was a job where you had to get on with things and manage people in a certain way. You had a lot of responsibility and things moved fast. He'd been the DCI for nearly five months, taking over the role after DCI June Thornton had gone. He ran things differently to how she had, but everyone in the office seemed to be getting used to his way. They didn't agree with his methods but nodded and smiled. He had a scar on the right side of his face from a knife attack when he was only weeks into his training. It didn't improve his looks, that's for sure.

'Tell me...' he said to them.

Byrd sighed. 'House fire, boss.'

Fuller waited, stared hard at them.

Byrd continued. 'Looks like petrol was used. It wasn't an accident.'

'How many dead?'

'Four. Father, mother, and two sons.'

It was Fuller's turn to sigh. He looked down at the desk and stayed silent for a moment. The detectives waited.

'I knew it wouldn't last,' he said, shaking his head.

'What's that?' Tanzy asked him.

'We've had three great months, three'—he held up three fingers—'months. Darlington was on the rise. Our figures have been great compared to what happened a few months ago.'

Byrd felt his skin warming and decided to keep silent. It was all about the figures to Fuller. All about how his team weighed up against the other constabularies. God, it wasn't a bloody competition and it bloody pissed Byrd off.

'Anyway, what do we know?'

'Fire was started at the base of the stairs. With the carpets being doused in petrol, it took no time for it to spread up the stairs. According to Hope and Tallow, and Harry Law, who also agreed, that the carpets had also been covered in petrol before the fire had started.'

'So, whoever did it, had gone into the bedrooms whilst they were sleeping?'

'Seems so,' Tanzy said.

'Jesus. Takes balls that.'

'When I was there, I was speaking to a guy who called himself Roger Carlton. He was looking at the ceiling in the dining room and told me about the fire. Turns out, after speaking with Harry Law, that no one by that name works for the fire department. When we went to look for him, he'd gone. The back gate was open.'

'How on earth did he just walk in?' Fuller said, frowning, picking up his coffee and taking a sip.

'We don't know.' Byrd this time, shrugging. 'But we found something.'

Fuller waited.

'Credit to DC Leonard. He found a camera at the end of the yard. We traced the wire back and found a little black box at the end of the kitchen. Fortunately, it doesn't look like the fire had reached the kitchen. We've handed the box to Mac in DFU. He said he'd check it out straight away. We'll head over when we leave here.'

DFU stood for Digital Forensics Unit.

'Okay. What do we know about the victims?' Fuller leaned back into his chair.

'So far, not much. We need to do some digging.'

'Forensics?'

'Still at the house.'

Fuller nodded. 'Keep me updated.'

Byrd and Tanzy stood up, left the office, and sat down at their desks. According to a neighbour, they obtained the name Danny Walters and searched that first. Several results came up, so they narrowed the search to Darlington. There was only one. He was forty-one years old.

A little later, after several cups of coffee, they'd built up a profile for him. He worked at B&Q as a customer service assistant and had no previous criminal convictions. He was a straight shooter, according to the facts.

'Why him, though?' Tanzy asked, looking at the same info on his screen. 'No previous trouble. Did a level six diploma in Business Management and used to work in the engineering sector as a commissioning engineer. He seems pretty normal.'

'They always do, Ori.'

They continued to dig.

'How are Pip and the kids?' Byrd asked.

'Good. She hasn't touched a drop for six months now. She received her badge last week and came home with the biggest smile on her face. She's feeling much better about herself and life in general.' Tanzy's wife, Pip, had had issues with drinking and had constantly been hitting the bottle over the past few years. She says it's down to her father, the way he used to treat her and her mother. Violence. Sexual abuse. The stories weren't pleasant.

'The kids are great too. Jasmine will be eleven soon, still knows everything. And Eric is loving his Lego. Should have seen the tower he built for me last night. Told me he wanted to put it beside my bed so I could wake up to it every day.'

Byrd smiled. 'Kids, eh.'

'You'll soon find out, Max.'

'I will. It won't be long.' Byrd clicked his mouse a few times, then asked, 'How's the judo going?'

'Good. They're coming on.' By 'they' he meant his students.

Tanzy had done Judo since he was six years old. Recently he'd started tutoring at the Dolphin Centre with beginner classes but now helps with some of the advanced classes, too. At six foot two, weighing barely twelve stone, with a six-pack that every man envied and most women desired, he was a hit with the ladies. His short – almost bald – hair took no maintenance and trimmed goatee enhanced his beautiful narrow face.

Byrd, however, wasn't possessed with such looks. His hair was much longer – which looked like it hadn't been brushed today – and he was clean-shaven. Months ago, you may have said Byrd was overweight, and if he was being honest with himself, he'd agree, but he'd continued to play football with his friends twice a week and started taking care of himself. The two stones he'd lost a few months ago had stayed off, and he was feeling fit again. He'd never had the six-pack that Tanzy had, nor did he care, but settled on being content.

'You fancy it?' Tanzy asked him.

'Judo isn't for me, Ori. I'll stick to football.'

Tanzy threw a smile his way, knowing it was a previous topic they'd discussed.

On the desk next to Byrd, the phone rang. He picked it up.

'It's Mac. I've had a look at the camera footage from Napier Street.'

'Anything interesting?'

'You need to see this.'

8

Tuesday Afternoon
Police Station

Byrd and Tanzy immediately went to see Mac, who was waiting for them at his desk. He had positioned two chairs for them in front of his computer screen.

Mac was approaching the age of forty. He'd been doing digital forensics for nearly twenty years; there was no one in the force as good as him. Due to the nature of his job, which involved sitting at a desk for most of the day, he'd put on weight. They often had seen him eating chocolate bars or noticed empty crisp packets on his desk.

Without a word, the detectives sat down and pulled themselves in. Byrd noticed the black box they had retrieved from the kitchen earlier that morning on the desk next to his keyboard with a wire plugged into it from the computer.

'Watch,' Mac said, clicking several times.

On the screen, there was a date. Today's date. He took the mouse, clicked on the time bar at the bottom, and dragged it just past eight am. The camera had the ideal view of the French doors that led to the dining room and the back door leading to the kitchen. A minute later, the man who called himself Roger Carlton stepped out quickly and headed towards the gate then vanished.

'Go back,' Byrd said. 'Pause it on his face.'

Mac did. Byrd looked at Tanzy.

'That the guy you spoke with?'

'Yeah.'

'How tall was he?' Byrd asked Tanzy.

Tanzy thought for a moment. 'He wasn't six foot. Maybe five, ten.'

Because of the yellow composite helmet he was wearing, they couldn't see his hair properly but could tell it was long. The visor on the helmet was pushed up, shielding his eyes but the moustache stood out like a sore thumb.

'Is that tash real?' asked Byrd.

'It looked real,' said Tanzy.

'Tom Selleck would be proud of that,' Mac noted.

'What time did you speak with him?' Byrd asked.

'Just after eight.'

'Go earlier this morning, see what time he got there.'

Mac had already done this before calling the detectives and stopped the time at 7.49 a.m., then pressed play. Roger Carlton appeared on the camera a moment later, coming from the right where the back gate was. He walked up to the back door, pulled out a key, and opened it.

'Where did he get the key from?' Tanzy asked, confused.

Mac smiled, closed the video, then hovered his mouse over another file, and clicked open. 'Watch this.'

They both frowned at the time and date at the bottom of the screen, indicating it was two days earlier.

'What's this?' Tanzy asked.

Mac pointed at the screen. At 2.03 p.m. on Sunday, the back door opened, and a man stepped out with some kind of cleaning device. It was roughly two feet high and a foot wide. Most of it was made of see-through plastic. The liquid inside was black. The man stepped out and immediately Byrd and Tanzy knew it was Roger Carlton. He stood in the corner of the yard near the back door and pulled off the top of the unit, then picked it up and tipped the contents down the drain.

'What on earth is he doing?' said Tanzy.

'So, he was there two days ago?' asked Byrd, a deep frown lining his forehead.

'It certainly looks like him,' Mac said, with a shrug.

Roger turned and, before he went back into the kitchen, they got a view of his face. His moustache was clearly visible, and the thick mop of black hair too.

Mac scrolled the time back, and they watched it multiple times.

'Why was he there cleaning the carpets two days ago?' Tanzy asked, confused.

'That's when he must have taken the key,' said Byrd. 'Did Harry Law say what time they'd got to the house?' The question was for Tanzy.

Tanzy nodded. 'He said just after five. A call came in by a neighbour opposite. Said they got up to go to the toilet just after half four and had seen the flames through the front bedroom window.'

'And Roger returned just before eight?'

Mac nodded. 'There's something else…'

The detectives waited.

Mac closed the video screen, found another file in the folder, and double clicked. The screen opened up showing the same shot of the back yard. The only difference was the date told the detectives it was two days before that. And the time was 8.13 a.m..

'Friday? He was there on Friday, too?' Byrd asked, noticing the date in the corner.

Again, Mac nodded, and focused back on the screen. A man, very similar to Roger Carlton, entered the screen from the right, and made his way to the back door. He then pulled out a small case, lowered to his knee, grabbed a tool from it and used it to open the lock. Once the door opened, he went inside for approximately seven minutes, then came back out. Similar to the Sunday and earlier this morning, he looked the same: the mop of hair and Magnum PI tache.

'He's got some balls, this guy,' Tanzy noted, shaking his head.

Silence grew around them for a while.

'So, no one, apart from you, saw him in there?' Byrd said to Tanzy.

Tanzy shrugged. 'I don't know. Why?'

'Surely, if one of the firemen had seen him, they'd have known he wasn't one of them. It's almost like he knew when to come back.'

'He could have been around the front, watching them going in and out of the front door.'

'It's possible he knew they wouldn't be in there at that exact time. And it's possible he knew who Harry Law was.'

'But the question is,' said Tanzy, leaning back a little, 'is why he was there. What was he looking for in the kitchen? I don't know how long he was in there, but when I stopped at the stairs, I heard him in there opening and closing drawers. Then he appeared in the dining room and started looking at the ceiling.'

Byrd frowned, thinking hard.

'This makes no sense to me,' said Mac, raising his brows. 'Why was he cleaning the carpets on Sunday?'

Byrd smiled.

'What's funny?' Mac asked him.

'He wasn't cleaning the carpets at all. He was putting chemicals on them. He didn't need to go into their rooms last night and pour petrol on the floor, because he'd already covered them in chemicals. Even though they may have dried, it would have made the carpets burn more fiercely.' Byrd sighed. 'This attack had been meticulously planned. We are dealing with someone very dangerous here.'

9

Tuesday Afternoon
Police Station

The detectives returned to their desks with the notes they had made. Mac had taken several screenshots of Roger Carlton leaving the house and a few from his time there on Sunday afternoon, emptying the contents of the cleaning device into the drain, and had emailed the images to both Tanzy and Byrd.

Back at their desks, they opened the images and had another look. Neither of them had seen him before nor did he look familiar. They both concluded that the moustache and his hair were both fake.

Byrd took the responsibility to email the best image of him to their media representative and included DCI Martin Fuller in the email. The faster they got this on the news, the quicker someone could get in touch with any information.

The time was ticking on. Tanzy had phoned the senior forensics, but they had not picked up their lab phone. He decided to walk down. The lab would have been empty, was it not for the forensic trainee Amanda Forrest, sitting at her desk.

'Hope and Tallow not back yet?' Tanzy asked her.

She told him they hadn't returned from Napier Street yet and would be a few more hours. He thanked her and went back to the office. Before he found his desk, DC Leonard called his name as he passed.

'What is it?' Tanzy walked over to Leonard's desk.

'I've done some digging on the name Roger Carlton. There are only fifteen people in the UK with that name. It shouldn't be too long to narrow it down.'

'Good,' said Tanzy, standing at the desk. 'Check everything. You know the drill. Social media and such.'

Leonard nodded and continued clicking and typing. Tanzy returned to his desk and told Byrd that Tallow and Hope were still not there. It was an extensive job analysing a crime scene from a forensic point of view. Everything took time. Tallow and Hope were very meticulous and methodical in the way they did it and worked superbly together. It wasn't always like that. When they were matched up, all they did was argue and disagree with each other. Most likely because they were opposites. Emily Hope was single, liked getting tattoos, drinking, and loud music. She took no shit and wouldn't bat an eye if she upset anyone. Jacob Tallow was different. He led a quieter life, always had. He had a wife who worked at a local DIY store and was equally as bland as he was. However, his plain persona was almost a good trait because he didn't waste time talking shit and got straight to the point. Everything was black and white. He focused on the facts and did his job as thoroughly as anyone. They shared a similar work ethic and had learned to enjoy each other's company.

Usually, at the crime scenes they attended, Tallow would video everything before they started working. That way, they could watch the video later in the lab if they needed to. After that, they would do everything they'd been taught. In this case, finding four burnt victims in a house fire didn't take much analysis of how they died. The bodies, however, because they had been involved in a crime, would be sent to the basement of the hospital where pathologists would look at them and think beyond the burns.

For the areas of the house that hadn't been affected by the fire, such as the front door and back door, they'd check for fingerprints on the handles, footprints inside and outside the house, fibres of clothing that had fallen off the suspect, bodily fluids, such as sweat, urine, or blood, that may be found. It was a demanding process.

Byrd was typing up his report at his desk. Before DCI Fuller was in charge, DCI Thornton wanted everyone to write a report, whether you had just joined the force as a fresh PC or an experienced detective with twenty plus years under your belt. She said it helped her see how people thought and how they got their ideas on paper. Others thought it was a tactic to see if everyone's story matched up, to make sure she knew exactly what was going on. When Fuller took charge, his superiors had told him it was something he would like to continue to do, to push the individual reports.

Tanzy sat down and sighed. 'Coffee?'

'Not right now. I need to finish this.'

Tanzy concentrated on his report. The office was busy. The fire at Napier Street had certainly got people moving around and chasing things up.

Just as Byrd had finished his report, he heard footsteps to his left. He looked up to see PC Amy Weaver standing there with a concerned look on her face. Tanzy edged back to see her.

'Amy, what's wrong?' Tanzy asked her.

'Boss, you need to see this,' she said, seriously.

'Let me just—'

She shook her head. 'No, you need to see this now. Both of you.'

Frowning, Byrd and Tanzy stood and quickly followed Weaver back to her desk.

10

Tuesday Afternoon
Police Station

Standing in front of Weaver's desk was DC Leonard, DC Cornty, and DS Stockdale. They moved back a step to let Weaver sit down on her chair, and pulled herself in.

Byrd and Tanzy approached.

Worried eyes fell on them.

The detectives had a feeling whatever it was, judging by the concern radiating from the three who were standing silently, it was a serious matter.

Tanzy stopped next to Stockdale and looked down at the computer screen.

'What's happening, Amy?' Byrd asked, stopping next to Tanzy.

'This has been uploaded to YouTube, sir,' she explained quickly. 'It has over twenty-five thousand views so far. It's also shared on multiple other social sites like Facebook, Twitter, and Instagram. It's a video.'

Byrd frowned. 'A video? Amy, we don't have time for this.'

'Sir, you might want to watch this one,' DI Leonard said seriously.

Byrd regarded his tone and nodded, then turned towards the screen. 'Okay.'

Amy moved the mouse cursor around the screen and double-clicked to enlarge the video so it filled the whole screen. The still shot was dark. In the top half of the screen, there was a long, rectangular window. In the window, there was a small silhouette of a figure with a hand up high on the glass. The features of the face couldn't be seen, nor could any great details of what the image was.

But then she pressed play.

Tanzy and Byrd watched it for the first time with wide eyes and didn't say a word throughout. It was the fourth time the others had seen it and they were just as disturbed as they were the first time around. The video lasted for forty-five seconds. When it finished, Byrd breathed deeply and asked her to play it again.

'Jesus,' Tanzy said, then gasped.

The title of the video was 'Element one'.

'What on earth is element one?' Tanzy asked no one in particular. They all shook their heads in confusion.

Amy looked back at him and said, 'Read the comments, boss.'

Judging by the way the others didn't lean in meant they'd already read them, so moved out of the way for Tanzy and Byrd to have a read. Their eyes scanned the dozens of comments in the thread.

Jay89 - Rest In Peace little person.
Dom454 - Jesus, someone said this was Darlington – anyone confirm this?
ElaineJef01 - What an awful way to go.
RuthDal – Oh God, can you imagine how that would feel?

Byrd slammed the desk with the side of his fist causing everyone, including Tanzy, to jump. 'Is this what I think it is?'

Weaver shrugged, not wanting to say anything to further his anger. Leonard and Stockdale stayed silent. Seldom had they seen anger from Max Byrd before.

'Did this bastard do this and then video it from the alley?' Byrd asked.

Again, no one spoke.

'Does anyone know?' he shouted, slamming his hand on the desk again.

'We don't know, sir,' Weaver said quietly.

'Watch it again,' Byrd said to her.

She turned with sad eyes and scrolled the time bar back to the beginning. At the start of the clip, it showed the small figure, who Byrd and Tanzy now assumed was one of the sons, clawing at the window frantically. Behind him, the room was glowing colours of red and orange, energetically dancing on the walls and ceiling behind him. Through the speakers, they could hear his high-pitched screaming, his desperation to escape but not having the power to do so. With nowhere to go, the only thing he could do was wait until the flames consumed him. As the window got brighter, the boy hit the window for the final time before his little body disappeared. The glass then illuminated with an orange flare and the whole room shone like the sun. His crying then stopped and all that could be heard was laughter from the person who recorded it. Then a voice said, 'Fire, fire, fire, fire…' repeatedly.

They all felt physically sick. Byrd and Tanzy both knew from being at Napier Street earlier how horrific this crime had been and if they were in the same position, how awful it must have been to be inside and felt the severe pain that they'd endured. But to see the little boy clawing at the window and hearing his shrieking pain built a fit of anger in them they hadn't felt in a very long time.

'Jesus Christ!' Byrd screamed, turning, and punching the wall behind him. The whole office became deadly silent. Everyone glared at him, wondering what on earth was going on.

Tanzy turned and watched him, panting hard and holding his wrist. 'Max?'

Byrd breathed heavily, resting his forehead on the wall near where he'd damaged it.

'Max, you alright?' Tanzy said, resting a palm on his back.

Byrd turned slowly, opened his eyes, and noticed everyone looking at him. The ones who had stood up abruptly to see what the commotion was about sat back down immediately when his gaze fell on them. Byrd looked at Tanzy and gave a small nod.

'I'm sorry for that, guys, I...' He shook his head and said nothing else. Tanzy looked back at Weaver and asked her the name of the user that had uploaded it.

'RCarl20 is the person who uploaded it,' she said.

'Okay, we need to find this fucker ASAP,' he said, addressing Weaver, Stockdale, and Leonard. They all nodded and listened further. 'I've emailed the still shot we have from the camera positioned at the back of the yard that picked up the guy calling himself Roger Carlton. We need this on the news.' He looked at Weaver specifically. 'Get this out on our Facebook, Twitter, and News update accounts.'

She nodded. 'Sir.'

The others dispersed towards their desks, leaving Tanzy with Byrd, who looked like he was going to be sick, his body slightly bent forward.

Tanzy put a hand on his shoulder. 'You okay, Max?'

Byrd took a deep breath, stood up straight, and managed a nod. 'Yeah. It's a sick thought Claire and I are bringing a child into this world with sick bastards like this around.'

Tanzy forced a smile and looked him in the eye. 'We'll get him. We always do.'

Byrd half smiled and, with a new lease of motivation, he said, 'Right, come on, let's find him.'

11

Tuesday Afternoon
Police Station

DCI Fuller had been on to them about updates. Unfortunately, they left him disappointed, so he stormed back into his office and slammed the door.

'Dickhead,' Tanzy muttered under his breath.

The time was approaching three p.m.. Mac, the DFU guy, had asked them to give him until three p.m. to see what he could come up with.

Byrd and Tanzy logged out of their computers, stood up, and made their way across the office towards the opposite side, where they entered the corridor, and a minute later, opened Mac's door. He was sitting at his desk to the right of the small room. His workspace was cluttered with empty chocolate bar wrappers and two empty coke cans. The bin underneath the desk, near his feet, was overflowing and needed emptying.

He coughed, quickly grabbed the wrappers, bent down with a struggle, and forced them into the bin.

'You had enough time?' Byrd asked him, eyeing the mess of the room. It wasn't just the desk that gave his OCD a shiver; the whole room lacked TLC. The shelving unit behind was filled with books and containers. Byrd, at a quick glance, sure he saw food in them and shivered at the thought of how long they'd been there for but decided not to mention it. In the past, they'd had conversations about it and Byrd had told him to take better care of himself, including his workspace. Tanzy had mentioned it to Byrd last week and it was something Byrd had been meaning to do. But for now, they had other pressing matters.

'Yeah, yeah. Come in,' Mac said, waving them in.

He edged back a little, allowing Byrd and Tanzy to stop in the centre of the room. On his desk, there were three computer screens. On the right one, was the YouTube clip they had seen earlier of the footage recorded from the man who called himself Roger Carlton. At the bottom of the clip, it told them the username: RCarl20.

The middle one contained some complicated digital graph that neither Byrd nor Tanzy understood. The left one was a word document with several paragraphs of notes, but the detectives weren't close enough to read them.

'You look well,' Mac said to Byrd. 'Kept the weight off?'

Byrd nodded. A few months back, they'd spoken about losing weight. Although Mac hadn't changed his excessive habits and serious lack of physical exercise, Byrd had. Football twice a week and walks with Claire had seen to that. He'd lost two stone and had managed to keep it off.

Wasting no time, Byrd said, 'What have you found?'

'Well, the username, RCarl20, is a new user. It subscribed to YouTube only two weeks ago. It has no display picture or any attached information. The video had been uploaded at five thirty-six this morning.'

Knowing there was a vast number of views when they watched it earlier, Tanzy asked him how many views it had now.

'On the channel itself, nearly seventy thousand.'

'Shit. That is not good.'

'No.'

'I'm surprised that YouTube hasn't taken it down yet?'

Mac looked up at Tanzy. 'They will soon. However, I can see the digital patterns of the algorithms. They tell me it's circulating on Facebook, Twitter, and Instagram.'

Byrd frowned. 'Is it possible to trace the IP address of the user RCarl20?'

'It certainly is. I have the IP address of the phone it was uploaded on. Here, have a look.' Mac leaned to the left, pointed to the furthest screen. The detectives squinted at the number which meant nothing to them. 'I have tracked the IP to the service provider. They told me it was uploaded from a Samsung S10 device.'

'Who's the owner of that phone?' Byrd said.

'Roger Carlton.'

'From the IP address, can we see the location of the device when it was uploaded?'

'We can, but…' Mac paused.

The detectives frowned at him and waited.

'The upload came from Oldbury, in Birmingham.'

'Birmingham? How is that possible?' Tanzy wanted to know.

'Two ways. Either the video had been sent to the device registered of Roger Carlton which was in Oldbury at the time of the upload, or he's used some kind of IP diverter.'

'IP diverter?'

Mac nodded.

Byrd sighed. 'We need to get on to Leonard, see where he is with these profiles.'

Tanzy agreed with a nod, then looked back at the right screen. 'Does the video look right?'

'What do you mean?' Mac asked.

'It's real, isn't it?'

He nodded confidently. 'Without a doubt. I often see videos that have been tampered with. You can tell if it's fake. Any little mistake stands out to someone who knows what they are doing. To make sure for my analysis, I ran it through Vidreel'—an app that savvy techs used to check a video's authenticity—'and can confirm it's real.'

'Okay. Let us know if there's anything else you find,' Byrd said, standing.

They backed out and walked back towards the office. As they entered, Tanzy veered off to the left in the direction of DC Leonard, who was leaning forward, concentrating on his screen through the narrow reading glasses he'd recently started wearing. The unknown continual headaches he'd been getting, according to the doctor, could be down to needing glasses. So, when he struggled with the basic eye test with a local optician, he wasn't surprised to hear the blonde-haired forty-something tell him he needed them. Tanzy had never got used to him in glasses yet.

'Jim,' said Tanzy, pulling a chair out and sitting down next to him. 'What have we got?'

'From the fifteen registered names of Roger Carlton, the closest we have is in Hull.'

Tanzy squinted. 'Hull?'

Leonard glanced his way. 'Yeah. Only one of them is in the PNC. He's thirty-nine. Attacked two teenagers in a park last April.'

'Location?'

'Westminster, London. His registered address is in Crawley, West Sussex.'

'Any from Oldbury, near Birmingham?'

Leonard shook his head, wondering what was so important about Oldbury.

Tanzy looked defeated. 'What about the PND?'

The PND (Police National Database) is a large database of people that have done something that the police have previously investigated but from their findings, no arrests were made. The PNC would pick up someone who, in some form, had committed a crime and had been arrested.

'Five of them,' Leonard said. 'Closest one is Oxford.'

Tanzy thought for a moment. 'Do some more digging. I want to see pictures. When you have them, send them over. I want to run them through facial recognition in and around Darlington. If one of the fifteen is our guy, we'll get him.'

12

Tuesday Night
Darlington

On the desk in front of him, there were dozens of photographs clustered in no particular order. He ran his small, dark eyes over them, slowly changing from photo to photo, absorbing each scene in detail. The colour of their clothing. The shade of their skin tones. The way they moved, especially the eldest son, who shuffled with the slight limp. The way the sunlight shone down on their innocent, clueless faces. The brickwork of the house behind them had stood there for decades, not knowing the next day would be a witness to a horrific murder.

He then looked down at the photo in his hands. It was the last photo he took of them. They had no idea it would be the last ever piece of happiness captured in the still shot, which he'd keep in a file tucked away forever. They were leaving the house, heading for their car. Danny Walters was in the process of opening his driver's door, with a smile across his face as if they'd cracked a joke about something funny. They weren't laughing now, though.

He smiled, remembered he'd parked down the street when he'd taken the photo. Watching the house for a couple of days, he had got used to their routines, their little habits. Friday morning, he'd watched Danny Walters head to work just before eight. That was the benefit of the summer months. The mornings were nice, warm. There was no fuss, heading out ten minutes earlier to de-ice the windows and get the car warmed up. Minutes after Walters had left, his missus, Jessica, and their sons, Mark and Peter, came out shortly after. They walked a few paces, then got into a red Renault Clio, then a moment later, they were gone.

The man got out of his car and locked it, then made his way to the bottom of the street and took a left up the alley. He counted the houses along to make sure the numbers matched up and he had the right house. Luckily, the gate wasn't locked, so he walked straight in and made his way to the back door. He lowered to his knee and used his tools to open the door. He went straight through the dining room and up the stairs into the bedroom at the front. From his pocket he pulled a small, sealed plastic bag filled with black liquid, slid the lock across, and poured half of it on to the carpet, spacing the drops to cover a decent area. He then went into the back bedroom and did the same. Once satisfied he went downstairs and placed a business card on the front door mat as if it had been posted like any other letter, then turned, made his way back through the house, locked the back door with his tool, then went back to his car.

Later that day, he got a phone call, asking if he'd go round and see if he could clean their carpets. The business card he'd left on their door mat advertised a carpet cleaning service he was confident it would do the trick. So, he went there to have a look at the awful mess in the two bedrooms, watching the confusion on Jessica and Danny's face, wondering where these marks had come from. He told them he'd need some strong chemicals and would return on Sunday to do the job. When he went back, he took the back door key and checked there were no locks on the gate when he was emptying the cleaning unit in the outside drain.

It was simple really.

He placed the photo on the desk, then leaned to his right, grabbing a piece of paper. On it, were four boxes. Above the empty boxes was the word 'Element' and, with a pen, he put a cross in the first box, whispering, 'Fire, fire, fire…' over and over.

Then he looked at the next empty box, staring at it for a long time, knowing that soon, he'd be able to put a cross in that one too.

13

Tuesday Night
Darlington

A few minutes away from home, DI Byrd ended the call with Tanzy and sighed. It had been a long day. They'd been discussing Roger Carlton and how Tanzy had sent the still shot of him to the media team, who would inform the local news channel and The Northern Echo, hoping to make the front page of tomorrow's paper.

They finally had the chance to speak to Tallow and Hope, who'd finished at the house and made it back just after five. It was an equally long day for them too. They'd taken all the samples they would need and had told Byrd and Tanzy they'd have the results back by tomorrow, especially for the substance on the carpets which aided the burning process.

Byrd had been in touch with Harry Law again, asking for any further findings from a fire investigator's point of view. He confirmed what they already knew: the fire had been started at the base of the stairs and had been fuelled by petrol. Tanzy nor Byrd could decipher that smell but Harry was adamant it was petrol. He also told Byrd he expected the forensics to confirm there was a flammable substance that had been used to clean the carpets, and to keep him up to date with what it was.

Byrd slowed the car and angled around to the right, following the slight bend, then dabbed the brakes, pulling up onto the kerb. He was shattered. It was only nine o'clock. The smell rising from the passenger seat was divine, and he couldn't wait to get inside and eat it.

Once he was through the door, he took off his shoes and made his way into the kitchen. Claire was sitting at the kitchen table reading her Kindle. Byrd placed the bagged food on the worktop to the right and went over to her, bent down, and kissed her forehead.

'How're my favourite people?' Byrd asked.

Tiredly, she smiled and lowered her Kindle to the table. 'He's wearing me out,' she said, rubbing her pregnant belly with both her hands.

Byrd placed a hand over hers.

'What's in the bag?' She looked past him to the contents on the worktop.

'Your favourite. I didn't know if you'd had something to eat but I got it anyway.'

'I have already eaten, but I'm eating for two now, so…'

Byrd kissed her again. At the counter, he pulled a plate from the cupboard and plated her some food up. Since she fell pregnant, Claire had developed a desire for chicken parmesan, which was strange, as she hadn't thought much of it beforehand. Women often got like that while they were pregnant; developed strange, unexplainable cravings that made no sense at all. When she told Byrd about her new hunger about the food she'd usually turned her nose up at, she explained that her mother had told her when she was pregnant with her, she had been obsessed with mint imperials. And when she couldn't get them, she'd chew on chalk. They both laughed at that one.

Byrd poured a dollop of sauce on the side of her plate, made her a drink, and carried them both over to the table. She tucked into the food as if she hadn't eaten in days.

'What are you reading?'

She chewed her mouthful of food, and said, 'Recursion. Blake Crouch.'

'Crouch?' Byrd asked, standing at the worktop, filling his own plate. 'Like the footballer?'

Claire frowned. 'No… American guy. Sci-fi. One of the best reads this year, apparently.'

Byrd took a seat opposite her. 'Is that so?'

She smiled and forked a load of food into her mouth. They ate in silence for a few moments. 'You had a good day?' she said.

Byrd wiped his mouth with the back of his hand and shook his head. 'No, not really.'

Claire, in hindsight, didn't have to ask. She'd been with Byrd for two years now, and each time he walked through the door after his shift, the look on his face alone would tell her if his day had been good or not.

'Wanna talk about it?' she said.

'Not really.' He smiled. 'Thanks though.'

She nodded and continued eating.

Byrd glanced up at the clock to his left; the time was approaching ten p.m.. He told Claire he was getting a quick shower then he was going to watch the news. She said she'd wash up and be waiting for him in the living room.

By the time he walked in wearing his dressing gown, he noticed she'd paused it for him. He'd been longer than a few minutes, which was usually the case. Through the window, the sun had almost dipped behind the houses opposite leaving the street in the falling dusk.

As he sat down next to her and relaxed on the comfy sofa, she pressed play.

'Good evening,' the news reporter in the blue suit started. She was late thirties with straight, blonde hair that sat nicely on her small, round shoulders. Her almost perfect, flawless skin reflected the lights on the studio around her, and her smile showed her well-looked after white teeth. 'Our first story takes us to Darlington where we've learned the devastating news that a family of four have tragically lost their lives in a house fire in a terraced street in the centre of town. During the early stages of this investigation, the police and fire service had found evidence that suggests the fire to be an act of purposeful malice. We have been notified that forensics have been at the scene to aid the police in their investigation. We have confirmation that the victims are forty-one-year-old Danny Walters, his wife, Jessica Walters, aged forty. And their two sons, Mark and Peter, sadly only aged eleven and six. This news comes as a massive shock to the town and police have sent us a photo taken from a camera at the property which shows an individual at the house on three separate occasions. Police believe he is the man responsible.'

The enlarged photo which Tanzy had sent to the media team filled the screen. The still shot had captured the man walking back towards the rear gate, his long mop of dark hair and ridiculous looking moustache plain to see.

'If anyone recognises this man, please get in touch with Durham Constabulary with any further information. They believe this individual goes by the name of Roger Carlton.'

The screen minimised, returning to the blonde haired reporter in the studio, who after giving a sad smile directly towards the camera, moved on to the next story.

Claire used the remote to mute the sound and looked at Byrd, who was focused on the screen. She now knew why he hadn't had a good day. Usually, he'd phone her several times during the day, but today he hadn't. And when he didn't, Claire knew he was busy with something very important.

'Wanna talk about it?' she asked softly, placing a palm on his shoulder.

He looked down at the carpet under the television. 'It was awful.'

She rubbed his shoulder but didn't say anymore, knowing him well enough that if he wanted to talk about it, he would.

Byrd leaned in, kissed her, stood up, and went upstairs to bed. For the first time in nearly six years, he'd fallen asleep within a minute.

Then he woke at half past two when he heard something. He shuffled up, his heart beating quickly, looking around the dark room. A slither of light was creeping in through the curtains from the streetlight outside. To his right, Claire was sleeping peacefully on her side.

For a moment, he thought he'd been dreaming and had woken, imagining it had been something to worry about. But the longer the silence continued, he was convinced it was nothing. He lowered his head to the pillow, closed his eyes, hoping he'd fall back to sleep.

Then he heard it again. There was no denying it was the sound of someone downstairs.

14

Tuesday Night
Newton Aycliffe

When Tanzy walked through the front door, Eric and Jasmine both hugged him as if they hadn't seen him in weeks. Tanzy put his bag down near the door, lowered to his knees, and put his arms around them. Eric excitedly told him he'd been sewing at school, then grabbed the square of fabric from the unit near the stairs to show him. It was a flower made from four different colours. Tanzy didn't have a clue how to sew, so even though Eric was ten, he was very impressed.

'That looks brilliant, mate,' he said, kissing his warm cheek. 'Have you showed mum?'

He nodded, smiling widely.

Tanzy turned to Jasmine, who told him about a game she played with her friends at dinnertime. Similar to stuck in the mud but they had to crawl under their legs instead of their outstretched arms.

'Mum has a surprise for you,' Eric said, laughing, nodding his head back and forth, his blonde hair rocking on the top of his head.

'She does, does she?'

Eric and Jasmine both nodded shyly.

'Where's Mum?'

Jasmine turned her head quickly, her long dark hair whipping the air, and pointed to the kitchen. Tanzy found his feet and smiled, wondering what it could be. In the kitchen, Pip finished washing the last plate and placed it on the draining board. She was wearing her grey tight-fitting jogging pants and a short-sleeved purple t-shirt.

'Hey,' he said, happy to see her.

Jasmine and Eric followed him in.

She turned and smiled. 'Hey, yourself. How was your day?'

'Well, we'll talk about it later.' He glanced behind him, spotted the kids looking up at him with mischievous eyes. 'What's going on?'

Pip moved across the kitchen floor, her bare feet silent on the tiles, and hugged him tightly. 'I have a surprise for you,' she whispered in his ear. Her emerald eyes glistened against the modern lighting under the cupboards to his left. Her dark, shiny hair rested on her shoulders.

'Do you?'

'Well, it's from me and the kids.'

'It isn't my birthday until next month.' He smiled and rubbed his perfectly trimmed goatee.

'Kids, go and get it for daddy.'

They left and returned a few moments later with a rectangular box covered in Toy Story wrapping paper.

Eric handed it to him. 'Open it, Daddy.'

Tanzy lowered to his knees and placed the box on the floor. He ripped the paper off and was surprised to see a Makita cordless drill.

'A drill?' he said, unsure why they'd bought him a drill.

'Well, you did mention that you couldn't finish the project in Eric's room because your drill broke,' Pip explained. 'So, I ordered one from Amazon for you. Hope it's the right one.'

Tanzy stood up, looking at the picture on the case. It was pretty much the same one as he had. And she was right, he did need a new one. After seeing something in one of her fancy magazines, Pip decided it would be good to build Eric a den in his room. Roughly head height, nestled in the corner with a ladder he could climb to access, a place for him to go to read or watch films on his iPad.

Tanzy had been building it for a while now, mainly when he had a day off, but it seemed to be taking forever.

'Now you can finish his den,' Pip said, smiling.

Tanzy grinned and looked behind him, noticed Eric clapping his hands excitedly. 'Yeah, that's great,' he said to him, although his words weren't filled with as much enthusiasm as they could have been.

'Daddy will soon have it done for you, Eric,' Pip said to him.

Eric hugged Tanzy and ran off upstairs, thrilled. Jasmine left too, returning to the dining room where she'd been watching the television before Tanzy arrived home.

Tanzy and Pip talked about their day, leaving out the descriptive details. What they'd witnessed at the house fire was beyond words. He told her how Max had punched the wall in the office.

'That's not like him,' she said.

'I know. I think the stress of the baby is catching up with him.'

'What did Fuller say about it?'

'He said he'd have to pay for the damage.'

Pip made a fair-enough face and flicked the kettle on. She made coffees and they both sat down. Tanzy looked at her and said, 'How are you doing?'

'Yeah, I'm good.'

'No, I mean, how are you doing?' he said seriously.

She frowned at him, unsure what he meant. In the cupboard behind them, Tanzy had noticed a bottle of vodka at the back. It was a bottle that had turned up no later than last week. When Pip started back at AA, Tanzy had made sure that they had no alcohol in the house so nothing could tempt her. He knew all too well how easy it was to have a bad day and turn to drink. The months of hard work and effort gone in a single moment. But he'd noticed this bottle four days ago, and three days ago, he noticed there was less vodka in it than the day before. Then yesterday, there was even less. He knew this because he'd made a thin pen mark on the side of the glass, just thick enough for him to see it.

'I'm okay,' she said, but her body language told a different story.

He nodded slowly, stood up, went to the cupboard, and opened it. After moving some tins and jars aside, he pulled out the bottle of vodka, returned to the table, and placed it down in front of her.

He watched her throat bulge and her eyes widen as he took a seat on the chair. It didn't take long for the silence to become uncomfortable.

'I er…' she muttered.

'What?'

She fell silent, looked away from him.

'Six months, Pip.' He stood up, went over to the cupboard, and pulled out an empty glass, then placed it next to the bottle. 'You really want to go back to this? Go ahead. We'll move the kids out, send them to your mums. I'll stop at Max's, and you can drink all of it, Pip.'

She frowned at him.

'You've been doing so well. Don't fuck this up now. But if this is what you want, go ahead.' He pushed the glass towards her.

She stared at him, then at the bottle.

'I'll leave it up to you.' He stood up, leaned over to kiss her forehead, left the kitchen, and went upstairs for a shower. After he got out, he checked on the kids, then returned to an empty kitchen. He checked the living room and dining room. She wasn't there either.

'Pip?' he shouted.

He opened the front door and looked out. Her car was still there. Back inside the house, he went down the hall, through the living room, and opened the back door. At the recycling bin, there Pip stood, gazing out on the garden.

Tanzy slowly approached.

Near her feet, he noticed the paving stones were soaked. He silently reached past her, opened the bin lid, and inside, found the empty vodka bottle. He closed the lid and held her close.

'Thank you,' he whispered.

They went inside, sorted the kids, and settled on the sofa to watch a film. Before midnight, they were in bed and went to sleep.

At half-past two in the morning, Tanzy's phone beeped, waking them both. The text message was from Byrd.

'Who's that?' Pip said, groggily.

'A text from Max. He says there's someone in his house, and if I don't hear from him in five minutes, I need to ring the police and head over.'

15

Tuesday Night
Low Coniscliffe, Darlington

Without waking up Claire, Byrd silently got out of bed, grabbed the dressing gown from the back of the bedroom door, and put it on. He took a few steps towards the bed, leaned over, and opened his bedside drawer, the sliding mechanism moaning in the darkness, but it wasn't enough to wake Claire. He had never used the truncheon he'd put there all those years ago or the torch either. After he grabbed his phone and placed it in the large pocket of his gown, he gently opened the bedroom door and stepped out onto the landing, the truncheon nestled firmly in his right hand, the torch, turned on, in his left.

He leaned over the banister to look downstairs. It sat in darkness. The sounds that woke him up were louder now, he was sure, but couldn't work out where it was coming from or what it was.

The past couple of weeks Low Coniscliffe had been subject to a few break ins. It wasn't a congested, busy place. Everyone knew each other. So when people had knocked on Byrd's door asking what was going on or who was responsible, he didn't have an answer. He'd lived there long enough to know the majority of the folk who lived here and surmised it wasn't anyone in their little community that was responsible but went around knocking. It must be people outside of town, seeing an opportunity. One of the neighbour's cars had been taken, and other people had had jewellery and laptops stolen. Whoever it was had worn gloves and overshoes, leaving no prints at all.

Several people had bought cameras to protect their property, while others had fixed their broken burglar alarms. The small village hadn't seen its share of crime so people were now wary of this once very quiet place.

Byrd stopped at the top of the stairs and listened hard. The noise was coming from the kitchen. A thumping sound? He directed the light down into the hallway, illuminating the darkness as he took the first step, then the second, followed by the third. The sound, if anything, was getting louder. His truncheon was extended to its capacity, raised slightly, in case he needed to swing it. Once he reached the wooden floor he peeked around the post at the bottom of the stairs, looking down the hall towards the kitchen, seeing the moonlight cast a haze of dull grey light through the closed blinds, giving the table and kitchen appliances a look of mystery about them.

With the noise still present, he tiptoed along the hall, his torch shooting its beam of brilliant light into the space.

The noise stopped dead.

'If anyone is in here, make yourself known,' Byrd said. 'You are on the property of a police officer who is not afraid to use the weapon in his hand.'

He stopped a few feet from the kitchen door. The light at the end of the torch didn't show anything unusual in the narrow section of the kitchen he could see. He stepped in, hitting the switch on the left, the space lighting up under the six bright spotlights above.

It was empty. He looked to his left towards the back door. It was closed. He could see the slither of the lock in place, knowing it hadn't been breached.

He frowned in confusion, looking around.

'Hello?' he said again.

He quickly turned around, shining the torch back into the hallway, feeling there was something behind him, but apart from the coats hanging on the hook and the shoes on the low-level rack next to the door, it was empty.

Moving closer, light on his bare feet to the centre of the kitchen, his eyes flitted left and right as he tried to remember the sound; he was sure it was a thumping sound. Everything was in its place. Nothing had moved.

He was about to relax and go back upstairs when he heard it again and froze. It was coming from the garage. With a sudden wave of anger, he dashed to the garage door, flicked the lock open, and barged it open with his truncheon held high.

An array of tools and garden furniture were under the torchlight, but the thumping sound was coming from the left. He aimed the light towards the sound and suddenly stopped, his heart beating hard and fast.

Then he smiled, laughed quietly to himself.

He flicked on the light and noticed the timer had thirty-four minutes left of the cycle. The clothes he'd put in before were meant to start in the morning, so Claire could take them out, and get them dried. He must have set the timer wrong.

He did a quick visual around the well-lit garage. The door at the back, leading to the garden, was closed, as was the garage door itself at the front.

Happy there were no monsters in his house, he locked the garage and turned the kitchen light off. Before he climbed the stairs, for peace of mind, he checked the handle on the front door and froze, immediately feeling the icy fingers crawl up his spine when the handle dipped and the door opened inwards.

'Jesus!' he whispered in panic.

As well as putting the wrong timer on the washing machine, he'd left the front door unlocked too. What was he thinking? He shook his tired head, had a quick peep outside. The dark street sat silent and still. He closed the door, grabbed the keys from the small table, and locked it.

Before he went upstairs, he checked the living room and dining room, then tiredly made his way back upstairs.

As Byrd reached the top and turned for his bedroom, the person crouched down behind the living room door sighed and smiled to himself. He'd wait until Byrd fell back to sleep before he made his move.

16

Wednesday Morning
Darlington

Tanzy was late out of the house and told Byrd he'd meet him at B&Q just after eight. He hadn't slept well, especially being woken at half two when Byrd had told him someone was in his house. A few minutes later, he'd received a text message saying there was nothing to worry about and went back to sleep.

Tanzy stepped out of his Golf and closed the door. He paused to look at his purchase. It was similar to his last but had all the mod cons, and the colour was a darker shade of grey. Pip was envious but to compensate, she drove his Mercedes CLS 350 when he was at work. Other than taking the kids to and from school, she didn't use it much, so Tanzy wasn't too concerned about her racking the mileage up.

Walking across the car park, he was surprised how full it was, wondering if people actually had jobs to go to. He spotted Byrd's X5 near the entrance in one of the 'load and go' bays.

The sun was up and about, shining down brightly, a mirage of reflections from angled car windscreens and polished roofs. It had been warm over the past few weeks and according to the weather reports, would only get warmer. It would be a record for May, the experts predicted.

As he approached the black X5, he made eye contact with Byrd through the driver's wing mirror, who opened his door and dropped down, wearing black trousers and a very thin dark blue jacket. His hair had been gelled and his moisturised skin shimmered in the morning light, although noticeable dark semi-circles sat just under his eyes.

'Morning, Max.'

'Morning, mate,' Byrd replied.

'You look shattered.' Tanzy stopped in front of him.

'I am. I kept hearing things all night. Didn't sleep well at all.'

'Thanks for waking me at half two.'

They shared a smile.

'Don't know what's wrong with me. I went back up then heard something again, but knew I'd already checked the house. Strange thing is, is when I went back upstairs, I checked the door and it was open. I'd forgot to lock it.'

'You know what that is, don't ya?'

Byrd waited, frowning.

'Old age,' Tanzy said, winking.

Byrd playfully jabbed his arm, and they turned and headed for the entrance. At the reception desk, a small woman, probably in her fifties, with blonde hair and a wide smile showing coffee-stained teeth asked them how she could help.

Byrd took charge. 'Can we speak to the manager, please?'

'Sure. Can I ask what it's regarding? Maybe I can help.'

'It's about one of your employees. Danny Walters.'

Her smile faded quickly. 'Oh. Okay, I'll call him.' She picked up the phone to her right and told the person on the other end that the police were here to speak to him about Danny. She placed the phone back on the receiver and told them he'd be a few minutes.

Byrd and Tanzy smiled and stepped back, spending their waiting time looking at the deals strategically placed on the low level stands near the entrance door. It wasn't long before a short guy in his late twenties appeared with a practised false smile.

Byrd extended his hand and shook it firmly. 'Can you spare a few minutes to speak about one of your employees Danny Walters?'

The man nodded several times. 'Of course, anything we can do to help.'

From his response it was obvious he was aware of what had happened to Danny. He led them from one end of the shop to the other and went through a door near the trade entrance and climbed some steps, took a left, then, a few metres down a narrow corridor, opened a door to an empty room. There were a couple of chairs and a table, but other than the clock on the wall, it was empty. Most likely used for one-to-one meetings.

He introduced himself as Peter Gilbert, then sat down, waiting for the detectives to speak first.

'So, I'm sure you're aware,' Tanzy started, taking the only seat on that side, 'that Danny and his family tragically died in a house fire?'

Peter nodded. 'Yes, I watched it on the news. We are devastated. He was a lovely man. Been here longer than I have.'

'How long is that?'

Peter explained he'd been the manager for almost four years, and Danny had been there at least ten years before that. 'He worked in the plumbing aisle. Did his time as a plumber but work had dried up and he got a temporary job in here until it picked back up but didn't leave. Said he enjoyed it and liked the people.'

Byrd, standing beside Tanzy, nodded. 'Can you tell us if he'd ever mentioned any problems he'd had outside of work? I'm sure you know we are investigating this fire as an act of intent.'

Peter thought for a moment. 'I can't say he ever did. We talked most days that he was here. He was an upbeat guy. Everyone liked him.'

'What was he into, any interests?'

'He said he liked his online games, used to play a lot with his friends. I don't see the fascination, but I know many people his age do. It isn't unusual. Have you found anything that can help in finding who did this to him?'

The detectives waited before answering. Then Tanzy said, 'We have a few leads we are chasing. Do you know anyone here who were friendly with him?'

'I'd say just about everyone. As I said, everyone liked him.' Peter shrugged, indicating he could offer no more on the matter.

Byrd and Tanzy both stood and in turn, shook his hand, asking him if he can think of anything else, to ring the number on the card that Tanzy handed to him. He told him he would, then led them back out on to the shop floor. Moments later, they were outside. It was still hot with not a cloud in the sky.

Byrd didn't say much on the way back to the car and it didn't go unnoticed.

'You okay?' asked Tanzy, looking his way.

Byrd held his gaze. 'Yeah. Why?'

'Just don't seem yourself.'

When he stopped at the car, he turned to Tanzy. 'I'm just nervous about the baby, I think. It upsets me that… ahh it sounds soft. I—'

'You don't need to be all macho for me, Max. What is it?'

'My mum and dad won't get to see him. It upsets me the way the world is, that I'm bringing a baby boy into this mess.'

Tanzy placed a palm on his shoulder. 'The world is the way it is. It will never change. I'm telling you that having kids is the best thing you'll ever do. If you're worrying it will be hard, it will be, but it's amazing.'

Byrd nodded, appreciating his words of encouragement. 'Let's head back to the station, see what mood Fuller is in this morning.'

When Byrd got into his car, his phone rang in his pocket. He leaned to the side, pulled it out, noticing Claire was ringing him. It was unusual because she'd always text when he was at work unless something was wrong.

'Claire?'

'Max, did you go out the back door this morning?'

Byrd thought quickly, realising he didn't. 'No. I got a quick shower, grabbed a bite, and went straight out the door. Why?'

'Because my laptop isn't here. And the back door isn't locked. I think someone's been in the house.'

17

Wednesday Afternoon
Police Station

Once they'd spoken with Hope and Tallow, Byrd and Tanzy had learned all the evidence had been collected from the house fire at Napier Street. After DNA had been taken from the four of them, matching with their identities, their bodies had been sent to the undertakers. The need for detailed post-mortems was unnecessary considering the nature of their deaths.

Peter Gibbs, the lead coroner for Darlington and Durham, had been on the phone, going through what had happened. It wasn't very often these house fires happened, and even less so, to take a family of four, so he went to the house to have a look himself.

Hope had told Byrd that, after analysing the samples taken from the house, due to the fire, there wasn't any other DNA found, which surprised Byrd as Roger Carlton had been there several times. Byrd had asked about prints on door handles, knowing he'd opened and closed the back door several times when cleaning the carpets on Sunday. But, looking back at the camera footage, the man had covered his tracks, wearing gloves to minimise his trace.

They did find something.

A footprint.

Located at the back door near the mat, they cross-referenced the pattern and found it didn't match up with any of the family's footwear. She told Byrd she would find out the type of the trainer and get back to him once she knew.

DCI Fuller popped his head through his office door, telling both Byrd and Tanzy he wanted a word with them.

They stood up, went inside, and sat down in the two empty chairs.

'Updates please, gents?' he asked, wasting no time.

They filled him in on the footprint that had been found and said they are waiting on forensics to find the model.

'Keep me updated with that. What else?'

'That's it for now, sir,' replied Byrd, itching his chin.

'Where are we on the missing women?' pressed Fuller, clearly agitated.

Four days ago, on Saturday night, four women had left The Grange bar and had got into a taxi. It was the last time anyone had seen them. A string of queries had come in a day later from worried family and friends, saying they hadn't seen them. The police had managed to come up with a list.

Theresa Jackson. Lisa Felon. Sarah Mckay. Lorraine Eckles.

Byrd and Tanzy had spoken to the husband of Sarah Mckay, who said Sarah had texted him saying she was leaving The Grange but was heading to Lisa's house afterward for a few drinks. When he woke the following morning she wasn't there, so tried ringing her but her phone was off.

Byrd had got in touch with the manager at The Grange, who checked the CCTV, and had seen four women matching their descriptions leaving the bar just after two in the morning. With that information, Tanzy had spoken to Jennifer Lucas at the Town Hall control room who had followed them on the nearest camera, watching them climb into a taxi near Joe's Bar. A red Skoda Octavia. Registration plate SN66 4LL. They found out the taxi was registered to 1AB, so Byrd had been to their office and spoken to the young, tattoo-covered, blonde-haired female sitting with the headset on who told him the name of the driver and his address. Byrd and Tanzy had knocked on his door the following day and he told them he remembered picking them up but had dropped them off in a lay by just past Morton Park. Apparently, from listening to their conversation, the driver assumed someone else was picking them up. The driver told them he was sorry he couldn't offer any further help and said he'd driven straight back into town looking for more fares before the bars closed for the night.

'No one has seen them, sir,' Tanzy said. 'We have obtained their pictures and as you know, the media have shown the public but nothing yet. We have updated our Facebook page and Twitter feed with it multiple times. We are receiving messages about how sad the situation is but there's nothing to go on.

Fuller sighed heavily and sat silent for a moment. Then he said, 'Have we found our Roger Carlton yet?'

'According to our data, the closest Roger Carlton lives in Leeds.'

'Facial Rec?'

Byrd shook his head. 'Nothing.'

'He may be wearing a wig and a fake moustache,' added Tanzy.

Fuller forced a smile, dipped his shoulders into the back of his chair. 'Do the public know about Roger Carlton yet?'

They both nodded, and Tanzy elaborated. 'His picture and name are on the news. We're waiting for anyone to come forward with any information.'

'Okay. Well, that's—'

The door behind the detectives opened. They both turned.

DC Leonard was standing at the door. 'Sir, someone thinks they know who Roger Carlton is.' It was aimed at Tanzy, more so than Byrd or Fuller.

'They still on the phone?'

'She's waiting in reception, boss.'

18

Wednesday Afternoon
Police Station

Within a minute, Byrd and Tanzy entered the small reception at the front of the building, where a woman, in her early thirties, dressed in a black pencil skirt, a white blouse, a black blazer, and high heels, stood before them. If she told them she was a lawyer, they wouldn't have second-guessed it. Her straight dark hair sat nicely on her shoulders, either side of an attractive, stern-looking face. Maybe a lawyer after all.

Byrd stepped forward and extended his hand. 'Hi, I'm DI Max Byrd.' He turned and used his hand to indicate Tanzy, who stepped forward. 'And this is my partner, DI Orion Tanzy.'

After she shook Byrd's hand, she repeated the process with Tanzy and told them her name was Samantha Verity.

'We have been aware that you may know Roger Carlton?' Byrd asked.

She nodded several times. 'Is there a place where we can talk?' Whatever she wanted to say, she wasn't comfortable saying it there, knowing it would take a while to explain herself.

The detectives led her through a door, down a corridor, and into a room on the right. It was a box room, with a table in the centre of it, two chairs on either side. There was no window and didn't feel very welcoming.

'Please, take a seat,' Tanzy told her, motioning either seat with his hand.

As Samantha sat, Byrd, who was still standing, asked, 'Can I get you a coffee?'

'Yes, please. Milk. No sugar,' she replied, followed with a smile.

Byrd nodded, left the room.

She settled herself in and looked a little nervous. Tanzy waited until Byrd's return so made small talk about the weather, and the recent building development near the new cinema. Byrd soon returned with three coffees and placed them all down on the table.

'So, what can you tell us, Samantha?' Byrd said, not wasting any time, knowing Tanzy would've waited.

She blinked a few times. 'I heard about the fire in Napier Street, about how the family all died. I saw it on the news actually. Then the still shot of the man in the backyard. Roger Carlton. The name Roger Carlton doesn't exist. At least not that I know of.'

The detectives frowned, unsure where she was going with it.

She noticed their confusion. 'Sorry, I'm not explaining myself well. Many years ago, I went out with a guy. He was obsessed with this American show.' She rocked her head back and looked at the ceiling. 'God, I can't remember the name. There was a character in it called Roger Carlton. The guy I used to date loved it. He always watched it. He always said if he could change his name it would be Roger Carlton. From the photo on the news, he was wearing a wig and a fake tache. The character in the American show did the same.'

'What's he called? Your previous boyfriend.'

'Mackenzie Dilton,' she replied clearly.

'Does Mackenzie Dilton have an address? We'd very much like to speak to him urgently.'

'He used to live on Victoria Embankment when I knew him. I fell pregnant with his baby but we lost it when I was six months along.'

Byrd gave her a sad smile, uncertain if she regarded it as a good thing or a bad thing.

'Oh, don't worry, it was for the best. I can promise you that.'

Her words insinuated she had more to tell.

'I'd been seeing him for a couple of years. Things were okay. We'd spoken about marriage and having a family but then he got weird.'

'Weird how?'

'He started spending a lot of time on his computer. He didn't want to go out and have fun anymore. He completely shut me off. All he cared about was his stupid computer.'

'What did Mr Dilton do for work?' inquired Tanzy.

'He worked for an IT firm, based somewhere in Newcastle. He's got a degree in some IT thing, I'm not sure the name. Programming or something.' She waved her hand, expressing little understanding or interest.

Byrd and Tanzy absorbed her words.

'I'm not sure if it was because we lost the baby, but we lost interest in each other and finally called it a day. It wasn't that he was a nasty man, it's just... he didn't prioritise his things well. And his obsession with his computer, well, that got too much for me.'

'What did he do on his computer?' Tanzy asked, curiously.

'Games, I think. But then sometimes, I think he did things he shouldn't have been doing.'

'What makes you say that?'

'A few times, I walked in without knocking or without him knowing I was there, and he went ballistic, telling me to eff off and that it was his time. I'm not entirely sure, but he became obsessed with it. A few months before we split up, there was this look in his eye. A dark look. As if there was another side of him that he hadn't shown me yet.'

'Had he ever been violent with you?' Byrd said, leaning forward, placing his palms on the desk.

She shook her head. 'No.'

'When was the last time you saw him?'

She narrowed her eyes in thought. 'About six months ago. I passed him in the street. He saw me but looked the other way as if he was ashamed of what he'd become. We stopped seeing each other two years ago.'

'Does he have any family living in Darlington?'

'Not that I know of,' she said. 'He has a sister that lives somewhere down south and a brother who lives in the Midlands. He didn't see much of them.'

'Do you still have his mobile number?'

'Unfortunately not, I deleted it. Sorry.' She genuinely looked apologetic.

'What number on Victoria Embankment did he live?'

She told them. Byrd took out his phone and made a note.

'Is there anything else?'

'Not at the moment. Have you got a card in case anything else comes to mind?'

Byrd leaned to the left, pulled a card from his right pocket, and handed it to her.

'Thank you.'

She rose to her feet, and Tanzy walked her to the reception, then she left. Back in the office, they mentioned to Fuller that they were going out. They stepped out into the sun and made their way over to Tanzy's Golf.

19

Wednesday Afternoon
Victoria Embankment

Less than two minutes later they knocked on the door that Samantha Verity had said belonged to Mackenzie Dilton. They waited a minute then knocked again when no one answered. Taking a step back they looked in the window to the right, then leaned back, trying to see into the windows upstairs. There was no movement or sudden twitching of curtains.

To the house on their left, a door opened and a man in his seventies stepped out with a thick coat, ready for winter, with a walking stick that looked older than he did.

He froze as if he was playing musical statues and looked at them through large, jam-jar glasses. 'Can I help you?'

Byrd smiled. 'We're looking for Mr Dilton. Do you know if he's in?'

'Oh, wack-job willy?'

Byrd frowned. 'Who?'

'It's not his real name. It's a nickname we have for him – my wife and me. He was a strange one.'

'What makes you say that?'

'He didn't speak much. Spent a lot of his time inside playing on his computer. His bedroom must have backed on to our room'—he pointed upwards towards his bedroom in case the detectives weren't sure where that would be—'and he used to keep us up most of the night. We complained on several occasions but it didn't make a difference. He carried on as he wanted.'

The elderly man gingerly made his way to the black, iron gate, and slowly pulled it towards him, then stepped down carefully onto the path. He lifted his free hand up to his face to shield it from the blinding sun.

'Can you tell us any information about him – where does he work?'

'He worked from home I think. Something to do with that stupid computer of his.'

'Did he have many friends? Or a girlfriend maybe?'

'From what we saw of him, I don't think so. He hardly came out of the house. Only for shopping, because every time he came back, he had bags in his hand. And, he wasn't the type to stop to say hello. To be honest, I don't think he was all there.' He raised a finger to his temple and made small circles with it.

The detectives nodded, waiting for more.

'Oh, there was a woman who used to visit him,' the man said. 'Only came a handful of times while he was there. Could have been a girlfriend, although I can't be sure.'

Tanzy raised the notepad, ready to write something. 'Did she have a name?'

The old man told them he didn't know it but she had blonde hair and wore glasses, which Tanzy quickly jotted down.

'So, if he's out, what time does he usually return home? We can pop back later,' Byrd said.

The old man smiled. 'You'll be waiting a while. He hasn't lived here for six months. The place is empty now.'

Byrd sighed heavily. 'Great. Does a landlord own it?'

The man shrugged. 'How am I supposed to know? Anyway, I need to go. She'll be wondering where the meat is. She's cooking dinner later. I'm not missing it. And I can't be arsed with the earache.'

'Appreciate your help, sir,' Byrd said, with a forced smile.

The elderly man and his stick headed along Victoria Embankment towards town. Wherever he was going, judging by his pace, it would take him a while.

Byrd turned back to Tanzy. 'Well, that's great. Back to square one.'

Tanzy was going to reply but his phone rang in his pocket. He plucked it out to answer. 'Hello?'

'Boss, it's Amy.'

'What's happening?'

'I found the trainer the man who called himself Roger Carlton was wearing at Napier Street.'

'That was quick.'

'It's an Adidas Samba trainer.'

Tanzy closed his eyes, knowing they were sold in hundreds of shops from here to London. 'Okay. We'll be heading back soon. We'll catch up then.' He put his phone away and headed towards the Golf. Byrd followed.

'So,' Byrd said, putting on his seatbelt, 'we have four missing women, a house fire that has killed four people, a missing man who is very likely the man responsible for it, and an address which he doesn't live at.'

'You're missing the Adidas Samba trainers?'

'Oh yeah, the trainer that could have been bought in any shop in any town in the whole country.'

'We'll check with HM Land Registry, see who the house belongs to.'

Byrd nodded toward Tanzy. 'Good shout.'

'Other than that, the investigation is thriving...' Tanzy turned on the engine and edged out, made his way towards Victoria Road. 'How's Claire, you spoken to her?'

'Yeah, she's okay. Just shook up a little. I popped home to see her on my dinner and made sure all the doors were locked and nothing else had been taken. I might have forgotten to lock it last night, but I can't remember going out. Not even to empty the bin.'

'Hadn't there been some break-ins around your street?'

'A couple. I've knocked on most doors, asking if people had seen anything. Whoever is doing it, is a ghost. I'm going to buy more locks today, put them on when I get home. The last thing we need is her worrying and not feeling safe. Won't do the baby any good at all.'

20

Wednesday Evening
Darlington

Although it was summer, the large room was cold and dark. There wasn't a single speck of light from anywhere, not even from the small, one-way window on one of the walls. If there had been, they'd see the fading sun offering the last of its falling light, as another day had come to an end.

The floor was cold and hard. One of them had mentioned it felt like concrete to touch, but the others weren't sure.

On the floor, along one of the walls, there were several bed covers laid out for them, which they'd spent the majority of their days sitting on in silence, mentioning the odd word now and again. The covers weren't thick but it kept them off the cold floor.

In the first few days, after waking up and realising they were without their phones or any possessions, they investigated the room. They'd learned many things. The room was square-shaped. The walls were made from concrete. In the centre of the room, there was a plastic bag with items inside. The scary thing was they couldn't see a thing, didn't know what the items were. From feel and smell, they assumed it was food. Packets of crisps, drinks, and chocolate bars. When hunger got hold of them, they had little choice but to tuck in. Item by item, the bag became lighter, so they rationed their supplies, unsure how long they'd be there for. There were still a few drinks inside and other wrapped goodies and decided to only eat when they were starving.

When they first woke up, they all panicked. It took them a while to finally calm each other down, realise the situation they were in. One of them recalled their last memory. They had been dropped off by the taxi after leaving town and were waiting for Ronny, one of Lisa's friends, to pick them up to go to the house party afterward. They were all wasted, could barely stand up, but they recalled getting into the small van, but after that their memories are blank. They woke up here.

They were tired and bored. Almost to the point of giving up. They'd screamed and kicked and punched the walls out of frustration but it was pointless. Each day, they woke up and did it again, but their cries for help were absorbed by the cold, dark, damp, unforgiving room.

'I can't feel my feet,' Lisa said.

'Me neither,' said Sarah.

'You awake?' Lisa asked the other one.

'Yeah, I'm here,' Lorraine replied weakly, shuffling a little to get comfortable.

It had been three days since they'd heard from Theresa. Lisa had realised that Theresa hadn't been talking much, so had called her name and received no answer. They'd checked the whole room in the dark, using their searching hands to feel the cold floor and walls but it soon dawned on them that Theresa was not there anymore. Somehow, she'd vanished. None of them can remember when or how – maybe when they were all sleeping? They realised they weren't getting out and had accepted their fates on the sixth day.

On the opposite wall to where their make-shift beds were, they used the wall and floor area for the toilet. The foul smell, along with the damp brickwork, had worsened as the days went on, but they'd become immune to it. Even their individual bad smells had almost become a comfort to one another. Strange how only last week, they were leading their own lives.

It seemed like a lifetime ago.

'I need to pee,' Lisa said, slowly climbing to her feet, using the wall behind to aid her. Because she hadn't moved, her bones felt like they were brittle, her muscles had almost forgotten how to function. She padded across to the other side with her arms outstretched until she reached the opposite wall, then pulled up her skirt, and the sound of her urinating echoed in the large, empty space.

She returned to Sarah and Lorraine, dropping on the floor near them.

'We're not getting out of here, are we?'

Lorraine leaned over, blindly reaching for her hand, and finally found it. 'I don't think so,' she whispered.

Lisa shuffled in and held her friend tight, battling against the cold that wasn't giving up, and started to cry.

Through the small rectangular window high on the opposite wall where they were crying, two men watched them. The glass was one-way, appearing jet black on the room's side, not allowing anything in, so the women couldn't see them or know they were being watched.

'Which one are they going to pick this week?' the man on the right said, rubbing his chin, and returned to the chair near the desk. He was thin, wore glasses, had eyes darker than the midnight sky. He placed his hand on the desk, gently tapping the wood near the keyboard with his long fingers.

'I'll check the votes,' the other said, pulling himself closer to the computer and taking hold of the mouse. He was taller and wider. The run-around, the one who did the leg work. The muscle. He clicked on the voting panel to check the scores.

On the screen, there were three pictures. The images had been duplicated from their social media accounts. They needed the players and watchers to see what they were looking at. Under each picture was a percentage, and because they were down to three, their score was split three ways.

'They seem to like Lisa,' said Brad, checking the figures. 'They like watching her cry. Her vote is low. They want to keep watching her.' Up in the corner of the room was a night vision camera recording twenty-four seven.

Mitch took his focus off the window and glared at Brad and the computer screen. 'Looks like it's Lorraine?'

Lorraine's score was forty-six percent.

Sarah's was thirty percent.

And Lisa's was twenty-four percent.

'Lorraine is up next. Start the gas. Get her prepped for Friday,' Mitch told him.

Brad nodded and leaned to the left. On the wall, he took hold of the gas valve and turned it on. Soon they'd all be asleep, and he'd go in to get Lorraine.

21

Wednesday Evening
Low Coniscliffe

Claire, tired after she'd finished the ironing and washing up, went straight to the sofa. She picked what she wanted to watch, settled in, and focused on the brand new fifty-inch TV they'd recently bought. Byrd had listened to her moaning about how she couldn't see it properly from the sofa, telling him they needed something new. Something bigger. Whether that was the case, or whether it was her friend, Mary, who'd told her *they'd* just bought one, and she felt jealous. Either way, they'd bought a new one.

Byrd, for a change, had decided to join her, sitting down on the other sofa; the one in the bay window. He seldom spent his evenings like this but figured it'd be nice to spend some time with her. He occasionally glanced over, watching her. It melted his heart how she subconsciously rubbed her belly.

Her son. *Their Son*. Alan.

He felt emotional. The thought of bringing a child into the world and not having his parents crushed him more than words could describe. Not only for the support they'd give him, but for the happiness they'd feel, seeing their first grandchild. It's a shame they would never feel that love.

It angered him. Not that they'd miss out on his child, but that his sister had been taken twelve years before and hadn't been given the chance to give them a grandchild either. Poor Anna. She was two years younger than Byrd. All his life he'd protected her. Any issues with boyfriends, she'd gone to Byrd first.

He thought back for a few moments, reliving their childhood in his mind, how they used to go out on days with mum and dad; how they'd spend their time in the car arguing about the next song they'd listen to. Then, when she was twenty-seven and he was twenty-nine, he got the phone call.

He remembered as if it was yesterday, standing in the kitchen when his mobile rang. It was Tanzy. Answering it the same way he always did, he felt broken after Tanzy had told him what he'd found. A dead body. His sister, Anna. Multiple stab wounds to her stomach and chest. Byrd took a week off work, roaming the streets, knocking on doors, and became obsessive. It certainly changed Byrd in a couple of ways. He appreciated his life more. Each day he woke, he tried to remember that Anna hadn't, and that he should be grateful for another day to live. Eventually, a few leads had led him to the man responsible. He'd cornered him in an alley. Just the two of them. The rage inside him wanted to grab the man's head, smash it off the cobbles on the ground below, but he was determined not to throw his life away. He cuffed him, dragged him to the station, and the man was sentenced to twenty-five years.

He pushed the thoughts from his mind and absorbed what was happening on the screen. Claire was intrigued with Sci-fi – not spaceships and aliens kind of sci-fi, more strange happenings type of sci-fi. They both watched a little boy holding a teddy anxiously walk into a cave in the middle of the night.

'Do you think he'll come back?' she asked, keeping her attention on the screen.

Byrd looked over to her and pondered the question, unsure whether she meant the boy on the screen or the person that broke in and took her laptop.

'The doors are secure,' he replied, assuming she meant the latter. 'Are you sure you haven't misplaced your laptop?'

She turned her head to him and frowned. 'I'm not stupid, Max.'

'I'm not saying you are, but everyone misplaces things,' he said, his voice even.

'I've looked all over. You have as well. It's been taken. The back door was open.' She sighed, then focused back to the TV.

Byrd didn't reply. Instead, he thought hard about whether he'd locked the door last night, but then he couldn't ever remember going out. Not yesterday anyway. Unless it had been left unlocked from the last time it was opened, which had been several days ago.

'You need the cameras working again,' she said, matter-of-factly. And she was right. Byrd had a camera fixed above the door, looking down the driveway, but for some reason, it hadn't been working properly. He'd checked the wiring. To him, it looked okay, not that he knew much about electrics.

'The house is safe,' he said finally. 'No one is getting in.'

22

Thursday Afternoon
Police Station

Byrd and Tanzy were at their desks. They'd already had lunch and spent much of their morning speaking with forensics about the house fire in Napier Street. There'd been nothing new found or no further leads. The most promising lead had been when Samantha Verity had come to the station, telling them she recognised the man on the still shot at the Napier Street property, stating he was wearing a wig and fake moustache, similar to the character he was obsessed with. Roger Carlton. And that his real name was Mackenzie Dilton.

A team had been looking for Mackenzie Dilton. There were seven in the whole country. It wasn't a very common name at all, which worked better for the police. The issue was that the closest address registered to Mackenzie Dilton was Liverpool. Within Darlington, there was no trace of a Mackenzie Dilton, but it did give the police a real name to work with and a name to give to the public. Last night, when he'd left Tanzy's house and got home, Byrd had watched the news, where the reporter had updated viewers on the name 'Mackenzie Dilton' and if anyone knew him or his whereabouts, to let the police know immediately.

Byrd had personally spoken to the IT firm that Samantha had told them that Mackenzie had worked for. The manager there, a Mr Jonas Black, had told Byrd that Dilton was a quiet man, a man who kept himself to himself. He'd worked there for a few years but handed in his notice around six months ago. Didn't give a reason. Byrd asked him what address they had for him and it turned out to be the address that Samantha had said, the same address that was empty.

The door behind them opened and Fuller popped his head out. 'You two. In here.' His tone wasn't very positive, nor did it give them a feeling it was going to be an uplifting conversation.

Byrd and Tanzy locked their computers and went inside the DCI's office. They took a seat in the two empty chairs opposite him.

'Updates, gentlemen? Start with the fire?'

Tanzy spoke first, telling him there were no further leads from a forensic point of view. He mentioned the trainer that PC Amy Weaver had matched to a pair of Adidas Sambas but also stated that they could have been bought in hundreds of shops anywhere in the country.

'What about the missing four women?' Fuller said, tapping the desk with his thick fingers. It was clear Fuller was becoming impatient. Earlier, when Fuller's door had been open an inch, they'd heard him on the phone. Sounded like a conversation with the superintendent about progress, saying how they weren't any further forward.

Tanzy shook his head in reply to the question.

'There are too many open cases right now. We need to start closing them. I'm getting heat from above and you know what happens when I get heat from above?'

They didn't need to answer. They both knew that shit rolled downhill.

'Work harder...' he said.

Byrd and Tanzy nodded and left, closing the door on their way out.

Byrd sat down. Tanzy stopped at his desk chair and told Byrd he would go see DS Stockdale, see if he was any further forward on the case of the four missing women.

The office was full. A wave of mixed conversations danced from wall to wall. Keyboards were tapping, mugs of coffee and tea being raised and lowered back on desks.

DS Phil Stockdale sat at the opposite end to where Byrd and Tanzy sat. His desk was the closest to the wall. Through the window next to him, he had a nice view of St. Cuthbert's Way, watching cars and vans pass by.

As Tanzy rounded the last row of desks, he noticed Stockdale was hunched over, looking at something on his desk. It was obvious he hadn't heard Tanzy approach because when Tanzy spoke, he jumped and fumbled with something in his hand.

'Oh, hi, boss.' His face reddened. 'Didn't see you there.'

Stockdale had short black hair, clean shaven, and was thick-set. When people learned he used to play rugby, it didn't come as a surprise to them due to his stature.

Tanzy stopped in front of him, watching him curiously. 'What you up to?'

He looked at his phone and shook his head, then placed it into his pocket. 'Ahh, nothing.'

Tanzy was aware that Stockdale previously had issues with gambling in the past. It had almost ruined his marriage after the thousands of pounds he'd wasted, digging himself into debt. He made a promise to his wife and also to Tanzy that he wasn't doing it anymore.

'How – how can I help, sir?' Stockdale said, the colour of his face turning back to pink again.

'Any further on the four missing women?'

Stockdale sighed, looking up with his emerald eyes. 'No, sir. Not yet. I need to make some calls.'

Tanzy nodded and turned, then stopped. 'Phil…'

'Yeah?'

'If you need help with something, you only need to ask me. As well as your supervisor, I'm here to help you as a friend. With matters inside and out of work. You know that, don't you?'

Stockdale nodded appreciatively and watched Tanzy return to his desk. Stockdale pulled out his phone and unlocked it, then immediately logged out of the site, then deleted his internet history.

23

Friday Afternoon
Darlington

Jane Ericson smiled to herself in the rectangular vanity mirror in the bedroom of her fourth-floor flat. To call it a flat would be a lie, although it wasn't much more. When advertised, her eyes had lit up when it had been labelled a 'Luxury Apartment' in the window of the estate agents situated on Duke Street. She'd immediately taken a fancy to it, whether it was the flat itself or because it had been given such a fancy name. Of the two bedrooms, her bedroom was the biggest. The other bedroom, almost half the size, was filled with open rails of clothing and sealed boxes. Hanging dresses, t-shirts, and garments along one wall, and the other, contained a shelving unit filled with folded items, such as skirts and jogging bottoms.

Her phone pinged with a text message on the vanity unit in front of her. She'd been waiting for the reply and smiled. Picking it up, she noticed it was from Suzie. She read the message, Suzie confirming that she'd meet her in William Steads at seven-thirty with the others.

It had been a few weeks since they'd all been out together and promised to be a good night. She knew most of them from school, and even now, eight years on, most of them were friends and made the effort to see each other on a weekly basis.

The time was four-thirty. She had a few hours to go and had already been showered and put her foundation on. She stood up, made her way over to the bed, and sat down, pulling her closed laptop toward her. She opened it, logged on, and waited for the ancient thing to boot up.

Once the internet page loaded, she clicked on her book-marks and found the page, then waited nervously. It was the second time she'd done this and hoped it would excite her as much as the first time. The screen came up. There she was, sitting in the chair. Up in the corner of the screen, there was a small list of usernames, people that were join-ing the session. She noticed her name, Ericj4, second on the list, although the list didn't indicate any relevance of order.

After the session ended, she sighed heavily and slumped a little. Then she got to her feet, went back over to her vanity unit, finishing her make up. She made a quick phone call to her friend, asking when she was pick-ing her up, then checked her bag a few times to make sure she had everything for her night out.

The time was approaching 7.15 p.m.. She stood at the front door of the flat and checked herself in the dark pur-ple maxi-dress that she'd chosen to wear, complimented by black high heels. Her dark hair had been curled, ring-lets nestled over her shoulders and down her chest. Her green eyes stood out like emeralds against the jet-black eye shadow and eyeliner.

Somewhere outside, she heard a car horn beep several times. Then a text message pinged on her phone in her small bag, her friend, telling her she was outside. Jane grabbed her keys, opened her door, locked it, then got in the lift in the hallway.

As soon as Jane stepped inside the lift, she pressed the button, turned to face the front, and waited for the lift to take her down four floors.

Mackenzie Dilton watched her through the camera up in the corner. He'd hacked into the CCTV of the flats and had taken control of the system. Usually, the cybersecu-rity of such a modern block of flats would have been much harder to access, but whoever had set it up, hadn't done the best job, although he wasn't complaining.

Judging by her choice of outfit, it wasn't hard to guess where she was going. He'd seen the purple maxi-dress in her small bedroom when he was there yesterday, checking the electrical wiring that had played up the day before. Fancy the chances of her electrics not working properly and him putting a business card in her letterbox the same day. What a coincidence.

Roger Carlton electrics.

Yesterday he had been to have a look around the flat, aimlessly checking the sockets and switches, pretending he knew what he was doing. When she received a phone call and went into the kitchen, he'd taken out his listening device and placed it under the desk where her laptop was. Then, being the hero he was, he checked the main supply from the consumer unit on the ground floor, flicked the switch, and voila, the power came back on. The trip to her flat was also useful to know if she lived alone, which, after asking her if having no electricity would affect anyone else in the flat, she told him she did live there alone.

The time on the office wall clock told him it was nearly 7.30 p.m.. He got up, went to his bedroom to put on a shirt, jeans, and some shoes. He then headed out, into town, in the direction of William Steads.

Hours later, Jane stumbled home, disorientated, stuffing cheesy chips into her mouth from the white Styrofoam container in her hands. Garlic sauce dripped down her chin onto her maxi-dress, but she didn't notice, nor did she care. She was going home after a really good night.

She turned left into Trinity Road and started dawdling up the incline as if she were a baby learning to walk, struggling to stay in a straight line, her strides not quite in sync, feeding the chips into her mouth as she went.

Stanhope Park sat in darkness on her left. A few eerie murmurs came from somewhere in the park, but she ignored the sounds, not bothering to look. Whoever they were, if they stayed out of her face, there wouldn't be a problem. Without looking for approaching vehicles as she came to the end of the path, she crossed the road on Vane Terrace, then stepped up onto the kerb in the direction of her flat.

The sounds of her heels occasionally scraping off the path every couple of steps reminded her she'd had too much wine, but she'd had fun and that's all that mattered, apart from the disagreement with Lexi about an American television show. Funny thing was, she couldn't even remember what it was about.

Mackenzie Dilton waited next to the pillar at the opening of her apartment car park, watching her coming towards him. The darkness around him was a blessing, although, in her current state, her blurred vision would probably mistake him for a tree, or a strange-looking plant pot.

He watched until she was only metres away, then hid back in the shadows, waiting till she passed. As she did, he could hear her heavy breathing through the struggle of walking and eating at the same time. The smell of her perfume still lingered around her like an invisible bubble, albeit not as strong as it was when he was standing next to her in Green Dragon a few hours before. She'd spotted him at the bar and shouted, 'Hey, you're the electrician!' They idly chatted for a little bit before she introduced him to a few of her friends, who smiled because that's what people did to be nice. Each place she and her friends went to, he was there, watching in the shadows.

Waiting.

Waiting until she made the short walk home.

She unevenly made her way to the front door, then stopped before it, remembering she'd need a key to get inside. She closed the half-eaten chips container and fumbled with her bag, lifting the flap too quickly, causing her phone, keys, and several coins to fall out and cause a racket on the floor.

Dilton stepped out from the dark and made his way over to her.

She didn't hear him coming.

24

Early Saturday Morning
Darlington

'Let me help you with that,' Dilton said.

Jane Ericson wearily turned after hearing the voice behind her and squinted at him as he approached. Although she was plastered, there was a flash of recognition. She'd seen him somewhere before.

He bent down, picked up her items, and handed them carefully back to her, apart from her keys.

She grunted something inaudible.

'Sorry?' he said.

'Trician…' She hiccupped violently. It threw her body forward a few inches, then she smiled. 'You electrician…'

'That's right. I'm just coming home. Do you want me to open the door?'

She nodded three times, her head feeling loose on the top of her shoulders like it wasn't connected properly. Like a Churchill dog on a car's parcel shelf. He slowly moved around her, took a few steps toward the door, then used her key to gain access. He held the door open and waited, then jumped forward to grab her when she tripped over herself and started laughing. Some of the chips fell out onto the floor.

Leaving them, he guided her in, letting the door close, looking up at the windows of the surrounding flats. There was no one around.

The corridor was familiar. The lift was to the right. Beyond that was a cupboard.

He guided her toward the lift and pressed the button, then said, 'Wait here.' He moved over to the cupboard, opened it, and leaned inside.

'Was' that?' she slurred, leaning against the wall, looking down at the bag in his hands. It was the type you'd take to the gym, long, narrow, black in colour.

'Oh, this? I forgot it earlier,' he said, with a smile.

She stared at him, her eyes glassy and half-open as if she could fall asleep at any moment. Seconds later, the lift door pinged open, the sound echoing in the silent building.

'Let me help you.' He gently took hold of her arm and led her inside, then placed the bag down to his right, so he could support her weight to prevent her falling. He leaned to the left and pressed the button for floor four on the control panel. In a sober state, she would have questioned why he was there. Or why he had pressed the top floor. She'd have known he didn't live on the fourth floor because *she* lived there, and there were only three flats on that floor. Unless he was helping her?

The doors pinged closed and the lift sluggishly started to ascend.

'Wait a second,' he said, letting her go for a moment, bending down to his bag. He unzipped it, pulled out a full head mask; it had a built-in filter around the mouth area with a large space for the eyes made from glass. The top and rear of it was made from thin flexible rubber.

'What is that?' she asked him, swaying unsteadily as the lift went up.

He smiled, then placed his hands inside, pulled it over and onto his head, making sure the bottom of it provided an even seal around his throat and his neck.

'You look like a spaceman,' she joked, a thin smile lining the edges of her mouth. 'Looks cute.'

'I'm glad you like it,' he said in a distorted voice. He then bent down to the open bag and pulled out a spray can. It was the size of a WD40 can but instead of having a push spray mechanism at the top, it had some kind of circular pin. He placed his forefinger into the ring and yanked it upwards.

It didn't take long for the green gas to come out of the top and start filling the lift.

Jane looked confused, seeing the green mist start to fall and pool in the bottom of the lift, quickly rising.

'It's like green rain…' she said, kicking it playfully.

Dilton stood watching her with wide eyes. He didn't move or change his focus. He knew the lift was filling, now up to their waistline.

'Have you ever suffocated?' Dilton asked her.

Her eyes narrowed and she shook her head. 'No. I go to bed now. Tired.' Her words were becoming more incomprehensible.

She coughed a few times until it become continual. Worried, she dropped her small bag to the floor of the lift and put both her hands to her mouth. Her phone, some coins, her ID, and items of make-up fell out under the green mist, rolling across the floor in all directions.

She couldn't breathe now, not getting enough oxygen. Dilton watched the panic in her eyes. Her frantic eye twitching, her sudden body jerking forward and backward realising she wasn't getting the air she needed to breathe. It was only getting worse.

'You can't breathe, can you?' he whispered. 'You're getting no air.' His eyes wrinkled at the edges as he smiled behind the mask.

She clawed at her throat, willing it to open up to allow some clean air inside. But the green mist was up to their chest now, taking over, depleting the level of oxygen inside the small space. She turned, banged on the lift door several times with a clenched fist, then hit the buttons on the control panel, but each time, weaker than the last, until finally, she cried out as the green mist filled her mouth.

She took one last breath and collapsed on the floor of the lift.

25

Saturday Early Morning
Darlington

When the lift reached the top floor, the doors opened. Before committing to fully stepping out, Dilton leaned out to check the small corridor.

No one there.

Absolute silence. He grabbed the bag and threw it out first, then went back and placed his hands under her armpits, dragged her out slowly, and lowered her to the floor. He gathered her items up, put them in her bag and dropped them inside his holdall.

Once at her flat door he removed her keys from his pocket, unlocked it and edged it open.

Once he was inside, he pulled off the mask, then went back out for the bag and for Jane then closed her door. He flicked on the light switch to his right and the short, narrow hallway lit up with cold, bright light. The bathroom was to his left. The kitchen / living space was straight ahead. And to the right, two doors led to the bedrooms. For one, he had to admit, it was a cozy apartment – he'd thought the same yesterday.

Leaving her curled up on the floor, he walked into the kitchen, made his way over to the left toward the French doors that led out to the small, rectangular balcony. The area was only two feet out, four feet wide. A viewing point at best, surrounded by a black, metallic railing. Dilton imagined it would be the perfect spot to stand and drink a cup of morning coffee, watching the town wake up, the noise gradually growing with early morning commuters on their way to work. With the double doors locked, he used the built-in lock to open it, and without making a sound, he gently pulled them towards him.

Night air gently slapped his face, noticeably cooler compared to how it felt on the ground level. He closed his eyes, took a lungful, and slowly breathed out like he had all the time in the world. The view was amazing, he had to admit, seeing for miles around. Although it was just after three in the morning, the night sky had a vibrant quality about it, the sun hovering just below the skyline, eager to rise from the east for another hot summer's day.

He looked down at the balcony railing for a moment. The railing was made up of thin cylindrical metal poles that were fixed to the base of the balcony, spaced three inches apart, going vertical to the handrail, which was flat, roughly two inches thick.

Finally, he nodded, happy about his decision.

He went back into the hallway, and picked Jane up, using her armpits to drag her flaccid body across the living room. He lowered her for a moment to readjust his stance and picked her up again, this time higher, toward the height of the railing.

'Jane?' he whispered.

No response. She was still unconscious.

He smiled, then very carefully, lifted her onto the balcony railing, placing one of her arms over the outside of it, then did the same with her right leg, so the top of the balcony rail was against her chest, stomach, and in between her legs. Her head was tipped to the left towards the flat, so, to balance her weight, he shuffled her centre of gravity to the outside of the railing.

Once he was sure she was balanced, he took a step back.

Her left arm and left leg were hanging inboard, and her right arm and leg hanging over the edge, four floors up.

'When you wake up, Jane, don't panic,' he whispered. 'Or you might just fall.' He went inside, grabbed her phone from her small bag and placed it on the floor of the balcony. Pressing the button, he saw it had plenty of battery remaining.

He went back inside, locked the French doors and on his way out of the flat, he turned off the light and shut the front door. He took the stairs all the way to the bottom and stepped outside at the ground level at 3.34 a.m.. Jane was still balanced on the railing. Deciding his work was done, he smiled.

At 6.01 a.m., DI Byrd's phone rang. His eyes flickered a few times until he realised what it was. He sat up quickly, rubbing his eyes from the morning sun that had crept around the edge of the half-closed curtains.

It was DC Phillip Cornty.

'What the hell does he want?' he muttered.

He accepted the call. 'Phil, do you know what' —

'Boss. You need to come. We have a very delicate situation on our hands.'

26

Saturday Early Morning
Darlington

Byrd pulled up in his X5 at the address which Cornty had given him, red-eyed and tired. He hadn't slept well; kept hearing noises downstairs at home and, on several occasions, had investigated to find a quiet, house with no intruders lurking in the shadows. The whereabouts of Claire's laptop were still unknown, and she'd claimed on her insurance that it had been stolen. He checked all the doors and windows before he left, happy Claire was safe inside, asleep upstairs, nestling their baby boy who, in three months, would be here. Whoever had entered his home the other night, if that's what it was, wouldn't be getting in again. He'd managed to fix the cameras which he could access remotely on his phone, informing him of anyone approaching which gave both of them peace of mind.

Trinity Road was a quiet road. There were cars scattered along the street on either side, their windows reflecting the bright morning sun. As he unclipped his seat belt, a car pulling into the road up ahead caught his eye. A Golf. Tanzy's Golf. He watched Tanzy angle over and stop just in front of him. They made eye contact and nodded, then stepped out. Byrd, although it was a Saturday, dressed in his usual smart trousers and shoes, but instead of a shirt, he'd put on a black t-shirt and worn a thin black jacket over the top. His hair had been dampened and brushed to the side.

'You going to a funeral?' Tanzy said.

Byrd cracked half a smile at his mistimed joke. 'Let's hope not.'

Tanzy was more casual, wearing trainers, blue jeans, and an open thin, dark blue jacket, showing a tight white t-shirt. He wouldn't look out of place in a fashion magazine, with his trimmed goatee, piercing blue eyes, and tanned bald head.

They both moved toward the entrance of the flats that Cornty had described, looking up, trying to see what had been explained to them, struggling in the low sun that dominated the morning sky.

When they arrived at the pillars that were either side of the entrance, they noticed a cluster of people standing in the middle of the car park, in front of the building's front door, glaring up with concern on their faces. Some of them on the phone, some of them silently staring up into the sky at the woman balanced on the handrail.

Tanzy and Byrd stopped at the small crowd and looked up, using a palm to shield their eyes from the sun.

'Jesus,' Byrd whispered.

To the right, DC Cornty heard the detectives approach and looked their way.

'Morning,' he said. 'We got a call from a runner who spotted her from Cleveland Terrace just over half an hour ago. Just hanging like that.'

Byrd and Tanzy craned their necks to look up.

'Is – is she dead?' Byrd asked, squinting in the morning glare.

'We don't know. When dispatch received the call, the woman explained what she could see and cleverly advised the operator not to approach with sirens in case the loud sounds woke her up.'

Byrd nodded. It made perfect sense.

Tanzy looked around at the people. 'Where are these people from?'

'The guy in the suit lives on the third floor. Was on his way out when he saw the runner standing in front of him, looking up with a worried look on her face. He said he doesn't know her but has seen her around, coming and going.'

Near the short chubby guy in the suit, there was an old lady, dressed in running gear but was holding a small dog on a lead, who seemed to be itching to finish his run, doing small energetic circles around her feet.

There was another couple, in their fifties, probably on a morning walk, and just beyond them, a bald guy dressed in shorts and a hoody.

'We need to get something set up,' Tanzy said to Cornty. 'If she is alive and wakes up, we need to make sure if she falls she lands on something soft. Or at least clear these people so they don't get hurt. Has the fire department been notified?'

Cornty shook his head.

'Get on it,' Tanzy instructed, disappointed with him. Cornty nodded, pulled his phone out, and stepped back a few paces.

'What on earth is she doing up there?' Byrd said. 'Is she drunk? Had she tried to jump and fell asleep? Is she dead already?'

Tanzy shrugged. 'We need a negotiator down here. If that's what her intentions are.' He looked over to Cornty, who had made the phone call to the fire brigade. 'We need the fire lads out, get an extended ladder up there. If we can't get through that door, that'll be the only way, Max.'

Byrd agreed. Tanzy then went over to the man in the suit from the third floor. He was holding a black briefcase and looked like the banker or lawyer type. 'What floor is she on, the fourth?

The man, who Tanzy guessed was in his fifties judging by his hairline, turned. 'Yeah, the fourth. I'm on the third.'

'Can you let us in the building? We need access to her flat.'

'Sure.'

Tanzy turned his attention to Cornty, who'd finished on the phone. 'What's happening?'

'Back up is coming now. I've told them to approach quietly.'

'Okay, we need to move these people back. If she falls now, she'll land on them.'

DC Cornty moved forward, and one by one, asked the people to move back. Everyone complied. To the left, they heard a murmur of voices, five people passing the pillars at the edge of the property with one thing in mind: to get a closer look at the woman balanced on the balcony. Tanzy immediately made his way over to them with his palms out. 'Please, I need you to leave. This is a very delicate situation. The fewer people the better.'

One of them, a man dressed smartly in chinos and a tight-fitting black jumper, said, 'What's going on here?'

'What's going on is that we have a delicate situation. And I'm asking you, as a police officer, for you to please leave and let us deal with it.'

They all stopped before him. 'What about them?' a woman said, pointing to the handful of people in the car park watching. 'Why can they watch?'

'They live in this apartment block. So please,' he said, his tone now firmer, 'leave. Let the police handle this.'

They pulled a face, reluctantly turned, and left the property, stopping on the path outside to watch from there which Tanzy knew he couldn't do anything about. The more people here, the more chance of waking or disturbing her. He went back over to Byrd who slipped his phone into his pocket.

'Negotiator is on his way,' Byrd informed him.

Tanzy nodded. 'The guy in the suit will let us in.'

'Cornty can control people down here. If we can get in her apartment and open that door, we could pull her back before she wakes.' Byrd and Tanzy went over to the short guy in the suit. 'Can you let us in now, please?'

The man nodded, pulled his keys from his pocket, and shuffled over to the front door of the building. Once he let them in, he went to the lift and pressed the button. Within seconds, the doors pinged open and the suit, Byrd, and Tanzy stepped inside. After the button for floor four was pressed, the doors closed, and the lift started to rise.

They stepped out but the man stopped to think and decided to go to the door on his right. 'Judging by her window, this should be the door.'

'Do you know her name?' Byrd asked him.

He squinted. 'Could be Lorraine. Or Jane. I'm not one hundred percent certain.'

Tanzy took out his phone and phoned the station, telling them to check the occupant of an address and to update them on their intentions of getting inside her apartment.

'Yeah, I'm sure it's this one.' The suited guy moved back, allowing Byrd and Tanzy to stop at the door.

Byrd tried pushing the door, then tried the handle. It was locked but worth a try. He checked Tanzy wasn't directly behind him, took a few spaces back, then lunged forward with his right foot into the left side of the door against the lock and handle mechanism. The door shook with a loud bang but it stood firm. He tried again and failed.

A door to their right opened. Out stepped an elderly man. 'What on earth is going on?' He wore a long, blue dressing gown and thick-framed glasses sat on the end of a thick nose. It seemed they'd interrupted his newspaper reading, judging by the folded Northern Echo in his hand.

'I'm sorry, sir,' Tanzy said. 'Don't worry, we are the police. We need to get inside. The woman is in danger.'

'What's wrong with Jane?'

'She's on her balcony. We need to get inside to help her.'

He eyed them suspiciously for a moment. Although he recognised the suited man as someone who lived on the floor below, he asked, 'Can I see some ID? You don't dress like you're with the police.'

The guy had a point. Tanzy looked like he'd do well on a catwalk and Byrd looked like he'd been to his gran's funeral. Tanzy pulled his ID from his pocket to show him. Once satisfied, the elderly man said, 'Don't kick that door again. You might break it.'

'But we need' —

'I have a spare key,' he said, stopping Tanzy short.

'Thank you.'

The guy went inside. It felt like three hours had passed before he came back and handed Tanzy the key. It was a single key linked to a keyring with a photo of Benidorm's seafront.

'What's her full name?'

'Jane Ericson.'

Byrd pulled two pairs of latex gloves from his pocket and handed a pair to Tanzy. They both pulled them on and used the key to open the door. Byrd went in first, followed by Tanzy, then the guy in the suit. Tanzy turned, advised the suit guy to stay back to give them room to work and think.

Immediately to the left they spotted the French doors and saw Jane positioned on the balcony. From inside her flat, they could see how perfectly balanced her weight must have been, and it wouldn't take much for her to become unbalanced.

Byrd tried to slide the door open but it wouldn't budge.

'The lock,' Tanzy said, pointing to the mechanism near the handle. Byrd, for a moment, felt stupid, then flicked the lock down, and very slowly slid the door open. Just as he did, a loud ringtone rang out, coming from a phone positioned on the floor of the balcony.

It was so loud, it stirred Jane, who opened her eyes suddenly, staring wide eyed at the phone.

Byrd froze, watching her, listening to the ringtone. He didn't want to speak or disturb her or call her name, knowing it could cause an unfortunate sudden movement that could literally tip her over. But she panicked, realising she was on her balcony handrail.

Then it happened so fast.

Byrd lunged forward to grab her left hand but missed.

And she fell four floors down to the concrete below with a sickening thud, the awful sound followed by a string of screams and panic from the people on the ground.

27

Saturday Morning
Police Station

'You missed her?' DCI Fuller asked Byrd after hearing what had happened.

Sadly, Byrd nodded. 'It happened too fast. I missed her by inches.'

Fuller leaned back, sighed heavily, and looked up at the ceiling. Byrd and Tanzy didn't say anything. Fuller wasn't intending to come in today, but after Byrd had phoned him less than an hour ago, informing him about Jane Ericson, he had no choice. He didn't look amused about it either, not that it was Byrd or Tanzy's fault.

The sunlight coming in from the window that overlooked St. Cuthbert's Way to the left had warmed the office for most of the morning. Fuller looked hot and bothered in his coat, but for some reason, he hadn't taken it off. A simple phone call and an emailed report would have done. He'd promised his missus and kids they were going to the beach and weren't pleased to hear he'd have to go down to the station to be personally updated about another death in Darlington.

'We don't need this shit.' Fuller's tone was grim, straight to the point. It was his usual tone, so it came as no surprise to Tanzy or Byrd. 'So, as well as a house fire that killed a family of four, and four missing women who haven't been seen in nearly a week, we now have this?'

Byrd and Tanzy didn't reply, knowing it was a rhetorical question.

'And nothing in the way of leads?'

Again, the detectives stayed silent.

'Please talk me through this again,' Fuller said, seeming like he had other things on his mind. 'You managed to get into the flat using the key from her neighbour, then saw her on the balcony. Then as you opened the door, the phone rang on the balcony and woke her up?'

Byrd nodded, confirming his analysis so far.

'But she panicked, realising she was balanced on the handrail and went over?'

'Yeah.'

Fuller thought for a moment. 'Who phoned her?'

'This is one of the reasons why I phoned you,' said Byrd. 'I needed to tell you personally.'

'Go on…'

'The number in her phone was saved as Roger Carlton.'

'The same name linked to the house fire, who we suspect could be Mackenzie Dilton?'

Tanzy and Byrd both nodded in unison.

'Sonofabitch…' Fuller dipped his head, looking down at the desk. 'We need to find this fucking Mackenzie Dilton. He's playing games with us. Do we know how she got up there?'

'Not yet. There are several possible scenarios,' said Byrd, who'd discussed this with Tanzy earlier at the scene after she'd fallen. Fuller waited for it. 'We'll be able to determine if she had consumed alcohol after the tox report, meaning she could have been out in the town, came home, and for whatever reason, collapsed in that position.'

Fuller made a face.

'I know. It doesn't seem likely,' admitted Byrd. 'Or… she was taken home, knocked unconscious, and carefully positioned there for her life to be determined whether she woke and leaned to the left or the right.'

'Where is Jane now?'

Byrd informed Fuller she had been taken to the hospital for the pathologists to have a look at her. It was obvious, judging by the nature of what happened and the state of the body, the fall had caused her death. But they needed to check to see what happened before then. Had she been drugged? Excessive levels of alcohol?

'Did the building have cameras?' asked Fuller.

Byrd nodded. 'We spotted a camera in the lift and in the entrance door. DC Cornty is speaking with the maintenance team to see the footage from last night and early this morning.'

'Why did the phone ring when it did?' asked Fuller. 'Seems a coincidence it was when you almost reached her?'

Tanzy nodded several times as if something had clicked. 'It's as if whoever did it, was watching, waiting for that exact moment, knowing that ringing her would wake her.'

'Are forensics there?'

'Yes. Forensics are checking the apartment for any prints. Tallow and Hope said they'd be in touch later. Tallow wasn't happy he had to come in.'

'Nature of the beast, unfortunately.' Fuller shrugged, implying he wasn't pleased to be here, either. 'Good work, you two. See what the cameras tell us and see what Tallow and Hope find.' He then noticed something on Tanzy's face. 'What is it, Orion?'

Tanzy turned to Byrd. 'Remember the people watching below, the people near us?'

Byrd bobbed his head.

'The bald guy in the shorts and hoody, remember him?'

Byrd said he did. Byrd rarely missed anything.

'Didn't Samantha Verity, from seeing the clip from the still shot on the camera at Napier Street, say she was certain that Roger Carlton was Mackenzie Dilton, and she was one hundred percent sure he was wearing a wig and a fake moustache?'

Byrd nodded. It finally clicked. 'Same height, same features…'

'I knew when I saw his face, there was something familiar about him. I'd spoken to him on the morning of the house fire. When I saw him this morning, he recognised me. But he didn't have dark, brown eyes. He had bright blue eyes. And a thin goatee.' Tanzy fell silent for a second. 'They were contact lenses. He was in disguise. Mackenzie Dilton was there, standing with us, watching Jane.'

'He knew exactly when to make the call,' Byrd said. 'As soon as he saw me at the French doors from below, he phoned her, knowing the call would wake her and there'd be a good chance she'd panic and would fall.'

28

Saturday Late Afternoon
Low Coniscliffe, Darlington

On the sofa in the living room, Claire was tired, her eyes barely staying open, watching the television fixed to the wall above the fireplace. Little Alan had started moving in her belly more recently and, although getting as comfortable as she could, she hadn't been sleeping very well on a night.

The front door opened. She looked toward the hallway, seeing Byrd appear. 'You okay, Claire?'

She smiled and looked back at the television. 'Has anyone seen anything?'

He padded a few steps in but didn't sit down. 'No, no one. Rick and Mary down the road have a camera that shows much of the street, but we couldn't see a thing. No one has heard anything in a few days. Nothing else has gone missing. Probably just a passer-by, trying his luck.'

'Hope so,' she said slowly. 'Can I have something to eat?'

'What would one like?'

'Up to the head chef. Surprise me.'

Byrd smiled, turned, and left the living room, then took his shoes off and positioned them near the front door under the piles of coats. It had been a long day. He went into the kitchen and grabbed some pasta and sauce from the cupboard and set it away in the oven.

His phone rang in his pocket. He was half expecting the call and answered it.

'Hi, Jacob,' said Byrd.

'Hey, Max,' replied Tallow.

'All done at the flat?'

'Yeah, we finished a little while ago.' Tallow paused a moment. 'In the way of prints and traces of DNA, there's nothing out of the ordinary that stands out. Have you seen the camera footage yet?'

'No, not yet. Still waiting on the maintenance man to call.'

'Okay.' Byrd leaned over to check the pasta in the oven, which was cooking away nicely.

'We did find something interesting in the bedroom though,' Tallow then said.

'What's that?'

'Under her desk, there was a bug stuck to the underside of it.'

'A bug?'

'A listening device. Something you guys know all about.' Tallow then explained what it looked like and Byrd agreed it was very likely a remote listening device. 'There was also a business card positioned on top of her closed laptop.'

'What type of business card?'

'An electrician's card with the name Roger Carlton on it.'

'Roger Carlton...'

'Yeah.'

Byrd fell silent for a few moments, thinking hard. Without seeing the cameras and finding out if Jane Ericson had gone up to her flat by herself, it was obvious that Roger Carlton aka Mackenzie Dilton had been in her flat at some point. If so, there was a similarity with the fire at Napier Street and his frequent visits there before the actual murder. This had been planned, similar to the last one. And not only that, Mackenzie Dilton had been there at the scene with them, same as he was in Napier Street, posing as a member of the fire department. It was like he was checking on his work, making sure his plan had worked as he intended.

'Also, there's something else,' Tallow said. 'On the back of the Roger Carlton card, it said to look at this laptop.'

'Where is the laptop?'

'I spoke to Orion. He told me to contact Mac from DFU. Mac said he was working today, so when we dropped off some samples to the lab, I left the laptop with him, telling him that Tanzy had requested a check on it to see if anything stood out.'

Byrd was surprised that Tanzy hadn't mentioned it.

'Okay, thanks for letting me know. Good work, Jacob. Enjoy the rest of your weekend.'

'I'll try.' Tallow hung up the phone, and the line went dead.

Byrd put the phone back into his pocket.

A little while after, he took out the pasta and plated some up for Claire, who, when he walked into the living room, found her asleep. He smiled, placed the plate down onto the coffee table with some cutlery and stood for a moment, watching her, the way she held her belly, holding their son, comforting him as he grew inside. He leaned down, placed a palm on her stomach and kissed her forehead. He couldn't wait to meet Alan. His only regret is that his parents wouldn't have the chance to see him but that's something he'd have to get over.

29

Saturday Evening
Darlington

Mackenzie Dilton sat at his desk, his hand on the mouse, clicking and scrolling. There was a deep focus in his eyes. When he concentrated, nothing distracted him. He knew what he wanted and knew how to get it.

Danny Walters had been pretty straight forward. Everything had gone to plan. Killing his family in the process was unfortunate, but he wouldn't dwell on it too much. It was Danny's fault.

Jane Ericson had been a breeze too. As long as he continued to stay focused and prepared, the plans would fall into place.

But, he had to admit, he was cutting it fine.

Earlier that morning had been the second time that DI Tanzy had seen him. Whether or not the detective inspector had noticed him was a different matter, but he knew it was a dangerous game to play, being there at the scene, involving himself when, perhaps, he didn't need to.

The difference was he wanted to make sure his plan had worked.

After his preparations, he needed to check they were dead. When DI Byrd had opened the French doors four floors up, he called Jane's phone. He knew what ringtone would blast out because before he left in the early hours, he'd downloaded the ringtone, then checked it would be loud enough.

And boy was it.

As soon as the phone went off, as well as seeing the anxiety in Byrd's serious face and his pathetic attempt to reach for her, he watched Jane twitch, then panic, and it didn't take long for her to fall over the edge. In less than a second, she hit the floor with a sickening splat.

Even he admitted it wasn't pleasant.

But when everyone jumped back in terrified shock, he casually placed his phone into his pocket and walked away. Everyone had been too concerned with Jane's mangled body down on the concrete to notice him disappear.

For a moment, he stopped what he was doing, looked at the printed sheet of paper to his left, the names underneath Danny Walters and Jane Ericson. He went through the names in his mind, thinking about who was next and how he'd implement his plan. It needed to be right.

Moving on, deciding he'd come back to it later, he finished editing the video on the screen. He watched it over and over, making a few tweaks, and finally smiled, happy it was ready to go.

He opened YouTube and logged in. He wasn't worried about being traced because he'd protected himself and his location, his IP address changing every ten seconds, bouncing around the globe, making it almost impossible for the most intelligent of IT wizards to trace.

He clicked on UPLOAD and sat back, waiting for the download bar to reach one hundred percent. He leaned back, smiled, and closed his eyes. He couldn't wait for the havoc it would cause.

30

Saturday Evening
Low Coniscliffe, Darlington

A few hours later, Claire had woken up, feeling hungry. Byrd warmed her food, brought it into the living room and placed it down on the coffee table in front of her.

'There you go,' said Byrd. 'How are you feeling?'

She shuffled up to a sitting position and leaned forward to grab the bowl of pasta bake. 'I'm tired, Max.'

He took a seat next to her, smiled, and rubbed her back for a moment. 'I can't wait to see him, you know. I wonder what he'll look like?'

'I bet he's a chunk, like you!' she said, with a playful grin.

'I'm actually categorised at an ideal weight now,' replied Byrd. And he was right. After losing two stone there wasn't much left on him. He wouldn't be on the cover of Men's Health magazine, or modelling swimwear, or would never be as finely tuned as Tanzy, but he was doing well. Certainly, an improvement to what he was like six months ago. He felt better, felt sharper, fitter. He enjoyed football, being able to run longer and quicker.

'I know,' said Claire, rubbing his thigh lovingly. 'You've done so well. It's my turn to be a fatty now.' She patted her stomach with her free hand.

Byrd leaned to the side to check his phone.

'You expecting a call?' Claire frowned at him. 'It's nearly nine.'

'I'm waiting for someone to ring me about the cameras at the flat today.' Byrd had told Claire the basic story of what happened earlier this morning, but, as he normally tended to, missed the not-so-pleasant details, like almost reaching Jane Ericson before her body fell four floors onto the hard concrete with a stomach-churning smack. He knew, after weeks of feeling sick because of the pregnancy, it wouldn't help her cause. She seemed to be worse on mornings, frequently waking, feeling nauseous. Sometimes she was sick, sometimes she wasn't.

Claire nodded and turned back to the television.

On cue, Byrd's phone rang. He didn't have the number saved, but stood and left the room, then pressed AN-SWER and wandered into the kitchen.

'Hi,' the voice said, 'is this Detective Inspector Max Byrd?'

'That's me.'

'Hi, my name is Joseph Peters. The maintenance man for the flats at Trinity Road.'

'Hi, Joseph.' As Byrd entered the kitchen, he glanced up at the clock to see the time. Asking him what had taken him so long was on the tip of his tongue.

'Apologies I am calling you now. I've been having issues with my phone. Only got it working over an hour ago and heard the awful news about what happened earlier. Is it true you want to see the footage from the cameras?'

'Please, if that is possible.'

'Well, it is possible. But I'm afraid they won't be of any help.'

Byrd frowned. 'How so?'

'Both cameras – the one in the entrance door and the camera in the lift – don't show anything between three am and four am.'

'You're joking?' Byrd hung his head and pressed a palm to the side of his temple.

'I wish I was. As soon as the clock on the screen goes to three am, it immediately changes to four am. There's an hour missing. I don't understand it myself. I can't explain it. It's never happened before.'

'Okay.'

Joseph Peters stayed silent for a while.

Byrd was about to hang up but thought of something. 'Can you access the cameras now? Where are you?'

'I'm at home. But yes, I have access to the cameras from my home. Because I'm maintenance, we set that up, so I could control it from here just in case. What is it you need?'

'The victim's name was Jane Ericson,' Byrd said. 'In her flat, we found a business card in her bedroom with the name Roger Carlton on it. It stated Roger Carlton was an electrician. However, we have sufficient reason to believe that the individual is linked to an urgent issue that the police are currently dealing with. I suspect that, over the past few days, he went to her flat. Would it be possible for you to check the camera for the previous three days to see if you can spot something unusual? Or someone inside the building who doesn't belong?'

'Erm, yeah, I suppose I could.' He didn't sound too keen.

'How many cameras are there?'

'Just two. One in the lift and the other covering the entrance and exit door. If anyone, other than the people who live there, came in, I'll be able to recognise them. I have a good idea who should be there.'

'Great, thank you,' said Byrd. 'If you spot something, don't hesitate to call, day or night.'

'It would be my pleasure, Detective Byrd,' he said, now sounding more upbeat.

Byrd wasn't sure if the sarcasm in Peter's tone was deliberate or he'd imagined it. Either way, Peter ended the call, and Byrd placed his phone down on the kitchen worktop and sighed heavily. Just as he was about to pick the phone up and head toward the living room, it rang, the ringtone echoing in the silent kitchen.

It was PC Amy Weaver. He frowned. It was unusual for her to be phoning him at this time, especially when she wasn't on shift.

'Amy…' he said, answering.

'Sir. Sorry to bother you…' She sounded flustered.

'What is it, Amy?'

'There's another video on YouTube. My God, you need to see this.'

31

Saturday Evening
Low Coniscliffe, Darlington

Byrd immediately went upstairs to his small, quiet office. His laptop was closed on the desk as he walked in. The desk was pushed up against the wall under a small window and, to the right, was a shelving unit filled with documents and smaller boxes that he hadn't touched in months. He forgot what was in them.

He took a seat on the chair he seldom used and opened the laptop which he rarely needed. If he did, it was to finish off reports he hadn't completed at work. His usual things, such as emails and browsing online, were done on his phone.

'You at your computer?' Amy Weaver asked.

'Yeah. Hold on.'

'I've emailed it to you,' added Weaver.

'How did you find it?' asked Byrd, waiting for the screen to load that seemed to be going slower than usual.

'It was on Facebook. A friend tagged me in it.'

'Jesus.'

The laptop caught up to speed and the plain desktop screen appeared. There were a couple of folders in the top left-hand corner, one labelled 'Pictures', the other 'Documents'. Underneath the folders was an internet icon. He clicked it twice and waited. Weaver stayed on the line but said nothing. Once the internet finally loaded, he opened his emails and found the one she'd sent at the top of the list, above the email offering him penis enlargement pills and diet shakes for 'great' results. He clicked on the link, and for the next minute, he remained silent, watching carefully. At the end of the clip, he realised he'd held his breath and let it out suddenly. 'Jesus Christ, Amy.'

'I know, Max,' she said quietly.

'Thanks for letting me know. I need to ring Ori.'

Byrd hung up and watched the video again. He then found Tanzy's number and pressed CALL.

'Max, what do I owe—'

'Ori, I'm sending you a link. It's a video. You need to stop whatever you're doing and watch it.'

Tanzy didn't reply for a moment, and judging by Byrd's tone, knew its importance. 'Okay, hold on.'

There were sounds of shuffling through the phone, then a beat of silence. Tanzy said, 'Okay, the laptop is open. How've you sent it?'

'Check your personal emails.'

Tanzy opened the email and clicked on the link.

'Tell me when it starts,' said Byrd.

'Yeah, it's started,' Tanzy informed him.

Byrd pressed play and they watched it together on their own screens. At the bottom of the video, the title of the video was *Element 2*.

'What is element 2?' said Tanzy.

The video looked like it had been edited and didn't flow perfectly, clearly showing different times of the day and background activity. The camera positioned high up in the corner of the poorly-lit lift picked up the man who stepped inside, carrying a holdall of tools. He then leaned forward and pressed a button on the control console, then took a step back, revealing his thick head of hair and a ridiculously looking moustache, which Byrd and Tanzy now both knew, was fake.

'That's Dilton!' noted Tanzy. 'See the time, Max. Half four the day before.'

'I see it.'

The next scene showed Jane Ericson walk into the lift, dressed up ready for town, wearing a purple maxi dress, her dark hair curled, resting on her slender shoulders. It wasn't long before she disappeared. The time was just after seven the night before.

'Max, what—'

'Just watch, Ori...'

The video changed to another scene inside the lift. This time, it was ten past three earlier that morning. Jane Ericson, carrying a half-eaten tray of chips and her small handbag, stumbled inside. She used the wall of the lift to steady her weight, which didn't take a detective to work out she was drunk.

To the right of the screen, an arm came into view and placed a black holdall down onto the lift floor. Judging by the size of the arm it looked like a man who was also wearing a shirt. Unfortunately, they couldn't see a face. A few seconds after, the figure lowered to the area where he'd placed the bag and pulled something out.

'What's that?' Tanzy asked.

When the man moved in full view of the camera, Byrd and Tanzy noticed he'd put on a mask, covering the whole of his face and top of his head.

'What the hell is that?' Tanzy whispered.

The man then leaned down, picked up some variety of can, unscrewed the lid, and green mist started to fill the lift. Jane Ericson didn't seem fazed. If anything, her drunken state found it funny, judging by the smile curling up the side of her face. Very soon, the screen turned green, the mist eventually taking over.

'What on earth is that, Max?'

'I have absolutely no idea, Ori.'

In the next scene, it was daylight. Outside. The camera or recording device was angled up, showing Jane Ericson balanced on her balcony. Somewhere off the screen, the sound of beeping was heard, then a final beep. The video then showed the balcony door open on the fourth floor and, out of nowhere, the phone rang.

Jane Ericson then fell to the ground with a splat. The video captured every second of it. Then a voice said, 'How unfortunate,' before it cut off.

Byrd's face grew hot.

'So, he recorded it, then put it online for the world to see. Again!' shouted Tanzy. 'We need to stop this before it goes viral.'

'It's already gone viral, Ori.'

32

Sunday Morning
Newton Aycliffe

Tanzy made two coffees. One for Pip, one for himself. He brought them over to the kitchen table, placing them both down, and took a seat opposite her. Pip smiled thanks and looked down, scrolling through something on her phone. The kids were outside playing in the garden. Eric was kicking the football against the side wall of the garage, the repetitive banging borderline annoying, and Jasmine was playing with a water set that Pip had bought recently, the sound of water splashing onto the decking every so often.

As Pip continued to scroll at whatever she was looking at, Tanzy's phone rang. He plucked it out from his jogging bottoms and answered it.

'Ori, it's Mac,' the voice said.

Mac from DFU.

'Hi, Mac.'

'I've been looking at Jane Ericson's laptop.' He fell silent as if he was doing something else. 'I need to show you something.'

'Okay, can you email it over? I can have a —'

'I need to show you now,' Mac said, cutting him off. 'Are you at home?'

Tanzy frowned. 'I am…'

'Good. I'm near yours. See you in five.'

Tanzy, with curiosity, opened the door, and standing there with a laptop under his arm, looking a little scruffier than usual, was Mac, wearing a faded jumper a size too small and jeans with a tear at the knee which looked like he'd had for years.

'Hey, Ori,' he said, with a smile.

'Come in,' Tanzy said, stepping back, motioning him in with a hand.

It was the first time that Mac had been to Tanzy's house. Whatever Mac was going to show him, Tanzy knew was important, otherwise it could have waited until the following morning.

'Just through there,' said Tanzy, pointing to the kitchen. 'Can I get you a coffee?'

Mac told him he would love one and pulled a seat out at the table that Pip had just left, plonking himself down and opening the laptop on the table. Without asking, Mac took the half-eaten pack of biscuits and helped himself.

No wonder you're in the obese category, Tanzy thought to himself.

Minutes after he'd made the coffees, Tanzy took a seat next to Mac, who explained to him he'd found something weird.

'Weird?' asked Tanzy, confused.

'Well, when you know where to look, you can see how long people spend on certain websites. Behind the scenes, if you like'—he waved it away rather than getting too technical—'and the data tells you that.'

Tanzy gave a gradual nod, not really following. 'Okay…'

'There's a certain website which she'd visited. The problem with the site is that, apart from an empty word box near the top of the page, there's nothing else. The site itself carries a huge source of data.'

Tanzy held up a hand. 'Hold on, hold on. I'm lost, Mac.'

Mac smiled. 'Have you got Wi-Fi?'

'Who doesn't,' joked Tanzy, then told him the password so Mac could connect to it.

'Let me show you.' In the blank bar at the top of the page, he typed in the address and tapped ENTER. The site came up immediately.

'At the end dot com?'

'Yeah,' said Mac, nodding. 'But look.' He angled the laptop so Tanzy could see it clearer. 'See this page. It's a black screen, apart from that login bar.'

'Yeah?'

'But a page like this, with no additional drop-down menus or no visible linked pages, should have a small internet presence. The data volumes coming from that server should be minimal.'

'But…?' Tanzy said, unsure.

'It has the capacity to run a large page with multiple drop-downs and a mass amount of media, such as videos and images.'

'So, why is there only the username and password login option?'

'That's what I was wondering,' admitted Mac. 'Whatever she was up to, she needed a password to access, which I assume, would take her beyond this page and on to whatever is lurking behind this page.'

'Is there a way to get past this?'

'I've tried dozens of words and phrases. Every time I press enter, the search bar clears and I have to try again.' He pulled the laptop closer to him. 'What I have done, though, is search for the site on Google. There are a couple of forums that came up. Here, have a look.' He pushed the laptop closer to Tanzy, who read the comments in several threads.

He frowned, worriedly. 'What on earth was she watching on that site?'

33

Monday Morning
Police Station

Most of the team had either heard what happened over the weekend on the news or had been told. They waited nervously in room 103, a long rectangular room with windows on one side, allowing a substantial amount of daylight in. A whiteboard filled most of the wall near the door, with a projector fixed to the ceiling just above it for presentations or videos.

This morning was going to be used for just that. An update on latest news and current affairs.

The tables in the room were positioned in a 'U' shape. Fuller had said, with Tanzy and Byrd's approval, that it would make everyone feel important and a part of the team. In previous roles, he'd implemented such ideas instead of rows of desks, experiencing the people at the back didn't involve themselves as much as the ones at the front.

As Tanzy and Byrd looked at their colleagues, the morning sun shone brightly through the windows, illuminating most of their tired faces. Byrd went over to the window, used the pull cord to lower the blinds a little.

On the desks furthest away from them was DC Cornty, DC Tiffin, PC Andrews, and PC Weaver. The right side was filled by DC Leonard, PC Grearer, DS Stockdale, and PC Timms. On the left side, were the lead forensic officers, Jacob Tallow and Emily Hope. Next to them, the forensic trainee officer, Amanda Forrest. And next to the forensic team, closest to the door, was DCI Fuller. He didn't always attend the meetings, but after the events from the weekend, he'd made the effort. He liked to know his team was up to speed with current affairs and equally, enjoyed hearing their views and ideas on how to solve them.

Byrd returned to the centre of the wall and stopped near Tanzy, who had set up the laptop with a presentation they'd both put together earlier.

'We'll make a start,' Byrd said, grabbing the small black remote from the table. Tanzy pressed a button on the laptop and the whiteboard filling with a page titled 'Current affairs' and the date underneath it.

'I'd first like to say I hope everyone had a good weekend.' He waited for nods but there were only a couple. 'Unfortunately'—he turned to the screen—'not everyone did.' He clicked the first slide. 'As some of us know, Jane Ericson, a twenty-six year old female fell from the fourth floor of her balcony to the ground. She died immediately.'

The slide on the screen showed everyone the area of concrete where she'd landed, covered in a small, faint pool of dried blood. The next image was a photo taken of the balcony from ground level, indicating the height of the fourth floor.

'That's a long way down,' DC Cornty commented.

Byrd ignored him and continued.

'In addition to this, another video has been uploaded to the internet. Some of you may have seen it, some may have not. Hands up who's seen it?' Half of the hands went up. 'We managed to save it before it was taken down. For those who haven't seen it, here goes.' He looked back at them. 'Viewer discretion is advised.'

Most of them nodded, readying themselves. The video was the same one Tanzy and Byrd had watched yesterday, starting with when Jane Ericson entered the lift. The time changed in the bottom corner suddenly and, on the screen, standing to the left, obviously under some influence of alcohol, was Jane, leaning to the side. In addition to Jane, there was what appeared like a man's arm, but not much could be seen in terms of his face or any distinctive features. They watched him disappear for a few seconds, then green gas started to fill the lift until they couldn't see Jane anymore.

'What on earth has just happened?' DC Anne Tiffin asked, the first time she'd seen it.

Byrd or Tanzy didn't respond and continued to watch. The next part was taken from ground level, looking up at Jane, who was balanced on the handrail of the balcony. Tanzy discreetly glanced up at Byrd while he watched it.

'Is that you, sir?' DC Cornty asked.

Byrd immediately snapped his head at him and stared. Many eyes widened and glared over at Cornty. Byrd didn't say anything, holding his gaze, but Cornty, cockily, matched it. Byrd was professional and didn't answer his question, looking back at the screen just in time for when the phone rings. A second later, Jane loses her balance and falls to her death.

'Jesus Christ!' Tiffin shouted, covering her mouth with her hands.

'That is a long way…' DC Cornty whispered.

Before Byrd exploded at him, Tanzy jumped up and said, 'So, we have a similarity here, guys.' All eyes found Tanzy. 'We have two murders and we have two videos. Investigating the scenes, we can also confirm we have the name Roger Carlton too. As we also know, a female called Samantha Verity came forward informing us she'd had a relationship with Roger Carlton, who, in fact, is called Mackenzie Dilton. She said he was obsessed with an American show where one of the characters was called Roger Carlton. She also said he was strange and there was something off about him. The first time we came across Roger Carlton was at the house fire at Napier Street. I spoke with him – he was posing as one of the fire investigators, but after speaking to Harry Law, their supervisor, he didn't know the name or see the man in question. Secondly'—he looked over to forensics—'thanks to our forensic team, we found a business card on Jane's laptop. It was an electrician's business card with the name Roger Carlton.'

DC Tiffin raised her hand.

'Yes, Anne?'

'If the videos were uploaded to the internet, can we not trace it? Or the IP address of the device that uploaded it?'

Byrd and Tanzy both smiled, appreciating her train of thought.

'Unfortunately not,' Byrd answered. 'We spoke with Mac in DFU and he said he did his best to trace the IP address with the ISP but the—'

'The ISP?' questioned DC Leonard.

'The internet service provider,' answered DC Cornty. All eyes fell on Cornty for a moment, so he elaborated. 'Everyone is assigned an IP address by their Internet service provider.'

'That's true,' continued Byrd, 'however the IP address was never fixed and the service provider didn't recognise the address of the upload.'

Leonard frowned. 'Meaning what exactly?'

'That Roger Carlton, a.k.a Mackenzie Dilton found a way to make sure his IP address was untraceable. Mac said he's come across it but only on rare occasions. The address seemed to bounce across providers, leaving no fixed location. We are assuming he's based here in Darlington, but according to his IP address, he could be in India, then ten seconds later, in America.'

There were a few confused faces but no one said anything on the matter.

'Do we have any intel on the whereabouts of Mr Dilton, yet?' asked DCI Fuller over from the left, sitting casually with one leg over the other.

'Not yet, sir,' responded Byrd. 'We spoke with the company he worked for, an IT firm up in Newcastle.' Fuller was aware of this but appreciated it was for the benefit of the team. 'Said he hadn't worked there in months.'

'Did Samantha Verity give an address for Mackenzie Dilton?'

'She did. Orion and I went there. Victoria Embankment. A few minutes from here. No one answered but we spoke with a neighbour who said he hadn't seen him in months. Turns out, judging by the information I received from HM Land Registry, that the house isn't owned by Mackenzie Dilton anymore. It used to be until ten months ago when Geoff Adamson purchased it. I went to the house on Friday to speak with him. He explained how he bought the house from Mr Dilton and that was the last time he had seen him, and unfortunately, didn't have any contact details, as everything was done through their solicitors.'

Fuller nodded but it was clear by his facial expression he was less than impressed with how things were going.

'Anything on the fire at Napier Street?' DS Stockdale asked.

Byrd turned towards Tallow, Hope, and Forrest in search of anything further on their findings. Tallow shook his head.

'What about the four missing women?' Fuller asked quickly.

Byrd and Tanzy had heard him on the phone in his office to the superintendent, Barry Eckles. Judging by their heated conversation, it appeared Eckles was pressing him hard and didn't hold back in expressing his disappointment so far. The call had ended by Fuller saying 'I understand' before he hung up the phone.

'No sign of them, sir. I've spoken to their families over the weekend to give them updates, a way of informing them they are our priority.'

Fuller gritted his teeth and pushed his lips out. It wasn't looking good for them. And judging by what was going on in Darlington, they all thought the same thing: it wouldn't be long before another body turned up or went missing.

34

Monday Morning
Essex, South of England

Linda Fallows made coffee and toast, then sauntered into her conservatory, placing them both down on the small table next to her chair. She grabbed the TV remote and settled into it. The sun was up and high in the sky, brightly shining through the glass windows of the conservatory. She'd had it built three years ago, ready for her retirement.

It wasn't long before Rusty, the black lab she'd had for eight years, came bouncing in from the kitchen, no doubt smelling the burnt bread lingering in the air. He loved toast. Not only toast but jam on toast. It was his favourite.

'Good morning, you!' she said, leaning forward, rubbing under his chin and top of his head. There was nothing but love in his dark, brown eyes as he looked up at her waiting patiently. 'You want your breakfast?'

He moved his head eagerly as if he understood.

'Here you go…' She grabbed a slice and fed it to him. It was gone within seconds, but he seemed happy. Rusty was a brilliant dog. She'd bought him as a puppy when her husband, Gary, was alive. They used to go walking with him over the fields and down by the river. Rusty was Gary's idea. He knew cancer would take him eventually and wanted Linda to have company when it was his time to go. And he wasn't wrong. Neither were the doctors. Six months after getting Rusty, Gary passed away. Liver cancer. The only saving grace was that, in the end, it happened quickly.

Rusty looked happy and lowered to the floor, dropping his head between his front legs, looking towards the television. He did this most mornings. It was their routine. Linda had always wondered what he could see on the television, or whether it was just colours but either way, he enjoyed it, and no doubt enjoyed her commentary about what was happening.

Linda, after reading some fiction, went up to bed early, then got up at 4 or 4.30 a.m.. It was something she got used to and when she rose, she always made breakfast and sat in the conservatory, catching up on the news she'd missed from the night before. Using the remote she found the news saved in her recordings and pressed play. She liked the national news, liked to know what was going on around the country, not only in and around Essex.

She watched the news desk reporter inform the public about a killer in Darlington, who'd set fire to a house, murdering a family of four, and was now the likely suspect in the death of a young woman who had fallen from her balcony from the fourth floor.

She raised a hand to her mouth. 'God... that's awful, Rusty.'

From her left, she grabbed her iPad and searched for murder in Darlington. A string of results came up. She slowly scrolled down the list, clicked on the link with the headline 'house fire – a family of four burns to death', and pressed enter. At the bottom of the page, it mentioned a YouTube video, titled 'Element 1', explaining that it was live footage recorded from the scene of the fire. She opened up YouTube and typed it in. Nothing came up. It had been taken down.

She pressed return and found herself on the list of results again, seeing headline 'Woman falls to her death' underneath. She clicked it, read up on Jane Ericson to learn exactly what'd happened to her. Due to further investigation from the forensic team after seeing the deadly gas from a camera inside the lift, they assume it was most likely an asphyxiant gas that depleted the level of oxygen inside the small space. The green colour could have been added for effect.

There's mention of another video posted to the internet, titled 'Element 2'. Linda opened up her app and searched for it, but it was either blocked or had been deleted.

'Never mind, Rusty,' she said to the dog. 'It isn't there.'

When she finished watching the rest of the news, she stood up, went to the kitchen, and made a coffee. On her way back to the conservatory she stopped to stare at the photos on the wall. There were dozens of them, all six inches by four, dotted around the wall in no particular order. Some were of her family and friends, and others were of her and Gary.

Finally, her focus fell on the one of her and Chief Constable David Gilling, when she'd received an award of recognition at the annual Police awards from several years ago. She was so happy and proud. Single-handed, she had interviewed and successfully got inside the mind of Tony Crawley, the man who'd kidnapped and killed multiple teenage girls, but had given the name of the last victim who he'd kept alive. Because of her, sixteen year old Bethany Tate had been found, and sent home to her family, safe and sound, albeit with a few scratches and a story she'd tell people forever.

She remembered the awards evening very vividly; David Gilling standing at the front of the smartly dressed crowd, commending her efforts and determination, labelling her one of the best criminal psychologists he'd ever had the pleasure to work with. After that, she'd decided to retire, take her pension, and settle down to a quiet life, where her biggest danger would be Rusty smothering her for more cuddles.

The morning passed and it was almost lunch time before she made her decision. She'd been thinking about it all morning. Once she'd fed Rusty, she picked up her phone and dialled the number she'd memorised from earlier.

After several rings, it was answered.

'Hi, my name is Linda Fallows. I'm wondering if I can speak to one of the lead detectives who is dealing with the recent murders in Darlington?'

'Hold on,' the operator said, 'I'll put you through.'

'Thanks.' Fallows waited half a minute before she heard a firm voice.

'Hi. This is Detective Inspector Max Byrd of Durham Constabulary. Who is calling?'

'My name is Linda Fallows. I'm a retired criminal psychologist.'

'How can I help you, Mrs Fallows?'

'You can't,' she said. 'But I have a very good feeling I can help you.'

35

Monday Evening
Darlington

Lisa Felon and Sarah McKay were cuddled together on the dark, cold floor. They had got over the fact they wouldn't see Lorraine again. It had been four days since she'd been there. Four horrendous days that, without any awareness of the time or light inside the dark space, had felt like weeks. They had tried to keep count of the days. At times, it was all they could think about, but they'd given up. They were tired, dirty, and hungry. They still didn't know how they'd got there and had stopped trying to work it out. One minute, they were getting into a minibus to take them to a party, the next, they woke up in this dark room without the ability to see or even begin to understand the situation they were in.

After two of them had vanished, their confusion worsened, understanding less about what was happening.

Watching them through the one-way mirror high up on the wall, were the two men responsible for putting them there. Mitch and Brad.

'They've given up, haven't they?' Brad said, standing at the window, peering down on them.

'What do you expect, Brad?' replied Mitch. 'If I was in there, I'd have given up too.'

Brad shrugged, turned, made his way back over to the desk where the computer screens were positioned, and sat down on the empty chair. 'Who are they wanting next?'

Mitch, watching the computer monitor, said, 'Votes are really close so far. See what it's like on Thursday.'

'I think we should mix this up a little,' suggested Brad.

'How?' Mitch swivelled on his chair, smiling, curious about what he had to say. 'What ideas do you have?'

'Nothing yet, but people will start to get bored if we keep things the same. We need to mix it up every so often. Maybe throw in a curveball of some sort. It'll get them all excited, won't it?'

'I'll think about it,' considered Mitch.

Both men focused on the screen for a while, looking at the various profiles. A message popped up in the lower right-hand corner.

'Ooo is that another one?' asked Brad, recognising the notification sound.

'Looks like it. We need to keep it quiet. It can't grow too quickly. I'd love it to, but it will attract too much attention.'

Reluctantly, Brad nodded his head.

'We'll put them on the reserve list for the next lot. There's so many to choose from.' Mitch smiled widely. 'We'll pick a selection when the time is right.'

'Sounds good,' agreed Brad. A moment later, he said, 'Hey, I was thinking.'

'Yeah?'

'You don't think what happened to Danny Walters and Jane Ericson had anything to do with this, do you?'

Mitch frowned at him. 'How could it? This is untraceable. Trust me. No one will get beyond the firewall. Have you seen the film Inception?'

Brad squinted, wondering where he was going with it. 'I have…'

'It's like that. A dream within a dream within a dream. This site'—he jabbed a finger toward the computer screens—'is like that. Even the best IT wizards won't find it.' Mitch's eyebrows shot up. 'They're paying through bitcoin. Trust me, it's untraceable.'

Brad nodded, absorbing Mitch's words. 'How does the bitcoin work?'

Mitch waved it away. 'You don't need to worry about a thing. It's a safer way of doing things, Brad.'

Brad wasn't sure but nodded again. He pointed to the screen. 'How's it looking?'

'The vote's tilted. They want Sarah now.'

Brad grinned. 'How many votes is that so far?'

'Three hundred and six.'

Brad smiled wider. 'We're doing well.' He stood up, went over to the window again. 'Seeing as Danny and Jane aren't going to be joining us anymore, are we going to let two more players in?'

'We are. I'm checking their profiles now. I'll pick two of the voters later. But for now, I need to go to work. How long are you staying?'

Brad looked down at his watch. 'Not long, the missus will be expecting me soon. By the way, have the three remaining players voted?'

'Two have. The other is online but they haven't decided yet.'

Standing up, Mitch yawned and stretched. 'Can't be bothered with work tonight. When you leave, turn off the lights, and lock up. Leave this system on. Might be good to keep playing the video from Friday. It'll keep them entertained.'

Brad nodded. It made sense. 'We'll need some more, won't we?'

'We will. Look around town on Saturday night. With a little persuasion and charm, you'll be able to pick up a few drunks in town that would be happy to go to a house party.'

'You got it, boss. See you tomorrow.'

An hour passed. Brad was still there, watching the women down on the floor through the glass. Through the microphones they'd positioned in the room, he could hear their tired, exhausted whispers.

He moved over to the left, stepping around the desk, and, reaching for the valve fixed to the wall, he opened it. Through the vents positioned in several locations around the dark room, gas silently filled it, and after three minutes he turned off the valve, grabbed the plate of food they'd prepared earlier, opened the door, went down the dark steps, and along the corridor. He picked up the mask from the floor and put it on. Then, using the key from his pocket, he opened the door and picked up the tray of food. The light from the hallway illuminated their peaceful faces; it would have been a pleasant sight if not for the rancid smell of urine and faeces hitting his nose. He gently placed the tray of food on the floor near them, and left, locking the door on his way out.

36

Tuesday Morning
Police Station

After Tanzy and Byrd had been into DCI Fuller's office to give an update on current investigations, it was safe to say he was less than impressed with how things were going. He barely spoke a word. Instead, he listened to them explaining the four women were still missing and forensics hadn't found anything further at the house fire they didn't already know.

The only links between the two murders was the posted videos to the internet and the name Roger Carlton, who they knew to be Mackenzie Dilton.

'Have we found Dilton yet?' Fuller asked, his tone flat.

Byrd shook his head. 'We've searched and searched. His picture is with the media. His last known employment was working for the IT firm up in Newcastle.'

Fuller sighed, leaned back. He was wearing a thin black jumper, something that fitted him better when he was a little slimmer, the bottom of his stomach appearing over the edge of the desk.

'So, we aren't doing very well, are we?' Fuller raised his hands to his face and rubbed hard.

'But, we may have something that can help us,' said Byrd.

'That so?' Fuller seemed sceptical.

'I spoke with someone yesterday. A woman called Linda Fallows. She's from Essex. A retired criminal psychologist. Seems to think she can help us with the investigation regarding Mackenzie Dilton and the videos posted to the internet.'

Fuller frowned, and for a moment, said nothing.

'What is it, sir?'

'I'm sure I've heard that name before,' Fuller said. He leaned to his left and wiggled his computer mouse. The screen came to life, and using the internet search bar, he typed in her name, clicked ENTER. 'Yes, I thought the name was familiar.'

'Who is she?' enquired Tanzy, finding a sudden interest.

'She received an award a few years by the chief constable for her hard work and diligent efforts in finding a missing victim. The killer had confessed to her whereabouts, and the girl was saved.'

Byrd and Tanzy nodded their approval.

'And she thinks she can help us track our guy down?'

'That's what she says.'

'Are you going to send her some information about our current findings, see what she comes up with?'

'Better than that, she said she's coming up.'

Fuller seemed surprised. 'From Essex?'

Byrd nodded. 'Told me she'd be here sometime this morning.'

Fuller smiled thinly, feeling a trace of hope inside. 'Good. That's good. Hopefully, we can make some progress with—'

There was a knock on the door.

Fuller said, 'Come in.'

PC Amy Weaver entered. 'Sir, there's a Linda Fallows here to see you, Max.'

Wasting no time, Byrd, Tanzy, and Fuller stood and went through to the office to find a very slender woman with long, well-kept blonde hair, who Byrd assumed, to be in her fifties. Despite the warmth of the morning and it being summer, she was wearing a long brown cardigan that went down to her knees, black jeans, and high brown boots. She had a very attractive, thin face, with prominent features: high cheekbones, and a thin nose that sat below bright blue eyes.

Byrd extended a hand. 'I'm Detective Inspector Max Byrd.' Immediately, even though she was older, he found her attractive. She had something about her; charisma and confidence that Byrd assumed had stemmed from her years as a criminal psychologist before she retired.

'It's nice to meet you, Detective Byrd. I am Linda Fallows.'

Fallows then shook Tanzy's hand, then Fuller's, who both introduced themselves with the professional courtesy when addressing someone in the force you didn't know.

There was an uncomfortable silence, then Fuller checked the time on his wrist, and said, 'I have a meeting I need to attend to. I'll leave you in the very capable hands of our detective inspectors, Max and Orion.'

'Thank you, DCI Fuller.'

Even without knowing she was from Essex, her accent was a giveaway.

'Thank you for coming all this way,' Byrd said, with a smile. 'Can I get you a coffee or tea? Water?'

'Coffee, please. Little milk. No sugar.'

'Okay.' Byrd turned to Tanzy. 'Should we go to meeting room 101? I'll grab the coffees, meet you in there?'

Tanzy nodded.

Byrd made his way across the office towards the canteen. Tanzy asked Fallows to follow him. As she did, curious eyes from behind desks watched her, noticing her new face.

Once inside room 101, Tanzy motioned to a chair across the desk. Fallows took off her coat, revealing a long-sleeved black t-shirt that enhanced her slim physique, and hung it on the rear of the chair before she sat down. They made small talk, discussing what time she'd arrived in Darlington and where she'd stayed last night. She even told Tanzy about leaving her dog, Rusty, with her next door neighbour.

It wasn't long before Byrd came back holding a small tray. He placed the three coffees down on the table and asked if she wanted a biscuit. She said she didn't, which didn't surprise Byrd, judging by her figure.

'I'll waste no time, Detectives. It seems like we don't have much of it,' she said. 'Have you heard of the four elements?'

37

Tuesday Morning
Police Station

'The four elements?' Tanzy asked, a frown lining his tanned forehead.

Fallows, sitting with one leg over the other, nodded.

'You mean fire, air, water, and earth?' said Byrd.

'That's right.'

Tanzy glanced to Byrd, feeling like he was missing out on something very important.

'I'm aware of there being four elements in the world,' said Byrd. 'Everything is made up of the four elements. I'm no expert, though.'

Next to Byrd, Tanzy looked lost. 'You need to tell me what you're talking about, Max.'

Byrd, without waiting for Fallows to explain, added, 'It originated from the ancient Greeks, who believed that everything was made up from four elements. Air. Water. Fire. And earth.'

'That's right,' Fallows agreed. 'But more importantly, this theory had developed in scientific terms and the meaning that it gives to our earth. For example, the air is a gas, water is a liquid, the earth is a solid, and fire is plasma.'

'The states of matter?' asked Tanzy, remembering something about it from school over twenty years ago.

'That's right. The way the atoms in each object or matter are made up of these four elements. It's everywhere. Earth could be defined by wood, rocks, metals, and ice. The liquid is water but could be hot lava. The gases are oxygen and nitrogen, which are the main gases we breathe.'

'What about plasma?' asked Tanzy before she had the chance to speak, not able to think how plasma fits into it.

'The plasma, to put simply, could be fire. But on a sci-entific level, we could think of lightning, solar wind, the sun, neon signs, and fluorescent lighting. These four ele-ments are everywhere.'

Tanzy and Byrd both nodded, but they weren't sure where this was going. They'd enjoyed the few moments of education but didn't understand what she was getting at. Fallows could see this on their blank faces.

'You're both wondering why I'm telling you all this?'

They nodded in unison.

'Well, the first victim died in a house fire. The Walters. That's our first element. The second victim, from reading it correctly, fell from four floors up onto the concrete. She—'

'So that's earth?' Tanzy asked, jumping the gun.

'I could see how you would think that. Because she hit the ground, which, as we know, is solid. But reading the report, she was gassed inside the lift beforehand, wasn't she? That's what knocked her unconscious to begin with?'

Byrd frowned, glancing at Tanzy for a moment, then back to her.

'How do you know that?'

'Because I read the report, Detective.'

'How did you read the report?' Byrd exchanged a look of confusion with Tanzy. 'Our reports are only for us to see, no other forces.'

'I asked someone to request it.'

Byrd leaned back a little. 'Who?'

'A friend of mine.'

'I thought you were retired?'

'I am,' she admitted. 'But I still have friends in Essex.'

'Why did you feel the need to access the report. This, as you know, happened in Darlington. What interest would you, or anyone else from the Essex police department have to request the report?' Byrd's tone had turned sour after learning what she'd done, now unsure of her motives.

She held up her palms. 'Listen, I can see how this looks. But rest assured, I'm here to help you.'

They absorbed her words for a moment. 'On what grounds did you have to request the report?'

'After seeing both videos on the internet about the fire and the fall, I needed to know if the fall was because of the earth, which in that situation, was our solid element. As it turned, out the victim was gassed out in the lift beforehand, so I'm assuming it's the air element.'

Byrd didn't reply straight away. All he could think of is who from Durham Constabulary had authorised the report for Essex police to get a hold of it.

'What are you saying, Mrs Fallows?'

She looked at Byrd. 'Please, call me Linda. Mrs Fallows seems too formal for someone who speaks the way I do.'

She had a point.

'What are you saying, Linda?'

'I'm saying that's two of the elements down. There are two to go. Water and Earth.'

'Why do you think that? Surely, if what you're saying is true, that everything links to the four elements, is it possible you're trying to make it fit when in reality, it doesn't? Maybe you're just trying to fill in your retirement time with something to do?'

Tanzy craned his neck to Byrd, knowing it wasn't a nice thing to say. He could tell his words had upset her a little.

'Well, Detective Byrd...' She hung her head for a moment, then lifted her gaze to meet his. 'I would agree with you. And I don't blame you for thinking that. I would think the same if I was you.'

'But?' asked Byrd, knowing there was more. Two hundred and fifty miles was a long way to travel for nothing.

'Because, Mr Byrd, when I watched the videos, I knew,' she said.

'Why?'

'Because I've seen this happen before. And I'm not letting the sonofabitch get away with it again. Not this time.'

'What happened?' asked Tanzy.

'Let me start from the beginning,' she replied.

38

Tuesday Morning
Darlington

Rachel Hammond hadn't been awake long. She'd finished at three in the morning and once she'd got home, she'd taken a quick shower, then went straight to bed. Her shifts at the factory were unusual. On a week-to-week, zero-hour contract, it was the manager who decided what shifts she was given. If the orders weren't very high and he didn't need a full shift in, he'd tell her not to turn up. The only problem with that was if she didn't work she didn't get paid; it wasn't the end of the world because of the inheritance that her grandfather had left her. Plus, she had other things to do. Going out. Partying with her friends.

She went downstairs and saw a leaflet on the doormat. It was unusual because the post didn't normally arrive until the afternoon, so she assumed it was a pointless leaflet, someone trying to offer another pointless service. She picked it up and made her way down the narrow hall, through the dining room with it in her hand.

The first thing she did when she woke up, regardless of the time, was make a coffee. She needed it to wake her up and get her mind going. She looked at the large selection of coffee pods neatly positioned in the rack, decided on a caramel latte, then grabbed a mug from the side and placed it on the ledge under the nozzle. She lifted the top of the machine and placed the pod into the holder, clamped it down, and pressed the button. A whirring sound filled the kitchen.

While she waited, she turned back and noticed the flyer on the worktop. She leaned forward to have a look at it to pass the time.

'That's cheap,' she muttered to herself, then pulled her phone from her dressing gown, found her friend's number, then pressed CALL.

'Hey, it's Rachel…'

'Hi, what's up?' said the voice on the other end.

'You know last night we were talking about getting a hot tub for my birthday this weekend, then decided there wouldn't be enough time?'

'Yup?'

'Just got a leaflet through the door. A company renting out hot tubs on short notice?'

'How short is short notice?'

Rachel carefully lifted her mug from the holder and placed it on the side. 'I don't know. I'll ring the number. If I can get one for Saturday, I'll have you lot around.'

'Brill. Let me know what they say.' Her friend hung up.

Rachel typed the number into her phone and pressed CALL. 'Hi, I'm ringing about hiring a hot tub.'

'Hi. When's it for?' It was a man's voice.

'This weekend. Saturday. A party on the night.'

'Yeah, there's a couple available. How many people is it for?'

Rachel thought for a moment. 'Five, possibly six.'

There was a long silence.

'Hi, is anyone there?' asked Rachel, frowning.

'Sorry, I'm just thinking which one would be best suited for you. We have one. I can pop over on Friday to set it up so it's all ready for the Saturday. Would that work for you?'

'That would be great. I have the Friday and the whole weekend off,' she said excitedly.

'Great. Can I take a name and address?'

She told him.

No One's Safe

'I'll be there Friday morning.'
'See you then, Roger.'

Mackenzie Dilton smiled and hung up the phone. Roll on Friday, he thought, smiling to himself.

39

Tuesday Morning
Police Station

Byrd and Tanzy gave Linda Fallows their undivided attention, desperate to know what she was going to say and how she could help them with the investigation. So far, in terms of finding any substantial evidence, or a big enough clue to lead to an arrest, they'd come up short.

After she took a sip of coffee, she carefully placed it down on the table in front of her.

'Nearly seven years ago, I was involved in something similar. Actually, at the time, I was a Detective Inspector before moving into the psychological side of things. The way criminals thought and acted. As well as my degree in criminology, I went on to study psychology. The way the mind worked and what made people tick excited me. To combine them was something my peers suggested a career in which I would thrive in. I'll be honest, I loved being a DI, running my small team. As you guys know, every day is different and, let's just say, every day can be very interesting.'

Byrd and Tanzy smiled and nodded, knowing exactly what she meant.

She continued. 'It all started with the fire. It was horrific. A father, mother, and daughter were burned. Similar circumstances. Days after, we witnessed a drowning. The victim had been drowned in the bath, left there for several days until a concerned friend, who had arranged to do something with her the previous night, was suspicious when she couldn't get hold of her, then went into her house using the spare key she had for emergencies, she found her in the bath, still with her eyes wide open, staring up at the ceiling. Several days after that, a man was found inside his car after leaving work after a late shift. Just after midnight, we learned that a man had crept up behind the car and climbed into the back seat just as the engine had been turned on, a deadly gas, according to the forensic team, had been released. The victim died quickly.' She stopped for a moment. 'And lastly, a male victim was found by a dog walker who passed him one morning, partially buried in the woods.'

Byrd and Tanzy absorbed her serious words.

'Where did these events occur?' asked Byrd, narrowing his eyes.

'Places close to Essex, hence why our team picked it up.'

Tanzy nodded, then said, 'Why do you think they are linked?'

'Not only can I see the four elements here, but there's a bigger similarity.'

The detectives waited.

'They were uploaded to the internet. After each event happened, a day later, a video was uploaded online for the world to see. We tried our best to track it, but we couldn't. We even had our best IT guys on it. They said the user name couldn't be tracked or the person who uploaded it had installed some type of blocker.' She shook her head. 'I can't remember the technical term they used.'

Byrd took a deep breath. 'Did you identify the suspect seven years ago?'

She shook her head again. 'Unfortunately not. But the username of the person who uploaded it was 'Rcarl20'. The name will always stay with me. Since then, I've looked for anything about fires, drownings, and people being gassed. When I saw the article on the house fire and the woman falling that happened in the same town within a few days, it got me thinking. Then when the article mentioned the videos that had been uploaded, it's all I thought about. The last thing I wanted to do was get involved. I have a quiet life now, I'm retired. I've put all the crime scenes and insane people this country has to offer behind me. But...' she stopped, looking at the table for a moment.

'But you decided to request the files of our investigations anyway?' Byrd was annoyed at her but at the same time, didn't blame her. He thought about what he'd do if it was him.

'I can't let the man responsible get away with this again,' she replied firmly. 'If it is him, he's ruined so many lives. I can't let him do it again. So, Detectives, what I want – or should I say, need – is for you to believe that you have witnessed the fire and the gas. Very soon, you may well be witnessing water and earth.'

'In what way?' Tanzy asked curiously.

'That I don't know. But if what I believe is true, then you're going to have more deaths on your hands very soon.'

Byrd hung his head, lost for words. Tanzy didn't say much either, letting the silence fill the room, which was broken when there was a knock on the door. They all turned towards it when it opened.

'Boss?' It was DC Leonard, breathing heavily.

'What is it, Jim?' Tanzy said.

'Something has been found on the A66, in the middle of the road. We need to go.'

40

Tuesday Late Morning
A66, outside of Darlington

Before Byrd and Tanzy had left the station, they went to see Fuller, telling him what they'd been told. He immediately logged off his computer, jumped up, and left the office. Byrd asked him about Linda Fallows, about what they'd do with her, after explaining very briefly what she'd said and what an asset she could be for them. Fuller had agreed to allow her to go along, if of course, they were happy with that. Maybe she could assist in assessing whatever they were about to see.

They joined the A66. Byrd put the X5 into third gear and put his foot down. Tanzy was riding shotgun, holding the phone to his ear, speaking with DC Leonard who was already there, getting a few minutes head start. Fallows was in the back, sitting in the middle, leaning forward, anticipating what was waiting for them.

'Only a mile or so from the roundabout,' Tanzy said, relaying the info, then ended the call, lowering the phone to his lap.

Byrd nodded, maintained a steady sixty. They passed a temporary sign position on the side of the road saying, 'Incident Ahead – Route Diverted'.

Up ahead, Byrd eyed two marked Peugeots parked diagonally to prevent any traffic getting through. In front of the cars, there was tape that had been fixed to the central reservation to a tree on the opposite side. A few metres in front of the tape, was a large sign positioned in the centre of the road, stating 'Diversion' with an arrow pointing to the left. Next to the sign, PC Amy Weaver stood with her arm permanently outstretched towards Darlington Road, directing vehicles through Sadberge.

Byrd slowed gradually, watching the car behind him, making sure the driver of the red Clio had noticed his brake lights in the bright sun that was shining down in their direction, then angled over into the right lane and came to a gradual stop just beyond the sign. Weaver immediately recognised his car and moved to the left so she could direct the cars that came behind him.

'We stopping here?' Fallows said from the back seat, staring through the windscreen at the tape set up and the cars parked diagonally.

'Yeah.' Byrd turned off the engine and opened his door. Tanzy climbed out of the passenger door and stepped down onto the road. They turned, looking back along the A66, watching the cars approach and slow under PC Weavers instruction and the diversion sign. Tanzy, for a split second, imagined the feeling of being catapulted into the air by a car that didn't slow and plough into him, wasting no time in moving around the front of Byrd's X5. A moment later, he was joined by Byrd and Fallows, who, instead of appearing confident like she did when speaking to them at the station, looked a little apprehensive. Maybe the thought of witnessing the third kill she'd told them could happen very soon.

From one of the parked Peugeots, PC Josh Andrews opened the door and smiled at Tanzy as he made his way over to them.

'You got here fast,' Tanzy said to him.

'Not fast, ya last.'

Tanzy smiled at the small joke between them.

Andrews was a tall guy and in good shape from recent gym visits. He was good-looking, his hair was always gelled and brushed over. His clean-shaven face made space for his square jaw and good posture, making him appear taller than he really was, which was a modest six foot one, an inch under Tanzy, but an inch taller than Byrd.

'What's the story?' asked Tanzy.

'Just up ahead, sir. A call came in from a man who was driving along with his missus. The rear doors of a van that was driving in front of them opened, and something hit their windscreen. They almost veered off the road and came to a sudden halt. The guy got out and found the object that hit them.'

'Where is he now?' Tanzy asked, looking around, seeing no sign of the man and woman in question.

'Parked at the petrol station further down the road. Anne is speaking with him and his wife.'

'How far down is the road shut off?' Byrd asked, knowing there was a turn off not far away.

'We've blocked off Stockton Road that joins the A66. For the moment, we don't know how far down we need to look.'

Byrd agreed that should be a sufficient distance.

Tanzy peered around him and saw the rear of the forensics van that was parked further down. 'Who's here?'

'Tallow, Hope, Forrest. DC Leonard and DC Cornty. Think Cornty was first here.'

Tanzy nodded, and turned, hearing footsteps behind him. He introduced Linda Fallows to Andrews. They shook hands briefly and shared polite smiles, although Andrews had no idea who she was or the reason for her being there.

Byrd and Tanzy and Fallows ducked under the loose plastic tape and passed through the small space between the front of the cars, then walked down the empty road. It was surreal in a way, the road that was usually filled with passing cars was silent and still. The sun was shining above them, beating down in waves.

Once they reached the forensic van, they went around it, and wasn't long before they noticed Jacob Tallow thirty metres up, dressed in white coveralls and wearing a face mask, kneeling at the right side of the road. His attention was on something near the kerb. Byrd and Tanzy could see the object but not quite make out what it was.

Beyond him, roughly twenty metres down, over to the left, were Emily Hope and Amanda Forrest, dressed the same. Hope was bent over with Forrest standing beside her, a camera in her hand, snapping whatever Hope was looking at down on the road.

A hundred metres along, Tanzy noticed DC Leonard and DC Cornty slowly walking along the edge of the road, one either side, peering down at the grass verge.

'What have they found?' Fallows asked, slowly trailing Byrd and Tanzy, but intrigued by the sight of forensics. She then stopped, experiencing a series of mixed feelings. The excitement of a crime scene, along with the familiar sicky feeling in her stomach that she'd never quite managed to deal with. But today was different. Today, she felt not only that, but she felt a deep sadness. The realisation that what she'd done in her career, however many criminals she'd caught, or killer's minds she'd gotten into, that the world moved on. And there were criminals still out there, doing this to people. She only hoped the butterflies in her stomach would lead to finding some evidence that she could use to catch the killer she failed to catch seven years ago.

'You okay?'

Fallows looked up, snapped out of her lost gaze, and smiled at Tanzy. 'Yeah, sorry.' She started walking again and once she levelled with them, they carried on.

Upon their right, the senior forensic tech, Jacob Tallow was still kneeling at the side of the road. He heard footsteps and looked to his right, eyed Byrd and Tanzy, then noticed Fallows a step behind them.

He stood up, stepped away from the grass.

'Hey, Max. Hey, Orion.'

'Pleasant day for it,' commented Tanzy, stopping near him.

'Just got a whole lot better.'

Byrd smiled at his sarcasm, then turned his body towards Fallows and said, 'This is Linda Fallows, a retired criminal psychologist of Essex Police.'

Tallow nodded and pulled down his mask. 'A pleasure to meet you.'

Under different circumstances, they would have shaken hands, but they were both professional to understand the situation they were in and formalities could come after.

'What have we got, Jacob?' said Tanzy, looking away to where Tallow had just been kneeling.

'See for yourself,' he replied.

Byrd and Tanzy, side by side, came forward to see the cylindrical object. It was quite thick, roughly a foot wide and at least ten inches long. The outside part was pale white, but the ends were more of a pink colour with specks of dark red and white hard bits.

'What is it?' asked Byrd, frowning.

'Pathology will have a better idea but if I were to guess, I'd say it was the top of someone's leg.'

41

Tuesday Afternoon
A66, outside of Darlington

Over an hour after Byrd, Tanzy, and Linda Fallows had arrived, the forensics team had collected a total of fourteen body parts. Each part had been photographed in the exact position they'd been found and carefully picked up and bagged for further testing.

Knowing each part could potentially make up the anatomy of a human body, Tallow cleared a space in the rear of their van and placed a plastic sheet down. Then, with each body part, placed it in the position he thought it would go.

So far, they had both feet, both calves, one knee, both thighs, both hands, two separate pieces of flesh that resembled the stomach, a forearm, and two upper arms.

'What's missing?' asked Byrd, appearing at the rear of the van. Tallow looked down at the separated body and said, 'The head. One of the arms. Chest. Shoulders.'

Byrd said nothing. Mainly because he was speechless. Who on earth would do this?

'Can you see a similarity here, Mrs Fallows?' asked Byrd, turning his head towards her.

'Please, call me Linda.' It was the second time she'd said that. Byrd could hear by her tone she didn't want to say it a third time.

'Sorry, I'm used to formalities.'

They exchanged a brief smile.

'No, Max. If I'm being honest with you, I can't.' She looked back to the neatly positioned parts in the back of the van, then at Tallows who studied them for a moment, feeling slightly attracted towards him. Tallow wasn't typically good-looking, but he was tall and thin. He had a slightly bigger nose than usual, but it made him look different. And, what she found sexier than anything, was his level of concentration. The sun beat down hard. The day had warmed to the high twenties but Tallow didn't seem fazed by it.

She angled her gaze back to Byrd. 'Can I have a word?'

Byrd nodded. 'Sure.' They stepped away from the van far enough so their conversation was between only themselves, but Tallow left the van and wandered back down the road; they were still missing parts to search for.

'What is it, Linda?' said Byrd.

'There's no link here to what happened in Essex.'

'How can you be sure?' Byrd frowned at her. Not in a questioning, I-don't-believe-you way, but more in a curious way, hoping she'd explain.

'I can't see the elements here. As we know, we've seen fire and air. There's no water or earth here. This, in my opinion, Max, is something entirely different.'

Byrd listened but with a pinch of salt. Regardless of what she'd seen or hadn't seen before, it didn't have any effect on his thoughts. He would, like he did with every case or crime scene, focus on the facts, disregarding presumed speculations, which more often than not, led them down the wrong path.

'Okay,' he said. 'We'll see how Orion is doing down there.'

She nodded and followed his lead. They passed Hope and Forrest who were rummaging through the grass verges down on the left. Further down, PC Timms and PC Grearer were over to the right. They waved a hand as Byrd passed.

A few hundred metres down the road, they took a left into the petrol station. It felt strange doing it on foot and gave Byrd the feeling that although the road behind them was silent, a car could pull in at any second.

Tanzy was over to the left, speaking with a man and woman, who were standing in front of their car. Byrd could see the red blood on their windscreen as he approached with Fallows. Tanzy, with a notepad and pen in his hands, turned and nodded at him. The man and woman followed his nod, noticing Byrd and Fallows approach.

'This is Detective Inspector Max Byrd,' Tanzy said, introducing them. In turn, they shook Byrd's hand and told him their names. The man who introduced himself as Rick was Byrd's height and had a shiny, tanned skinhead. The top of a tribal tattoo crept over the top of his red t-shirt on the side of his neck. On his legs, he wore black shorts which didn't reach his knee. He was muscular, his width definitely belonged to a motivated gym-goer. The small, thin woman, who said her name was Paula, also sporting tattoos, stood with him.

Tanzy had been speaking with them for a while now, had had their side of the story. In brief, he updated Byrd and Fallows, occasionally nodding to the couple with certain points but Tanzy pretty much nailed it.

They'd told Tanzy in detail how they'd been driving along behind a blue Volkswagen Transporter when, for some reason, the rear doors opened and something hit their bonnet then came up and hit the windscreen, leaving the red smudge mark that Byrd noticed on his way over. They stopped and pulled up at the petrol station, then the man had walked back to see what the object was. When he found the hand a few inches inside the grass verge, he phoned 999 immediately.

'Did you manage to get a registration plate?' Byrd asked.

The man sighed. 'I've already told your colleague,' he said, pointing toward Tanzy, 'that I didn't. It all happened so fast.'

Byrd held up a palm, apologising for asking again. He wasn't sorry. It was something he did after knowing Tanzy had already asked the same question, to see what answer was given.

'Where do you guys live?' asked Byrd.

'Darlington. Just off North Road.'

'Where are you heading?'

'Billingham. I have family there,' replied the man sharply, a sign he was becoming impatient. 'Listen, can we go now? We've answered all the questions you've asked. We need to get to Billingham. Our family is waiting to go out for dinner and they'll be wondering where we are.'

Byrd, without replying, moved over to get a better look at the windscreen. In doing so, he caught a glimpse at the registration plate and took out his phone. He texted someone at the station to run the plate.

'What are you doing?' Rick asked. 'Your colleagues have looked already.'

Byrd turned to Tanzy. 'Have forensics took a picture and a sample of the blood?'

'Yeah. Tallow has been down.'

Byrd nodded and took a few steps back, turning to give them his full attention. He was about to say something when his phone pinged. He excused himself for a moment and looked at the text message. Rick and Paula sighed heavily and eyed him disapprovingly.

'I'm sorry about this,' Tanzy said to them, knowing exactly what Byrd was up to.

Byrd opened the message. The information about the car was legitimate. The car belonged to a Rick Jacobs. It was both Tax and Tested. Byrd turned back and pulled a card from one of his pockets. 'If there's anything else you can think of, I'd appreciate a call. You're welcome to go. Enjoy your dinner with the family. Sorry to have kept you.'

Rick forced a smile and wasted no time getting into the car. Paula traipsed around the other side and got into the passenger seat and within seconds, they were gone.

The detectives and Linda Fallows walked back up the quiet road towards the forensics' van. On their way, they looked up to see if there were any cameras. There weren't.

'Do you think you could have a word with Jennifer Lucas at the town hall?' Byrd said to Tanzy. 'I know it's out of her range but she'll have contacts, won't she? See if we can trace the blue Transporter.'

'I'll get in touch with her,' Tanzy said, plucking the phone from his pocket. He found her number and made the call, drifting over to one side.

Byrd looked at Fallows. 'How are you holding up?'

'It's hot today.' A thin film of sweat lined her forehead. 'But I'm okay.'

Tanzy spoke for a few minutes on the phone, explaining to Jennifer Lucas about the situation. She told him she knew who to call and that she'd get back to him with any footage that could help with their investigation.

Back at the van, Tallow and Hope were discussing something. Hope nodded several times then shrugged, then turned when they heard the detectives approach.

Byrd noticed their confusion about something. 'What have you found?'

'We haven't found the head yet, if that's what you're wondering...' Hope replied. 'But, it doesn't make sense.'

'What doesn't?' Tanzy said, intrigued.

'I don't want to speculate,' she said. 'But we'll see what pathology has to say.'

42

Tuesday
Outskirts of Darlington

As soon as Brad heard the loud noise behind him, he looked through the rear-view mirror and noticed the van's back door had swung open.

'Shit!'

Knowing he'd placed the body parts on the floor near the door, he immediately thought about the chances of them falling out. He switched his focus back on the road in front of him, almost ramming into the car in front which for some reason had suddenly slammed on the brakes and pulled hard on the steering wheel to avoid the almost certain collision.

'Watch where you're going!' he shouted at them, undertaking them in the left lane. It was an elderly couple driving an old Micra.

He looked in the side mirror at what was going on behind, and noticed a car come to a sudden halt, objects dancing on the road before it, falling from the rear of the van, bouncing on the tarmac, going in every direction.

Instantly he felt sick. What was he going to do? He couldn't stop the van in the middle of the A66 and walk back up to collect the body parts. He had to get away.

'Shit!' he shouted again, banging his hand so hard on the steering wheel, the horn blasted for a few seconds. He put his foot down and reached eighty, then took the next left turn near Long Newton, taking him around to the left and over the bridge. The rear doors had slammed closed but it was too late. At the mini roundabout, he took a right, and a hundred metres down the road, he pulled over, put his hazards on, and jumped out quickly. He raced to the back of the van and opened the doors to look in the back.

'Oh… no,' he whispered, placing both hands on his head, knowing most of the body parts weren't there. For a moment, he felt numb, then he started to shake. A car whizzed past, startling him from a second until he realised what it was, then the road fell deadly silent as the car disappeared into the distance, leaving the sound of his thumping heart and the pounding in his ears.

He'd messed up big time.

There was no way he could go back.

The police would be on their way.

With shaking hands he pulled the phone from his pocket, found the number, and pressed CALL.

'Yes, Brad…'

'We have a big problem, Mitch.'

'What?'

Brad explained what had happened.

'You, Brad, are an absolute idiot! Go back to HQ and don't do anything until I get there.'

43

Wednesday Morning
Police Station

When Linda Fallows returned to the station yesterday, she contacted an ex-colleague from Essex Police, who kindly granted her full access to the files they had on the murders she believed were linked to the recent happenings in Darlington. After speaking with DCI Fuller, Byrd and Tanzy had both decided she could be an asset and were happy to keep her there with them.

It was undeniable that Byrd and Tanzy were capable detectives but even the best detectives missed things.

Fallows used one of the empty computers at the back of the room, just across from Tanzy. She accessed her emails and forwarded the information she'd received from Essex to both of them. They read through the reports on the murders that Fallows had briefly spoken about yesterday, and Byrd and Tanzy had to admit, there were similarities between them, although a different location, and seven years apart. They understood Fallows' desperation in catching the man who got away seven years ago.

It had just turned nine. Byrd and Tanzy were standing at the front of the meeting room to brief everyone on what had happened yesterday. Fuller was sitting in his usual chair, the one closest to the door as he was normally the last one to arrive.

Byrd stood with the black remote and pressed the button.

As the first slide came up, DC Cornty, sitting on the right, asked, 'Sir, I was wondering – probably the same as other people here – who's the lady?' He pointed to Fallows who was sat next to Fuller, with one leg over the other.

Byrd narrowed his eyes at his smart comment, and said, 'The *lady* is —'

Fallows stood up abruptly, interrupting him. 'This lady is called Linda Fallows. She is a retired criminal psychologist who, for the last seven years, have helped Essex Police get into the minds of criminals and killers. Prior to that, she was DI, and has over forty years' experience in police and criminal activity, predominantly for Essex Police. She is here because she believes the house fire and the woman falling from the flats are linked, not only to each other but to previous murders that happened seven years ago in the Essex area.'

The room fell silent immediately. Byrd and Tanzy couldn't help but smile at each other and looked over to Cornty. Everyone else did too. The smug look on his face was replaced with embarrassment. Fallows sat back down.

'That a good enough explanation for you, Phillip?' DCI Fuller asked him.

His cheeks reddened so much, Tanzy and Byrd felt sorry for him.

'Yes, sir,' he replied quietly, looking away, towards the floor.

'Okay,' Byrd said, 'glad that's settled then.' He looked at the board behind him. 'We know the current situation with the missing four women. And we know about the fire at the Walters' house, and Jane Ericson falling from the flats. The focus of this meeting is about what happened yesterday on the A66. As some of you know, a couple were behind a blue Volkswagen Transporter near the Sadberge turn-off, when the rear doors of the Transporter opened and something hit their windscreen. They stopped to check it out and found a human hand.'

What had been found yesterday had become common knowledge so it didn't come as a shock to many. However, some weren't aware of the details why the meeting had been called, so due to the importance of transparency within the department, keeping everyone in the know was paramount to its success.

Byrd was about to continue but noticed DC Cornty looking down at his phone. He waited for a few seconds. Cornty heard the silence and looked up at Byrd, who scowled at him.

'Are you finished, Phillip?'

Cornty apologised and put his phone back into his pocket.

'Hope, Tallow, and Forrest swept the road and grass verges,' Byrd went on. 'With the help of Eric and Donny, there were fourteen body parts that were found. Forensics are currently working with the pathology department at Darlington Memorial Hospital to find out exactly what is going on.'

Byrd pressed the fob. The next slide was a photo of a piece of flesh, which the detectives knew was the top of someone's leg. The following slide showed various body parts.

'No head?' DS Stockdale asked.

'Not yet. We believe we have found all the pieces that had fallen from the back of the van.'

DC Anne Tiffin raised a hand.

'Yes, Anne?' said Tanzy, looking her way.

'Do we have any information on the van?'

'Not yet. I reached out to Jennifer Lucas from the Town Hall yesterday. She works in the control room and monitors the CCTV devices in and around the town. She's checking and will get in touch when she knows.'

Tiffin nodded her thanks to his reply.

'So, now it's time to formally introduce Linda Fallows.' Byrd motioned her forward with a hand. She stood, moved past Fuller and joined Byrd and Tanzy at the front of the room.

She looked directly at DC Cornty as she spoke for a few moments then looked around the room. 'As you now know, I'm Linda Fallows. I believe a string of murders that happened seven years ago in the Essex area are linked to what Darlington is currently experiencing. The cases I'm referring to are the house fire and the fall from the block of flats.'

She went on to explain her theory that each murder involved one of the elements. Fire, water, air, or earth. She answered a string of questions from Cornty, who Tanzy and Byrd surmised was being awkward, and then a few from DC Tiffin and PC Weaver, who were genuinely interested. She explained the videos being uploaded online and firmly believes that this is the killer that the Essex Police didn't catch.

'I've given Max and Orion full access to the files and reports Essex have on the murders in case they may come in handy. We need to find this man.'

She received several supportive nods around the room.

'And rest assured,' she added, 'I'll do everything I can to help and make sure we catch this sonofabitch.'

44

Wednesday Afternoon
Darlington Memorial Hospital

Byrd and Tanzy arrived there just after one. They made their way across the busy car park toward the entrance door under the high, hot sun. According to the weather forecast, it would reach thirty degrees but if anything, it was hotter.

There was a woman in her mid-forties standing a few feet from the entrance door, dressed in a pink fluffy dressing gown, with a cigarette in her hand. In the other, was a phone, raised to her head. She spoke loudly and abruptly, complaining about the doctors and nurses who she felt weren't doing a good enough job for her. Byrd knew patients or personnel weren't allowed to smoke on hospital grounds. It was common courtesy but he decided to let it go, knowing they had bigger issues to deal with.

Byrd went through the sliding doors first, followed by Tanzy. The air-con in the corridor was cool and welcoming as they passed a handful of doctors and nurses who were walking the opposite way, some of them looking down at clipboards with furrowed eyebrows as they went, whilst others were on the phone. Some, the detectives knew, were consultants, dressed in tightly fitted shirts and smart trousers. He'd come across them before, especially when his parents had passed away. They tended to have that confidence about them. That superior specialist knowledge could only be gained through decades in the business. On the flip side, bar their arrogance, they were a credit to the NHS.

The pathology department was down a long corridor and off to the left. After passing through the double doors, they stopped at the small desk. An attractive, thin dark-haired woman in her early thirties, dressed in a smart shirt, looked up from her computer over the top of her glasses.

'Can I help you?' she asked in a soft voice.

'Here to see Arnold Hemsley,' Tanzy said.

'Do you have an appointment with Doctor Hemsley?' she said, raising her eyebrows.

'He's expecting us. I'm Detective Inspector Orion Tanzy of Durham Constabulary. This is my colleague Detective Inspector Max Byrd.'

'One moment, please,' she replied with a smile and returned her focus to the screen. A moment later, she pointed to the double doors to their left. 'Through there. Been here before?'

'Too many times, unfortunately.'

They went through the doors, took a right, and walked along a quiet corridor until they reached a door with the sign on saying, 'Dr. Arnold Hemsley'. Tanzy knocked twice, and after hearing something inside, he opened it.

'Hello, Arnold,' said Tanzy.

Hemsley was a slight man in his fifties with a bald head, appearing hardened by a lifetime of working long hours and eating very little. His teeth were tainted with cigarettes and a heavy supply of coffee when he smiled, and the crow's feet lining his eyes when they were closer showed he may have been older than fifty.

'Detectives,' he said, standing, and shaking both of their hands. Similar to previous times they'd been here, his handshake was firm, carrying a strong character. Byrd was always told by his father you could judge a man's character by his handshake. If their handshake was weak, the man had no backbone. If a man had a strong hand-shake and looked you in the eye, he was more than likely a man you could rely on.

'Come this way,' said Hemsley, who stepped out of his office, then led them along the corridor, through the double doors into the lab. Standing at the rectangular table where the neatly positioned body parts they found yesterday, were Tallow and Hope, dressed casually. There was no sign of the forensic trainee Amanda Forrest. Most likely, she was back at the lab or with the crime scene manager, Tony McCabe, going over her reports. On the opposite side of the table was Peter Gibbs, the H.M. Senior Coroner for the Darlington and Durham area.

The detectives had been in the room on several occasions so far in their career. But never had they seen a dismembered display such as this. On the majority of occasions, the body on the table was intact.

The room was square-shaped and probably the cleanest room the detectives had been in. A clinical smell hung in the air and air conditioning gave it that fresh, cool feel. The temperature was a few degrees lower than the corridor which made Byrd shiver a little until he got used to it. The floor appeared to be linoleum but Byrd knew, after reading into things when he struggled to sleep at night, that it was specially designed so it was suitable for a lab. It had to be smooth, non-slipping, easy to clean, and lastly, resistant to chemicals and fluids. The walls were painted white but had a sheen finish, which Byrd also knew, was a special coating that allowed it to be cleaned and was resistant to foreign objects.

Along the back wall, were two low-level sinks, with emergency cleaning fluids and an eyewash station fixed to the wall. Next to the sink, was a metal tray used to place objects such as body parts or other not very pleasant materials on. Beside the tray, was storage shelving and a cupboard clearly labelled, filled with chemicals the pathology staff needed to use. Further down there was another sink which could be used to wash hands, and beyond that, a door that led to a small corridor where there was a toilet and shower facilities for staff before or after their shift.

'Let's begin,' said Hemsley, stopping at the table next to the coroner Peter Gibbs.

Hope and Tallow moved along to make room for Byrd and Tanzy, exchanging professional nods but didn't say anything. They focused on Hemsley.

'After inspecting these parts yesterday and running the tests we needed to, I can confirm these parts belong to the same person. We know, however, this doesn't make a complete human body, so as we assume, there are other parts out there that are yet to be found. The interesting thing I found was, as Jacob and Emily pointed out, is that this is very unusual.'

Byrd frowned. 'Unusual how?'

'Well, let me start by what we know. It's a woman. Without having the head here or the pelvic bone, I know this because of the size of the hands. They belong to a female who's somewhere between a teenager up to her thirties. It's fully grown and the skin also tells me her age.'

'Sorry, Doctor, if I may – how can you tell?'

Hemsley paused, looking at Tanzy. 'After you hit your twenties, the skin on your hands show signs of losing moisture. As you know, older people lose oils and minerals in their skin – we see in our parents and grandparents if they're lucky enough to still be with us. They often use hand creams to replenish the oils lost that, unfortunately, come with growing old.'

'How have the parts been cut, Doctor?' asked Byrd.

'The cut lines appeared to be from an electric cutter or something you'd used to cut meat. Not your average household cutting device but something stronger to get through the bone. Each part has been cut the same way. To make these cuts, the person had time on their hands.

They weren't rushed. Each cut shows the same pattern on the flesh and was done at a slow pace.'

Tallow and Hope knew this, as they'd been briefed on this beforehand, assuming something similar. They weren't experts on dismembering parts of the body but they were aware and fully understood the science and process behind it.

'But... each part is different. Each part tells us something unique.'

'How do you mean?' asked Tanzy, with a quizzical frown.

'This person has been tortured before they were cut up,' Hemsley replied. He then leaned over, pointing to one of the hands. 'See that mark?'

Byrd and Tanzy leaned closer.

'This is a burn mark. It looks like it's been done with some kind of blowtorch.'

'Something a plumber would use to heat and solder a joint?'

Hemsley looked up at Byrd. 'Exactly. And this part.' He pointed to a piece of flesh. They remembered from the scene where Tallow had said it could have been the top of someone's leg. 'This has been crushed. Something'—he raised his hands in the air, his palms facing each other, and moved them closer—'has crushed this part.'

'Like a vice?' Tanzy said, tilting his head.

A nod from Hemsley. 'Something like that, yes. The skin is stretched and muscles have elongated. And see here...'

The detectives looked at where he pointed. 'Bruises on the skin,' he went on. 'This, which we know is the forearm, had been strapped. I doubt the victim wore her watch that tight. She's been tied down to something while this happened to her.'

'Do we know the victim yet?' Byrd asked Tallow.

'We do. It's Lorraine Eckles. One of the missing four women we are looking for,' Tallow said.

When the four women had gone missing, Byrd and Tanzy had requested samples of their DNA to be taken from their homes, with the permission of their family, to hold on the database in case they potentially found something they could match it with. Unfortunately for Lorraine Eckles and her family, the DNA of this female matched with hers.

Byrd sighed heavily and hung his head. 'So, we have found one of them.'

Across the table, Peter Gibbs looked confused.

'Sorry. There were four women who went missing at the same time last weekend. They haven't been seen or located.' Byrd pointed to the table. 'Until now. We've found one of them.'

'Question is,' said Tanzy, 'will we find the others in time before they end up like this?'

45

Wednesday Afternoon
Police Station

When Byrd and Tanzy returned to the station they grabbed a coffee from the canteen and made their way through the office to their desks. They found Linda Fallows sat across the walkway at the desk, on the phone, speaking quietly. They heard a little of the conversation which sounded like she was giving someone instructions on what time to feed a pet.

She ended the call, put the phone down, and said, 'Hey. How was it?'

Because she wasn't officially employed directly by Durham Constabulary, she wasn't allowed to go to the hospital to see the body parts, so stayed at the office to do some research.

'How you getting on?' asked Byrd, passing her, placing his coffee down on his desk.

She stood up, went over to them. 'I've made a list of places.' She showed Byrd and Tanzy the list.

'What's this?' said Tanzy, peering down at the paper on the desk she'd put in front of them.

'Well, as I believe we are waiting on earth and water, I've made a list of ways someone could die by water. The most obvious is drowning. I've listed the rivers and ponds in the local area.'

'Must have taken a while,' said Tanzy.

She nodded. 'I've also been in touch with Jennifer Lucas at the Town Hall asking if these places are monitored with the town's CCTV system.'

Tanzy was impressed, eyeing the places on the list.

South Park Lake.

Brinkburn Pond Nature Reserve.

Drinkfield Marsh Nature Reserve.

Cleasby Lake.

River Tees.

River Skerne.

The list went on and on.

'What did Jennifer say?' Tanzy asked her, noticing ticks next to some of them.

'The ones with the ticks have CCTV in the nearby area.'

'Good work,' Byrd said to her, nodding. He meant it. It was refreshing to see someone doing something off their own back instead of being asked. 'I'm going to see the rest of the team, give them an update on what the pathologist found.'

He stood up to walk away when she said, 'What *did* they find?'

Byrd stopped, turned, and looked down on her. 'Four women went missing last weekend. Forensics checked the DNA and it matched with one of them.'

Fallows genuinely appeared sad, tucking a few strands of long blonde hair behind her ear. 'Anything about the four elements?'

'Vic had been burned in various places. Other parts suggested they'd been squeezed or compressed in some way. Apart from that, no.'

Fallows nodded and Byrd walked away. He came to DC Leonard's desk first, who was sitting on the right, tapping away at his keyboard. He pulled the seat out and sat down, gave a quick recap of what happened at the hospital. When he finished, he got up and went to DS Stockdale who was sitting a few rows past Leonard.

'Phil...'

Stockdale jumped, quickly tapping a few buttons on his phone, and threw it down on the desk. Whatever he was doing, it was obvious he didn't want Byrd to know about it.

Byrd frowned at his unusual behaviour. 'Have you done your report?'

Stockdale started moving around, organising items on his desk, and stared at his computer monitor, which was open on his emails. 'Not yet. Just doing it now, sir.'

'Show me…'

'Show you?'

'The report you said you were just doing?' Byrd edged closer. Stockdale didn't move. It was obvious he was trying to come up with something quick. 'You weren't doing a report. You were on your phone. So don't lie to me.'

Stockdale's face reddened. 'I er – I was just messaging a cousin.'

'Would you be happy for IT to check that?' Byrd grabbed the nearest empty chair and sat down next to him. By Stockdale's lack of answer, he assumed that was a no. 'Listen, Phil. I know Orion has been over this with you a few times now. What you need to remember is that you're here to work. You get a decent wage. Fuller is pressing Orion and me about these individual reports and thinks you guys are not doing enough.'

Stockdale was about to reply when Byrd stuck a palm up to silence him.

'I know you have issues at home. With your marriage.'

Stockdale gave a small nod and looked away for a moment.

'And I know the gambling issue. How is *that* going?'

Stockdale sighed a little, his shoulders giving away the answer before he spoke. He said, 'I'll be honest…'

'That's what we want, Phil.'

'Not good at the moment. I bet most days. The missus is talking about us separating and me finding somewhere else to live. If I don't change.'

Byrd wasn't a betting man. He knew from his earlier years wasting money in betting shops there was only one winner when it came to betting. The odds were never good enough. But he also understood the addiction. Similar to smoking, or drinking, or vaping, it became something your mind and body tricked you into believing you needed.

'Listen, it's easy for me to say never do it again because I don't share that addiction. So, I won't. Ideally, you should, but I know it isn't as simple as that. You know the number you need to call, don't you?'

In the police, it's known that almost half of the police force, at some point in the last five years, have taken sick leave due to a mental illness. Policing is both demanding and stressful, seeing and witnessing potentially traumatic situations daily can take its toll, driving individuals to do things they wouldn't normally. However, they must be aware, that there is help available if needed. More often than not, members of the police don't seek this help because they tell themselves they need to be strong and capable to do their job correctly. What they should understand is by addressing any issues and getting the help required, they can get better and have a bigger positive impact on the community there are working in.

Stockdale nodded. 'I know the number, sir. Thanks.'

'Don't hesitate to call it. You have mine and Orion's support.' Byrd stood up. 'Once you finish the report, send it to Fuller. He's wanting to read it, okay?'

'Boss,' he replied with a nod, then pulled himself in to start the report.

Byrd patted his back and moved on, looking across the office. He was about to get DC Cornty's attention but PC Weaver walked towards him from the right, carrying a cardboard box, roughly a foot by a foot in size.

'Boss, this is for you,' Weaver said.

Byrd frowned. 'What is it?'

'I don't know. I can't see through the box, sir.' Weaver smiled.

'Thanks.'

Weaver nodded, returned to her desk, and Byrd carried the box back to his desk.

After Tanzy asked Jennifer Lucas about the mysterious blue van, he was disappointed to hear she couldn't trace it. She said she'd contacted Cleveland police and explained the situation, then received some contact details for the individual who worked the cameras in the Cleveland area, who told her they'd get straight on it.

'Are there any cameras before it changes to Cleveland after the body parts fell from the van?'

'There's nothing. Seven cameras were installed on the A66 closer to Middlesbrough to monitor traffic and help with the infrastructure but that was a year or two back. Angela, the woman I spoke with, said she'll check the cameras to that nearest point and let me know if she finds the blue van.'

'Okay, thanks. Good work,' said Tanzy.

'We haven't found it yet...'

'You will, I have faith,' he replied.

'Hey, need to go. I'll be in touch.'

The line went dead and Tanzy placed his phone back into his pocket.

Byrd came back with the box that PC Weaver had handed him. 'What did Jennifer say?'

'She hasn't located it yet. Said there are no cameras where it happened. She's contacted Cleveland Police and spoken to a woman who monitors the cameras, who'll be in touch when they find it.'

'Good...' Byrd placed the box on his desk to the right of his keyboard and pulled his chair over to sit down.

'What's in the box?' Tanzy frowned. It wasn't often they got deliveries.

'Weaver has just handed it to me. I'm not sure. It's quite heavy.'

The cardboard box was sealed at the top with what appeared to be sellotape. On the side, it had a large, printed label saying, 'DI Max Byrd, Darlington Police Station, Durham Constabulary'.

'Ooo, I'm excited,' Tanzy said, edging closer.

Byrd peeled off the tape and opened up the flap to look inside. He immediately took a step back.

'What is it, Max?'

Byrd didn't reply. He just stared inside.

'Max, what's in the box?' Tanzy said, this time louder.

After Byrd didn't reply again, Tanzy pushed his chair out, stood up, and leaned in to have a look. 'Here, let me have – Jesus Christ!' Tanzy stumbled back a little and gasped. 'What the hell.'

46

Wednesday Afternoon
Police Station

DCI Fuller walked out of his office to find Byrd and Tanzy both stood, staring into the box.

Fuller frowned, wondering what they were doing. 'What's up?'

Byrd and Tanzy didn't acknowledge him.

Fallows, who was sitting at the desk across the walk-way, stopped typing and looked over, curious to what had grabbed their attention.

'Max? Orion?' Fuller edged forward. 'What are you looking at?'

Byrd placed his palms on top of his head and sighed.

A few people sitting at nearby desks also stopped typing and glanced over, intrigued. Fuller came up behind them. 'Hey, what's in the—'

He fell silent immediately, seeing the contents of the box.

'I think we need Tallow and Hope...' whispered Byrd. He took a step back, grabbed his phone, and made the call. 'Jacob, we need you and Emily in the office right now.' He then explained to him what was inside the box and Tallow told him not to touch anything and they'd be straight there.

The back end of the office, apart from Tallow and Hope, had been cleared. Fuller, Byrd, Fallows, and Tanzy had moved closer to the front, telling people what they'd found in the box. Weaver gasped, placing her hands to her mouth, disgusted she'd handled the box before handing it over to Byrd.

'Who does it belong to?' DC Leonard asked them.

'I don't know,' Tanzy said, who seemed to be in a daze.

'I think it's her. Judging by the photo.' Byrd pointed down at Weaver's computer. 'Get up the pictures of the missing women. The one we sent over to the media.'

Weaver nodded, pulled herself into her desk, and typed with trembling hands. Within a few moments, the four images were up on her screen. She slid along to make space for Byrd and Tanzy who leaned forward to look at them.

'It could be her...' Tanzy said.

Byrd stood and looked over to his desk. Tallow waved him over.

'Max, we'll take the box to the lab,' said Tallow when he was within earshot, It'll give us a chance to get some fingerprints off it. We'll also get a blood sample from it and send it to the hospital to see if it matches with who we think it is.'

Byrd stared in the box at the human head. She had long, matted dark hair. The cut had been just under the chin, showing thick clots of blood and multiple severed tendons.

'That okay?' Tallow said.

Byrd snapped out of his daze and focused on Tallow. 'Let us know what you find.'

Tallow nodded and, with gloved hands, carefully picked up the box and made his way through the office back to the forensics lab. All eyes were on Tallow and the box in his hands.

Tanzy returned to his desk and asked Byrd, 'You alright?'

Byrd nodded. 'Yeah. What the hell is going on in this town?'

'Never a dull day in Darlington, Max, you know that.'

47

Wednesday Evening
Low Coniscliffe

'Thanks for tea,' said Byrd, walking into the living room, dressed in a t-shirt and shorts.

From the sofa, in her usual spot, Claire said, 'No problem.'

The curtains were drawn but the room was still well-lit from the remaining daylight outside.

'Are you alright?' Byrd asked. 'You look a little pale.' Instead of sitting down, he padded over to her and placed his hand on her cheek. 'You're quite warm.'

'I don't feel very good, to be honest. Haven't felt right all day.'

Byrd offered to run her a bath but she declined, saying it would make her feel too hot and sick. She'd rather stay in front of the television for the night, watching Lost with Matthew Fox, an American show she'd never seen before but heard it was good from one of her friends. Byrd hadn't seen it but watched it for a little while, occasionally glancing at her, concerned how pale she looked.

'You sure you're okay?'

She turned her head slowly to him and managed a thin smile. 'I'm fine, Max. Just tired I think.'

'I can take you to bed if you want, get settled for the night. You can watch the television up there?'

'I'm fine, thank you.'

They watched the pilot episode. A group of people had crash-landed on an island in the middle of nowhere. Some died, some survived, waking up on the beach, not knowing what had happened. Luggage, clothing, and people were everywhere, some covered in blood, with body parts missing while others were untouched. Parts of the plane had been ripped off during the crash. The main character, Jack, was helping someone who was struggling to breathe. Byrd assumed he was a doctor.

Claire made a strange sound. Byrd looked over.

'I feel dizzy. I'm going to be sick,' she whispered, then tried to shuffle up. Byrd jumped up, went over, and gently grabbed her arm to aid her.

'Here, let me,' he offered.

'No.' She frowned at him. 'I'm fine. I can go myself.'

'I'm trying to look after you, Claire.'

'I can do it myself,' she said quickly, brushing his hand away.

He held his palms up. 'Okay. I'm here if you need me. Just tell me what you want.'

It wasn't like her to be that abrupt with him. Byrd put it down to the pregnancy hormones and certainly wasn't going to push it. He wanted to make sure she was okay and followed her out of the room and watched her struggle up the stairs. He waited at the bottom, heard the bathroom door close, followed by the sound of heavy retching that filled the house and made him wince.

He returned to the living room to check his phone. There was a text from one of his friends about five-a-side football at the weekend. He replied to him, then checked his personal emails. After that, he opened the security app, checking the camera out the front which covered the driveway and road, and noticed a car pass. It looked like Roger's Bentley, a guy who lived five doors down. Pleasant bloke. One of the ones who walked his dog three or four times a day and always said hello. He changed the camera to look what was happening out the back of the house. The camera was positioned just above the back door, covering most of the garden.

He was so focused on his phone he hadn't heard Claire come back into the room.

'Max…'

He looked up at her.

She was standing, hunched over with both hands on her stomach. Below, around her groin, there was blood. A lot of it.

'God…' he said.

'Max, I think something's wrong with the baby.'

48

Thursday Morning
Police Station

Tanzy arrived just after seven, applied the handbrake and glanced to his right, noticing Byrd's X5 wasn't in its usual spot. He rarely got to the office before Byrd did; Tanzy could probably count on his hand how many times in the last year he'd beat him; not that it was a race.

Tanzy remembered once, after getting an earful about how Byrd always arrived first, they said the one who turned up last would have to buy the breakfast the following morning. So, to make sure he was there first, Tanzy set off half an hour earlier, smiling and checking the time on the dash until he hit a deep pothole driving along the A167 from Aycliffe. He had to pull over and change the tyre. By the time he'd arrived, Byrd's X5 was already there.

Tanzy scanned the car park for Byrd's car with curiosity but failed to see the X5. He went in through the sliding double doors, passing the receptionist, Lisa, who looked up and waved. Lisa had been there for a few years now. Tanzy didn't know much about her but she seemed pleasant. Apparently, she'd had a little trouble with past boyfriends and was currently single, and according to some, spent most of her weekends living a completely different life than she did during the week. Each to their own.

After grabbing a coffee, Tanzy made his way through the office, stopping to speak with DC Leonard, DC Cornty, and DS Stockdale, who were at their desks, located a few metres apart. They told him that the senior forensic, Jacob Tallow was already in the lab, and had received the fingerprints from the box they found the head in yesterday and the results of who it belonged to. Tanzy or Byrd would do a conference at some point later today about the identity of who it is. Doing conferences was something Tanzy didn't like, and no matter how many times Byrd had let him do them to build up his confidence, it hadn't worked.

'Thanks, I'll go down and see him,' Tanzy said, turning away, noticing Linda Fallows sitting at the desk that she'd been assigned to at the back of the office. Before he went to see Tallow, he walked down the central walkway and placed his coffee on his desk.

'You beat Max,' Fallows said, smiling.

'Doesn't happen very often, let me tell you.' He took off his thin, dark-blue jacket and hung it on the back of his chair. 'What time did you get in?'

'Just after seven, Ori.' She pointed to the screen. 'Been looking for information on Mackenzie Dilton. Not much is coming up though. The last known address is where you and Max went – Victoria Embankment. After that, there's nothing. No jobs after the IT position with the company in Newcastle. No social media profiles matched the images we have of him from the CCTV footage. It's like he's just vanished.'

Tanzy nodded.

Seven years ago, Fallows didn't know it was Mackenzie Dilton she was looking for or if it was the same man Byrd and Tanzy were after. She did, however, know the name, Roger Carlton. It was the name of the uploader who put the videos online seven years back.

'It's only a matter of t—'

Fallows stopped what she was saying and frowned at Tanzy, noticing he'd pulled his phone from his pocket and froze.

'What is it, Ori?' She swivelled fully towards him.

'Shit.'

'What is it?'

'Max texted me last night. I've only seen it now. He took Claire to the hospital. She wasn't feeling very well.' Tanzy fell silent and re-read the message. He didn't want to mention the part where Byrd had told him she had been bleeding and feared there might be something wrong with the baby, so didn't mention it to Fallows.

'Oh, no… I hope she's okay.'

When Tanzy didn't reply, she slowly turned back to her screen, continued typing and moving her mouse cursor across the screen.

It made sense why Byrd wasn't here. He pressed CALL and listened to it ringing until Byrd picked up.

'Hey, Max. It's Ori. Listen, sorry I didn't text you back last night. I've just seen the message now.'

'It's okay, Ori.' Byrd sounded flat and tired.

'Is… is everything okay, Max?'

Byrd didn't answer straight away and Tanzy didn't want to ask again.

'She was bleeding pretty bad so we went to the hospital straight away. The doctors had a look at her and did a scan. Luckily, the baby is still there and his heart is beating so that's the main thing.'

'Aww thank God, Max.' Tanzy tilted his head back and sighed in relief.

'But they don't know why she bled in the first place. So we're here now, doing more tests. And until the results come back, we have to wait here.'

'Okay, Max. Hope she's okay.'

'She's okay in herself. Just pain in her belly. She's been given some tablets. I spoke to Fuller early this morning so he's aware.'

'Is there anything you need me to bring?'

'No, we're okay, thanks, Ori. We're in our own room. There's a shop downstairs if she wants anything and I can go home to get anything else she needs.'

'Well, if there is, let me know, Max.'

Byrd thanked him and hung up. Tanzy put the phone back into his pocket and looked over to Fallows, who was staring at her screen but Tanzy had the feeling she was listening to his side of the conversation. 'They're at the hospital now. She's staying in for tests to make sure things are okay.'

She smiled and crossed her fingers.

Tanzy then left the office and went along the corridor to the forensics lab, knocked on the door, and opened it. Inside the lab, Tallow was hunched over his desk at the far side, typing away. After he finished whatever he was doing, which looked to be some type of report, he looked over and waved Tanzy in.

'Morning, Jacob.' Tanzy closed the door and went over, pulled out a chair, and sat down near him. 'Are the results back?'

Tallow nodded and slid along a few inches to the left to pick up a piece of paper from the desk. 'The blood and DNA came back matching Lorraine Eckles. The head is currently at the hospital with pathology.'

Tanzy nodded. 'No relation to the superintendent, Barry Eckles, is it?'

Tallow smiled thinly and shook his head.

'What about prints on the box? I know Amy handed it to me, so I'm assuming hers will be on it.'

Tallow handed Tanzy a smaller slip of paper which he'd handwritten a list of names on.

'Max, yours, Amy's, Phil's, and Lisa's.'

Tanzy studied the list. 'Lisa from reception?'

A nod from Tallow. 'That's right.'

'Which Phil?'

'Cornty.'

Tanzy nodded. 'I suppose if you were to send a box to the police station addressed to a detective, with a head inside, you'd most likely wear gloves.'

Tallow smiled. 'Well, that's what I'd do…'

Tanzy stood. 'Thanks, Jacob.' He looked around at the empty room, not seeing Emily or Amanda. 'Where're the girls?'

'Emily is getting coffee in the canteen. Amanda isn't here yet.'

'How's she getting on – Amanda?'

'She's coming on well. This job takes time, a lot of time. Tony is happy with her so far, so that's all that matters really. How's the great DCI Fuller coping in the big office?'

'He's… okay.' Tanzy winced a little. 'Under a lot of pressure from Eckles at the moment. He's always on the phone. Fortunately, or should I say, unfortunately, Max and I sit right near his door, so when he comes out, raging, he can vent his frustration on us. You don't know the half of it…'

Tallow laughed. 'I bet.'

'Anyway, thanks, Jacob.'

Tanzy left the lab and made his way back down the corridor, through the office, and took a seat back at his desk. The office was warm, the morning sun shining through the windows to his right. Not long after he sat down, DC Cornty appeared at his side, wearing a black tight-fitting shirt and black trousers. His hair was gelled slightly different today.

'Morning, boss,' he started, looking down on Tanzy through his square-framed glasses. 'Did you see forensics?'

Tanzy looked away from the computer screen and nodded up at him. 'I did.'

'Who does the head belong to?'

'Lorraine Eckles. One of the missing four women. The one whose body parts were laid out on the A66.'

'What about the prints on the box?' asked Cornty.

'No good. Mine, Max's, Amy's, Lisa's from reception, and yours.'

Cornty dipped his head and gave a beaten sigh. 'Never mind.'

'What are you doing now?'

Cornty explained he was looking for blue Volkswagen vans in the local area. 'I have a small list. There are three in Darlington. Going to knock on some doors later this morning, hopefully speak to the owners of them.'

'Take Leonard with you.'

Cornty was going to ask why but nodded instead. 'Okay, he's aware of what I'm doing so I'll let him know when I head out.'

'What's he doing right now - Leonard?'

Cornty frowned and looked down the office, seeing the top of Leonard's head where his desk was located. 'Think he's doing a report. I'm not sure, though.'

Tanzy smiled. 'How about DS Stockdale?'

'I – I don't know,' Cornty said. 'I haven't seen him for a while. He was on the phone earlier, speaking with some-one at his desk. Not sure who, though.' Cornty was about to turn but stopped, appearing he had something on his mind. 'Excuse me for asking, boss. Why the questions?'

Tanzy looked up at him. 'No reason, Phil.'

Cornty walked away back to his desk, wondering what was on Tanzy's mind.

49

Thursday Morning
Darlington

Brad locked the blue van and carefully looked around, making sure it was clear. He walked along the side of the building, rounded the corner then went to the front door. He was told to keep the van out of sight in case anyone noticed it. At the yellow double metal doors he used the key from his pocket to open it and went through, then locked it once he was inside.

He flicked the switch on the right-hand side. The wide hallway flooded with harsh bright light. He walked down the hall, his boots echoing off the hard wooden floor, until he reached a door on the right and opened it. The room where the two computers were.

He turned on the light, dropped into one of the seats at the desk and looked at how the votes were going so far.

'Ooo, interesting,' he whispered.

Sarah had fifty-six percent and Lisa had forty-four.

When he phone rang, he pulled it out. 'Hello?'

'How are things going there, Brad?'

'Okay, Mitch. Gonna be close on votes I think.'

'How they doing? They still alive?'

Brad concentrated on the screen.

'They're awake. Sat against the wall. Not saying much, though.'

'You fed them yet?'

'Just about to.' Brad went back over to the chair and sat back down. 'Hey, I was thinking…'

'Yeah…'

'We'll be okay, won't we?'

'How do you mean?' replied Mitch.

'I mean about the van, you know. 'Cos I messed up with the body parts. Think the police will trace us?'

Mitch didn't answer him, which sent butterflies through Brad's thick gut.

'Mitch, I mean—'

'They're fake plates anyway, Brad. Don't worry about it.'

Brad sat in thought for a moment, then said, 'They can't track us, can they?' He pointed to the computer screens as if Mitch was there, knowing what he was referring to.

'I've been doing computers all my life. There's no way the site can be traced, never mind traced back to you or me. It doesn't work like a normal website.'

'How do you mean?'

'You heard of the dark web?'

Brad frowned. He had heard of it, but that's as far as his knowledge went. 'Yeah?'

'It's like that.'

'Okay…'

'Don't worry, big fella.'

Brad smiled. 'Good. Just concerned for a moment there.'

Brad hadn't known Mitch very long. They had first met a few months ago in The Green Dragon pub in the middle of the town. It was a Friday night, the place was busy with loud music, fancy disco lights, and a DJ who didn't make much sense when he spoke but played some classic dance tunes when he finally put the mic down. Brad had gone for a smoke out the back. The place was busy, groups of men standing, laughing, and large groups of teenagers, smoking and cracking jokes to impress the people drinking with them. Brad was minding his business when Mitch came over, introduced himself, and asked him if he needed a job. Brad explained he had a job but asked what it was out of curiosity. When Mitch had explained he needed someone strong, he told him he was okay for work at the moment and Mitch handed him a business card anyway, telling him to call him if things changed. Things did change. Brad lost his job at Argos warehouse after an argument with a colleague ended up physical and he was sacked. As soon as Brad left he phoned Mitch asking him if the offer still stood. It did.

'Well, rest assured, Brad. It's safe. The police won't track the van and the computer site is untraceable. Trust me.'

'Good. I'm just worried, that's all.'

'What about, Brad?'

'Well, when I heard about Danny Walters and Jane Ericson, I started to think someone knew...'

'Go feed the girls mate, keep them alive, okay. I'll get over there this afternoon at some point. Remember, only two more to go and we'll have enough money for ages, Brad.'

Brad smiled, placed the phone down on the desk, went over to the valve on the wall, and turned it on. When Lisa and Sarah slid down the wall and fell asleep, he turned the gas off, then used a button on the wall for the fans to clear the room before he went down.

Grabbing the tray of food from a desk to the left, he made his way through the door, down the set of steps illuminated with the blue neon hand rail, through another locked door, and into the dark room. Sarah and Lisa were in a deep sleep over to the left as he entered. He placed the tray of food down on the floor near them and walked out.

'It'll be the last meal for one of you,' he said then walked out and locked the door.

50

Thursday Evening
Dolphin Centre, Darlington Town Centre

Usually, the police held their conferences at Darlington Business Centre but tonight would be different. The manager of the business centre had informed the police that, due to severe damage caused by a small, rowdy crowd they had in two days ago, the walls, chairs, and tables had been broken. The manager apologised and told them it would be fixed as soon as possible.

Because of this, Press Office got in touch with the manager of the Dolphin Centre to ask if there was enough space in one of their function rooms. Fortunately, up on the second floor, near the football courts, was a room more than capable hosting a press conference; it also catered for wedding receptions and political events.

Sitting in the rows of chairs in the middle of the room were reporters, members of the public, and town officials. At the front, sitting behind the long rectangular desk, made from three desks connected from end to end, was DI Orion Tanzy. Next to him was a very attractive woman in her mid-thirties, dressed in a blue two-piece suit with long, dark hair. She was responsible for organising it. On the other side of Tanzy, was a man representing the PR department of Darlington Borough Council, who'd asked to sit in, wearing a plain, black suit with a black tie.

The woman in a blue suit stood and raised a palm, quietening the idle chatter until silence descended on the room.

'Thank you all for coming here tonight,' she started, her experienced voice loud and clear. 'I can only apologise it isn't in our usual place. I've been told they are renovating.' She paused a moment, looking down at the clipboard in her hands to collect her thoughts. 'This meeting is concerning current events in Darlington. We, as the people of this town, should know that this town is safe and that our police force is doing everything they can to keep it that way. Recently, in my opinion, and I'm sure the opinions of others, this town has experienced things which make us feel unsafe. Tonight we have DI Orion Tanzy from Durham Constabulary with us, to explain what's been happening, and to hopefully reassure us that our town will be soon safe to live in.'

Her words hovered over the crowd.

Tanzy felt his blood pump around his body and his cheeks warm, knowing it was his turn to stand up as soon as she sat down. He hated these things, hated the spotlight. Byrd was better speaking to groups and Tanzy wouldn't deny it.

He forced a smile and slowly found his feet, feeling the stares of the people watching him. The cameras clicked, quickly illuminating the room in stabs of lightning. He took a breath and introduced himself first, then said, 'I'd first like to say that Durham Constabulary are doing everything they can to catch the person responsible for the murders of the Walters family. We believe the same killer was involved in the cause of the death of Jane Ericson when she fell from four floors up. We think —'

'Is it true a detective should have reached her but missed, which led to her death?' a reporter said, sitting in the middle, two rows back. A woman with ginger frizzy hair, holding a recording device out in front of her at arm's length.

'I'm not sure where that information came from, but the detective you're speaking of reached out for her the best he could. Unfortunately, Jane Ericson panicked and lost her balance. Regardless of who was standing at that apartment door trying to grab her, she'd have fallen.'

'What leads have you got on the person responsible – it's a Mackenzie Dilton you're looking for, isn't it?' The question came from a man in his early sixties with whispery grey hair and whose face was blotchy with red skin.

'We are led to believe, by a witness who came forward, he's called Mackenzie Dilton. She also had informed us that the name Roger Carlton, a name linked with the video uploads and a name he used when I spoke to him at the scene of the fire, was a name of a character he used to love in an American series when they dated years earlier. We have been to his address and been notified by a neighbour they haven't seen Mr Dilton for almost a year now. The address in question, according to HM Land Registry, doesn't belong to him anymore.'

'Is that all you have on him?' the same man asked, disappointed.

Tanzy shook his head. 'Mr Dilton's last known job was for an IT firm based in Newcastle. I've spoken with the manager there who confirmed Mr Dilton was in their employment but hasn't been seen for the last six months. The address given by the member of the public who came forward was confirmed with the IT company.'

'What did Dilton do at the IT company?' a voice asked but Tanzy couldn't place it.

Tanzy looked in the general direction where the voice came from and said, 'He was a software expert.'

'Is that why you aren't able to track the videos he uploaded?' asked the same voice. Tanzy shifted his head but he still couldn't see who asked the question.

'That's correct,' admitted Tanzy. 'Whatever he's done, he's made it very difficult for our IT employees to track it. But we believe we are getting very close.' Tanzy didn't want to go into details about how the IP addresses kept shifting every so often, making it almost impossible to trace. And the fact that they were nowhere near locating him. 'On a positive note, we also have help from an for- mer employee from Essex Police force, who believes there are similar links to something that happened in Essex seven years ago. I'm not willing to go into details but in- forming you to ensure you know we are doing the best we can.' Tanzy fell silent, swept the rooms with his eyes, searching for the next question.

'What about the four missing women?' the ginger- haired reporter asked, still holding the device out in front of her.

A man stood quickly to the left. 'Yes, what about them. What about my Lisa? Lisa Felon?'

Another man behind him stood. 'And my Sarah? Sarah McKay? Where are they?'

Tanzy took a deep breath, carefully thinking about an answer.

'Whose body was found on the A66?' the first man asked, his face serious and red. His shoulders raised and fell quickly, his hands shaking by his side. 'Why aren't the police telling us what's going on?'

Tanzy forced a thin smile, scratched the top of his tanned, bald head. 'I can assure you we are doing every- thing we can. Please—'

'Who does the body belong to?'

Tanzy didn't think this was public knowledge yet but it's only a matter of time before word gets around this town. 'We haven't clarified that yet, sir. We need to speak to forensics and the pathology department at the hospital. We're still waiting on official identification. As soon as we know, we'll inform the public.' Tanzy then nodded, indi- cating he was ready for another question.

'In your opinion, Detective, are the public safe?'

Tanzy thought long and hard about the answer. He didn't want to worry them but at the same time, he didn't want to lie. 'Being honest, I'd say no one's safe.'

51

Thursday Evening
Darlington

Mackenzie Dilton picked up his phone from the kitchen table and called her. It wasn't long before she answered.

'Hello…'

'Hi, is that Rachel?' he said in a chirpy, upbeat voice.

'Yes…' she sounded hesitant.

'It's Roger Carlton. I'm just confirming you still require the hot tub for tomorrow evening. I've had a couple of calls from potential customers who are wanting some tubs over the weekend, but as you are booked in, I'm just confirming your slot.'

'Oh, hi, Roger,' she said, her voice becoming friendlier. 'Yes, please. I'll need it for Saturday night. Did you say you'll pop by tomorrow to set it up, to make sure everything is working?'

'That's right,' Dilton said. 'It'll be late morning I'd say. I have plans in the afternoon with family.'

'That's fine. I'm in all day. Whenever it is, I'll be here.'

'Great. See you then.'

Dilton hung up and placed the phone on the table, then stood up, made his way over to the worktop, where there was a bag. He pulled the zip open and peered inside. The lights on the underside of the top cupboard allowed him to see everything in there. He reached in, checked he had everything he'd need for tomorrow. Needles. Two knives. Thin clear tubes. A mechanical pump. Several coiled hoses. Sheeting. Rope. Two jugs. An extension lead. Duct tape. Two small boxes. A catheter with a pre-lubed needle and case.

He nodded, zipped it back up, then lifted the bag over to the back door, and dropped it carefully down near the large plastic tank.

Minutes later, he was up in his office, sat down at his desk with his laptop open, looking at a social media profile for Rachel Hammond. He'd been looking at her photos from this year. By the looks of it, she'd been all over the place. Egypt. Cyprus. Turkey. Spain. It was only June.

Dilton was jealous. The last time he'd been on holiday was Greece over ten years ago. A small place called Lindos on the island of Rhodes.

His phone rang. He pulled it from his pocket and answered it.

'Hey.'

'How you doing, Mack?' said the voice.

'I'm good. How are you?'

'I'm great, thank you. How are things… progressing?'

'So far, so good,' he said. 'Fire and Gas are both done.'

'I know. You did well. I heard about it. What's next?'

'Water.'

'When?'

'It's happening tomorrow,' he said, proudly. 'Then there's one more after that.'

'Have you planned it all – will it work?' said the voice.

'Yes. Everything is planned. It will work. They will get what's coming to them.'

'I'm not questioning that one bit, Mack. You've done yourself proud.'

'Thank you…'

'What's up?' asked the voice, detecting something off.

'I can't believe how people can be. Why would they do it?' Dilton said.

'Well, it's for people like us to make sure these people are brought to sweet justice, isn't it? What will you do after earth?'

'The list starts again. There are too many of them doing it. I need it to stop.'

'Good luck, Mack. I'm praying for you.'

Dilton smiled to himself. 'Don't pray for me. Pray for *them*.'

52

Thursday Evening
Newton Aycliffe

Tanzy kissed both Eric and Jasmine good night and re-turned downstairs to find Pip in the kitchen clearing away the dishes. A smell of lavender hung in the air from the plug-in on the worktop as well as her sweet perfume. He stopped in the doorway to look at her. Her slim physique, her tanned hips, her long, dark, straight hair that tickled the base of her spine as she moved, putting the clean plates away.

'They asleep?' she asked, knowing he was standing there, watching her.

He walked in and pulled a glass down from the cup-board. 'They certainly are.'

'Thanks.'

Tanzy filled the glass with water and drunk it all. Then, as he turned, Pip got in his way, stopping him from moving away from the sink.

'Wha—'

She placed her finger on his mouth. 'Shh, Ori...' She then took the glass from his hand and placed it beside him on the worktop, then slowly pulled his shorts down to his ankles, and lowered to her knees.

'Pip, what are—'

She silenced him when she took him in her mouth. It wasn't something she'd normally do but he wasn't going to complain or interrupt her. Instead, he leaned back against the worktop and closed his eyes.

A little while later, after Pip had showered, she returned to the kitchen to find Tanzy sitting at the table, looking at his laptop.

'Do you ever stop?' she asked.

He shook his head. 'I don't. I need to finish this report. Today has been manic. Did you see the news?'

'You looked as handsome as ever.' She grabbed a snack bar from the cupboard, sat down opposite him and removed the wrapper. 'Some awkward reporters though?'

'They're ruthless, Pip.' He typed a few lines while she ate.

'Eric has been asking about his den.'

Tanzy pulled his focus away from his laptop to look at her. 'I haven't started yet. I've been so busy with work and everything going on.'

'He won't be happy with you.'

Tanzy rolled his eyes, knowing his ten-year-old son all too well.

'How are Max and Claire?' she asked.

He'd told her about Byrd not being there today because Claire had been bleeding and they'd gone to the hospital. Pip was going to text her but felt like, although it wasn't her intent, it would look like she was being nosey.

'As far as I know, they're still there. Max hasn't told me what's happening yet. He said the baby is fine though, which is the main thing, but they've done some tests and are waiting on the results coming back. You know how long these things can take.'

Pip nodded. 'Bless her. Let's hope things are going to be fine.'

After CSI New York had finished, Tanzy picked his phone from the arm of the chair and decided to ring Byrd for an update on Claire.

'Hey, Ori,' Byrd answered.

'How're things?'

'We're home now. Just got in actually. Walked through the door fifteen minutes ago. Was going to ring you.'

'Long day.'

'Longer for Claire.'

'How's she doing?'

'The results came back. Doctors say she has got Uterine Fibroids.'

'What are they?'

'Tissue around her uterine wall – the uterine is the womb where the baby grows. Says the tissue could have expanded during her pregnancy which has caused the heavy bleed.'

'What happens now?'

'She has to see a specialist. Where the fibroids are, if they grow too big, could affect the pregnancy. She has to go in every week to have them checked. If they grow too big, she'll have them removed.'

There was a moment of silence.

'Well I'm just happy things are okay, that the baby is, you know…'

'Makes two of us. What's been happening in the office then? Oh – how was the dreaded conference?'

Tanzy could tell there was humour in Byrd's voice, who was well aware of Tanzy's public-speaking fear.

'As good as any other time. Bloody dreadful. Whatever happens, you're doing the next one.'

'You got it, boss,' Byrd said, then laughed. 'Any updates?'

'I have two from today. First is we got the fingerprints from the box with the head in. No other prints than ours. The second is confirmation of the head belonging to the body parts we found on the A66. Lorraine Eckles. You back tomorrow?'

'Yeah. I'll be there.'

'Okay. See you bright and early.'

53

Friday Morning
Elton Road

Rachel Hammond had enjoyed her lie in because she seldom got one. She rose just after nine, had breakfast with a cup of strong coffee, then jumped in the shower, got dressed, and was in her office – a small spare room with a desk and a laptop – by ten.

Waiting for her laptop to boot up, she slid across the carpet on her chair and looked out the window, spotting Mr Weller next door, tinkering on with his garden, dressed in only shorts and a cap. For sixty, he had a terrific figure. According to his wife, he goes running three times a week, has done for years. When a ping came from the laptop, she slid back across, settled at her desk, and logged on to the website. When the screen changed, there they were. Two of them, awake, sitting against the back wall, in silence.

On the right-hand side of the screen, it showed the votes. Lisa had fifty-three percent and Sarah had forty-seven. It was going to be a close one because not everyone had voted yet. It showed the three players who were online, including herself.

RCarl20.

Spork11.

And herself. Hammr33.

But she did wonder where the other two had gone.

DWalt66 and EricJ4.

She didn't know these people, only their usernames, and she couldn't contact them directly. It was against the rules.

Above the list of three, was a tab saying 'Watchers'. Next to this, in brackets, was the number 488. She couldn't see their usernames but knew they were waiting for the next game. Until then, they couldn't play, only watch.

Outside, she heard an engine. She slid away from the desk, stood, and peered out the window. A white van was parked directly outside her house. She closed the lid of her laptop, left the office, and made her way downstairs to the front door.

'Hey,' she said, opening it, seeing a stocky, clean-shaven, bald man in his late thirties, wearing a pair of shorts and a tight-fitting top. He wasn't in 'gym' shape but was attractive. His dark brown eyes were unusual, al-most so dark, they sucked you in for a moment too long when you looked into them.

'Rachel?' he said.

'That's me. Are you Roger?'

'I am. Sorry I'm a little earlier than I said. I like to get a head start on the day.'

She playfully waved his comment away. 'Oh, that's okay.'

'Would it be possible to see where you want the hot tub first to make sure there's enough space?'

She opened the door fully. 'Yeah no problem. Follow me.'

He stepped up into a wide hallway and she closed the door. He noticed the stairs were up to the left and at the end of the hall, he could see the kitchen. There were a cou-ple of doors going off to the right. The décor was simple yet modern, whites and greens mixed. A large rectangular mirror was fixed to the wall on the right, positioned above the radiator.

'Please, this way,' she said, heading toward the kitchen. He followed her movements, watching her tanned, mus-cular legs contract as she walked. She sounded sexy on the phone and her appearance didn't disappoint.

'Mind the mess,' she said. 'I'm about to clean up.'

Dilton smiled as he followed her. People always said the same when you went into their house, regardless of if they hadn't cleaned in a week, or they'd just finished. It was a polite way of saying 'hey, this is my house. If it isn't up to your standards, then you'll have to accept it.' But everyone knew it was a thing that people said.

'So, have you got many booked in for today?' she asked.

He stared at the back of her head, watching her closely, pulling out one of the needles from his pocket. 'Yeah, I have seven booked in for today.'

She turned and made a 'wow' face. 'That's good. Just through here.' As she stepped one foot on the lino she felt the needle go into the right side of her neck. An instant reaction was to swat at her neck, thinking it was some type of wasp or bee sting. Dilton threw his strong left hand around her and pulled her close into him, her feet leaving the floor for a moment, and pushed the liquid into her neck. Helplessly, she shuddered and wriggled, struggling for several seconds until she lost consciousness.

Dilton removed the needle and dropped it on the floor. Without letting her hit the ground, he carried her into the dining room and looked around.

'This will be perfect.'

He admired her for a moment, unconscious on the floor. A minute later there were two quick knocks on the front door, then he heard it open.

'Hey, Rach.' A man's voice. 'Where are you?'

'Shit,' Dilton whispered.

54

Friday Morning
Elton Road

The man closed the door and looked down the hall, hoping to see Rachel in the kitchen, but the house was unusually silent. Usually Rachel had music on.

'Rachel, you here? I'm back from Judo.'

He took a few steps down the hall, then stopped, and looked upstairs. 'Rach?' He carried on down the hall and found something on the floor. 'What the...'

Dilton was against the wall in the dining room, close to the door, with a second needle in his hand.

The man picked up the first needle on the floor. 'What the fuck is this?' he said. 'Rachel, where on earth are you?'

Dilton's heart pumped quickly as he waited, hearing the footsteps approach. It would only be a matter of seconds. He had the element of surprise and would need to act quickly. As the side of the man's face appeared Dilton threw himself through the threshold with the needle first, stabbing him in the chest, using his size to take him to the floor, then managed to inject the syringe into him. it took seconds for the injected liquid to take effect.

Dilton gasped. 'Jesus.' He slowly got off him, feeling a rush of blood to his nose and temple where the man had struck him. He grabbed the man's hands and dragged him into the dining room, placed his body next to Rachel's.

Rachel woke up first. She tried to move her arms but realised she couldn't, then opened her eyes, seeing him in the chair opposite. His head was tilted back, his eyes closed, his body totally still.

'Aaron?' she whispered, not understanding what she was seeing. There was a strange smell in the air, like a cleaning smell, but she couldn't remember cleaning. There was a slight draught too, but the French doors to her right were closed, the curtains were pulled across, leaving the room darker than it should have been.

'Aaron? Aaron, wake up?'

Feeling groggy and sick, she couldn't remember what happened, her head spinning each time she blinked.

Aaron was positioned on the chair facing her. There was a gap of two metres. Behind him, was the doorway to the hallway. His arms were tied to the chair with a thick rope and there were several loops of rope around his chest and stomach which seemed to go around the back of the chair. His legs were also tied together in several places.

Then she noticed the tubes.

'What the fuck?' she said, frowning at her unresponsive boyfriend.

In his forearm, there were several tubes connected to what looked like catheters. She followed the tubes down to the floor, along to a little metal block on the carpet. On the other side of the block, there was a rubber pipe, similar to a hosepipe, which ran a few feet to the left side of a mechanical pump. A tube from the back of the pump that went to a large, black plastic box. She couldn't see what was inside.

Then she noticed the hose connected to the right side of the pump which came down under the table, then towards her, to another metal block, which split off into smaller tubes. The smaller tubes went along the floor and up into two catheters that were fixed into her own forearms.

She gasped. 'What the fuck. Help me!'

She wriggled and fought against the ropes but they were too tight.

In her hand, which she hadn't realised, was a small black box. It had a button on it. She stared at it, wondering what it was.

'Roger!' she whispered, recalling he was the last person she had seen. 'Oh, God. What happened?' She remembered walking into the kitchen to show him the back garden, then woke up here, tied to the chair with tubes sticking out of her arms.

'What the fuck is this!' she screamed, her anger filling the silent house.

She looked around for Roger Carlton. Then, out of the corner of her eye, she saw the writing on the wall to the left in a thick black marker pen. It covered most of it, nearly filling it from the ceiling to the floor.

It read:

Hello Rachel. I'm sorry things had to be this way, but you did this to yourself. You have sinned and it's up to me to put things right, so you can't harm again. As you may have noticed, there are tubes fixed to you. These tubes are connected to a mechanical pump which is connected to the large plastic tank over to your right. Inside the tank there is water. Just ordinary tap water, which isn't very good for you, believe it or not. Every seven minutes, the pump will turn for a few seconds and will pump approximately half a litre of water into your body. Now, this doesn't sound like much, but have you heard of water intoxication? Maybe you have. Maybe you haven't. This is when the body gets too much water and causes it to break down and not function. If water intoxication is severe, you will die. Because too much water causes the sodium levels in your body to dilute, leaving the sodium lining on your cells vulnerable, allowing water to penetrate them. If this happens to your brain cells, let's just say it will swell and prevent the flow of blood and oxygen to your head. First you'll get a headache, then you'll feel sick, then be sick, and let's just say the whole thing isn't a pleasant experience. In your hand, you have a small remote. This remote, if you press the button, will turn on the pump, sending water into your boyfriend's body instead of yours. If you don't press the button, then every seven minutes, half a litre will be pumped into both of your bodies until one of you die. And I can guarantee that will be you because he's bigger, and it'll take more water to kill him. Choose wisely. I'll be watching. Roger.

'What the fuck?' she whispered, looking down at the tubes, pump, and plastic tank. 'Is this a joke?' She looked around the room and noticed the small white camera on the table facing them. There was a red light flashing every few seconds, indicating whatever it was, it was probably recording them.

As she re-read the handwritten message on the wall, just before the last line, the pump to her right kicked in for a few seconds.

'Shit! Shit!'

She started shaking, feeling the liquid being pumped into her arm.

Aaron jerked wide awake in the chair opposite, his eyes wide, looking around the dim room. 'What the hell?' he mumbled, trying to move his arms and body but realised he couldn't. 'Where is he – where—'

He noticed Rachel in the opposite chair, tied up, with the tubes in her arms.

'Rachel – what the fuck is going on?' He clamped his eyes shut for a moment and tipped his head back. 'My head is banging.'

'Aaron, don't panic.'

'Don't panic? What is this…'

Rachel started to feel a headache coming on. According to the writing on the wall, it was the first sign of the body breaking down. She pressed the button in her right hand causing the pump to whir. She held it for ten seconds.

Aaron screamed, feeling the liquid enter his arms. 'Ahhh, what is that?' He tried to thrust forward but the ropes restricted any form of movement. 'Rachel, I don't feel well.'

'Just hold on,' she said, maintaining his eye contact, hoping he wouldn't see the writing on the wall but it was so clear, it was impossible to miss. He looked to his right, started reading it. When he reached the bottom, he glared at Rachel, then down to the black box in her hand. 'Rachel, why do you have that?'

She focused on him with tears in her eyes, knowing there were a few minutes until the pump would rotate and inject water into her veins. Instead of replying, she pressed the button. The pump whirred on.

'Rach – Rachel! Do not fucking press that button!' he spat at her. 'Don't you dare... turn it off!' He could feel the liquid pouring into his arm, filling his body slowly. It wasn't long before he was sick all down his front.

Rachel winced but held her finger on the button, the pump continuously going.

His skin started turning white. 'Rachel...' His voice was weak now. Then he was sick again. 'Rach – turn it off, please.'

She didn't want to do it but if it was a choice, she had to look after number one. If she didn't press it, he'd survive longer, meaning he'd live. She had to press the button.

He clamped his eyes shut and rocked his head back violently. 'My head. Please...'

Tears rolled down her face pressing the button again, holding her finger down onto it. She knew it was something she had to do and cried loudly, masking the wails of his pain.

Nearly half an hour later, Aaron was still, his head cocked to one side, his eyes bloodshot, looking down at the floor. His almost albino-like white skin had swelled and bubbled. She finally let go of the remote and dropped it on the floor.

Her head was banging from the emotions, tears, and crying. She sat still, without the energy to move, then angled her head to the writing, re-read the part where it said *choose wisely. I'll be watching.*

'Hello?' she said, barely audible. 'Roger…'

After seven minutes had passed the pump kicked in for a few seconds. Her eyes widened, feeling more liquid injected into her body.

She started screaming, realising this was a game neither of them would win.

Two hours later, she was dead.

55

Friday Late Afternoon
Police Station

Tanzy was sat at his desk with Linda Fallows, who'd logged on to Byrd's computer so they could be next to each other to save them shouting across the walkway. Fallows had been, for most of the day, looking over her old files from Essex Police concerning the murders that happened seven years ago, searching specifically for water and earth.

Drowning and a burial.

'I have a list of victims from seven years ago, Ori,' she said, handing over a list she'd handwritten on some plain paper.

At the top, it said 'fire', followed by three names. Norman Peters, Anna Peters, and James Peters. Man, wife, and child.

Then below, it said 'water' and named a female who'd been held under the water in her bath to drown. Theresa Forgan.

The third was 'gas' followed by a male victim who had been gassed out inside his car. Lewis Phillips.

And lastly, 'earth', followed by another male victim who'd been buried in the woods. Donald Cramer.

Tanzy's eyes narrowed at the list. 'Have you come up with – or did you at the time – a link between these people. Something they shared in common. Or was it random?'

She took the list back to have a look. 'I looked into every victim. Who they were. What they did as jobs. Their interests. But we couldn't see a pattern. It frustrated us like nothing before. It seemed, from what I gathered, a random list of people. I looked at this list for months on end. It drove me insane. My Super, at the time, had talked about taking me off the case because it's all I was doing. I'd stay up at night, thinking about it on a loop. I didn't have an image of what the man looked like who we were chasing – Mackenzie Dilton. I remember making my own image of him up in my mind. Had dreams about being at home and hearing something come up behind me and when his hand grabbed my shoulder or I felt his breath on the back of my neck, I'd wake up in a sweat.' She sighed and shook her head a little as if reliving the pain and effort she'd been through.

'There must have been something which linked them?' Tanzy picked up his coffee, took a sip, and placed it back down by his keyboard. 'Someone doesn't just go and kill six people on four different occasions.'

She shrugged. 'It's the first killer to ever elude me.'

'Do you think it was some type of ritual?'

'The four elements?' she said, frowning at him.

He nodded.

'I don't know. Perhaps.' It was her turn to sip her coffee, then silence descended on them. The other end of the office was busy. DC Leonard was at his desk, speaking with someone on the phone. DS Stockdale was on the right-hand side, near the window, at his desk, looking down at something. Probably his phone, Tanzy thought. PC Weaver, Andrews, Timms, and Grearer were dotted about, tapping keyboards, and idly chatting, winding down for the weekend. Despite the recent happenings in Darlington, people were smiling more than usual, happy to be away from the office for the weekend. Leave the problems at work. Switch off, get some normality back in their lives.

It wasn't so easy for Tanzy and Byrd, especially Byrd. He never switched off. Ever since his sister was murdered all those years ago, he'd been reborn into something almost unstoppable. An asset to any team.

'Where did Max go?' Fallows asked, remembering he'd left a couple of hours ago.

'He had to go home to see Claire. Make sure she's alright.'

'How is she?'

'Taking things easy.'

'She needs to. Carrying the baby and all.'

Tanzy agreed and stood. 'Excuse me a minute.'

Fallows nodded.

Tanzy rounded the desks, and joined the central walkway, heading towards the opposite end. Passing team members sitting on either side, he nodded and smiled, but his focus was on the back wall, where DS Stockdale was sitting.

'Phil?'

Stockdale shuddered a little. 'Jeez, boss. You scared me.'

'Did you go to the addresses we had for the blue VW vans?'

He swivelled towards Tanzy. 'Yeah. Jim and I went. There was one on West Crescent owned by a man in his late sixties. Crazy about VWs. Told us how he'd owned them all his life. Said he'd had that one for three years. He showed us in the back. All kitted out with a bed, sink, and toilet. Looked really smart.'

Tanzy wasn't interested in how smart it looked, and Stockdale noticed that by his face.

'Did you get a reg?'

Stockdale picked up a sheet of paper from the desk. 'There you go.'

'Does everything check out? Owner. M.O.T. Tax?'

'Yeah. It's clean. Belongs to a Mr Simms. There's eleven months M.O.T left and it's taxed.'

'Where did he say he was on Tuesday morning?'

'Told us he and his wife had been to the Lake District. Been camping for a few days. Got back Wednesday night. His wife, after she heard someone at the door, came out to confirm it.'

Tanzy said, 'Okay. What about the other one?'

Stockdale smiled. 'Owned by a twenty-seven year-old, blonde haired female.'

'Why you smiling?' queried Tanzy.

'Am I?' He waved it away and looked serious again. 'She bought it last year. Doesn't use it very much. Bought it for more of a memento to her father who was obsessed with them. When he died, she thought she'd get one to remember him by. Think it's kind of sweet.'

'Yeah, very sweet, Phil.' Tanzy wasn't in the mood for jokes today. 'There was a third one?'

Stockdale nodded. 'There was. We knocked on the door of a Mrs Anderson. A woman in her sixties answered. When we asked about the van, she started going crazy, asking why we hadn't found it yet. Said it was stolen last week and she's been on the phone to us, asking if we'd found it.'

Tanzy scowled. 'First I've heard about that one.'

'I know. I told her the same. But said I'd look into it and update her with what we know.'

Tanzy thought for a moment, thinking about why he or Stockdale wasn't aware of her missing blue VW van, the likely van that had the body parts in on Tuesday morning.

'Did you speak with Jennifer at the Town Hall?' Stockdale asked, winking.

'What's with the wink?'

'The wha…'

'You winked at me when you said have I spoken with Jennifer at the Town Hall?'

'I did?'

'Phil, you know you did.'

The silence was so awkward that Stockdale said, 'I heard from somewhere that you're always the one who phones her or goes down to see her.'

Tanzy frowned. 'Meaning?'

Stockdale shrugged. 'No meaning, sir.'

Tanzy sighed. He didn't have time for games. 'I need you to find that missing van, Phil. That's what I want you to do. How's that sound?'

'Sounds good.'

'Right. Get on with it then.'

Stockdale bit his lip and focused back on his computer screen.

Tanzy turned and went over to DC Leonard, who was tapping away on his keyboard. 'Jim,' Tanzy said, pulling the nearest seat out and sitting down. 'What's happening?'

'Did Stockdale tell you about the missing van?'

Tanzy said that he did.

'I've been on to Jennifer at the Town Hall,' Leonard said. 'She said she'd have a good look for it and she's input the registration plate into the system. If there's a hit, she'll get back to us.'

'Good.' Tanzy said nothing for a while.

Leonard noticed his moment of silence. 'Everything okay?'

Tanzy narrowed his eyes, said quietly, 'How's Phil getting on?' He pointed toward Stockdale who was sitting behind him.

'How – how do you mean?' Leonard leaned into him, making sure his voice was low.

'I... don't know. He's not himself. He's not as focused.'

'Maybe having a tough time at home,' added DC Cornty, who was sitting on the other side of Leonard. Tanzy leaned to his right to see beyond Leonard. 'Heard he's been on his phone a lot. Also, heard him talking to Donny about a bet he put on and nearly won but never.'

'Okay. Where's Donny?'

'Canteen with Amy. One last coffee before we pack up for the weekend.'

As Tanzy stood up, he saw Weaver dash towards him - without a coffee in her hand. Instead, she was holding her phone.

'Where's the coffee?' Leonard complained, looking up at her with his palms out.

Weaver ignored Leonard and focused on Tanzy. 'Sir, you need to see this.' She stopped next to him and showed him what was on her phone.

'What is it?'

'Another video has been uploaded by RCarl20.'

They watched it on her phone.

'Jesus,' Tanzy said.

56

Friday Late Afternoon
Police Station

Tanzy had asked Weaver to send Leonard the website address. As Leonard opened it up, everyone stood behind, watching his computer, seeing the video on a bigger scale. The camera was positioned roughly a metre high off the floor, showing a man and a woman sitting on two chairs, facing each other. They were tied in several places. They were both non-responsive, both quiet and still.

Behind them, black writing covered most of the wall.

'What does that say?' Tanzy said, pointing from over Leonard's shoulder.

Leonard, knowing what he meant, double-clicked the screen to enlarge it, but the writing was too small and blurry.

'I can't see it properly,' replied Leonard, squinting.

'No way of zooming in?' DC Cornty suggested.

'Someone get Mac,' Tanzy said to anyone.

'Sir,' Weaver replied, then dashed down the corridor towards Digital Forensics.

'Print screen it and save it,' Tanzy told Leonard. 'Hopefully, we can enhance the shot to see the words better.'

Leonard nodded and saved the still shot.

'Watch it again,' Tanzy said.

It was clear the video had been edited. The time in the bottom right corner of the screen kept changing, progressing forward as the video did. The whole video should have been nearly three hours long but had been compressed to thirteen minutes. It showed the couple, if that's what they were, waking up, the woman before the man.

She was on the left. When she woke, it wasn't long before she started panicking and screaming.

'What's with the tubes in her arms. Where do they go?' Cornty said, seeing the two small, clear tubes going towards and off the bottom of the screen.

'I have no idea,' Stockdale said. 'Are they going to her arms?'

'Like a catheter?' added Tanzy, nodding.

'Could be, yeah,' Stockdale replied.

It was moments later when Weaver returned to the office with Mac, who, judging by the crumbs on his t-shirt, had been eating crisps. Tanzy asked him to sit and watch the video.

'Jesus, what's this – is this him again?' Mac asked, noticing the name of the uploader being RCarl20.

Tanzy came from Mac's right and pointed to the screen. 'Can you see what's on the wall behind them? It looks like writing but we can't make it out.'

Mac leaned closer to the screen, trying to make out the black writing.

'Is there a way you can enlarge it?' asked Tanzy.

Mac used the mouse to copy and paste the address and fired an email over to himself. He told Tanzy he'd get straight on it and get back to him when he knew what the words said.

The woman on the screen woke up a little startled, sighing and getting her breath back. It took a few seconds for her to recognise the man – and the situation – in front of her. It wasn't long before a mechanical sound was heard.

'What the hell is that?' DC Leonard asked, furrowing his brows up at Tanzy, then to Cornty.

'Doesn't sound good, whatever it is,' replied Cornty, peering down over his glasses, with folded arms.

They watched on.

Linda Fallows appeared in the walkway. 'What's happened?'

'Your man is at it again,' Tanzy said, pointing to the screen.

She stopped next to Tanzy and focused on the screen.

It wasn't long before they learned the man's name was Aaron and she was called Rachel. Aaron kept telling her not to push the button, and it wasn't long before the detectives noticed something in her right hand, the hand nearest to the camera.

'Is that some kind of remote?' Tanzy wondered out loud.

Aaron then screamed, jerking his body back and forth, as much as the rope holding him allowed. The sound of the pump continued while she pressed the button.

'Whatever is happening, isn't good. He's in pain,' noted Tanzy.

'Is she doing this to him?' Leonard asked.

Tanzy wasn't sure so stayed silent.

'Does Max know about this yet?' Cornty asked.

Tanzy shook his head. 'He'll be back soon. He had to pop out for a little while.'

Footsteps were heard behind him. It was Mac, carrying a piece of paper in his hand. 'Hey…' They all turned. 'I took still shots and zoomed in,' Mac informed them, handing the paper to Tanzy, who took it to read.

'Those tubes are pumping water in their veins…' Tanzy told them after digesting what it said.

'Water?' Leonard frowned. 'Why water?'

'Here, read this…' Tanzy handed the paper to him.

A moment later, Byrd turned up, wondering why they were all standing by Leonard's desk, watching something on the screen.

'What's the big commotion?' Byrd said, stopping behind them.

Tanzy turned to him. 'Max, there's another one…'

Byrd sighed and placed both hands on his head.

'Not only that,' PC Eric Timms said from across the office as he dashed over. Byrd and Tanzy looked at him, eager to hear what he had to say. 'There's someone on the phone. She says she knows the woman on the video. She's Rachel Hammond, aged twenty-seven.'

'Does this person know Rachel's address?'

'Yeah. She does.' Timms handed over the slip of paper. 'Here.'

Byrd glanced down. 'Looks like we're heading out. Come on.'

57

Friday Late Afternoon
Elton Road

Byrd took Tanzy and Fallows in his X5 and Cornty went with Leonard in his Vauxhall Insignia. Stockdale said he'd travel alone and would meet them there.

The differences that Leonard and Cornty had seemed to be a thing of the past. What Leonard hadn't told him, is that he and Amy Weaver had been seeing each other outside of work. He hadn't mentioned it because Cornty and Weaver used to be a thing, but she'd broken it off a little while back, although it was obvious Cornty still liked her. Who could blame him? She was gorgeous. Her blonde hair was always pristine. Her blue eyes were the focus of her very attractive face, and that figure turned the heads of all men, even men who liked men. If Leonard was being honest, he was proverbially punching above his weight. Things weren't serious between them yet, but Leonard couldn't deny he was starting to fall for her. Time would tell.

Byrd turned into Elton Road, drove a hundred metres then slowed, looking at the house numbers. When he approached the number, he pulled over on the right, stopping at the semi-detached property with a brown-painted door.

The street, as usual, was quiet.

Byrd stepped out onto the grass verge while Tanzy opened the passenger door and stepped down onto the road. Fallows climbed out too, trailing them. They'd been discussing, on their way over, how they needed to stop Mackenzie Dilton. Fallows had weighed in, expressing her concern that now they had experienced *water*, it would only be a matter of time before he used *earth* to kill someone.

The house looked well-kept but carried a unique character in comparison to others in the street. The low wall at the front of the boundary that protected a modest neatly trimmed square of grass complemented the style of the bay windows, which were probably installed fifteen years ago but looked brand new.

They stepped onto the driveway, where a yellow Renault Clio, less than two years old, looked polished and new, glistening in the late afternoon sunlight. As they angled right towards the brown door, Tanzy stepped up first.

Behind them on the road they heard a vehicle pull up. It was Leonard and Cornty, who seconds later, got out, and eagerly walked up the driveway.

Tanzy knocked but after fifteen seconds of getting no answer, he tried the handle. The door opened. In his hand was the baton he'd grabbed from Byrd's glovebox.

'Hello?' he shouted as he entered.

Byrd, who was a few feet behind him, turned and directed Leonard and Cornty around the side towards the brown gate which spanned the width of the drive. He then told Fallows to wait at the door until he deemed it safe for entry – after all, she was his responsibility whilst she was here – and stepped inside.

The hallway was wide. The walls were white but shades of green gave it a little colour.

'Hello?' shouted Tanzy, looking up the stairs, then down the hall, seeing into the kitchen. He moved forward with the baton in his right hand, ready to attack if someone jumped out. By the time he'd got to the dining room, he lowered the weapon, noticing Rachel and Aaron in the chairs.

'Jesus,' said Byrd in the doorway, looking inside the dim room.

They were still tied up. The tubes and catheters were still in place, fixed to equipment down on the floor. There was a large, plastic tank next to the table – a similar size to a water tank you'd find in the attic before Combi boilers had taken over – with what looked like a pump in front of it, being powered by an extension lead that ran to a socket in the alcove.

The writing on the wall to their right was clearer and much bigger now. Byrd took a few steps in the room and skimmed over it to get a feel for what he was seeing. Tanzy passed him, going closer to the victims, and could feel the carpet underfoot was saturated with water.

Linda Fallows, ignoring Byrd's instruction, entered and gasped when she saw Aaron and Rachel sitting lifeless in the chairs.

'The skin…' Tanzy whispered.

Fallows grew closer. The skin on the back of Aaron's neck was white, almost translucent. 'The water's changed his skin,' she said.

Byrd finished reading and turned to see what Tanzy and Fallows were meaning. It was true. Their skin colour had changed, almost becoming see through and bloated. Byrd was about to comment on it when the mechanical pump whirred near the table.

Tanzy raised the baton quickly, angling his body to the sudden sound.

'Easy partner,' mused Byrd, realising what it was.

Through each openly visible orifice – their mouths, nose, ears – water seeped. It was like their bodies couldn't absorb any more, like a sink overflowing. It was the strangest thing Tanzy had ever seen. 'This is fucking weird.'

Fallows didn't like to swear but nodded in agreement, leaning down, taking a closer look at Aaron's forearm.

'We need Tallow and Hope here,' said Byrd.

Tanzy picked his phone from his pocket and rang Jacob Tallow, telling him the situation.

'Jacob said he's on his way with Emily,' Tanzy told them, putting his phone away.

'I'm going to have a look around,' said Byrd, turning slowly, leaving the dining room.

Tanzy, with his phone still in his hand, made a call to the undertakers too. After forensics were finished, the bodies would need to be taken to the hospital for further analysis by pathologists.

Once Byrd had swept downstairs, he went upstairs. The house, apart from Tanzy and Fallows discussing the colour of the skin in the dining room, was eerie silent. Off the rectangular landing, a bathroom was on the right. Straight ahead, there was a bedroom with the door open. To the left there were two further bedrooms, one of the doors shut, the other ajar.

He peeked into the empty bathroom, then headed straight into the bedroom with the open door. It was square. A single bed was against the left wall, a chest of cheap-looking drawers against the far wall, and a wardrobe was positioned to the right, next to the long, wide window.

He stepped back onto the landing, made his way to the bedroom at the end, and opened the door, finding a much smaller room with a desk over to the right. On the closed laptop, there was a business card.

He picked it up.

Roger Carlton Hot Tubs.

'Crafty bastard.'

Byrd sighed heavily. He could have screamed but didn't have the energy to. Roger Carlton - or Mackenzie Dilton as they know him to be – had used an excuse to get into someone's home. A valid excuse alluring people to think he was a normal guy doing a normal job.

A carpet cleaner.

An electrician.

A guy who rents out hot tubs.

Under his name, there was a handwritten message saying, 'Look at Laptop!'

Byrd dropped the card on the desk, found his phone, then dialled Mac. He didn't answer on the first ring but did on the second.

'Mac, you remember the laptop from Jane Ericson's apartment that you looked at?'

'I do.'

'I need you to do it again, please. I'm currently at the house where we saw the couple on the video. There's a card with handwriting on telling me to look at the laptop. I believe there could be something on it.'

'Okay, Max. Would you be able to bag it up and drop it off at some point over the weekend?'

'I'll bag it up and drop it off very soon.'

'How soon?'

'As in I-want-to-catch-this-fucking-killer soon. Probably within the hour.'

Mac sighed, as if he had plans, but said, 'Okay…'

Byrd wasn't impressed with his attitude and hung up the phone. He picked up the card again and looked at the back. His eyes widened. This card was different from the others. There was a number on it with a handwritten message: Call me.

Byrd typed the number into his phone, pressed CALL, and put it to his ear.

'Hello, Detective…' said the male voice.

'Roger Carlton? Or should I say Mackenzie Dilton?'

'Call me whatever you like.'

'I'll call you Mackenzie Dilton as that's your real name.'

'Suit yourself. How's the investigation coming on, Detective?'

'We're very close…'

'No, you're not. You're a million miles away. And let me tell you something...'

'What's that Mr Dilton?'

'It'll only get worse. Because I'm going to kill them all... one by one...'

'Kill who?'

'The ones who deserve it.'

'Deserve what?'

'I guess you'll have to wait and find out.'

Dilton hung up the phone and the line went dead.

58

Saturday Morning
Darlington

Brad opened the door of the computer room and carried the coffee holder containing the two cups over to the desk that Mitch was and placed a coffee down in front of him.

'Cheers.' Mitch picked it up and took a sip.

Brad removed the holder from the base of his take-out cup, threw it at the bin over to the right but failed miserably, hitting the wall instead. He took a drink of his Salted caramel latte and closed his eyes for a moment. 'Unbelievable.'

He noticed something on Mitch's face as he glared at the computer screen. 'What is it?'

'HammR33 wasn't online last night.'

'She didn't play?'

Mitch lowered his coffee and shook his head. 'No, she didn't.'

'Well, that's a waste of money, isn't it?'

'Spork11 and RCarl20 were there, though.'

'How many were watching?' Brad asked.

Mitch grabbed the mouse, clicked a few tabs, and found the figure. 'Just over a thousand. The most so far.'

Brad felt tingling in his chest and his smile widening. 'It's all working out, isn't it.'

Mitch smiled, agreeing with him but didn't look convincing. 'Why have players not turned up? Last night, neither did HammR33. I don't understand.'

'As long as we get paid who's bothered, Mitch,' noted Brad, greedily rubbing his hands.

Mitch gave a fair-enough shrug and looked at the screen on the right showing the room below. 'I wonder how long it takes her to realise she's alone?'

'She probably already does.'

'Where's Lisa?'

'She's in the van,' Brad replied, looking over. Their eyes met for a moment. 'I'm not stupid, you know, Mitch. I'll make sure the back door is locked this time.'

Mitch looked away from him, rolling his eyes. He knew Brad wasn't stupid, but he was a long way from Britain's next top scientist. He looked at the list of players.

Spork11.

RCarl20.

'We'll open the table tonight. We'll allow another three in to play.'

'I think we should up the price too,' said Brad. 'It's clearly popular with so many watchers waiting for their turn.'

Mitch turned back to the computer and considered it. It was a good idea. If they could make more money, then why not. To the right of the screen in the bottom corner, another notification popped up.

'They're coming thick and fast,' Mitch said, smiling.

Brad rubbed his thick hands together again, this time quicker. 'It's making the rounds.'

Each time someone clicked on www.attheend.com, a notification in the form of a small rectangular box came up in the bottom corner, with an IP Address, and underneath it, an option for either Brad or Mitch to press 'Yes' or 'No'.

He hovered the mouse over the box and decided to click 'yes' then smiled. It was another potential customer. He leaned back and sighed lightly, tilting his head into the leather of the high-backed chair.

'What's going to happen after Sarah is dead?' Brad asked, watching the screen. Sarah was sitting against the far wall with her knees tucked under her chin, shivering a little.

'We need more women. Preferably in their twenties. Nothing older.'

'When by?'

'This time next week,' Mitch told him. 'We'll need another four. Doesn't matter where from.'

Brad looked over to him and nodded, understanding his role. He knew Mitch had set this up; he was the brains behind this idea and had arranged the computer side of things. Brad was just the muscle. He would collect – or maybe taking women against their will using whatever violence he deemed necessary was a better fit – and bring them here, ready for the show.

They'd started so well.

The first group had been successful.

From the group of four, three of them were dead. They'd made thousands of pounds so far. For this to continue, they'd need to be clever and patient, not letting it go to their heads. Obviously, it was something they couldn't do forever but for now, they'd cash in whatever they could get. The ones unfortunate to be involved was collateral damage that Mitch was willing to make.

'Right, Brad. I need to head off soon. Feed Sarah and get rid of Lisa. Remember' — he turned to him and pointed — 'no excuses this time.'

'I know!' Brad spurted quickly.

Mitch nodded and smiled. 'Good.' He stood, pushed his chair in. 'Have a think about the next four, Brad. I'll leave that up to you. I'll be in touch.'

59

Saturday Afternoon
Police Station

Tanzy had almost finished his report. He picked up his coffee, drained it, and placed it back down by his keyboard.

The office was quiet for a Saturday. And hot. The sun had blazed through the windows all morning and had created a hot box because the air conditioning was only half working. It was making a sound but not actually doing what it was meant to. The maintenance man had been called and said he'd come in today at some point to have a look at it.

Tanzy glanced up across the office. Normally, there'd be a few more people in on overtime but there weren't many volunteers this weekend. The weather had been hot through the week and according to the forecast, it was going to peak on Saturday and Sunday, then it was going to get colder next week. Overtime looked good for the ones who volunteered but it wasn't mandatory. It would, however, enhance their upcoming appraisals, which was another thing Tanzy had to do today.

Most weekends, Tanzy or Byrd came in. It wasn't exactly in their contracts to do unpaid work but as time had passed, it had almost become expected of them. It was part and parcel of being a DI and they both knew that.

But as Byrd had been off looking after Claire, Tanzy didn't mind coming in. He had his report to finish and was hoping to catch Mac too. Byrd had informed him that he'd dropped Rachel Hammond's laptop off at his house for him to look at, also mentioning Mac didn't seem too keen on doing unpaid work in his own time.

Welcome to the real world, mate.

It wasn't just in the police force, but everywhere. Managers wanted more from their employees all the time. Standards were higher and competition was fierce. What didn't improve were the wages and that was something that Tanzy would have to grin and bear without making too much fuss. Life was, unfortunately, about pleasing the next in command. If you argued with them or made waves, it didn't go unnoticed.

If they were being honest, neither Byrd nor Tanzy had any great respect for DCI Fuller or particularly liked him, but it wasn't his job to be liked. It was his job to manage them.

Yesterday, the undertakers came to collect Rachel and Aaron and had taken them to the hospital to be further examined. It was obvious by the video how they died but they needed to make sure. It was not only clear that their man, Mackenzie Dilton, had been involved because of the video he'd uploaded but by finding his card on Rachel's laptop with a handwritten message.

Roger Carlton Hot tubs.

Byrd had told Tanzy that he'd phoned the number written on the back and spoken to him. He said Dilton told him he'd kill them all one by one. And that they deserved it. Byrd had tried ringing Dilton back but had no joy – it went straight to answerphone. He'd tried to trace the phone too but couldn't.

It seemed like Dilton knew how to play them. He knew how to stay hidden. Judging by the screen stills of the camera at Napier Street where the house fire was, the wig and tash were obviously fake. They did know his height and build, and that he had, from what Tanzy had remembered, dark brown eyes and a large nose.

Tanzy's phone rang. He looked at the caller, noticed her name.

'Hi, Linda.'

'You okay, Ori?'

He said he was.

'Just checking in. I'm bored at the hotel.' Fallows had said she was going to pop into town today and would phone either Byrd or Tanzy at some point. She had booked a few more nights in the hotel she was staying but wanted to get out for a while. Sometimes, she explained, it got too much for her, day after day – she wasn't used to it anymore.

'Nothing yet, Linda,' said Tanzy. 'By leaving his card on her laptop, it's obvious he wants us to have a look at it. Digital forensics is checking it now.' It reminded him he needed to pop along to see Mac. 'Are you enjoying our fabulous town?'

'I'm currently in the Cornmill Shopping Centre. Just been to Waterstones. I'm heading back to the hotel soon.'

'Good. Well, I'll let you know if I hear anything.'

'Speak soon.'

They both hung up and Tanzy placed his phone near his empty mug. He thought about the day before, finding the bodies that had been pumped with water, thinking about how strange it was, what it would have felt like to have water pumped into your body quicker than it was absorbed. Judging by the screams on the video it wouldn't have been pleasant. He also thought about how DS Stockdale acted when he turned up. He seemed fidgety, not quite himself. He'd been like that for a little while now, and no matter how many times Tanzy or Byrd had spoken with him, it hadn't improved. They knew he was having issues at home; he'd told some of the team himself about issues outside of work.

Tanzy stood, remembering that Stockdale had said he'd come in today to do his report. On his way down to see

Mac, he noticed he wasn't at his desk. He tried calling him, but it went straight to voicemail, so he left a message asking to send over his report when he had the chance.

Tanzy knocked on Mac's door.

'Yeah...'

He opened it and went inside.

Mac was sitting at his desk with Rachel Hammond's laptop open in front of him. There were several wires from her laptop to the computer and another wire connected to one of the screens on his wide desk.

Tanzy closed the door and thanked him for coming in. He replied saying it was no problem but Tanzy didn't need to be a detective to work out it was a burden on whatever he had planned for the day. Tanzy too had plans with Pip and the kids and had promised to be back by three as they wanted to go to Hardwick Park for a walk and soak up some sun before settling down for a film and takeaway later, so Tanzy wasn't here to waste any time.

'What have you found?' asked Tanzy, straight to the point.

'Remember when I checked Jane Ericson's laptop and found that website that contained much more than it appeared to have.'

Tanzy took a few steps towards him, frowning, trying to remember, then it clicked. 'Theend.com or something?'

'Attheend.com,' Mac said, turning slightly towards him. 'She's been on that site a lot, according to her history. The difference we have here in comparison to Jane Ericson's laptop is that when you go to the site, it comes up with a username and password option. Her username is already there. HammR33.'

'Spell that, please.'

Mac did letter by letter. 'We just need the password.'

'Can you not bypass it?'

Mac pushed his lips out, making a wet sound. 'Usually, yes. But not on this site. The firewall protection is something which MI5 wouldn't crack.'

Tanzy considered his words for a moment and grabbed a chair from his left, then sat down on it.

Mac leaned over, grabbed a pack of crisps from his desk, opened them, and started munching on them. Loudly. The sound of people eating made Tanzy want to punch the wall. He breathed slowly, trying not to let it bother him.

After Mac had finished, he threw the empty bag on the desk near another empty bag. Tanzy decided to let it go and not mention it – he would only get wound up. He was there to find out what was on Rachel's laptop, nothing more.

'So, what would you suggest we do with this then, Mac?'

The big man shrugged. 'I don't know, Ori. It's beyond my capability. Maybe we should send it away?'

'Okay. Yeah, maybe we'll need to. Thanks for coming in anyway and having a look.'

Mac immediately stood and left his office without saying goodbye. Whatever he had planned was obviously more important than cracking this case. Tanzy shook his head a little and stared at Rachel's laptop screen, open on the website www.attheend.com. If only he knew the password to access the site.

Still in Mac's office, he decided to ring Byrd. When Byrd answered, he asked how Claire was doing. Byrd said she was sofa-bound watching television and taking it easy.

'What's happening there, Ori?'

'Mac has been in looking at Rachel's laptop. He said about the site that she'd visited, that it was the same one as Jane Ericson had been on.'

'Can he access it?' asked Byrd. 'I remember him coming stuck with it.'

'Same scenario. He said the firewall is too strong to get in.'

'So we don't know what this website is?'

'We don't...'

'What is it?' asked Byrd, knowing there was more Tanzy wanted to say.

'Whatever it is, it's why people are dying.'

Byrd considered his words and had to agree with him. 'Very likely.'

'I wonder if Danny Walters had accessed the site, too?'

'His laptop would have been burnt in the fire. I didn't see any laptops there.'

'Or maybe it was there, but we didn't find it?'

'Maybe.'

'Leave it with me, Max. I need to get going...'

'Where are you going?'

'To Napier Street. Where this all started. If he had a laptop, it wasn't collected in evidence so must still be there. I'll ring you soon.'

'Good luck.'

Tanzy ended the call, stood up, and put his phone away. He left Mac's office and headed along to the evidence room. After speaking with Rebecca and signing out the sets of keys that belonged to Danny Walters, he went outside in the warmth of the Saturday afternoon and walked over to his car.

Soon, he pulled up outside the burnt house in Napier Street, got out, and locked his car, then used the key from evidence to open the door. The smell of charcoal was strong as he made his way down the narrow hallway, pulling on a pair of gloves.

The stairs in front of him were severely fire damaged. He took a right at the base of them and made his way through the dining room to the long, narrow kitchen. Drawer by drawer, he pulled them open, then tried the cupboards. He found no laptop. He sighed, returning to the base of the stairs. Looking up at them, the smell of pet-rol and burnt flesh came back to him.

He was almost certain there was no laptop found in the house inventory that forensics had come across. He knew Tallow and Hope were on the ball so if Walters had a lap-top, it hadn't been left somewhere obvious.

He entered the front bedroom and couldn't help think-ing about the mother and son who had died in there. He pictured them, the way they held each other over in the corner, the way the mother's eyes had frozen, looking down at her small son, all bloodshot and black.

He shuddered at the thought of it as if they were still there inside the room, somehow watching him, begging him to find something that would help figure out who did this to them. His first thought was the wardrobes. There were two of them, one on either side of the chimney breast, built in to the alcoves. He went to the left one, gen-tly grabbed the metal handle, and pulled it towards him. Inside, objects were burnt but not as severe as inside the room. In the bottom half, there were bags of clothes and a suitcase which, when he lifted, seemed to be empty. On the middle shelf, there were smaller boxes, some of them cardboard shoe boxes, half-burnt, while others were made from hardened plastic that had melted and distorted with the heat. On the top shelf, it appeared empty. He rose on his tiptoes and ran his palm across it but found nothing.

'Shit.'

Going over to the opposite side, he checked the other wardrobe. Other than more clothes, a large box filled with games, and a large plastic tub of toys which were black-ened with smoke, there was nothing else.

He left the bedroom and searched the rear bedroom where he found a built-in wardrobe over to the right of the room, the front of it black and flaked. He pulled it open with a slight crack and looked inside, seeing a rail of clothing and below, boxes of burnt games. One of them was Kerplunk, a game he remembered playing with his own dad many years ago.

He closed the wardrobe, backed away, and checked around the room, looking for places where a laptop would be but came up short. Back on the landing, he saw a door directly in front of him, unsure how he'd missed it when he was last here. It was more than likely a cupboard, he assumed. He pushed down the handle but it was locked, then he noticed the keyhole.

'Shit,' he muttered, trying to pull the door towards him harder this time but it wouldn't budge.

Then he thought of something and pulled the set of keys from his pocket, tried one and the lock turned. He opened it to find a wooden ladder, then looked up, seeing a closed hatch above him. On the wall to the left, there was a light switch which he pressed, but nothing happened. Then he realised the electricity was off because of the fire. He stepped fully into the cupboard, started to climb the steps.

When he reached the top, he pushed the hatch up as far as it went and looked into the room, brightly lit with sunlight coming from an attic window. The room which was big, spanning the full width of the house. The floor had been boarded and lined with a carpet that had seen better days. He climbed up and stood fully, the angled roof inches from his bald head. Up there it was warm and clammy, although there was a window, the still, stagnant air was a sign it hadn't been opened for some time. Mostly the room was empty, apart from the old wooden wardrobe against the wall that backed on to the house next door. He went over and opened it.

On the shelf in front of him, there was a laptop.

'Bingo.'

As he reached for the laptop, he paused, hearing something below. He couldn't be certain but it sounded like footsteps. He listened harder, angling his ear to the open hatch.

It was probably something outside.

Then he realised it wasn't. Someone was walking up the stairs.

60

Saturday Afternoon
Napier Street, Darlington

Tanzy stayed perfectly still, staring at the open hatch, listening to the approaching footsteps until the house became silent. Had he imagined it? He couldn't be sure. Very slowly, with the laptop in his hand, he took a few paces towards the hatch.

'Orion?' he heard someone say.

He frowned. The voice wasn't familiar.

'Orion? Are you up there?'

He appeared at the hatch and looked down. 'What are you doing here?' He crouched down, finding his footing on the steps, and descended them. 'How did you know I was here?'

'I spoke with Max,' Linda Fallows replied. 'He said you were here. I tried calling but it kept going to answerphone.'

'I've had no missed calls,' he said, stepping onto the landing, taking out his phone to check it. 'Must be a bad signal around here.'

'I was going to go back to the hotel, but when Max said you were here, I put it into my phone and realised it was only a few minutes away.'

'What's that?' Tanzy asked, pointing to the bags in her hand.

'Few bits. Some make-up. Nothing too exciting,' she said, then pointed to the laptop he was holding. 'What's that?'

'Danny Walters laptop.'

When they were back at the station, they handed the keys over to Rebecca in the evidence lock-up and went into the office. Tanzy glanced left, looking for Stockdale, but he wasn't there. He still needed Stockdale's report from the previous day to forward on to Fuller, who'd no doubt, be looking for it first thing Monday morning.

Tanzy sat down at his desk, placing the laptop in front of him, and Fallows sat on Byrd's chair and leaned in, interested in what they'd find.

He opened the laptop, pressed the ON button.

She was close enough for him to smell her perfume. It was nice. Her blonde hair was long and had been straightened. Her face was nicely done. Her green, emerald eyes were highlighted by dark mascara and eye shadow, easily knocking ten years off her. It was the first time that he'd felt a hint of attraction towards her, which he considered a little weird and strange.

The laptop whirred a little, and the screen came alive. 'Here we go,' said Tanzy.

Without requesting a password, the screen changed to the laptop's background, showing a couple of columns of folders on the left-hand side. Tanzy placed a finger on the mouse cursor and navigated to the internet icon, then double-clicked.

He knew he was way off Mac regarding computer knowledge but knew the basics. If the website that Mac had found on both Jane Ericson's laptop and Rachel Hammond's laptop was on this one, then it was clear the website was the only thing they'd found linking Danny Walters to those two.

The internet wouldn't open.

'Don't we have to connect it to the Wi-fi?' Fallows said, unsure.

'Ahh, of course.' Tanzy connected it, entered the Wi-Fi password, and tried again. This time it opened. He went to the tab at the top of the page and opened the history. The last visited address was www.attheend.com.

'Bingo,' he said. 'It's the same website the other's used.'

When the page came up, it was a different scenario to Rachel Hammond's laptop. The username was there – Dwalt66 – and a password had been automatically saved disguised as eight small asterisks.

'Is that the password?' Fallows asked, leaning closer.

'Looks that way.'

'Go on it,' Fallows encouraged.

Whatever this site was, Tanzy knew it had something to do with why they'd been murdered. It was the only link they'd figured out. He pressed the ENTER key and it went to the next screen.

A welcome message came up, saying 'Hello, Dwalt66.'

'What the hell is this?' Tanzy whispered.

On the left of the screen there was a box, showing a live camera feed of a dark room, revealing a woman sitting on the floor with her back against the wall. Near her, there were food wrappers and an empty drink bottle.

'What the hell is this?' Fallows said loudly, shocked by what she was seeing.

Tanzy didn't reply, instead looked over to the right. At the top, it had a box with the title 'Current players' and under the title, there were three names.

Dwalt66.

Spork11.

RCarl20.

He pointed to RCarl20 and said, 'He's our guy. That's Mackenzie Dilton. That's the same user who uploaded those videos online. He's a part of' – Tanzy raised his palms towards the screen – 'this. Whatever this is.'

Under the names, it had '6 days until next game' and underneath that, was a separate tab with the word 'watchers' on. In brackets next to 'watchers' was the number 1023.

'What the fuck is this?' Tanzy said, placing his palms on his head. It was so warm in the office, he felt sweat running down his back.

'I don't understand,' Fallows said. 'Some kind of game?'

Tanzy didn't know what to say because he didn't fully understand it. He edged a little closer, trying to see the girl on the video feed better, but couldn't make out her details. He picked up his phone to ring Byrd but as he dialled the number and put it to his ear, the screen changed back to the first page again, asking them to input the password again.

Tanzy jerked back. 'No! Where did it go?'

Fallows looked at the screen.

Username – Dwalt66.

Password – please enter.

'Shit. Where's it gone?'

Across town, Mitch had noticed Dwalt66 had logged on. It had appeared as a notification in the bottom half of the screen. It was a good job he glanced at it because him and Brad were discussing where they'd get the next victims from.

'Hold on a second,' Mitch said quickly. 'Dwalt66 is online.'

'How's that possible?' Brad frowned and slid his chair over. 'He's dead, isn't he?'

'Hold on,' said Mitch. 'I'll find the IP address, see where it is.'

It didn't take him very long to locate the current IP Address of Dwalt66.

'Oh, hell no!' Mitch shouted, then quickly tapped the keyboard. 'There. They are logged back out. They can't see anymore.'

'What's wrong – who was it?' Brad said, confused at what was happening.

'It wasn't Dwalt66 watching. It was the police.'

61

Monday Morning
Police Station

Tanzy was the last one to enter the meeting room. He could feel all eyes watching him, including DCI Fuller's, as he closed the door and made his way to the whiteboard. A little earlier he'd heard Fuller in his office, speaking with someone on the phone. The way he was talking and the language he used indicated it was not a friendly conversation. Tanzy and Byrd had heard him defending his team, so they assumed it was Barry Eckles or possibly someone higher, asking why the results weren't coming. They had a point. There were too many open investigations with too many unanswered questions and minimal leads.

'Morning,' said Tanzy addressing the room. He stopped next to Byrd, who greeted him with a nod.

'Morning,' PC Weaver replied.

'Morning,' DC Leonard added.

No one else said anything. Saying good morning in that context was more of a courteous rhetorical statement, especially if he'd already spoken with some of the individuals beforehand.

In the meeting was the usual team, plus Linda Fallows, who'd just arrived. The senior forensics, Jacob Tallow, and Emily Hope were there, too, as was the forensic trainee, Amanda Forrest.

Tanzy nodded at Byrd, who was holding the remote. Byrd pressed the button and the first slide appeared, telling everyone the day, date, and a title 'Updates' underneath.

'I hope everyone has had a good weekend and had some rest,' Tanzy started. 'This week will be a busy one. To the ones who don't know, we found Rachel Hammond in a property on Elton Road on Friday, tied to a chair sitting opposite her boyfriend, who was also tied up. There was a video posted online by RCarl20, the same user who uploaded the house fire video and the shocking footage of Jane Ericson falling from the flat, indicating it's his third victim and —'

'Sixth victim,' DC Cornty said.

Tanzy jerked his head towards him. It was too early for his sarcasm and witty cleverness. 'I'm sorry, Phil?'

'It's his sixth victim, sir.'

Tanzy frowned.

'Four victims died in the fire. Then Jane Ericson. Now Rachel. That makes six. Actually seven, if we include her boyfriend, Aaron.'

Byrd sighed loud enough for only Tanzy to hear. DCI Fuller, who was sitting to the detective's left, in the seat he usually sat in, glanced over to him, also not impressed by his comment. It didn't help that the air con wasn't working either. The room was hot and stuffy, the air stagnant and irritating.

Tanzy took a deep breath. 'His third occasion, shall we say?'

Cornty nodded his approval.

'So… his third occasion. We know from Jane Ericson that Mackenzie Dilton, the man we are looking for, left a business card on her laptop. It was an electrician's card with the name Roger Carlton. We know that Roger Carlton is a character who he admired from an old American show.'

Several nods responded.

'Eric, you wouldn't mind opening that window, would you?' DCI Fuller asked Timms, who was closest to it. 'It's too hot in here.'

Timms nodded, went over to the window, and opened it, then returned to his seat.

'On Jane's laptop,' Tanzy continued, 'Mac found a frequently visited website called www.attheend.com. He tried accessing the site but said it was very strange. Apparently, it had layers upon layers of security he couldn't break through. I did some digging but didn't find a thing on www.attheend.com, so I can't be sure what it is. What I can be sure of is, when we found Rachel Hammond and after searching the house, there was another business card upstairs, on top of her closed laptop. The business card was Roger Carlton Hot tubs. Now we believe Mackenzie Dilton posed as a guy renting out hot tubs this time and got in her house that way.'

PC Weaver raised her slender hand. Her hair was different today. Curled. She looked stunning.

'Yes, Amy?' said Tanzy.

'So, he posed as a carpet cleaner, then an electrician, now a guy renting out hot tubs?'

Tanzy nodded.

'Seems so,' added Byrd.

Weaver gave a sad smile.

'The business card that he left on her laptop had a number written on, along with a message. The message said look on the laptop and to call him.'

'Did you phone the number?' PC Andrews asked, over to the right.

Tanzy said, 'Max did,' then turned to him.

'It was him. Mackenzie Dilton,' informed Byrd. 'He told me that he would kill them all.'

'Who?' Fallows said over to their left, sitting next to Fuller.

'He said everyone who deserves it.'

Silence filled the large room for a few moments.

'What did you find on Rachel's laptop?' DC Anne Tiffin asked.

Tanzy nodded. 'The same website as we did on Jane's laptop. But as before, we couldn't access it.' He turned to Byrd, who pressed the button. The screen behind them changed. 'It comes up with this.'

On the screen, it showed the website www.at-theend.com. Apart from the message in the rectangular box asking for a username and password, the page was blank.

'What is it?' Fuller asked, leaning forward.

'The site that both Rachel Hammond and Jane Ericson had been on.'

'Do you know the password or login?'

Tanzy shook his head at Fuller. 'Unfortunately not.' He then turned to the room. 'After noticing the same website, it got me thinking. What if Danny Walters had also been on this site.'

DC Anne Tiffin nodded in agreement, as did Amy Weaver.

'We didn't find a laptop in the house, Ori,' Tallow said.

'I know. I went there to check, though, just in case. You're right, Jacob, with what you're saying. There was no laptop downstairs or upstairs. But on the set of keys that evidence had, there was another key which opened what looked like a boiler cupboard on the landing.'

'I remember seeing it. Tried it but it was locked,' Tallow replied.

Tanzy smiled. 'There was a set of ladders that led to an attic. Up there, was a wardrobe, and inside, a laptop, which I assume had been hidden out of the way of the children. We brought it back to the station – Linda and me – to have a look. Danny Walter's last visited site had been attheend.com, so we clicked on it. His browser had some-how saved his username and password login so we logged in.'

The room suddenly became dead quiet, everyone listening to what was coming next.

'There was a screen on the left, showing a woman sitting on a blanket on the floor of a room with her head tucked into her knees. The room looked big but empty. There was only her. It was as if her being there was not her choice. On the right-hand side of the site page, there was a tab with the word players. There were three names. One of them was Danny Walters's name. I remember that one. Dwalt66. The others I can't. Under that tab, there was another tab saying, 'Watchers' with a number over a thousand. Then, out of now where, it logged me out taking me back to the first page. I didn't know his password so couldn't get back on. It did say, however, six days until the next game. That was Saturday morning.'

'So four days from now?' Fuller replied. 'Friday is the day. Whatever game this is, it's happening Friday.'

Tanzy nodded, although he wasn't sure enough to confirm anything.

'Do you think this is Mackenzie Dilton?' asked PC Weaver.

Tanzy's nod wasn't confident. 'I'm led to believe it is, although I can't be certain. If this is the link between Danny Walters, Jane Ericson, and Rachel Hammond, which so far seems to be, then perhaps Dilton knows.' Tanzy paused and frowned suddenly.

'What is it?' Fuller asked him, noticing his expression change.

Tanzy scowled, turning to Linda. 'Linda, did you see RCarl20 as one of the players?'

She thought for a moment, her thin blonde eyebrows arching towards the centre of her forehead. 'I don't know… maybe, Ori. I can't be sure.'

'It went off so quickly. But I'm going to stick with my gut and say that one of the players was RCarl20.'

'So he's playing the game too – whatever game it is?' Tiffin probed.

Tanzy offered a simple shrug.

'So,' Fuller said, standing abruptly. 'In four days, there's a game?'

'Seems so, sir,' answered Byrd, unsure of why Fuller had stood.

'Whatever this fucking game is isn't good and will probably lead to another death. And I'll tell you something, after the conversation I've just had with Barry Eckles, is something I can't let happen. It would be bad for all of us. And I mean all of us. Now, get your fucking acts together and find Mackenzie Dilton.' He turned, picked up his chair, and threw it into the wall, causing a loud smack. A few of them flinched, Linda Fallows more than anyone as she was closest to him. The plaster on the wall dented and fell away in small pieces to the carpet.

Fuller left the room and slammed the door behind him.

There was an uncomfortable silence in the room until Byrd asked, 'Any questions?'

62

Monday Late Morning
Police Station

Byrd and Tanzy returned to their desks, followed by Linda Fallows, who took a right and sat down on the desk across from them.

She caught Tanzy's eye, pointed towards Fuller's office, and whispered, 'He doesn't seem very pleased.'

Tanzy rolled his eyes, implying it was nothing to worry about it.

'So,' Byrd said, getting comfortable, 'what's our plan, Ori?'

Tanzy leaned back a little, thinking. 'We need to know what this website is.' He then sat up straight. 'I've looked and looked. There's nothing on it.' He pulled himself in and started typing away.

Byrd considered his response and turned to his own computer. Before doing anything, he picked up his phone and phoned Claire to check up on her.

Fallows wheeled herself over to Tanzy, stopping next to him. 'We've had water, fire, and air, Ori.' Tanzy turned his attention to her. 'Earth is next, I'm sure of it.'

Tanzy nodded but didn't want to believe it. But, as things stood, he couldn't deny it was a possibility unless they got their arses in gear, found out what was on the site and Mackenzie Dilton's involvement.

'We'll see,' Tanzy replied quietly to her.

She rolled herself back across the aisle to the desk she was using. 'I'll do some more digging on earth, Ori. See what I come up with.'

First, Tanzy checked his emails, looking for the reports from the people who were at Rachel Hammond's house on Friday. He was missing one report.

DS Stockdale's.

Narrowing his eyes, he checked his emails again but couldn't find his report. He stood up, peered over the desks, searching for him at the back but was nowhere to be seen. He frowned as he sat, trying to remember if he'd seen him in the meeting.

He angled his body to Byrd, who had just ended the call with Claire.

'How is she?'

Byrd nodded. 'She's good. Her friend Becca is there keeping her company. The doctor gave her some pills for the pain.'

'Good.' Tanzy paused a moment, not wanting to move on too quickly. 'Have you seen Phil Stockdale today?'

Byrd thought for a few seconds. 'Don't think so. Was he not in the meeting?'

'Did you see him?'

'Now I think about it. No, I didn't.'

'Weird.' Tanzy glanced down at his watch. 'There's no reason for him not to be here?'

'Unless he's out and about?'

'He didn't report in this morning,' Tanzy said. He turned to Fallows. 'Have you seen DS Stockdale this morning?'

'Which one is that?' she replied, with a shrug.

'Never mind.' He stood. 'I'm going to look for him. I need his report on what happened at Rachel Hammond's house on Friday. Plus, I'm not too sure he's in the right frame of mind. I need to see how he's doing.'

Byrd looked at him in understanding. 'You worried about him?'

Tanzy gave a small shrug. 'A little, Max. Yeah. I'll see where he is.'

He left Byrd and Fallows, made his way down the aisle toward the other end, a spring of urgency in his step. From the walkway, he couldn't see Stockdale at his desk, only his empty chair. He turned around and asked Leonard, 'You seen Phil today?'

Leonard glanced up at him, said he hadn't.

Tanzy moved past Leonard, and stopped next to Cornty, who was typing an email. 'You seen Phil today?'

Cornty pressed SEND and swivelled quickly on his chair. 'No, boss. Not today.'

'Okay.'

'But...' Cornty added with a finger in the air.

Tanzy was mid-turn so swivelled back. 'Yeah?'

'I'm sure he said something on Friday about taking his kid to the opticians.' Cornty nodded. 'I'm sure he did.'

Tanzy looked at Leonard, who had stopped doing typing. 'You hear him say that – about the opticians?'

Leonard said he hadn't. 'Sorry, boss.'

Tanzy left the office, made his way down the corridor, and went to reception. Lisa was sitting behind her desk, reading something positioned behind her computer screen out of sight, which Tanzy guessed was a woman's mag. She dragged herself away from whatever it was and looked up hearing his approaching footsteps.

'Hey, Ori,' she said, cheerfully.

'Is Phil Stockdale in today?' he said, straight to the point.

She considered the question, then grabbed the mouse and looked down at the screen in front of her. The woman's magazine that Tanzy assumed was in fact a textbook on Criminal Law. He smiled inside for getting it so wrong.

A few moments later, she said, 'Doesn't look like he clocked in this morning, sir.'

Tanzy thanked her and went out to the car park. Among the cars, he couldn't see Stockdale's. He picked his phone from his pocket, found his number, and frowned. There was a missed call from Stockdale last night at 10.27 p.m.. Tanzy couldn't remember it, wondering why he hadn't realised or answered it. He called him but it went straight to the answerphone.

'C'mon, Phil. Where are you?' he whispered to himself.

Just before he put his phone away it rang. The number on the screen was one he didn't recognise, ending in two four seven. He accepted the call. 'Hello?'

'Is that Detective Inspector Orion Tanzy?' It was a woman's voice, sounding concerned.

'Speaking. Who's this?' Tanzy asked, frowning, watching cars and vans pass by on St. Cuthbert's Way through the fence.

'My name is Joan Stockdale. Phil is my husband.'

'Okay…'

'This might sound strange, but have you seen him today?'

'I – I haven't. One of the guys said he might be taking his son to the opticians?'

'Our son? Josh?'

'I… don't know,' admitted Tanzy, feeling bad he didn't know his son's name.

'Josh is at school. He doesn't even have glasses. There'd be no reason to take him to the opticians.'

'Joan, when was the last time you saw Phil?' Tanzy started slowly walking up the path.

'Last night. He said he needed to clear his head to think. Recently, he's…'

'He's what, Joan?' Tanzy stopped to concentrate on her response, blocking out the sound of the passing traffic along the main road.

'He hasn't been himself. He's been spending a lot of time on his phone and his laptop. I' — she sighed heavily — 'I think he might be gambling again. Has he said anything to you or his friends?'

Tanzy thought hard, knowing Stockdale hadn't quite been himself but knew he had to be careful the way he answered. The last thing he wanted to do was worry her more than she already was.

'He hasn't, no.'

There was silence on the call for a long moment.

'You there, Joan?'

'Yes. Yes.' She started to sob a little. 'I just need to know why he never came home last night. We kind of argued and he went, saying he needed to clear his head. I went to sleep, assuming he'd be next to me when I woke this morning but he wasn't. I've checked the house. He wasn't here.'

'Is his car at home?'

'Yes. It's still here,' she replied quickly. 'That's the weird thing about it.'

Tanzy fell silent in thought. 'Let me make some calls, Joan. I'll find him, okay?'

'Thank you.'

Tanzy hung up and called Stockdale again. It went straight to voicemail.

63

Sunday Night (Night Before)

'Please, just tell me what's wrong?' Joan Stockdale said to her husband with her hands out wide, desperate to know. She had just got out of the bath and was wearing a thin, blue dressing gown. Her dark hair was damp, tied up in a loose ponytail.

Phil was sitting at the kitchen table in a t-shirt and jogging bottoms, vacantly staring, making minimal eye contact with her. He hadn't said much to her all day, even when she'd tried to speak to him or when Josh had tried showing him a game he was interested in, all Stockdale did was smile at him. He seemed lost, vacant.

She wandered over, took a seat next to him, and took hold of his hand. He edged away slightly, causing her to sigh.

'Please, Phil. Just tell me what's wrong?' she begged him.

He stared silently at the table.

'Is it the gambling again?' she said softly. 'Because if it is, we can get help again.'

He considered the question for a long moment, then shook his head slowly. 'No.'

'What is it – is it work? Too much pressure?'

Again, the question seemed to take a while to sink in. Stockdale was in a trance. Something was on his mind.

'I just need to go for a walk.' He edged out, then stopped. 'Yeah. Work is hard at the moment. There's a lot of shit coming down from Fuller. We have our appraisals coming up soon.'

She smiled sadly at him.

'I'm not gambling again. I promise you that.' He found his feet. 'I need some air. I need to get out.'

She frowned, looked up at the kitchen clock. 'Phil, it's after ten… where are you walking to?'

'I don't know.'

'It'll be getting dark soon.'

'I won't be long. I just – just need some air. You go on up to bed. I'll be up soon.'

He stood up, grabbed a thin jacket from a hook near the back door and put it on. From the table, she watched him carefully.

'I'll wait for you to come back.'

'I won't be long, Joan.' He left the kitchen, went down the hall, and out of the front door.

Ten minutes after leaving the house, he found himself walking past Cockerton Green. It was quiet and still warm. The earlier heat had stuck around a little, but as the sun was almost out of sight, it had started to dip in temperature. He passed the row of shops, and crossed near Cockerton Club, then continued along the path, past the new housing development being built on, the front of it barricaded with a line of temporary metal fences stuck into grey, rectangular blocks. The houses weren't finished but were close, waiting for the finishing touches. It amazed him how fast houses went up nowadays, especially after the foundations were laid.

He looked right and left before crossing over Deneside Road and had a quick nose in the window of the antique shop on the corner as he passed it. He never understood how it stayed in business. He'd never seen anyone inside of it.

Just before he reached the roundabout, a car slowed behind him and stopped. He looked to his right, hearing it slow. It was a blue Ford Focus. New model. Once it had stopped, the passenger window lowered, and inside, a man leaned towards him, his upper body over the gear stick.

'Excuse me, mate,' the man said.

Stockdale stopped, took a few steps towards the car, and leaned over.

'Can you tell me where Pierremont Road is?'

Stockdale thought for a moment, then pointed straight ahead. 'Take a left here and it's literally one hundred metres on either your right or left, depending on where you need to be.'

The man in the car smiled, then sighed. 'I knew it was around here somewhere.'

Stockdale frowned for a moment, realising the man looked somewhat familiar, but he couldn't place him. His big brown, dark eyes. The large nose. He'd seen him somewhere he was sure of it.

'Thanks, mate.' The man raised the window, checked the traffic behind, and pulled out.

Stockdale continued walking, thinking about the man. Then it clicked. He recognised him from the video from Napier Street. It was Mackenzie Dilton. He took out his phone and found Tanzy's number, pressed CALL. It went unanswered. As Stockdale rounded the corner, approaching the tennis courts on his left, he was going to try again but noticed the Focus had stopped up on the left, just next to the park entrance, just beyond the tennis courts.

The lights were turned off. There didn't look like there was anyone inside.

He looked around the car, trying to spot him.

When he grew closer, he heard footsteps inside the park. Through the railings, he saw the man, walking along the path away from him.

'Hey, wait!' Stockdale shouted, then picked up his speed and took a left into the park, seeing him just ahead. There wasn't much light inside the park, the high, surrounding trees blocking most of the remaining daylight.

'Hey!' he shouted again.

The man took a right out of Stockdale's sight.

Stockdale broke out into a jog, focusing down the path. It got darker the further he went but he kept his eyes on the path, noticed it branched off to the right, and from where he'd last seen the man he believed was Mackenzie Dilton, assumed he'd gone that way.

He angled right but there was no one there.

He looked around quickly, battling the growing darkness.

'Hello?' he said, quieter this time.

No response. The park was absolutely silent and, although he was a fixed-set man, it made him feel uncomfortable. If he was being honest, a little vulnerable. He turned around, looking behind him, and grabbed his phone, found the torch app. The light was good but not bright enough to see very far.

'Where's he gone?' he said to himself.

'Looking for me?' he heard a whisper behind him.

As he turned, he felt the hard impact to the side of his head; a hot, searing pain that felt like his head was on fire. With nothing he could do about it, he fell to the ground and his world went black.

64

Monday Afternoon
Police Station

Tanzy returned to the office, finding Fallows sitting on his chair next to Byrd, both reading something on his computer screen.

'Stockdale's car isn't here,' said Tanzy. He stopped behind them, focused on the article on the screen. It was about the 'Earth' murder that happened seven years ago near Essex, the case Linda Fallows had been heavily involved in. 'What's this?' he asked.

Fallows turned. 'Just going through this article written by a local paper down our way. About the guy who was buried in the woods.'

'Earth?' asked Tanzy.

She nodded. 'Yup.'

'Max, I've tried ringing Phil but it's going straight to voicemail.'

Byrd turned, looked up at him with concern. 'Have you spoken with his wife?'

'Funny you should say that.'

Byrd's eyes narrowed.

'She's just rang me asking if I'd seen him.'

Fallows stopped reading the article and turned her attention to Tanzy.

'She says he went for a walk last night to clear his head. Apparently, he and his missus, Joan, argued, then he said he needed some air. That was just after ten last night. She'd told him she was going to bed but would wait up for him. But when she woke this morning, he wasn't there.'

Byrd's frown deepened. 'Where's his car?'

'It's at home. First thing I asked.'

'Okay. Had she tried ringing him?'

Tanzy nodded. 'Yeah. A few times. Can't get hold of him.'

'Isn't like him?'

Tanzy had to agree. Fallows looked worried, wondering if his absence had something to do with Mackenzie Dilton. If he'd already gone missing, was it too late for Stockdale? Or was it something totally innocent? A logical reason why he wasn't there and his wife hadn't heard from him.

The door opened behind them and DCI Fuller asked, 'Have you found him yet?'

'Who sir?' asked Byrd.

'Phil Stockdale. Cornty said he wasn't in today. Any sign of him yet? I'm needing his report from Friday?'

'I spoke with his wife,' Tanzy said, then told him about their conversation.

Fuller's face changed in thought. 'His phone goes straight to voicemail?'

Tanzy nodded.

'And no one's seen him today, so far?'

Tanzy shook his head. 'I've checked with Lisa at reception. He hasn't clocked on today either.'

Fuller was about to comment on that but noticed DC Leonard dashing down the aisle towards them. Leonard looked alarmed, holding his phone out in front of him.

'Sir,' he said, addressing Byrd and Tanzy, not Fuller. 'Look at this.' He held his arm out to show them both his phone screen.

Fallows stood up and joined them.

'Is – is that Phil?' asked Byrd.

'It looks like it,' said Leonard.

'Where the hell is he?'

65

Monday Afternoon
Police Station

It was a video uploaded to the internet. A close-up of a man's face.

'Can we get it up on the computer?' Tanzy asked. 'Make it bigger?'

Tanzy dragged the page up to see the web address, then held his finger down to copy it. He closed the app, opened his emails, and forwarded on to Byrd.

'I've sent it,' said Tanzy, nodding towards Byrd's desk.

Byrd sat down at his screen, found the link, and clicked it open, tapping his foot impatiently off the floor. Tanzy, Fallows, and Fuller waited impatiently behind him.

'What is it?' Fuller asked quickly, not needing to be a detective to figure out it was something very important. He'd also heard Byrd ask if it was Phil.

The website opened on the screen, showing a close-up of Phil Stockdale's face, illuminated by a dim light. The camera was fixed in position. Stockdale, judging by his face, the way his skin sagged under the pull of gravity, seemed to be on his back and behind him was a dark surface that looked to be some type of fabric.

Byrd noticed under the video the name of the uploader: RCarl20.

'It's him, isn't it?' Fuller said, pointing at the name.

Fallows turned, nodded sadly.

'Bastard.' Fuller leaned forward a little to get a better view. 'What's he doing?'

Stockdale was on his back, his eyes darting around as if trying to work out what was happening. His upper body rose and fell with quick breathing. Panic was clearly setting in. Whatever the reason he was there, it wasn't out of choice.

'Why is he moving like that?' asked Fallows.

'He's tied up,' Leonard said.

If he was tied up, it was out of camera shot.

'Is he in a box?'

Fallows turned to Byrd. 'Like a coffin?'

Byrd snapped his neck at her as if realising something. 'Earth? Buried. It makes sense.'

'Where the hell is this happening?' Fuller shouted, his voice reaching the far end of the office. People looked up from their desks with curious eyes, wondering what was happening. PC Amy Weaver came over to join them.

'Jesus. Is that Phil?'

'Yes,' Byrd replied to her, keeping his eyes on the screen. He then looked up at Leonard. 'Jim, go get Mac!'

Leonard broke away from the desk and ran through the office, curious eyes following him until he reached the door and went into the corridor. Once Leonard reached his door, he quickly knocked and opened it. Inside the office, there was no sign of Mac.

'Shit.'

He checked the canteen, found a couple of PCs talking and having their lunch. He closed the door and made his way down the corridor, then down the flight of stairs, passing Jacob Tallow, the senior forensic, on his way back to the office.

'Have you seen Mac from DFU?'

Tallow shook his head. 'Haven't seen him all day. I've phoned him too but he didn't answer. I thought it was strange, to be honest.'

Leonard thanked him and returned to the office. 'He isn't there.'

Byrd and Tanzy continued to watch the video. Stockdale wriggled in whatever space he was in. Fuller placed his hand on his head, watching in horror, thinking about what they were going to do.

The video was ten minutes long. It reached nine minutes, then a voice spoke on the video.

'Hello, Detective Inspector Max Byrd and Detective Inspector Orion Tanzy. I trust you are watching and both listening.'

Byrd and Tanzy froze.

'How does he know your names?' asked Fuller.

'By now, you may have realised you are watching one of your own,' the voice continued. 'Detective Sergeant Phillip Stockdale. I'm sorry I had to do this to him, but it's the least he deserves for what he's done.'

Dilton's words played over in all of their minds.

'What's he done?' Weaver asked, looking at them one by one but they ignored her, keeping their focus on Byrd's computer screen.

'As you may or may not see, Phil is tied up. He can't move. The enclosed space he is in, is in fact, a coffin. In approximately thirty minutes, the oxygen supply to the coffin will stop. And I don't need to tell you what happens when you don't get oxygen.' Dilton started to laugh. 'You can't breathe.'

Tanzy visualised him laughing and it boiled his blood.

'So, I hope you enjoy the show. Because as long as you keep enjoying it, the show will continue. Catch up soon, Detectives.'

The audio file that had been placed over the footage stopped and the video came to an end, reaching a total of ten minutes.

'In a coffin?' Weaver said. 'Why is…' she trailed off, battling with the million thoughts in her mind.

Byrd stood up abruptly, almost knocking into Fallows, and went to the window. He placed both hands on the top of his head and sighed.

'What time was the video posted?' Tanzy asked, grabbing hold of the mouse, and scrolling down. It stated the video upload time was 1.14 p.m.. He looked down at his watch. It was a little after two.

'How long would you last inside a closed coffin?' Weaver said. 'It wouldn't take long for the air to run out, would it?'

Byrd, standing at the window, turned and shook his head. 'An hour maybe. Two at the most.'

'So,' Tanzy said, thinking hard. 'We need to think of the obvious. If he's in a coffin, he might—'

'A cemetery?' Fallows suggested, finishing his trail of thought.

He nodded. 'Leonard, make a list of cemeteries in Darlington.'

'Okay, boss.' He left them, dashed down the aisle, and took a left, then sat down at his computer to make a list of cemeteries.

'We need to fucking find him!' Fuller shouted, smacking his hands together. Fallows flinched a little, unsure what the noise was initially. 'We don't have long,' he added, then returned to his office and slammed the door behind him.

A few seconds of silence passed. Tanzy took a deep breath, started the video again, and watched carefully, seeing if he could spot something that could help. If it's true what Dilton said, that he was inside a coffin, then the most obvious place he would be at is a cemetery. It would certainly be the fourth kill, the one that Linda Fallows had predicted, being 'earth'.

'Where was that man buried, Linda?' Byrd asked, returning to his desk. 'The one in Essex?'

'In the woods.'

'Not a cemetery?'

'No. The woods. Nowhere near a cemetery.'

'If the coffin is a normal size, how long would it take to use all the air?' Byrd said.

'Hold on…' Weaver asked, pulling out her phone. She tapped away, opening up an internet page. A few moments passed, then she said, 'The smaller you are, then there's more space for the air. The larger you are, the less space for air.'

Byrd pushed his lip out, knowing Stockdale was both tall and thick set.

'It says an average person under normal conditions could last up to five hours,' Weaver said.

'The problem we have,' said Tanzy, pointing at the screen, particularly at Stockdale's face, 'is that he's a large man, clearly panicking. The rise and fall in his chest indicate he's breathing quickly. That air, however much there is, won't last long in there.'

'Every breath he takes is decreasing the oxygen and increasing the levels of carbon dioxide,' Byrd added.

Weaver glanced up, and nodded, reading the same point on the site on her phone. 'That's true, Max. It says that here.'

A minute later, DC Leonard came back with a sheet of paper. 'Here.'

Tanzy took the paper and looked down the list.

There were three. West Cemetery on Carmel Road. East Cemetery on Geneva Road. North Cemetery on North Road. 'We'll need to split up to cover these – we don't have enough time.' He turned to Leonard. 'You and Amy go to North Road. We'll go to Carmel Road.' He stood, glared over the top of the desks, grabbed PC Grearer's and PC Timm's attention, and waved them over. They both looked at each other confused, wondering which one Tanzy was meaning but both stood, and started across the office.

'What's happening?' Timms said when he reached him.

'You seen the latest video?'

Timms nodded.

'Can you both go to East Cemetery on Geneva Road?'

'What are we looking for?' Grearer asked.

'We think Stockdale is buried in the ground inside a coffin. Go there. Look for any areas which look like they've just been laid. If you see anything, ring me immediately. Go.'

Timms and Grearer both nodded and backed away, grabbing their keys and jackets, then left the office.

Byrd said to Tanzy, 'Guess we'll start with Carmel Road?'

Fallows leaned over, noticed the top one. 'Where's Carmel Road?'

'Come on,' Byrd said. 'You can come with us.'

66

Monday Afternoon
West Cemetery, Carmel Road

Byrd decided to drive when they reached the car park and Tanzy rode shotgun, with Fallows in the back. Byrd reached the end of Park Place in seconds, took a left on to Yarm Road, and put his siren on, going through the next red light at the bottom of Yarm Road. They overtook a string of cars, quickly making their way around the ring roads, joining Woodland Road, then flew through the red lights at the crossroads of Greenbank Road.

At the end of Woodland Road, Byrd went left at the mini roundabout, pushing through the gears, hitting nearly fifty going up the hill, veering around a handful of vehicles. It wasn't long before he slowed and took a right into the cemetery, almost colliding with a car slowly pulling out, which forced Byrd to slam his brakes on, throwing them all forward. 'God…'

Fallows let out a quiet yelp as her belt dug into her shoulder and gripped the door handle to steady herself.

'Easy, boy!' Tanzy said, noticing Byrd's frustration.

The car moved out of the way of the entrance and Byrd went through.

'Jesus, this place is huge!' Fallows said, looking out the side window at the rows and rows of gravestones, then through the front windscreen at the length of the road. 'Does it go all the way back?'

'I'm not sure,' Byrd admitted. He hadn't been there in a while. His parents were buried at North Cemetery.

He slowed the car, pulled it over to the side so other vehicles could pass. He knew there was a car park further down but they had to cover all of it. 'We'll start here. See if there are any fresh burials.'

Tanzy jumped out. Fallows got out the back and closed the door.

They split up and started with the ones closest, taking a row each.

A man standing at the small building on the right, dressed in stained overalls, somewhere in his late sixties, stopped what he was doing. 'Excuse me?' he shouted over.

Byrd and Fallows were out of earshot, but Tanzy glanced his way.

'Who are you looking for? You shouldn't be parking there...'

Tanzy jogged over, pulled his badge from his pocket. 'Detective Inspector Orion Tanzy. Are you in charge? Do you know if there have been any burials in the last day or so?'

The man had whispery hair and a short, grey stubble, and eyed his ID with furrowed brows. 'There's been three today.'

'Okay.'

'Why?'

'We believe a police officer is in real trouble. We think he could be buried somewhere here.'

The man looked bewildered. 'We have names of all the people who have been—'

Tanzy shook his head quickly, silencing him. 'No. He's been buried alive.'

'Oh, God...' the man sighed, edging back. 'Here?'

'It's possible – are there any graves that have been dug, waiting for a burial in the coming days?'

The man looked around, thinking hard. There were multiple plots. 'There's a couple.' He turned, looking down the long narrow road as if searching for the plot in his head. 'If you go down the road. When you pass the crematorium, there are three spaces that have just been dug.'

Tanzy thanked him and started sprinting down the road, his feet slapping the dry concrete as he ran.

Byrd, who was carefully passing a row of graves, heard the noise and glanced up. 'Ori?'

'Where's he running to?' Fallows asked Byrd.

'I – I don't know.' Byrd had a quick look around at the graves near him. They all looked intact and settled as if they'd been there for years. 'Come on, let's follow him.'

Fallows met Byrd back on the narrow road and started slowly trailing after Tanzy. She wasn't exactly dressed for running in heels, jeans, and a white long-sleeved t-shirt, but Byrd went at her pace, watching Tanzy power on. It wasn't long before he disappeared from their view, taking a left after the crematorium.

'Where's he gone?' Fallows panted, a few metres behind Byrd, her voice wavering in an attempt to catch her breath.

'Keep up, Linda.'

'I'm trying…'

They passed the crematorium and Byrd glared to the left, seeing a cluster of trees and more gravestones. He couldn't see Tanzy yet.

After Tanzy passed the crem, he kept going, his eyes frantically darting around, trying to spot the open graves the man at the front mentioned. It wasn't long before he spotted them, about sixty metres down a walkway on the left.

But there weren't three. There were two.

Standing near them, was a bald man in his late thirties, around six foot tall. He had a stocky build, wearing a tight fitting black t-shirt, blue jeans, and white trainers, looking down at a grave. Only this grave he was looking at didn't have a headstone.

He heard Tanzy's footsteps and snapped his neck in his direction.

Tanzy kept going but had slowed a fraction, watching the man. He looked familiar. When the man had figured out who it might be, he turned and darted across the grass towards the wall.

'Hey!' Tanzy shouted at him.

There was no doubt in Tanzy's mind it was Mackenzie Dilton. He remembered his face from the house fire in Napier Street, remembered the way he moved, his body shape. By how he reacted and bolted off confirmed it.

Dilton had at least forty metres head start. Tanzy bolted after him.

Once Byrd and Fallows rounded the corner, they saw Tanzy sprint across the field, chasing someone.

'That's him!' Byrd shouted. 'That's Dilton.'

Fallows, struggling for breath, followed Byrd's finger, and noticed them on the field, heading for the wall at the back.

'Ori!' Byrd shouted, struggling for breath himself.

Tanzy heard his call and turned but kept running, pointing back at the walkway where he'd seen the buried grave.

Byrd shrugged, unsure what he meant.

Then his phone rang. It was Tanzy.

'Ori – what's happening? Who is it?'

'It's Dilton. I've got him. The guy at the front said there were three open graves. There are only two. Stockdale could be in there, Max. Check it out. I'll get this bastard.'

Byrd slowed near the two open graves, put his phone away, and noticed the third one that had been freshly filled, judging by the difference in colour to the ones near it. The others had settled to a lighter colour, no doubt dried by warmth and direct sunlight over time. This was a darker shade of soil as if just put down in the last day or so.

The area in front of them was roughly four feet wide, eight feet long. The ideal size of a hole that a coffin would fit into.

Byrd fell to his knees, panting hard, and starting digging at the soil, grabbing hand fulls and moving it out the way. He had no idea how deep it would go and didn't stop to think either.

Fallows, standing behind Byrd, bent over with her hands on her knees, breathing hard. She'd hadn't run like that in a long time. Over the field, Tanzy was only metres behind Dilton, approaching the far wall.

'I'll help Ori,' she told Byrd, who was throwing up the dirt like a man possessed, desperate to get to Stockdale, if he was under there.

Fallows struggled into a jog and headed across the field.

Tanzy was a few strides behind Dilton.

'Fucking stop now!' he barked.

Ignoring him, Dilton jumped up the wall, grabbing the top and heaving himself up. It was high, maybe six feet. Tanzy made it in time and grabbed his left foot, preventing him from pulling himself all the way over.

'Get here…'

Dilton kicked a leg out and caught Tanzy hard in the chin. As Tanzy stumbled, Dilton jumped the wall. Tanzy was dazed and disorientated. The kick to the face felt like a sledgehammer.

'Help me over,' he heard Fallows say behind him.

Tanzy leaned against the wall and interlocked his fingers for her to use as a step up. She got hold of the wall, used everything she had, and climbed it. Tanzy took a few steps back, took a quick run and climbed it with ease, dropping down the opposite side. There was a path that led down to an abandoned house.

They watched Dilton go inside.

'Come on, there he is,' Tanzy said, pointing through the bushes. 'Let's go.'

67

Monday Afternoon
West Cemetery, Carmel Road

Byrd was tired after only minutes of hard digging. His hair, face, and neck were drenched in sweat and his hands were burning. He sighed heavily, and pulled his jacket off, then continued to dig for a few more minutes, feeling the lactic acid burning in his shoulders from the continual movement. He was about a foot down, give or take, and had opened an area of roughly two feet. Then his fingers started bleeding.

He pulled his phone from his pocket and found DC Leonard's number, pressed CALL.

'Boss?' Leonard answered.

'Get to West Cemetery. I need help,' he panted.

'Okay... have you found Phil?'

'I hope so. I'm digging a grave up with my fucking hands. Think he's under it. Get here ASAP. Tanzy has gone after Dilton.'

'He's there?'

'Yeah. Get here now!' Byrd told him where the grave was and hung up, then found Weaver's number and told her the same. Then he rang PC Timms who he knew was with PC Grearer, relaying the same message. No doubt, they'd arrive at different times but Byrd needed all the help he could to dig this up. It could go down six feet and he had no idea where Tanzy or Fallows were.

After five more minutes, removing another few inches, he sat up, panting heavily. He couldn't go on like this. He'd have a heart attack soon. His fingers were bleeding badly now.

'Where the hell are they!' he shouted in pain.

'What on earth are you doing?' a voice said behind him.

Still panting, he turned to a man on the path. He didn't recognise him but it was the same man Tanzy was speaking with earlier, the elderly man with whispery hair near the front of the cemetery.

'Have you... got a... digger?' Byrd said in between breaths.

'You can't just start digging graves—'

Byrd threw his hands in the air in frustration, his whole body drenched in sweat. 'Sir! Have you got a digger?'

The man was taken aback and stared. 'We have one in the shed. Why?'

'Because I believe someone who isn't fucking dead is buried under here. Can you get the digger please?'

'I can't just—'

'I'm with the police. Please get the digger.' Byrd took a lung full of warm air. 'Please. I wouldn't ask if it wasn't a life or death situation.'

The man absorbed his concern and gave a brief nod, then turned, broke out into a jog away from him.

Turning back to the grave Byrd felt he was losing time. His hands were bleeding more, his cut skin breaking away.

'Come on!' he screamed to himself, fighting through the pain.

Footsteps approached him.

It was PC Timms and PC Grearer, dressed in their uniform.

'Jesus, boss,' Timms said, seeing how little he'd dug and the state of Byrd's hands.

'Fucking dig boys. Quick!' barked Byrd, stabbing a swollen bloody finger at the ground.

They wasted no time following his order and both dropped to their knees, one either side and started clawing away.

'Quicker,' he told them.

It wasn't long before DC Cornty and DC Leonard arrived. They settled in next to Timms and Grearer and started frantically scraping at the ground. After a few minutes, they were making progress. Byrd was relieved, but they still had a way to go. The coffin would be at least seven feet long and two to three feet wide. And God knows how deep it was. So far, they hadn't reached anything yet.

Nearby on the path, a couple in their fifties had stopped to watch them digging. They didn't say anything, just stared with their mouths open, wondering what they were up to. Behind them, they heard the sound of a mechanical vehicle coming towards them and moved out of the way when they saw what it was.

It wasn't as big as Byrd had assumed it would be. He'd visualised something you'd see on a construction site, capable of removing tons of earth for building large foundations.

'Move!' the man in the digger said, waving a frantic hand side to side.

They made enough space, stood back, most of them doubled over, struggling for air. Byrd was panting the heaviest, with his bloody palms pressed hard on his knees.

'You alright, boss?' Leonard asked him, placing a hand on his back.

The digger stopped in front of the half-dug grave. One of the arms moved and made a clonking mechanical sound. It was music to Byrd's ears. The huge claw tipped up, grabbed a chunk of earth, and pulled from the ground, making easy work of what they'd been doing.

After a few minutes of digging, the claw hit something hard, making a clunk.

'What's that?' Timms shouted.

Byrd, who had managed to get his breath back, took a few steps forward and leaned over the hole. He could see the lid of the coffin. 'There it is,' he bellowed. 'Keep going. Keep going,' he told the man inside the digger.

The man gave a concentrated nod from behind the plastic viewing panel and continued playing with the levers.

'Where are Orion and Linda?' Leonard asked Byrd, realising they weren't there.

68

Monday Afternoon
West Cemetery, Carmel Road

The house Mackenzie Dilton had gone into was narrow, small, and older than both Tanzy and Fallows. The brick-work made up of different sized stones had stood there a long time, weathering through decades of seasons and had looked better, but stood proud in respect to the build-ers who had once put it there.

The front door would have been in good nick if it did indeed have a front door, and not a gaping hole into a cold hallway made of a concrete floor leading to other open ar-eas.

It was a place Tanzy hadn't seen before, just off the path, beyond the hedges and overgrown grass, probably belonging to a janitor from way back.

When Tanzy and Fallows stepped onto the short path leading to the front door, he placed his arm out, indicating for her to drop back, allowing him in first. She slowed and did as he asked.

On his approach, he grabbed the truncheon he'd brought with him and looked through the open space with wide eyes, scanning for movement. The hard floor led to a room out the back from what he could see.

'Can you see him?' she whispered, fear creeping into her words. She was so close to finally getting Mackenzie Dilton, she could feel her heart pounding against her chest.

Tanzy shook his head, his heart racing too. His chin still throbbed from where Dilton had kicked it moments ear-lier, but he pushed the pain to the back of his mind. They needed to catch this sonofabitch, that was all that mattered. If what Dilton said to Byrd on the phone was true, and what he said at the end of the video of Stockdale in the coffin, he'd continue to murder people. He needed putting behind bars.

Tanzy carefully and quietly stepped through the worn, neglected threshold, the sides and top uneven with several visible sharp edges.

'Careful,' Tanzy whispered.

In the hall, the stairs went off to the left, and a corridor ran along the right-hand side, leading to a room at the back, with another door off to the right. The doorframes had decayed, leaving exposed rocky brickwork, and the walls were bare, mostly down to the brick.

Tanzy slowed and peeped into the first room, which looked like where the living room would be. It was bare, apart from bits of rubble scattered around the edges of the concrete floor. There was, however, a cluster of flattened cardboard in the corner with an old, brown stained sheet in one of the alcoves, telling Tanzy someone had probably slept here recently.

They backed out and checked the room at the end of the corridor. Exposed pipework was fixed under the window, made from lead, mangled, and crooked. To the left, was another open void, leading to outside.

'Check upstairs,' Fallows said behind him.

He nodded twice. 'Come on.'

Silently, they made their way upstairs. Tanzy was light on his feet, not only so Dilton wouldn't hear him, but to not disturb the old, battered wood on the stairs that looked like it could give way any second.

Fallows slowly trailed him a few feet behind. Just before Tanzy reached the top, she misjudged one of the steps, catching the front of her right foot on the fourth stair to the top, and stumbled forward into him.

'Linda…' he gasped. 'Careful,' he then whispered, placing a finger over his mouth.

She gritted her teeth in apology and nodded.

Tanzy stepped up onto the landing, or what was left of it, the gaps in the floor revealing aged joists and the hallway below. To his left, was a small room with an old rusty bath inside and a sink pedestal that had come away from the wall. The toilet over to the right was brown rather than white and smelt heavily of urine. In fact, the whole place did.

Backing away, he moved into the next bedroom, brightly lit by the light coming through a window to the left. Again, the room was empty, apart from a box the size of a shoebox in the alcove, made from hardened leather. He would have gone over to see what was inside if it wasn't for the noise they heard from the next bedroom.

A creaking floorboard.

They both froze, making eye contact with each other.

Tanzy got in front of her, and carefully made his way across the incomplete landing, switching focus between his footing and another ahead in case Dilton came flying out. When he reached the doorway, he took a left and stepped inside, the truncheon tightly gripped in his hand, fully extended.

In the corner, Mackenzie Dilton was stood, staring at him. He had nowhere to go. A window was to his left but didn't open.

'Dilton…' Tanzy whispered.

Dilton didn't say anything and appeared calm.

'You're coming with me,' said Tanzy, stepping into the room.

Dilton slowly shook his head. 'I have more work to do.' His voice was rough, raspy, full of determination.

Tanzy smiled widely. 'You've done enough.' He held the baton high up behind him and made his way over, watching Dilton carefully, anticipating what he might do. There was nowhere to go. He was cornered.

Fallows held off a little, not wanting to get too close to the monster who'd evaded her seven years ago but stared at him with wide eyes.

'I need you to put these on,' Tanzy said. He grabbed some cuffs from his pocket and threw them over to him. They landed near his feet, the sound pinging around the room.

'Go on, put them on.'

Dilton silently stared, defying his order.

'You either put them on or I'll make you—'

Tanzy felt the blow to his head a split second before he passed out and helplessly collapsed to the floor with a thud.

Dilton stared wide eyed at Fallows. 'Linda, what are you doing here?'

She dropped the brick she'd picked up near the door and smiled at him.

69

Monday Afternoon
West Cemetery, Carmel Road

As soon as the man in the digger had cleared enough earth around the coffin, he jumped out, grabbed two long straps he'd collected from the shed when he went to get the digger, and went to the open grave.

'Here, hold these,' he said to Byrd, who took them from him. The man then lowered himself into the hole, using his strong hands to steady himself onto the surface of the coffin with a thud. He'd dug enough earth bedside the coffin, so stepped down, the lid of the coffin now at knee height, and pulled the lid open quickly.

Byrd, Leonard, Cornty, Weaver, Timms, and Grearer watched him with wide eyes in anticipation from the ground above.

Inside, was DS Stockdale. He lay silently and still.

'Is he alive?' Byrd asked.

The gravedigger lowered his hand into the coffin and placed two fingers on the side of his throat to find a pulse. He looked back up and nodded twice.

'Right, let's get him out.' Byrd turned to Weaver. 'Amy, ring an ambulance, please.'

With tears in her eyes, she nodded and pulled out her phone.

The man in the grave lowered himself and, with his hands, dug some of the earth from underneath the coffin, just enough room for him to get the straps through. He struggled but managed to get one under, then moved down near Stockdale's feet and did the same. Once he'd got the straps under, he apologised to Stockdale, who looked to be moving a little more, and closed the coffin lid, then grabbed the other sides of the strap. One at a time, he threw them up.

'Help me up,' the man said, holding his hands up in the air.

Byrd grabbed one of his hands, Cornty grabbed the other and together, they heaved him up, almost pulling his old arms from the sockets.

'Great work,' Byrd encouraged him when he was out of the hole. He then took hold of one side of the strap that went around the top end of the coffin. Leonard went to the other side, grabbing the opposite end of it. Timms and Cornty grabbed the other strap, standing opposite each other, the six-foot hole in between them.

'On three,' said Byrd. 'One. Two. Three.'

They all started to pull up slowly. They knew it would be heavy but didn't expect to weigh the same as an elephant.

'Jesus,' Leonard said, struggling with the weight of it, his palms already burning. When the undertakers carefully lowered coffins into the hole, apart from doing it properly, with years of experience and training, they wore gloves.

A minute later, they had managed to lift the coffin above the hole and followed the gravedigger's instruction to pull the coffin away from the hole and lower it to the grass. Byrd opened the lid. 'Phil?'

He leaned in, placed a hand on his cold face. 'Phil?' He gently tapped his face. Stockdale's eyes flicked open for a second, but he didn't move.

'Amy, where's that ambulance?' shouted Byrd in her general direction.

'On its way, sir.'

Byrd nodded and looked back at Stockdale.

'Should we move him, boss? Get him out in the open?'

Byrd shook his head at Cornty. The idea was good, but he didn't want to risk moving him, not knowing if he was injured or not. 'Phil, are you hurt?'

Stockdale didn't respond.

Leonard told Byrd he would go find Tanzy and Fallows, see if they needed help. Byrd agreed and asked Cornty to go with him. They ran across the field towards the wall that Byrd said they'd climbed and jumped over it, landing on a man-made path on the other side.

'Where did they go?' Cornty asked, looking around. The path went under a cluster of trees in one direction, and in the other, bordered the stone wall until it went out of sight. In front of them, was woodland and clusters of bushes.

'In there?' Leonard said, pointing at the house Cornty had noticed through the hedging.

Cornty nodded and went first, stepping over the uneven ground and through the array of hedges until he reached the abandoned path leading to the house.

'Surely, they're not in there?' Cornty said, frowning.

'Worth a check,' Leonard replied.

As they stepped through the open doorway, they heard something upstairs. Floorboards creaking. They froze, looked at each other for a moment, then Leonard went first, making his way carefully up the stairs, mindful of the broken wood underfoot.

'Hello? Police here,' shouted Leonard, grabbing his truncheon from his trousers. Cornty grabbed his own, gripping it tightly in his right hand, a few steps behind Leonard. He reached the top and turned. 'Hello – is there anyone here?'

As he stepped onto the patchy landing, a shadow shifted ahead of him, causing him to look up. From the front bedroom, someone stepped out.

'Jesus, boss,' Leonard said.

Tanzy was unsteady on his feet, his right hand pressed firmly on the side of his head, covering the blood on his face.

'What the fuck happened, boss?' Leonard said, leaning in to have a closer look.

'Dilton. He was here,' Tanzy managed to say, wincing in pain.

'Where's Linda Fallows?'

Tanzy painfully shook his head. 'I don't know.'

70

Monday Afternoon
West Cemetery, Carmel Road

'You okay, boss?' Cornty asked Tanzy, helping him away from the house. Leonard was on his other side. They reached the wall.

'Think you can climb it?' Leonard asked Tanzy, staring at the cut on his head.

Tanzy nodded. 'I'll be fine.' With the aid of Leonard and Cornty, Tanzy managed to climb over the high wall and drop down on the other side. His head was thumping in agony. Leonard and Cornty climbed over a few seconds after.

'What was Dilton wearing, boss?' Leonard asked, finding his feet.

Tanzy slowly stood up, the blow to his head affecting his balance and ability to move one hundred percent. 'Black t-shirt and blue jeans,' he said, wincing at the pounding inside his head.

Leonard pulled his radio from his belt clip and spoke into it. 'We have a suspect in the nearby area of West Cemetery off Carmel Road, who we believe to be Mackenzie Dilton. He's just attacked one of our officers and is wearing a black t-shirt and blue jeans. Keep your eyes peeled.'

'How's the head, boss?' Cornty asked him.

Tanzy gave a slow shake of the head. 'Not good.'

'Can you remember where Linda went? Has he got her?'

Tanzy clamped his eyes shut as he struggled across the grass. 'She – she was behind me, and then I felt something hard hit me, then I was out…' Tanzy thought hard. 'There may have been someone else there.'

'Did you hear anyone else in the house?' Cornty asked.

'No.'

Leonard frowned, thinking of the possibility. If the only person who was there was Linda Fallows, could it have been her? What reason would she have to attack Tanzy? She'd travelled up from Essex to help them with the investigation, allowing them to see reports from a similar thing that Dilton could have been responsible for seven years ago.

It didn't make any sense.

Byrd heard what Leonard had said on the radio and told Weaver to wait at the car park they'd passed on their way in. It was about halfway up on the right hand side. 'If he travelled here in a car, he might go back to it. Black t-shirt and blue jeans. Go keep an eye out.' He grabbed PC Timms' attention who was standing with PC Grearer. 'Eric, go with her, please.'

Timms nodded and together with Weaver, went back to the path, and jogged along the narrow road to the car park.

Byrd looked away from Stockdale for a moment. 'Where's the ambulance at?' he asked no one in particular, then spotted Tanzy walking over with Leonard and Cornty. 'Ori…'

Everyone else looked over, noticed the blood on Tanzy's head and down his neck and arm.

'Jesus, Ori. What happened?' asked Byrd, frowning at the damage.

'I don't know,' replied Tanzy, lowering his hand for a moment. Byrd leaned in to have a look.

'Nasty.'

'I had him cornered, Max. He was right there. Then something hit me from behind.'

Byrd considered his words. 'Where was Linda?'

Tanzy smiled sadly. 'Behind me…'

A frown found Byrd's face. 'You don't think?'

Tanzy shrugged. 'Why would she?'

On the road behind them the sound of an ambulance siren was heard, gradually getting louder until it stopped on the grass to their right. Two paramedics jumped out, dressed in green, and ran to the back and opened the rear door. The driver picked up a walkie talkie from the dash and said something in to it. One pulled out a stretcher and the other grabbed a hip bag, looping it over his shoulder.

Byrd waved them over, pointing to the coffin. They nodded, dropped down on their knees beside it, and looked inside to assess the situation. The one with the stretcher placed it down on the floor beside the coffin and the other grabbed a few things from the bag and placed them down on the floor. They evaluated the position and wellbeing of Stockdale after checking his pulse and getting a rough story of why he was there.

On the count of three, with the help of Byrd and Leonard, they lifted Stockdale up and lowered him down on the stretcher. One of them grabbed a bag valve mask from the kit and place it over Stockdale's mouth with the expandable string around the back of his head, then started squeezing the bag to force some fresh air into Stockdale's lungs; something he was in desperate need of.

The third paramedic, the driver, who was talking on the walkie talkie, ran over, noticing Tanzy had been injured also. 'Let me have a look at you,' he said to Tanzy.

Tanzy lowered his hand to let him inspect the cut.

'What hit you – a brick or something?'

'Something like that,' Tanzy said quietly.

The blood was still flowing from the wound. 'Right, you need to come with us, too.' The paramedic turned to Byrd, assuming he was the man in charge. 'He's coming with us – we need to get this sorted. It's bad.'

Byrd nodded. 'Okay.' He looked at Tanzy. 'You want one of us to come along?'

Tanzy shook his head. 'No chance. Go and find the son-ofabitch.'

71

Monday Afternoon
West Cemetery, Carmel Road

Weaver and Timms reached the car park halfway down on the right. It wasn't big, totalling roughly thirty spaces, half occupied.

A bald man with a black t-shirt and blue jeans.

That's who they were looking for.

Up on the left, was a couple in their eighties, slowly plodding along with walking sticks. The man was dressed for the sun in a short-sleeved shirt tucked into grey trousers that appeared both too big and long for his legs. The lady walking beside him was slight, dressed in a blue two-piece and black tights over bony knees. It made Weaver feel hot just looking at her.

'Excuse me,' Weaver said, slightly out of breath. 'Have you seen a bald man in a black t-shirt and blue jeans?'

The elderly couple looked at her strangely, then gradually shook their heads. They probably didn't know what day it was.

'Okay, thanks,' Weaver said, moving on, scanning the area.

'A bald man in a black t-shirt you say?' a voice said from behind.

Weaver turned, as did Timms, and saw a man standing on the grass verge near a row of freshly laid flowers, with a watering can in his right hand, wearing a pair of thin, white overalls. Looked to be a caretaker.

'Yeah. Have you seen him?'

The man nodded twice. 'Sure. He was here a minute ago. Got into a blue Ford Focus.'

'You sure?' Timms asked, sceptical.

'Yes. He was running from down there.' The man pointed down the narrow road, back to where they'd just come from.

'Was he alone?' Weaver this time.

'Yeah. As far as I could see.'

'This blue Focus,' Timms said quickly, taking a few steps toward him. 'You didn't happen to see—'

'It was a twelve reg. Looked in good nick, apart from a scratch on the back passenger quarter.'

'You remembered that well?'

'As I said, he was running. It stands out in a place like this. It was parked just over there.'

They followed his finger to the empty space, then thanked him. Weaver pulled the radio from her hip. 'We have a possible vehicle for Mackenzie Dilton in the area of Carmel Road. Twelve reg. According to a witness, there's a large scratch in the back quarter, passenger side.'

She put her radio back and had a quick scan around. They left the man, made their way back to where they found Stockdale. The ambulance was parked up on the left with the rear doors open. Inside, DS Stockdale lay on a trolley with something over his mouth and a few wires coming from him. There was a jump bag fixed to a metal pole by his side, feeding him something but nor Weaver or Timms knew exactly what. To the right side of the van, Tanzy sat upright with a bag of something cold wrapped in a cloth on his head to keep the swelling down.

They took a left and returned to the grave where they found Byrd, Leonard, Cornty, and Grearer. They were talking about something but stopped when Weaver and Timms approached.

'Find the blue Focus?' Byrd asked.

'No.' Weaver frowned wondering how he knew but re-membered saying it through the radio, which was fed to anyone that was tuned in to the same channel.

Mackenzie Dilton took a left when he came out of the cemetery and powered through the gears along Carmel Road. When he reached Hummersknott Avenue, he veered left, following the winding road a few minutes until he reached Baydale Road, turned left, and stopped roughly fifty metres up at the side of the road.

It was warm inside the car. He cracked the window allowing mild air to seep in. Opposite, there were children playing in one of the front gardens, throwing a tennis ball between them. A boy and girl, a few years apart, likely brother and sister. He smiled towards them, thinking about what life would be like with a brother or a sister. He hadn't had the most privileged upbringings, missing out on what some would consider normal and because of that, it had maybe shaped him into what he was.

Lost in a state of thinking, he snapped back to the present when the passenger door opened. He glared to the left, watching her climb in quickly, and closed the door. She was panting for air.

'We need to ditch the car,' he told her.

'Why?'

He nodded at the radio. 'One of them said about a blue Ford Focus, twelve reg, with a scratch on the back.'

Linda Fallows sighed. 'We can just get another one. Right, come on, Mack. Let's get going. We have more work to do.'

72

Monday Afternoon
Police station

Byrd turned the engine off and pulled his key out, sitting for a moment in deep thought. Picking up his phone, he found Linda Fallows number and called it. As he guessed, it went straight to answerphone.

'God's sake...' he whispered. His head was battered. He didn't know what to think. Why would she travel all this way from Essex to help them with this investigation and do something stupid? She wouldn't, would she?

But where was she?

Had Dilton taken her? Killed her too?

Byrd had no clue, but he needed to know. Needed to find her. He pushed open the door and stepped down onto the tarmac. The day was hot, warmer than before. Sweating profusely, he took off his thin jacket and carried it in his dirty, bloody hand he'd need to clean when he got inside. Maybe get one of the first aiders to look at them.

Walking over to the entrance door, he remembered what Dilton had said on the video he'd posted online. *They deserved it.* That *he* deserved it.

What had Stockdale done?

He opened the door of reception, stepped inside, and smiled at Lisa behind the desk before heading for the door on the other side. It wasn't long before he was at his desk. Weaver, Cornty, and Leonard had made it back before him and were at their own desks. Weaver was telling another PC what had happened.

At his desk, he hung his jacket on the rear of his chair and sat down. His first job was to ring PC Josh Andrews to ask for an update on Tanzy and Stockdale, who he'd asked to accompany them at the hospital and keep him up to date. He knew Tanzy's blow was bad but not life-threatening. Regarding Stockdale, he knew he'd been without oxygen for a while, so it could take some time before he's one hundred percent. Following his recovery, questions would need to be asked on how he was there in the first place.

Andrews answered the phone on the second ring. They spoke for a few minutes, then Byrd thanked him and hung up, placing his phone down on the desk.

The door opened behind him. 'Max...'

Byrd turned to see a furious looking Fuller.

'In here.'

Byrd nodded, stood up, and went into his office. He closed the door, padded over to the desk, and sat down on one of the chairs. Byrd spent the next ten minutes going over the events of the day.

'Where is Fallows now?'

Byrd shrugged. 'I don't know, yet. I'm going to the Premier Inn she's been staying at.'

A nod from Fuller. 'What about Dilton?'

Byrd shook his head slowly.

'Max, we need to get a lid on this.'

Before Fuller carried on, Byrd said, 'On my way back, I contacted Jennifer Lucas at the Town Hall, explaining about the blue Ford Focus we were told Dilton got into. She's searching the local camera system and will get back to me when she knows something.'

Fuller didn't seem pleased, but it was a step in the right direction. They spoke a little more. Byrd explained how Tanzy was and the condition of Stockdale.

'The question is,' Fuller said, 'is why he was chosen. There must be a reason. I watched the video Dilton put online. I heard what he said at the end. That Stockdale deserved it.'

'I heard that, too,' countered Byrd. 'Andrews is there with them both. They are on the same ward, so is keeping touch with the nurses regarding both.'

Fuller thanked him and asked Byrd to let him know when he finds Fallows or hears anything back about the blue Ford Focus.

'Will do,' Byrd said, standing.

At his desk he sat down and leaned back, sighing heavily. It had been one hell of a day and it wasn't over. Before he decided to go to the Premier Inn to find Fallows, he decided to make a call. He needed to know who he was dealing with.

He spent a few minutes on the computer doing research, finding the number he needed and punched it into his phone. After he pressed CALL he put it to his ear and waited.

'Hello, this is Essex Police help desk. Clio speaking, how can I help?'

'Hi, Clio. My name is Max Byrd. I'm a Detective Inspector with Durham Constabulary in Darlington. I'm wondering if I can speak to one of your detective chiefs or maybe a superintendent? It's very important.'

Clio didn't reply for a moment, then said, 'Hold on one moment, please, Detective Inspector Byrd.'

There was a few moments of silence. Byrd looked around the office until he heard the voice.

'Hello,' said Clio. 'I'll have him call your switchboard at Darlington. Just to make sure you are who you say you are.'

'That's fair enough,' replied Byrd, a little frustrated time was being wasted. The call ended. Less than a minute later, his mobile rang, the call forward from the switchboard. He answered it.

'Hello, this is Detective Superintendent John Malice. Is this Detective Inspector Max Byrd?'

'Hi, John. Yes, I'm DI Byrd. I need some information, please.'

'Okay. What's the information regarding?'

'Linda Fallows. I believe she worked as a DI for so many years then went on to criminal psychology.'

A sigh from Malice.

'John?'

'Why do you need information on Linda Fallows?'

'We're looking for her,' Byrd explained. 'She came up last week to help us with a case we are working on. Something's happened. She's disappeared.'

'What happened, DI Byrd?'

Byrd explained the case they were working on and about Fallows.

'Jesus,' he replied. 'And you just let her walk in there, DI Byrd? Giving her full access to your files and resources.'

Byrd stayed silent. When it was put like that, it sounded ridiculous.

'Why didn't you phone us?' Malice said. 'You would have known about her.'

'I – I don't understand, sir? She told us she was involved in the case that happened seven years ago and she had retired. She wanted to help.'

John Malice sighed again. Byrd didn't like the sound of it.

'Max, Linda Fallows didn't retire. Her employment was terminated.'

'What for?'

'Let me explain.'

73

Monday Late Afternoon
Police station

'I have to admit I quite liked Linda,' Superintendent Malice said, 'but there was always... something different about her. And to say I'd never seen a change in her would be a lie.'

'How do you mean?' asked Byrd.

'She worked her way up to Detective Inspector respectfully. She did a great job in her previous roles. But I always had the feeling she wanted more.'

'A promotion – the next level?'

'Hmm, maybe not,' Malice said. 'I think that's why she went into criminal psychology. She had done that the past six years. And she was good at it. She loved getting into the minds of killers and criminals to understand what made them tick. Why they did what they did. But she wasn't as – I don't know how to say this – as hard as she should have been.'

Byrd wasn't following.

'She always looked for a deeper meaning why something was the way it was. Why a person would kill.' Malice paused a beat. 'So, as well as understanding why a criminal did what they did, she started to sympathise with them, began to understand their mind and found a soft spot in her heart for them and their actions. I could never prove it, but I felt like she was working against us.'

'How so?' Byrd was intrigued.

'She held things back. Information. Leads. She —'

'You mean on the four murders that happened seven years ago?'

'Yes. Particularly that one. She was a DI on that case. As a team, we'd come up with a few leads, but every lead she followed went cold. Every sniff we had at catching the sonofabitch was gone. Judging by what you've told me, it sounds like the same guy but as you know, we never caught him. I blame Linda for that. But not only that, when she took the role as a psychologist, she advised us – and the criminals – on what to do. On more than one occasion, someone had heard her telling a murderer that they acted not on impulse but because of a deeper reason, a reason which, when explained sympathetically, would sway a court case against us. This happened too many times. We warned her, but she carried on. We'd had enough. We had to let her go. She was getting in our way.'

'To summarise her, John, what would you say?'

'I'd say Linda Fallows is a very intelligent woman who always gets what she wants. I'd say don't be deceived by her but that's something we both know has already happened.'

'Okay… thanks.' Byrd felt so stupid he'd allowed her to come to Darlington in search for Mackenzie Dilton, now knowing she probably fed back the information and aided him in many ways. 'Any idea where'd she'd go?'

'Not a clue. If I was a betting man, I'd say she's helping your man, Dilton.'

Byrd sighed, tipped his head back.

'Be careful of her. She's very unpredictable, DI Byrd.'

74

Monday Late Afternoon
Police station

DC Leonard and DC Cornty had not only spent time doing their reports, they'd also got in touch with the train station and local airports to see if Fallows had booked anything. They'd also reached out to banks, asking if there was a Linda Fallows who had an account with them.

Barclays came back with a yes, confirming a Linda Fallows had an account with them who was based in Essex, however, there'd been nothing booked in the past few days regarding tickets or flights. After looking at her statements, which the bank was reluctant to hand over, they'd noticed regular household payments to utility companies and one for her phone. On several occasions, there had been money withdrawals in the last month. It was also obvious to see she was very wealthy, her bank account over the two hundred thousand pound mark.

'Someone's doing okay,' Cornty humoured when telling Byrd.

'Good work,' said Byrd. 'Keep going.'

It was getting late. The office was quieter than before, a few people had gone home. Byrd hung around and handed over the day's events to nightshift who were made up of several PCs and a DC who'd recently been promoted. Their task was to continue looking into Linda Fallows and Mackenzie Dilton in addition to whatever else the good town of Darlington had to offer.

On his way home, Byrd stopped off at the hospital to see Tanzy, who lay in a bed situated in the corner of the room, halfway down the corridor on the left, on the fifth floor. Byrd opened the door, spotted him straight away, and went over, absorbing the amazing view of Darlington through the wide window at the back of the room. Thinking about it, it was the first time he'd seen the town from up here. Under the setting sun and clear cloudless sky, it was beautiful.

'How are you holding up?' Byrd said to him.

Tanzy, who had a bandage wrapped around his head, smiled. 'Top of the world, Max. Thanks for asking.' They shared a smile. 'Did you find Dilton?'

Byrd smiled sadly and shook his head.

'What about Linda?'

Byrd said he hadn't, then gazed out of the window for a moment.

'Some view, isn't it?' Tanzy said, looking out, too.

'I spoke with someone at Essex Police,' Byrd said, then told him what John Malice had said about her.

Tanzy banged his fist off his bed, causing the man in the next bed, a thirty-something dark-haired man with his arm in a sling, to glance over. 'What about the hotel she's staying at?'

'Went there before. There's no one by her name staying there.'

Tanzy gritted his teeth. 'Why didn't we see it, Max?'

Byrd shrugged. 'She convinced everyone, Ori. Not just us.'

Tanzy looked away for a moment, disappointed with himself. It wasn't his fault. It wasn't anyone's fault. She'd manipulated them all.

'I spoke with Jennifer. Gave her info on a blue Ford Focus we believe Dilton got into. A guy standing near the car park at the cemetery said he saw someone matching Dilton's description get in and drive away quickly.'

'If there's anything to find, Max, she's the person that'll do it.'

Byrd agreed and asked him how his family was.

'Pip is good. I've just been on the phone with her. She said she'd try to get here later if her mum watches the kids for a bit.'

'When you allowed out?'

'Nurse said tomorrow.' Tanzy sighed, rolling his eyes. 'They need to keep me in because it's a head injury.'

'Just a scratch, Ori. Don't know why you're fussing over it.'

Tanzy reached over and playfully punched Byrd in the arm.

'You seen Phil yet? Andrews said he was down the hall.'

Byrd said, 'Not yet, Ori. I'm going to see him after I've left you. I need to find out why Dilton chose him. I need to find out what he's done. If he doesn't cooperate, then we'll have to bring him in.'

Tanzy winced, hated the thought of one of their own doing something they shouldn't have. 'Keep me updated. He's one of mine, Max. I need to make sure he's okay.' He paused a few moments. 'I just hope whatever it is, there's been a mistake. I really do.'

'Me and you both.' Byrd leaned over, tapped his hand on Tanzy's. 'Rest up. I'll pick you up tomorrow. You need anything bringing?'

'Pip will bring a few bits soon. Don't worry about me. Go see Phil.'

Byrd nodded and departed the room, taking a left down the brightly lit hallway. On his right, there was a reception desk with two nurses sitting behind it, both blonde, around the age of fifty, looking at separate computer screens. One of them looked up at Byrd and smiled, the other too absorbed to notice him. It wasn't long before Byrd reached the room and knocked twice.

When he heard a reply, he grabbed the handle, and opened the door.

It was a single room, the air warm and stuffy. The window at the end was closed but the blinds were open, the sun setting over Darlington casting an orange glow across building tops. Stockdale lay on a single bed to the right. Andrews was seated on the left in a single, low-level chair, facing Stockdale. From the hanging silence between them and serious faces, Byrd got the impression they'd been talking about something important. Beside the bed, was a table with a jug of water and several plastic cups.

'Hey,' said Byrd as he entered.

'Hi, boss,' Andrews said, turning his head to the door.

Byrd closed it, and stepped forward, focusing on Stockdale, who was awake, staring at the ceiling.

'How you doing, Phil?' asked Byrd.

'I'll survive, sir. You know me.' He sounded dull and flat as if he had no energy. 'They're keeping me in to see how my breathing is. Make sure my lungs are working properly.'

Byrd nodded, grabbed the spare chair next to Andrews, and dropped into it.

'How long you been here?' Byrd asked Andrews.

He glanced down at his watch. 'Ever since he was brought in. I'm starving.'

Byrd noticed the time. It was just after seven. 'Go and get something to eat. It's fine, I'm here. I think the café is still open.'

Andrews didn't need to be asked twice and left the room.

'How are you holding up, Phil?' Byrd said, this time more serious.

Stockdale looked his way with glassy eyes. 'I'm… okay.'

'What happened, Phil?'

Stockdale told him what happened the night before, how he went out for a walk and Dilton pulled over in the car at the roundabout on Woodland Road, asking for directions. He said he recognised him and called Tanzy but he didn't answer. Then he saw Dilton walk into the park and followed him. The next thing he knew he woke up inside the coffin. 'It was terrifying, sir.'

Byrd nodded in understanding, then asked a very important question. 'Why did he pick you?'

Stockdale looked away, not wanting to look at his superior. The silence that filled the small room was deafening.

'If there's something you need to tell me, Phil, you need to do it now.'

Stockdale swallowed hard, then over the following five minutes, told Byrd exactly what he'd done.

Byrd was speechless and glared at him with wide eyes. 'Jesus, Phil.'

75

Tuesday Morning
Police station

When Byrd had left the hospital last night after seeing DS Stockdale, he rang DCI Fuller immediately, telling him there was something important he needed to know.

'What is it with this department?' Fuller had said.

The question, Byrd knew, was rhetorical, so allowed Fuller to vent his frustration. Fuller then said he needed to figure out a way to keep this under wraps for a while, although that would be an impossible task.

Byrd pulled up in his X5, parked in his usual bay. The sun, already on the rise somewhere behind him, cast shadows of nearby cars on the tarmac below. He opened the door, stepped down onto the ground, feeling waves of sickness in his stomach, although missing out on breakfast hadn't helped. He'd left Claire on the sofa in the living room, with a few snacks and drinks. She told him her friend was coming over again, which was something Byrd didn't mind. It was as much Claire's house now as it was his.

He walked through the sliding double doors into reception and smiled at Lisa.

'Good morning, Max,' she said, with a smile.

The office was a third full. DC Leonard was at his desk, typing away quickly.

'Morning, Jim.'

Leonard turned to him. 'Morning, sir.'

'You hear about Phil?' Byrd asked quietly, knowing there'd be a chance he had but didn't want to catch the attention of others nearby.

He replied with a slow nod.

'Who else knows?'

Leonard looked to his right. Cornty hadn't arrived yet.

'Phil knows. Amy knows. A few others do. We were messaging about it last night.'

Byrd remembered he'd asked PC Josh Andrews to keep it quiet and was upset he hadn't done that. But it was an issue that would need addressing sooner rather than later so he'd have to accept it and move on.

'How's he doing?' Leonard asked.

'He's upset…'

'I can imagine.'

'I'm calling a meeting soon. I'll run through it all with everyone. It isn't pleasant but it's something we all need to know.'

Leonard nodded, and Byrd walked down the aisle towards his desk. Before he reached it, Fuller opened his door as if he knew he was approaching and asked Byrd to come inside. Before he did, he took off his jacket and hung it on the back of his chair.

Fuller's office was warm, the open window to the left not making a difference to the humidity. On Fuller's desk was an empty mug and a scrunched up cereal bar wrapper, among a pile of paperwork and a couple of photos he'd been looking at.

'How's Phil?'

Byrd gave him a sad smile. 'As soon as the doctors give him the all clear, we're bringing him in. Does Barry Eckles know about this yet?'

Fuller winced at the thought. 'Not yet, Max.'

'I'm holding a meeting at nine. I need to tell everyone what he told me.'

Fuller looked sceptical.

'They deserve to know,' insisted Byrd.

Fuller understood his point. There were, because of how Fuller had run the department, certain aspects he allowed Byrd and Tanzy to take charge of. Fundamentally, the big decisions were down to Fuller, but telling the team about this was down to Byrd and Tanzy. As Tanzy was still at the hospital, it would be Byrd's decision.

'How's Orion?'

'He was okay last night. He should have been able to go home but the doctors insisted he stayed in for further monitoring. He's just texted saying they're happy for him to come out. His missus is picking him up soon. He'll be here for the briefing.'

Fuller nodded his approval. 'I guess I'll need to let Barry know. It won't be long till it makes the rounds.'

Byrd, after the silence filled the office, knew it was his cue to leave. He stood up, put the chair in slowly, and made his way back to his desk. After turning his computer on, he sighed heavily, his frustration multiplied in the emptiness of the office.

No Tanzy.

No Linda Fallows.

The more he thought of her, the more anger built up inside him. For the next thirty minutes, he compiled a report and PowerPoint presentation for the upcoming meeting, and sent everyone email alerts, letting them know where to be at nine.

He saved the presentation on a memory stick, pulled it out from the computer, and stood up, then made his way across the office towards the meeting room.

'This should be fun,' he whispered, walking down the hall, approaching the closed door on the right.

76

Tuesday Morning
Police station

In the meeting room, there was a dark silence hanging in the air. Byrd closed the door, and as he walked over to the whiteboard in the centre of the nearest wall, he knew most of his colleagues had not only heard about Phil Stockdale being buried in a coffin, but that he'd told Byrd what he'd done, and more importantly, why.

'Morning,' he said loudly, building himself up for what was coming.

Everyone was there. On the email he'd sent out less than thirty minutes earlier, Byrd had stated everyone needed to be here, including the forensics team, who were seated to the left next to DCI Fuller.

Fuller looked sick, Byrd thought, a white complexion mixed with a look of dread and anticipation on how his team would react to the news. What Stockdale had done had been horrific.

Over to the right, DI Tanzy was sat on the end with a bandage around his head. Byrd turned to him specifically.

'How you doing, Ori?'

'All good, Max,' he said, with a positive nod and both thumbs up. He'd just arrived minutes earlier and had come straight through. Pip had picked him up from the hospital and dropped him off before taking the kids to school.

Byrd nodded and looked forward, falling into a moment of silence. He then padded over to his left, opened the laptop, and placed his USB stick in the side of it. It wasn't long before the screen at the front lit up.

It told them today's date and time. In addition to that, it said *Urgent Meeting* underneath it. The words grabbed the attention of everyone. Byrd grabbed the small black remote, took a few steps away from the laptop, and stood beside the screen.

Everyone waited.

'Firstly,' he started, his voice clear and loud, 'I want to thank everyone for coming in on such short notice. This meeting is not only going to be about what happened yesterday involving DS Phillip Stockdale, but what role he played over the past couple of weeks.'

His words were met by a few understanding nods but equal stares of confusion. He glanced over to Fuller, who frowned but nodded, agreeing full transparency within his team was for the best.

'Yesterday, Mackenzie Dilton's fourth video was uploaded online. I'm aware the majority of you will have seen it.' He turned to the screen, pressing the button, showing a close-up of Stockdale's scared face. 'This video was inside a coffin. As you can see, it's Phil. At the end of the video, we heard Dilton say the air supply had run out and he didn't have long left. We went from the time the video was uploaded and searched for local cemeteries. Luckily, our team acted quickly. By that, I mean all of you. Before I continue, I want to thank you all for your efforts yesterday. Our quick, decisive actions saved his life.'

He took a breath, pressed the button again. On the screen was an image of the grave he was buried in.

'When we arrived, we saw Mackenzie Dilton standing at a grave then he fled. With the help of the gravedigger, we dug up the earth and lifted the coffin above ground. We saved his life.'

He pointed around the room. 'Because of *this* team.'

Fuller nodded at him, appreciating his leadership.

'DI Tanzy and Linda Fallows then went in pursuit of Dilton, climbing the wall and giving chase. It wasn't long before James and Phillip went to help, but they came back with only Tanzy, who'd been attacked over the head.

A few stared at the bandage wrapped around Tanzy's head for a moment.

'Where did Linda go?' Jacob Tallow, the senior forensic officer, asked.

'At the moment, we don't know,' admitted Byrd. 'I've tried calling her. She's not answering.'

'What about the hotel she was staying at?' DC Cornty said.

'I went there last night. There isn't a Linda Fallows staying there.'

Cornty sighed, looking down. 'What about her phone – can we not track it?'

'Already tried. Mac can't locate it for some reason.'

'Where was Linda when you were attacked, Ori?' The question came from Emily Hope, the other senior forensic officer.

'She was behind me.'

Wide eyes circled the room, putting two and two together.

'We can't make assumptions,' Byrd said. 'But... based on what we know and the fact she's disappeared, it's hard not to think there's something off about this. In addition, I spoke with a Detective Superintendent from Essex Police, the same team she worked for, and was made aware that Linda didn't retire. She was too mentally unstable to work anymore. There had been theories about her helping criminals and advising them in policing matters to give them a better chance in court. Because of her, some had been freed to walk the streets.'

Several disgusted faces stared back at Byrd, which made him feel stupid for letting her in to help them with the investigation.

'Do you think she helped Dilton?' Cornty asked, adjusting himself on the seat.

'It's looking a very likely possibility.' Byrd looked down at the floor for a moment, collecting his thoughts, not allowing them to defeat the positive attitude he was desperate to keep a hold of.

'When Phil – and Orion – had been taken to hospital, Amy and Eric had gone looking for Dilton. We were told, judging by his clothing, that he'd got into a blue Ford Focus and left in a hurry. I reached out to Jennifer Lucas at the Town Hall with some info, hoping she'll track the car down.'

'What did she say?' Tanzy asked.

'Still waiting to hear back. She said she had to leave the office for a family emergency. Her mum had an accident. She's back in this morning, searching for it, so I'm hoping it's soon.'

'What happened to Phil?' PC Grearer asked.

'After Phil was taken to hospital, I went to see him. As we know, from the previous three victims, Mackenzie Dilton, or as he called himself, Roger Carlton, had left notes on their laptops asking us to look at them. According to Mac in DFU, there's a website called attheend.com. Mac said it's unusual because the website shows a home screen that is pretty much blank, with a box asking for a username and password, but the site contains massive memory. Something, which he explained, is beyond the login page. We wouldn't know what this is if Tanzy hadn't managed to get on, using the laptop from Danny Walters attic which had his username and password saved.' He looked over to Tanzy and nodded.

'Yeah, once we pressed enter, it took us to a screen showing a camera looking at a woman in a room. The floor was made of concrete and the walls were bare. Next to the camera shot was a list of a few players. RCarl20 was there. Who we know to be Mackenzie Dilton. Below that, there was a tab saying, watchers. Next to watchers was a number. Over a thousand. It then logged me out and I couldn't get back in.'

'What was it?' DC Cornty asked, frowning.

Tanzy shrugged. 'I don't really know. Some kind of a game. Whatever it is, I didn't have long enough on there.' Tanzy then looked back at Byrd, knowing he'd tell them what Stockdale had said.

'When I spoke with Phil, he told me he'd logged on to the website, and that he was a player.'

Several gasps were heard around the room.

'What did the player do?' Leonard asked, concerned.

'Phil said that players paid a lot of money to play the game. The game was hosted by unknown hosts. Only five players were allowed at any one time. The watchers, Phil explained, were online users wanting to play but had to wait for their turn. They paid a lesser amount to watch the game until the series of games finished and they'd get a chance to become a player.'

Weaver raised a hand to her mouth. 'Jesus. That's awful.'

'What happened in the games?' Cornty said.

'They decided how the person died.'

Byrd's words sent shivers among them. They all looked at one another, not believing Stockdale would be a part of this.

'Please, Max, go on...' Fuller encouraged him, wanting them to know the full story.

Byrd nodded. 'Each victim was placed in a chair, tied down, with a gag over their mouth. Each player, in turn, could tell the hosts what to do with them. He said in the first game, the victim had died in the end from fire. The username DWalt66 had instructed the hosts to pour petrol on her and burn her.'

Weaver physically gagged but stopped herself from being sick.

The senior forensic officers, Tallow and Hope, exchanged worried looks between each other.

'Then what happened?' Leonard asked.

'The username EricJ4 had told the hosts to put a bag over her head to starve the next victim of oxygen. The third murder involved a woman dying from water. One of the hosts, who was dressed in black with a black balaclava to hide their face, as the username Hammr33 had suggested, placed a tightly-fitting plastic bag around her head and filled it with water until she drowned. Only the players had a say what happened to them. Each player had a go at each victim. So far, Phil told me, there'd been three victims. There was one more to go.'

'So, if there have been three victims in this game, and Phil was meant to be Dilton's fourth murder, what did Phil do?'

Byrd took a breath. 'Phil told me the hosts had a lot of props. He'd asked the host to place a plastic box with a hole in the bottom just big enough for the victims head to fit through, and then asked them to pour soil inside so the victim wouldn't be able to breathe, then take it off just in time before they died. Phil's victim would have been the next one.'

'When did this happen?' Weaver asked, grimacing.

'According to Phil, every Friday night. There's one coming up this Friday.'

Collective sighs swept the room.

And then something strange happened.

Tanzy and Leonard both looked at each other and narrowed their eyes.

'You thinking what I'm thinking, Jim?' Tanzy asked.

Leonard nodded twice. 'I think so…'

'What is it?' Byrd asked, intrigued about what they'd figured out.

'You go first…' Tanzy offered.

'So if user DWalt66 had told the hosts to kill the victim with fire, it can't be a coincidence that Dilton set Danny Walters' house on fire, or that EricJ4 had told the hosts to place a bag over the victim's head and then she was gassed out in the lift before she fell from her balcony...'

Byrd nodded, now understanding. He looked at Tanzy.

'Or that Hammr33 had told them to place a plastic bag over their head and fill it with water. Then she and her boyfriend died by Dilton injecting excessive water into their bodies until they internally drowned?'

The realisation of what had happened hit everyone at a similar time.

'So,' Fuller said, 'you're thinking that Dilton, who we know was playing the game with them, had somehow figured out who they were and had taken some form of revenge on them?'

Tanzy nodded. 'That's exactly what I'm saying.'

The door in the corner opened suddenly and in came the receptionist Lisa. 'Max, there's a call for you...'

Byrd said okay.

Lisa walked in with a cordless phone that was usually sat on the desk at reception. 'She's tried to call you, but couldn't get through, so called reception.'

'Who is it?' Byrd asked but took the phone, putting it to his ear. 'Hello?'

'Max. It's Jennifer from the Town Hall.'

'Hi, Jennifer. Thanks for getting back to me. What do you have?'

'I have a very good idea where to find your blue Ford Focus.'

77

Tuesday Morning
Darlington

Brad bent down near Sarah, placing the tray of food near her leg. A ham and cheese sandwich, a packet of crisps, and bottled water. He'd even treat her today because she'd been so good and put a chocolate bar on there, too.

He picked up the empty tray and the empty bottle she'd squashed out of anger earlier that morning. Brad didn't blame her for it. He'd do the same. Being taken to a dark room with three friends in pitch black, then suddenly waking and finding one of them missing was no idea of fun. Especially when she didn't know where they'd gone or what had happened to them.

He stood up, looked down on her for a moment, feeling sorry for her. It wasn't pleasant what they had done, or what they'd do over the next few months, but financially, it was something he couldn't turn down.

He'd been thinking over the past few days about the next victims, making a list of five for the next set of games. After reaching out using a fake profile, the plan was still to meet them on Saturday. Joanne, the one he'd been speaking to, said she'd be out on Saturday and would message him to meet. Apparently, they had a lot in common. The plan was to drive into town, park the blue van somewhere, and hit the bars. Once he locates the women, he'd tell them there's a party at his house and on their way back, gas them out, using the same stuff they used in the room below when delivering their food or taking one of them for the games.

On his way out of the room, he closed the door and slid the bolt across until it reached the end, making a metallic pinging sound. He then turned with the empty tray by his side and made his way up the stairs.

The blue neon lights flashed from the angled ceiling and the handrail, illuminating the stairs as he climbed them two at a time. It reminded him of an old nightclub from the eighties.

Cheap, fun, and unmissable.

He opened the door at the top, took a left, then went through further doors until he reached the room with the computers in. He placed the tray with empty wrappers on a table to the right, then dropped into the chair at the desk, plucking his phone from his pocket to call Mitch.

'Brad,' Mitch answered. 'How's it going?'

'Just fed her. She'll wake up soon.'

'Good.'

'When are you getting here?'

'I have a lot on today, Brad. Are you alright holding the fort?'

Brad said he was. He had little choice. Mitch was in charge of all the money the players and watchers paid, so whatever Mitch wanted, Brad would do it to get his cut, which he was yet to receive.

'Yeah,' Brad said, 'whatever you need, Mitch.'

'Good. How's the list coming on?'

Brad told him about Joanne and the plan to meet them this Saturday. That he'd lure them into the van and bring them here.

'Keep up the good work, Brad. I'll see you soon.'

Mitch hung up the phone and the line went dead.

78

Tuesday Morning
Police Station

Byrd had passed on what Jennifer Lucas had said about the blue Ford Focus to Leonard, Cornty, and Weaver. It was seen on a camera leaving the roundabout on Haughton Road going up Barton Street. The only way out of that estate is under the bridge on Cleveland Street leading to North Road. There was a camera, Jennifer knew, because she'd looked at the same camera months ago when helping the police, positioned high up on the side of a factory next to the railway line, facing towards North Road. She'd waited at least half an hour, looking for the car but it didn't show, nor did it back on itself and come back down Barton Street to the Haughton Road roundabout it originally came from.

Although she knew Darlington like the back of her hand, she looked on Google Maps and made a list of streets within that small area. Judging by the list, it wasn't that small. There were ten in total with a few areas of industrial units, including a hefty number of garages where a vehicle could easily be hidden.

'Where should we start?' Leonard asked them.

Cornty, who was riding shotgun, looked down at the list of streets in his hand on the paper that Byrd had written for him. Weaver was in the back with her phone open on Google Maps, switching her focus between the road ahead and the electronic map in her hand.

'Could start with this one? Barton Street,' suggested Weaver.

Leonard nodded and drove on, slowly passing the timber place on the right. They were all looking around carefully and meticulously, scanning left and right.

'What year was it?' Leonard said in concentration.

'Twelve reg, Jim. N. A. 1. 2. O. P. P,' he said, referring to what Byrd had jotted down.

Over the next thirty minutes, they drove around the streets slowly, passing every house in the area. When they returned to Barton Street, they pulled over to the left. Haughton Road was roughly one hundred metres behind them.

The enthusiasm they'd driven over with seemed to have dissipated a little.

'No sign then?' Weaver noted sadly.

'Do you think if there had been, one of us would have said,' Cornty replied sharply.

The tone he used with her didn't go unnoticed with Leonard.

'Don't take it out on her, Phil.' Leonard stared at him and Cornty matched it. 'She's making conversation.'

Cornty swivelled a little towards the back of the car. 'Sorry, Amy. It's getting to me all this shit.'

She pursed her lips together but didn't say anything.

'It's getting to everyone,' said Leonard. 'This Dilton fucker. Fallows, wherever the hell she is. And now Stockdale is involved in this online shit...'

Cornty nodded and apologised again.

'It's fine, Phil,' Amy replied quietly.

'Looks like we'll need to—'

'Whoa!' Leonard snapped, stopping Cornty from finishing his sentence.

'What?' Weaver said, leaning forward from the back, her hands on the head rests of both front seats.

'There...' Leonard said, pointing down the street on the right, watching a man walk across the road further down.

'Him?' Cornty said.

He was bald, matching the height and width of the profile they had on Mackenzie Dilton. He took a right into Church Grove.

Leonard engaged the clutch of the silver Insignia and put the gear in first, checked for traffic in his wing mirror, and pulled out quickly, planting his foot to the floor. When they made the turn, they frantically scanned the area for the man who'd they just seen. He was wearing a red t-shirt and black shorts.

Leonard stopped. A cul-de-sac, nowhere to go. 'Can you see him?'

Weaver leaned back, methodically checking each house in turn. They'd been in the same street five minutes ago but didn't see a Ford Focus. 'I can't see him.'

'Phil?'

Cornty inspected the houses to the left of the car. 'Zilch...'

'Bastard.'

Leonard then asked Weaver for her phone, which she handed over. He craned his neck, looking at the map that was open on Google.

'What are you looking for?' Weaver asked.

Handing back her phone, he did a U-turn, returning to Barton Street again.

Cornty was baffled. 'What are you doing?'

'Show him, Amy,' said Leonard.

Cornty took the phone to have a look. 'What am I looking at, Jim?'

Leonard leaned over, pointed to the map. 'It's a cul-de-sac. There's no way out. I think we should sit tight watching, see what happens.'

'Why don't we just knock on doors,' suggested Weaver.

'Because if Fallows is helping him, she'll recognise us. They won't answer the door. We haven't the man power to burst down every door.'

Weaver made a *fair enough* face and leaned back.

'Who you calling?' Cornty said to Leonard as he plucked his own phone from his pocket.

'To let Max and Orion know.' He paused a beat. 'We have him cornered.'

79

Tuesday Morning
Police Station

'Okay. Thanks for letting me know.'

Byrd hung up the phone and slipped it into his pocket.

'Who was that?' asked Tanzy, staring at him.

'Leonard. He thinks they spotted him go into Church Grove but lost him. Reckon he's in one of the houses. They're waiting out on the road until backup arrives. Says he's blocked in.'

Tanzy nodded and stood up. 'Let's go.'

'We'll get Timms and Grearer there, too.'

'Good idea,' replied Tanzy as they both made their way to the office.

'Timms!' Tanzy shouted. 'Grearer. Let's go.'

PC Timms and PC Grearer, who were seated near each other on separate desks, stood up immediately. Tanzy filled them in on the situation about Dilton then, after they grabbed a few things, followed Byrd and Tanzy out into the car park. Byrd opened his X5, the sidelights flashing once, and jumped in the driver's seat. Tanzy got into the passenger seat and buckled up.

Grearer and Timms took one of the marked Peugeots and pulled out onto the road a moment after.

'You think it was definitely him?' DC Cornty asked Leonard, watching the opening to Church Grove.

'I'm pretty confident, yeah.'

'Good enough for me,' Cornty said, nodding.

'Are Max and Orion coming?' Weaver said from the back of the car.

'Yeah. Max said he'll request more backup. Once they're pegged in with nowhere to go, we'll go in.'

'What if they—'

'Look!' Cornty shouted, stabbing the warm air inside the car. 'Look.'

Leonard and Weaver watched the blue Ford Focus edge out and take a right, away from them.

'There she is, the bitch!' Leonard shouted, referring to Linda Fallows in the passenger seat.

'Think they saw us?' asked Weaver.

Leonard quickly pulled out and quickly accelerated through the gears. By the time they hit the bend, the Focus was out of sight, somewhere along the road.

'C'mon, Jim!' Cornty shouted, tapping the dash in frustration.

Leonard planted his foot and the car surged forward. Soon they reached the traffic lights just before the bridge.

The Focus shot down the ramp, through the lights, and raced up the other side.

Leonard gripped the wheel and pushed hard on the pedal, creeping in front of a car coming from the left. Weaver leaned back into the seat with her palms flat on the seats either side to stop her falling. In the front seat, Cornty held on to the door handle to steady his weight as Leonard powered under the bridge, the roar of the engine echoing off the brick walls on either side.

'C'mon, Jim!' repeated Cornty, watching the Focus reach the top of the incline and go out of sight.

'I am,' replied a frustrated Leonard. They sped up the hill and the car went airborne for a moment, sending butterflies through their stomachs. 'Ring Max. Tell him they're on the move.'

Cornty found Tanzy's number, and pressed CALL. 'C'mon. Pick up, pick up,' he said quickly, his heart rate through the roof.

'Phil?' Tanzy answered.

'They're moving towards North Road.'

'In the Focus?'

Cornty said they were.

The Focus whizzed by Aldi at sixty miles an hour. If a car pulled out, or a pedestrian crossed the road, the repercussions would be catastrophic.

'They must know we're behind them!' Weaver panted from the back seat, watching the speeding car through the front windscreen.

A red Clio pulled out of Aldi's car park just as Dilton and Fallows passed and slammed on their brakes, causing tyres to skid on the tarmac. People nearby froze and stared at the high-screeched sound.

'Jesus!' Leonard said, gasping at how close it was. On the opposite side of the road, there were no cars, so when Leonard's Insignia caught up with the Clio, he veered onto the other side, went around it, and pulled back in. The Focus took a sudden left onto North Road.

'He's fast. Must be an ST...'

Leonard frowned. 'Quicker. An RS may be?' He reached the turn and looked up at the traffic lights. They were on red. Cars from the right started to shift forward.

'They've gone left on North Road, Orion,' Cornty shouted into the phone.

'Got ya!' replied Tanzy. 'We're on St. Cuthbert's Way, heading to the roundabout.'

Cornty noticed the cars coming from the right.

'Jim?' Cornty said, patting his leg, seeing the approaching cars getting close. 'Jim...'

'Hold on...' Leonard floored it and guided the car left. The tyres almost lost grip and the car bounced, the rubber squealing on the road. The car approaching from the right, driven by a man in his sixties, rocked his head back in horror and slammed on his brakes, although Leonard was confident in making the turn.

Up ahead, roughly forty metres beyond the bridge, the Focus was weaving in and out of the traffic.

'He's gonna kill someone!' bellowed Cornty from the passenger seat.

'Sit tight!' Leonard answered, approaching the next car, and doing the same, mindful of the oncoming traffic.

'Easy, Jim,' Weaver said. 'Easy...'

'We need to catch them.'

The insignia passed Skin Deep tattoo shop on the right and approached the traffic lights near the petrol station. Again, the lights were red. The Focus swung wide and powered through, flying past stationary traffic, making it over before the cars from Eastmount Road turned onto North Road.

'Shit!' Leonard panted, immediately slowing the car to thirty, quickly assessing his options. Then cars turned from Eastmount Road and blocked his way, so he stopped to avoid an almost certain collision.

'Orion, they're heading along North Road towards the roundabout,' Cornty said into the phone. 'We've lost them. Stuck in traffic. Catch up when we can.'

'Okay. We're approaching the roundabout now,' replied Tanzy.

Byrd nodded as Tanzy relayed the message, keeping his eyes on the roundabout ahead, specifically the exit from North Road, knowing Dilton's Focus would appear any moment.

'There, there. There!' Tanzy screamed, pointing.

Byrd could see it. They flew out of North Road onto the roundabout, not caring about the traffic from their right, causing a black Fiesta to suddenly come to a halt and the car behind it, a white transit van, to collide into the back of it with a metal crunch.

Byrd watched Dilton pass in almost a blur. In the passenger seat was Fallows, who made eye contact with him for a brief moment, then the car was gone, Dilton going straight over, following the bus route into town.

'Where's he going?' snapped Tanzy.

Byrd flew around the roundabout and followed the bus route into town. They saw a flash of the Focus before it whizzed out of sight down toward Wilko's.

'Max. Put ya foot down!'

Byrd scowled, losing his patience. 'I fucking am!'

Without any warning, a bus pulled out from the left, nearly forcing them onto the path over to the right. Byrd managed to somehow keep it on the road, inches from the low kerb, barely missing a family of five casually walking by, and straightened out to take the left.

The Focus took a right at the next junction, heading towards The William Stead pub. Byrd followed.

'The car is in the middle of town,' Tanzy said into the phone.

'We're not far behind,' replied Cornty from the Insignia. 'Just at the roundabout now.'

'Head straight over. Bus route,' Tanzy replied.

The Focus took the right turn before it reached The William Stead pub.

'Why – what on earth...' Byrd whispered, slowing the X5, and followed him up the bank. The road ahead was clear. No buses. No pedestrian shoppers idly crossing the road. When the Focus went under the Cornmill, the exhaust echoed off the building.

Byrd nodded in agreement.

Before the Focus reached the turn, a taxi pulled out, causing it to slow allowing Byrd to close the gap.

'Easy, Max...' Tanzy warned him.

That part of town, although a well-used bus route, was always flooded with people crossing roads.

'He's mine!' Byrd shouted. The Focus veered around the awkward taxi which had suddenly stopped and started to make the turn. Byrd drove around the taxi and put his foot down, surging the X5 forward.

'Max!' Tanzy shouted with wide eyes, not knowing what was going to happen. They were going far too fast.

Byrd tightened his grip on the wheel and as the Focus was mid-turn, Byrd ploughed into the back quarter, sending the Focus into the concrete flower bed. The crash was so loud, everyone around froze and stared in horror at what had happened.

Byrd's airbag came up, smashing him in the nose with the force of a hammer. Tanzy's airbag exploded too, cushioning his face as he was jerked forward into the direction of the dashboard.

Silence surrounded them after the deafening crash faded into the town. Nearby people glared in shock with open, speechless mouths at the mess. Someone got their phone out to take a picture.

Byrd didn't move. Neither did Tanzy.

80

Tuesday Morning
High Row, Town Centre

'God...' Fallows whispered. 'Think my arm's broken.'

'Can – can you move?' Dilton asked, feeling a pounding in the side of his temple where he'd collided into the side window. He raised his hand, felt the warm blood gushing from the cut.

'I – I think so, Mack...' Fallows struggled to say.

When Byrd had crashed into the rear of them, sending the Focus forward into the concrete flower beds, she jerked forward, hitting her shoulder off the central console. She'd wailed in pain, immediately feeling like something terrible had happened. A bone breaking, for sure.

'Come on. We need to go.' Dilton turned around. The X5 was hard up against the rear, the bonnet crumpled and smashed up.

'Your head...' Fallows said, seeing the blood dripping onto his trousers and the inside of the car.

'Come on. We need to get out.'

He opened his door and, with just enough room to squeeze out, he pulled himself up onto his feet. Fallows opened the passenger door and slowly got out. Dilton noticed the front of the Focus hard up against the high concrete slab, the bonnet crushed.

He looked back at the X5. Tanzy and Byrd were both leaning forward, unconscious. Dilton rushed around the back of the X5 and appeared at Fallows' side. 'You okay, Linda?'

'I'll survive.'

Dilton took a soft grip of her arm and gently helped her out. 'Let's go before they wake up.'

Tanzy's eyes flickered a few times until he managed to keep them open, seeing the deflated airbag on his lap. His nose felt hot and sore, like he'd just been headbutted, maybe worse. He sniffed hard, tasting the blood in the back of his throat. To his right, Byrd was still out.

'Max?'

Nothing.

Then he heard a voice say, 'Let's go before they wake up.'

He followed the sound, the simple head movement causing a wave of almost unbearable pain. Dilton and Fallows moved down the side of the car, but Tanzy quickly grabbed the handle and threw his door open, unbuckled his seat belt and leaned out, leading with his left leg. As Dilton ran by, he kicked Tanzy's door closed, jamming Tanzy's knee between the side skirt and the door. There was a crack. Tanzy, sure it was a bone breaking, howled in agony and fell out of the car onto his back. He hadn't felt pain like it. He watched Fallows and Dilton dash across the road and run into The Cornmill Shopping centre.

'Max – Max!' he screamed.

Byrd stirred and jerked awake a moment later, sighing something inaudible.

'Max. Here!'

Byrd swivelled his stiff neck to the left, seeing Tanzy lay on the road through the open passenger door, wincing in pain. His knee was bleeding and swelling already.

'Get them. They've gone into the Cornmill.'

Byrd, after three attempts, pushed his door open and stepped down onto the concrete, a little unsteady on his feet, then staggered around the rear of the car to aid to Tanzy.

'Did you not hear me?'

Byrd frowned, unsure what he'd said.

'The Cornmill.' Tanzy stabbed the air in the direction of the entrance. 'Get them!'

Byrd nodded, trying to make sense of what had happened, and with a thumping head, dashed across the road towards the entrance.

81

Tuesday Late Morning
The Cornmill Shopping Centre, Town Centre

Dilton barged into the entrance door first and almost collided into an elderly man, somewhere in his eighties, holding a walking stick who was on his way out. The old man jolted back a few inches, glaring wide eyed at Dilton wondering what on earth he was doing.

Fallows managed to get through before it swung back and hit her, and swerved the man, who remained still, a look of disgust on his face at both of them. He shook his head and exited through the door.

'Come on, Linda!' Dilton screamed, almost at HMV.

In jeans and shoes, she wasn't really dressed for sprinting, but she was doing her best. For her age, she was quick.

Dilton hung back a little, waiting for her to level with him. 'Come on,' he repeated. When she reached him, he looked back at the door they'd just came through, seeing DI Byrd barge through, almost losing his balance in the process.

He grabbed her hand and they passed the perfume shop until they had a choice to make. They could take the escalator down to the ground floor. Or they could take a left, along to the next area of shops where JD Sports was.

They swung a left, barely missing a woman walking with two toddlers, who both seemed to be around the age of five.

'Watch it!' the mother blasted in revulsion, glowering at them as they ran past.

Fallows and Dilton continued on, their heavy footsteps slapping the floor, loud enough for nearby shoppers to stop and glare at them in wonder. They sprinted past JD Sports, almost into a group of teenagers who looked young enough to be skiving school.

'Stop them!' they heard Byrd shout somewhere behind. It sounded close.

He pulled on Fallows' arm, urging her to move quicker. They raced past Game on their left and headed toward WHSmith. Dilton's mind was doing overtime, thinking hard, wondering what to do, where to go. He knew they were being followed from his house to North Road because Fallows had said she recognised the registration on the Insignia. A guy called James she'd said. If back-up was coming, they'd no doubt have the exits covered. It was policing basics. So Dilton needed to think outside the box.

'Here! Take a right here,' he shouted, just before they reached WHSmith's. A set of open double doors led to a lift and a staircase down to the toilets. Dilton went through first, narrowly missing a woman in a wheelchair, dressed in a red coat and hat although it was nearly thirty degrees outside.

'Hey...' the woman said, sighing.

Dilton and Fallows reached the stairs, but instead of taking the stairs down, they went up, climbing them two at a time. He was much quicker than she was and reached the next level, scanning what was there. A closed door with a Yale lock.

'Shit...'

He went up the next lot, kept going until he was four floors up where he reached the emergency exit access to the roof. Before he went through, he stopped to hear where Fallows was. The level below.

Without waiting for her, he pushed the bar in and opened the door, went outside into the hot sun. It was so bright he had to cover his eyes with a palm to see what was out there. It was pretty flat in most areas, but noticed a long, angled window, which he recognised was the skylight giving natural light for the shoppers down below. Other areas contained cubed-shaped ducting probably used for HVAC systems.

A few moments later, Fallows barged through the door, red-faced and panting heavily, her blonde hair all over the place.

'Linda,' he said, going back to her. 'You okay?'

'Where – where are we going to go?'

'We'll hide up here for a while…'

She shook her head. 'No, Mack. We can't. Max is right behind us. We need to hide.'

82

Tuesday Late Morning
Roof top of The Cornmill Shopping Centre,
Town Centre

Byrd was two floors from the top before he stopped hearing Fallows' shoes slapping inside the stairwell, meaning she wasn't in the stairwell anymore. He was tired, his lungs gasping for air, his arms and legs burning. After a few exhausting seconds later, he reached the top level, seeing an open emergency exit door swinging gently in the breeze.

He burst out onto the roof, the light almost blinding him in the process. For a second, he shielded himself, feeling very vulnerable if Dilton had waited at the door and decided to attack him.

Fortunately, no attack came.

He stopped and glared around in all directions.

No sign of Fallows and Dilton. He absorbed the ducting lines and small metal items. To the right, he noticed a handrail at the edge, which, as he followed, ran the whole perimeter of the roof.

He took a few quiet steps away from the open door, pulled a baton from his pocket, fully extended it, and held it tightly in his right hand. Deciding to take a right, he tiptoed across the roof, scanning everything around him, trying to hear for movement.

As he stepped into the centre of the space, he realised the roof was bigger than he first thought. The view of Darlington beyond the handrails was admirable, to say the least. Further along, he came across a small shed made from brick, with a thick door on the front of it. There was a keycode panel at head height beside it, so wherever they'd gone, it wasn't through there. He backed away, turned, and moved along the railing, looking carefully through all the ducting lines.

Then he had an idea.

He lowered to the ground, his head still pounding from the crash minutes earlier and looked along the floor of the roof. The ducting sections, he realised, didn't reach the floor, instead were supported by metal brackets an inch off the deck.

Bingo.

There they were, roughly forty metres over to the right, hiding behind a large section of the ducting.

He stood, battling against his own spinning head, and slowly made his way over. He plucked his phone from his pocket and called Tanzy.

'Max…'

'Hey, Ori. They're on the roof. I've got them cornered. Where are you?'

'Still outside. I can't fucking move. I think they've broken my knee. Ambulance is here.'

'Leonard. Cornty. Where are they?' he whispered, not wanting to be heard.

'Inside the Cornmill looking for you.'

'Send them up. Staircase near the toilets. It goes to the roof.'

He took a quick, sharp breath, and moved over to the ducting ahead of him, slowly and carefully rounding the edge of it.

Dilton and Fallows edged away when they saw him, taking a few steps back towards the railings.

'Linda,' Byrd said. 'I don't understand.'

'There's a lot of things you don't understand, Max,' she replied, stepping in front of Dilton, as if somehow protecting him.

'Please explain.' Byrd stepped closer, but with each step, Dilton and Fallows backed away, getting close to the handrail on the edge of the roof. There were a few feet between them. Dilton noticed the baton in Byrd's hands.

'I don't need to explain anything to you…'

Before Byrd replied, Dilton pushed Fallows into Byrd and made a run for it. Byrd deflected Fallows' slap, knocking her to one side, and went after him. Dilton was quick, but Byrd equalled him, if not, quicker.

'Stop!' Byrd shouted, panting.

Dilton ran along the side of the handrail until he reached the edge. For a moment, when he disappeared, Byrd thought he'd gone over the side, but when he reached it, he realised there was another roof next to it, roughly two feet lower, a small access ladder between them.

'Stop!' Byrd screamed, but Dilton didn't slow.

Up ahead, was a large dome-like set of windows. Byrd recognised it as the huge skylight above the escalators near Primark.

Dilton reached it and jumped on top, then started moving up it.

'Mackenzie, don't!' Byrd yelled, not knowing if it was safe. 'Get off there.'

It would be engineered to withstand the weight of snow over the whole area but not necessarily the concentrated weight of a man.

Dilton ignored him, going higher.

'Max, leave him alone,' Fallows cried somewhere behind him.

Byrd ignored her plea and arrived at the base of the glass dome skylight. 'Fuck it,' he muttered, and raised his right leg, climbing on to it. Dilton was nearly at the top, and Byrd had noticed he'd slowed, almost coming to a stop.

Byrd carefully went up, keeping his weight on the PVC framework, avoiding any contact with the glass, just in case. It wasn't long before Dilton stopped and turned to him.

'Why?' Dilton asked.

Byrd frowned. 'Why what, Mackenzie?'

'Why are you chasing me?'

'Because killing people is illegal.'

'I'm doing you a favour. Can't you see that?'

'Well, whatever you're doing... it's against the law. You need to come with me.'

Byrd finally stopped on the angled pane, three metres from Dilton. He glanced right and left, realising he didn't really have anywhere to go.

'I'm going nowhere. There's so much more work to do...' he said, scowling at Byrd.

'Please, Mackenzie. You need to—'

Dilton lifted his right foot and stomped hard onto the glass he was standing on. The rectangular pane was large, roughly a metre by two metres.

'No,' Byrd begged, holding his palms out. 'Don't do that.'

Dilton lifted his leg and did it again, the sound of it startled Byrd, knowing what could happen if the glass went through. He looked below for a second, noticed the sea of people watching them from below, their faces glaring up in horror at the crazy guy standing above them.

'Do not do—'

Dilton did it again, this time harder.

The pane of glass crunched. A multitude of paper-thin cracks shot off in all directions away from where he stomped his foot for the third time. A few seconds later the glass collapsed in on itself and Dilton disappeared through it.

The loud thud of his body hitting the handrail of the escalator below was sickening. His body literally folding in two and blood cascaded in several directions, followed by the screams of innocent shoppers.

Byrd immediately turned away, clamping his eyes closed, not wanting to see the mess below.

Slowly, he lowered himself off the dome and turned to see where Fallows was.

She was gone.

83

Tuesday Late Morning
The Cornmill, Darlington

Byrd tried calling Fallows' mobile but it was switched off. On his way back down, he phoned Tanzy, who was in the rear of an ambulance with a paramedic looking at his knee. He said he'd heard the screams inside but didn't know what had happened.

Byrd filled him in and ended the call. He stepped out of the toilets and ran along towards JD Sports, his frantic footsteps bouncing off the shiny, tiled floor towards the mass of people standing near the glass handrail, gob-smacked by Dilton's body below. A couple of people were physically sick at the sight of it.

'I need everyone out!' Byrd shouted, his head high, projecting his voice.

A couple of people turned but most were fixated on Dilton's broken body below.

'Everyone out...'

To his right, he saw Leonard, glaring wide-eyed down at the mess. Leonard looked up after hearing Byrd's voice and ran over.

'Jesus, Max! What happened?'

Byrd quickly told him, then added, 'We need everyone out. Call for back-up. We need this shit cleaned up ASAP.'

Leonard nodded, took out his radio.

Byrd scanned the area, noticed Cornty on the other side, trying to get people to move. Weaver was near him doing the same.

'What a fucking mess,' muttered Byrd to himself.

A little while later, after the security staff of nearby shops had joined in to help the police clear the place, The Cornmill was empty. It was eerie, Byrd thought, standing at the glass handrail in silence, looking up at where Dilton had fallen.

Down below, the senior forensics, Tallow and Hope, were there in the white, overall clearing the place the best they could. They'd taken photos of the whole scene, and as usual, Tallow had taken a video for his analysis later.

The undertakers had been called to collect what was left of the body, and Peter Gibbs, the lead coroner, had also been informed about what had happened and turned up quickly. The colour had drained from his face as he approached Byrd.

'My goodness…' he said, raising a palm to his mouth.

There was no need for a police investigation, which Byrd knew, but he'd reached out to the security officer of The Cornmill to see if there was any cameras on the roof, just in case. Only Byrd knew what had really happened but seeing camera footage would eliminate the unlikely suggestion that Byrd had pushed him.

He also wanted to see which direction Fallows had run off in. She must have slipped past Cornty and Leonard. He planned to ask Jennifer Lucas about it later.

But for now, they had more pressing matters.

They needed to search the house where Dilton had been staying. They say to understand someone, especially a killer, it was best to start off in a place they spent a lot of their time because often, there were clues which hadn't been fully covered.

Byrd, after dealing with Fuller shouting in his face back in town, had kept his cool and told Weaver, Leonard, and Cornty to go to Church Grove to find the house which he was staying in. Before heading over himself, he went back to the ambulance to see Tanzy who was sat on a trolley with his leg bandaged up.

'What's the damage, Ori?' he asked him through the open rear doors.

A female paramedic with blonde hair in her thirties said, 'Excuse me,' and veered around Byrd, climbed into the back of the van and grabbed a small kit bag, then thanked him when she jumped back out.

'They said it could be bad, Max,' replied Tanzy, physically in pain. 'Won't know until I get an x-ray. It could be just bruised. Where's Fallows?'

'I don't know. Fuller isn't a happy man.'

Tanzy sighed, waved his hand. 'He's never happy, Max. It's the way he is.'

Byrd made a fair enough face. 'They taking you now?'

Tanzy nodded. 'Checking if anyone else needs any help before we go. Make me a promise, Max…'

'What is it?'

'Catch that bitch.'

'I'll do what I can, Ori.'

As Byrd turned, he stopped when Tanzy said, 'Never a dull day in Darlington, is there?'

Byrd smiled, agreeing with him with a shake of his head.

By the time Byrd had reached Church Grove in his battered X5 which, fortunately, was still driveable, the police had managed to locate the house that Dilton and Fallows had been staying in. They'd asked some of the neighbours where the bald man lived with the blue Focus. It wasn't hard.

Cornty and Leonard had kicked the door in and Weaver had followed, then with overshoes and gloves on, they searched the house until Byrd arrived, which wasn't long after.

Byrd pulled into the street and spotted Leonard's Insignia and two marked Peugeots over in the left corner in front of a nice-looking semi-detached house. Byrd got out, locked the door, and walked towards the house, feeling the stares of nosy neighbours from all directions, standing behind curtains, peeping out to see what was happening.

Byrd stepped through the broken red door that was open a few inches and called out.

Leonard appeared at the top of the stairs with a serious look on his face. 'Come up here, boss. There's something you need to see.'

84

Tuesday Early Afternoon
Church Grove, Darlington

Byrd followed Leonard into a small room at the end of the short, narrow landing. Once he was inside, it was obvious Dilton had used it as an office. There was a desk against the wall to the right, and above it, dozens of photos and bits of paper randomly pinned to the wall.

Byrd looked at it, seeing photos of Danny Walters, Jane Ericson, Rachel Hammond, and lastly, DS Phil Stockdale. Next to each photograph, there was information and details about them that Dilton had noted when watching them over the last couple of weeks. Stuck on the bottom of each photo, there was a yellow post-it note, a single word on each of them. The word, *fire* was under Walters, *Air* under Ericson, *Water* under Hammond, and lastly, *Earth* under Stockdale.

Pulling his eyes away from the wall, Byrd noticed an envelope in Leonard's hand.

In the centre of it, in scribbled handwriting, it said *FAO Max Byrd / Orion Tanzy*.

'What is it?' Cornty asked, stepping into the room. Byrd turned it over, peeled away the sticky flap, and reached inside, pulling out multiple sheets of A-4 paper.

Byrd dropped them onto the desk and sat down to look. The first page was a printed letter to Byrd and Tanzy.

To Max and Orion,
Firstly, I want to apologise for what I've done. The way I killed Danny, Jane, and Rachel, I must admit, wasn't pleasant. I'm

glad you found Phil before he ran out of air. I left you the message at the end of my fourth video in the hope you would find him. He seemed like a genuine man caught up in something wrong, but I hoped he learned his lesson for what he did. By now, I'm sure he's confessed to what he's done and is paying the price in prison for a long time, so either way, justice is served.

I came across the website which I know you're now aware of. www.attheend.com – it's pure evil. The people who did those despicable things needed to pay the price.

Yes, I admit, taking an eye for an eye isn't the way it should be, but after I witnessed what they'd done and what they said, it sickened me. So, I got them back.

By now, I'm either dead or arrested. So this is my way of saying sorry for what's happened. The games online that the players and watchers were involved in will go on, and I wanted to stop it, wanted to stop them from taking innocent girls and torturing them for money. It's wrong. I won't accept it.

Now, as you know, I'm not in a position to stop this anymore. This, now, is up to you Max / Orion, to finish this. If you look on my computer (username RCarl20 and password Dilton) – another apology about the RCarl20 and Roger Carlton. I was obsessed with a character growing up, and this Carlton guy, in my head, has been with me ever since – and look at the program that is currently running (LocateIP). It's a special tracking program from the US. It was expensive, but if it works, it'll be worth it to save them. So far, I haven't been able to locate the source of where these games are taking place. It could be anywhere in the world. Judging by the missing four girls, I have an idea it's somewhere in Darlington.

Go on to the program and see if it's worked. I'm hoping it's found the location of where the website originates from. Once it reaches 100%, their location will come up. You need to find them and stop them from causing more harm to innocent families.

Keep up the good work.

Best wishes,

Mackenzie Dilton.

'Jesus,' Byrd whispered.

'What is it?' Leonard said.

Byrd handed the letter over to Leonard, who started to read it. Cornty leaned in to read it too.

Byrd logged on to the computer and the program appeared. The current search bar had reached 97%, slowly crawling across the screen. Under the number, it stated *Location not yet found...* in bold lettering.

'Come on...' he said, looking above the monitor at the notes on the wall.

'Bloody hell,' Leonard said behind him. 'He's trying to stop it.'

'In other words,' Cornty said, pushing his lips out, 'he's a hero then...'

'I wouldn't go that far,' countered Leonard, who placed the paper on the desk and looked at the screen.

'It's nearly a hundred, then we'll know,' Byrd said.

Leonard and Cornty both nodded, watching the bar crawl across.

'I'm gonna check on Weaver,' Cornty said, edging back and leaving the room. Weaver was downstairs, checking through the cupboards in the kitchen.

'Hey,' Cornty said.

It took her by surprise and she jumped.

'Jeez... you got me there,' she said, placing a palm on her chest. 'What have you found?'

Cornty explained.

'We'll nail them!' she said positively.

Back upstairs, a little over fifteen minutes later, the bar had reached one hundred percent. It stated search complete and gave them an IP Address and coordinates. Byrd, from the right side of the desk, grabbed a pen and piece of scrap paper, and made a note of them. He then went on to Google and typed in the coordinates that the program had given and pressed ENTER.

The location came up.

'Bingo...' said Leonard, leaning over him.

'Ring this in, Jim.'

Leonard took his phone out and rang dispatch. Moments after, they went downstairs. Weaver was in the living room, hunting through a cabinet in one of the alcoves.

'We found a location for the online games. Just off McMullen Road. Where are Timms and Grearer?'

'Upstairs with you, I think. In the back bedrooms?'

Byrd appeared behind Leonard. 'We need to go, Amy. You go with Leonard.' He turned back to Timms and Grearer, who had followed Byrd down. 'Eric and Donny, you go together.'

They both nodded.

'Where's Phil?'

Weaver shrugged. 'He was here a moment ago.'

They went outside and found the marked Peugeot was gone.

'Eh? Where's Cornty gone?' Byrd said.

'He asked me for our key to the car, said he wanted to check something,' Timms said.

'Someone please call him,' countered Byrd.

Timms pulled his phone from his pocket and did as Byrd had asked. They all watched the blank look on his face. 'He's not answering, boss.'

'He was literally here a moment ago.'

Byrd thought for a moment. 'Amy, you come with me. Eric, Donny, you both go with Jim.'

They nodded and made their way to the cars. Byrd edged the front door closed. Later, they'd be back, but for now, they had to go to the place where the tracker had said.

Byrd climbed in his seat, pulled his door shut. Weaver got into the passenger seat and closed her door. While

Byrd turned on the engine and turned the car around, Weaver noticed a slip of paper down by her foot. She bent down, picked it up between two fingers, and scanned it curiously.

There was a list of names.

Max Byrd.

Orion Tanzy.

Amy Weaver.

Phil Cornty.

Lisa Shepherd.

'Boss, what's this list?'

Byrd pulled out of Church Grove, and glanced her way, seeing the paper. 'List of people whose prints forensics found on the box that was delivered to the station. One with the head in.'

Weaver frowned. 'I don't understand.'

Byrd looked her way. 'What?'

Weaver stayed silent for a moment.

'Amy, speak up. What is it?' Byrd was stern.

'I got it from Lisa when it was at reception then brought it straight to you and DI Tanzy in the office.'

'Okay…' Byrd was unsure what she meant.

'Phil Cornty didn't touch the box while it was at the station.'

85

Tuesday Afternoon
Church Grove, Darlington

'He didn't touch the box?' Byrd asked, turning onto Barton Street.

Weaver shook her head. 'No.'

Byrd grabbed the radio from the dash, pressed the button. 'Dispatch…'

'Go ahead…' the female voice replied.

'Can we get a location on vehicle November-Alpha-Six-Seven-Yankie…' His mind went blank for a second.

'PC,' whispered Weaver, helping him out.

'Papa-Charlie?' added Byrd, then nodded thanks towards her.

'Hold on…' replied the operator.

Approaching the roundabout at the bottom of Barton Street, Byrd angled left, not taking Haughton Road but the next one, the road heading to McMullen Road. The location of the IP address the program on Dilton's computer had told Byrd was an industrial property near Lingfield Point, close to the Tornado Way heading to the A66. He flew over the roundabout, the X5's three-litre engine roared as he put the gear into third and pushed his foot flat to the floor. The road ahead was clear, allowing him to open it up, approaching seventy within seconds.

Weaver straightened in her seat, grabbing the handle on the door to steady herself.

'DI Byrd,' said the female operator through the radio, 'the location of the vehicle is currently at Eastpoint Road in the Lingfield Point estate.'

'Thank you,' he replied, concentrating on the traffic lights ahead which were quickly approaching.

'Sir?' Weaver muttered, noticing he wasn't slowing down.

The lights were on red, with a line of cars waiting to go straight ahead.

Byrd didn't ease off the pedal.

Traffic from the left and right were crawling through the cross section, minding their business.

'Sir?' she repeated, this time louder, tightening her grip on the handle.

'Hold on, Amy...'

The left lane for cars turning left was empty. Weaver wondered if he was planning on taking that but found her eyes flicking towards the dashboard. The X5 was going somewhere between sixty and seventy. The lights were less than a hundred metres away.

As Byrd veered over to the left lane and reached level with the last car in the queue waiting to go, the lights flashed amber, then green. Byrd judged the first car would set off when they turned green, so dropped a gear and planted his foot, surging the big 4x4 onwards.

Weaver clamped her eyes closed, gripped the door handle so hard, her knuckles were sheet white.

'Hold on...' Byrd whispered and concentrated hard to avoid the oncoming kerb, pulling hard on the steering wheel. The tyres skidded a little, the sound of screeching ripped through the air but somehow managed it although the whole car shifted before it levelled out.

'Sorry about that.'

She opened her eyes and smiled shyly at him.

At the next set of lights, he took a right, a back way into Lingfield Point. They came to a roundabout, realising there was only the right turn to make, so traffic was minimal. There was a left turn but it was blocked off with four large boulders, leading to a half-built road.

They arrived at Eastpoint Road.

Weaver looked down at her phone in her hand. 'This is the road.'

'Keep an eye out for our Peugeot.'

She nodded.

He stopped the X5 at the junction, unsure to take a right or left. He scanned both ways. It was fifty-fifty, so he decided to take a right. The road went down until it reached a left bend, taking it around an old, abandoned building, something he'd noticed when driving along the main road.

Byrd carefully took the bend, cautious of oncoming traffic, when Weaver shouted, 'Hold on, hold on!'

'What – what is it?'

'Stop the car.' She pointed to a small parking area behind the building. Around it, were a few smaller buildings, the size of garages. If she hadn't been looking directly through the gap in between the buildings, she'd have missed it. 'You see it?'

Byrd did. He looked back at the road, deciding the best way to get to it. He followed it further, took a left to back on to himself, and pulled up behind the Peugeot. Next to it, was a blue Volkswagen Transporter Van.

'There's our van,' noted Byrd with a sigh, remembering it was the one they'd been looking for, the one the body parts had fallen out of on the A66.

It wasn't long before they heard a car nearby. Leonard's Insignia appeared to the left on the road they'd just driven down. Leonard spotted them and came to a halt behind the X5.

They all stopped and jumped out.

'Why is he here, sir?' Leonard said loudly, clear frustrated about the situation. 'He doesn't know where it is yet...'

Byrd nodded in understanding, knowing what it could mean.

'And, his phone is turned off,' added Weaver, stopping near Byrd.

They all padded towards the car, then looked around it. The car was sheltered, a small building to the left, and a large – what looked like an old factory – ahead of them.

'What's the plan?' asked Leonard, his heart rate through the roof.

Byrd scanned the area. 'There must be a door somewhere?'

'Over there,' Timms said, pointing to a set of faded yellow double doors.

They all went over to them. They looked like they'd been there for over a hundred years, judging by the rust that had taken over. The whole building, too, looked aged, weathered, and abandoned.

'What even is this building?' Leonard asked no one in particular.

'God knows,' Byrd said, trying to pull the handle on the right door, then the left. The door was locked.

'Whatever it is, it's up for let,' Timms added. 'Sign on the top up there.'

Grearer looked up for a moment, noticed the blue fabric banner.

'James... you got a crowbar in your car?' asked Byrd, looking his way. He nodded and went to the Insignia, opened the boot, and grabbed the crowbar. He ran back to the door and placed the sharp tip into the slight gap in the door. He pushed against it, the reluctant sound of metal responding to his efforts.

'Come on!' he whispered, putting his full effort in.

'Here, let me help,' Timms said, stepping forward, grabbing the bar at a lower point to Leonard.

'On three,' said Leonard. 'One, two, three.'

They both pushed hard. The lock cracked and the door edged open, the mechanism breaking in two, most of it falling near their feet. Leonard stepped back, keeping hold of the bar.

'You got your flashlights?' Byrd asked, peering inside, noticing it was very dark.

Timms and Grearer nodded, both pulling theirs from the belts.

'Let me have one,' said Byrd.

Timms handed his light over. Byrd adjusted his grip on it and pulled his baton from his belt too. 'Right, let's go…'

86

Tuesday Afternoon
Lingfield Point, Darlington

Byrd had told Weaver to stay near the door, just in case anyone tried to escape while they were inside. She nodded and called for more back-up. They had no clue what they were dealing with so the more help available, the better.

Byrd, Leonard, Timms, and Grearer went down the dark space, with Byrd and Grearer at the front holding the torches out in front. The corridor was long and narrow, with multiple doors on both sides, all closed.

'Hello? Police,' Byrd said loud and clear.

They moved onwards, further into the building, trying the handles of the doors but so far, every door was locked.

Byrd raised his hand suddenly. Everyone stopped and stared.

'Wha—' Leonard began to say.

'Shhhh….'

There was a rustling sound somewhere down the hall.

'Hear that?' Byrd whispered.

'Yeah,' Grearer replied.

'Come on.'

Slowly, they followed Byrd's lead, keeping their wits about them, trying door handles, and moving onto the next, trying to keep quiet. On the right-hand side, they came to a door Byrd was sure he heard something behind.

Byrd raised a palm again, put his head to the door and listened hard. There was the sound of a click on the other side, a similar sound to a door closing.

He tried the handle but it was locked. Stepping back, he raised a leg and kicked the left side of the door just below the handle. The door juddered but held. He did it again, this time, the door crumbled in on itself, the lock shearing with a crack.

Inside the room was bright, so he lowered the torch, but kept his baton held high, ready for anything that might try and surprise him. There was a large desk with two computer screens on top of it. Behind the screen, was a black window.

'What the fuck is this?' Leonard said, as he stepped inside, seeing the computer screens.

Byrd looked carefully around the room. To the right, a thin black coat hung from a hook on the wall. To the right of that was a shelving unit with various papers on them, nothing in any particular order. On the wide desk before them, was an empty chocolate wrapper and a half-drunk bottle of Pepsi. Whoever was here, hadn't been gone very long.

Leonard took a seat on one of the two empty desk chairs and pulled himself in. On the right monitor was a screen showing a camera looking down onto a room. He leaned forward, squinting.

'Is that a woman?' He turned back to Byrd. 'Sir. Have a look.'

Byrd, Timms, and Grearer came over immediately.

'Looks like it…' replied Byrd.

They saw the tab with the word *Players* on it, then underneath, another tab saying *Watchers*.

'This is exactly where it happens,' Leonard noted angrily, hitting the desk with a palm.

The rustling sound on the other side of the door over to the left caught their attention. They all stared, exchanging quick glances with each other. Byrd wasted no time and stepped away from the desk, then dashing over with the baton high up in his right hand, he grabbed the handle and pulled the door inwards.

He was well aware of the dangers when opening a door, not knowing what could be behind, so, through experience, he stamped his foot down near the open threshold but held off, missing the baseball bat that swung down from the right. And boy, was he glad he did. Judging by the speed and the crack when it hit the floor, it would have split his skull into two.

Leonard, Timms, and Grearer all froze, staring at the door.

A moment later, Brad stumbled through, raising the bat high above his head with menace on his face. Byrd kept a close eye on him, weighing him up, watching his movements. Brad was big and bulky and Byrd knew he'd have to be sharp to avoid another one of Brad's vicious swings, which would no doubt knock him into next week.

'Calm down,' said Byrd quickly. 'You don't want to do this…'

Brad didn't speak. He moved forward and raised the bat high above his head. Only when he was in the room he noticed Leonard, Timms, and Grearer, and realised he was outnumbered, but it was clear that he'd go down fighting.

'You need to put that down,' Byrd said, louder and clearer this time.

Brad's eyes flicked from Byrd to the others, then rested back on Byrd, as he was closer and posed a threat with the extended baton.

'Where's Phil?' asked Byrd.

Brad's eyes frowned. 'Phil who – you dare come near me!' he screamed at Leonard, noticing him edge closer from his left.

Leonard threw his palms up. 'Okay. Okay. Calm…'

Brad glared back at Byrd. 'I don't know a Phil. Now fuck off.' He raised the bat higher and took a step forward.

Byrd weighed up his options. The last thing he wanted was a clout from the big guy with a baseball bat, but he was a threat that had already swung for him. If he'd connected, it would have probably killed him.

He also knew DC Cornty was somewhere in the building.

As he figured, Brad swung again, but Byrd was ready, diving to the floor, just missing the bat that whizzed by his head. Once Brad was off-balance, Leonard acted quickly, charging towards him, knocking Brad off balance until he hit the floor. Leonard mounted him, using his left arm to block Brad, swinging the bat up from the floor. Without hesitation, Leonard laid into him, relentless pounding on his face until he dropped the bat and it rolled away a few feet.

Timms pulled Leonard off, dragging him up against his will. He was like a man possessed, wriggling like an animal.

'Jim – fucking calm down!' Timms shouted, struggling to hold his frantic arms back.

Byrd had rolled away and had climbed to his feet. Leonard finally lowered his arms and regained control of his breathing and uncharacteristic temper.

'I'm fine. I'm fine,' he said, pushing Timms off him, allowing the mixture of emotions that had built up over the past few weeks.

'You got him?' Byrd asked Timms and Grearer.

Grearer nodded, pulled the cuffs from his belt, and leaned down over Brad.

Byrd went to the open door and noticed the stairway going down. The handrail on either side was illuminated in soft blue neon strips. At the bottom, although it wasn't very well lit, he saw someone standing there looking up at him.

He didn't need to be a detective to recognise DC Cornty.

There was a sudden scuffle behind him in the room. Byrd turned quickly. Brad had managed to get up, wriggling Timms and Grearer off him, and charged through the open door directly at Byrd.

'Max!' Leonard screamed.

87

Tuesday Afternoon
Lingfield Point, Darlington

Byrd spun on his toes, seeing Brad charging right for him. He looked bigger against the light inside the room behind him, almost highlighting a rapid moving silhouette, growing bigger each passing second.

In his mind, knowing if he stayed where he was at the top of the stairs, he'd be flying down them. A hot wave ran through his body as he tensed and waited for him, steadying his feet, raising the baton high above his head.

When he felt Brad was close enough, he did two things almost at the same time. First, he swung the baton at Brad's face. Hard. This caused him to wail in pain as the end of the baton popped his nose, blood exploding from it instantly. And two, he dropped to his knees and rolled to the left, hurling himself into the wall.

Brad continued to travel and went tumbling past him, bouncing off the stairs, all the way down to the bottom with a huge thud.

Panting, Byrd rolled over and stood up.

'You okay, boss?' asked Leonard, stopping behind him, placing a hand on his shoulder.

Byrd managed a nod and stared down the stairs. There were four flights, with flat areas between each flight. It must have been thirty metres, maybe more. A long way to tumble.

The man at the bottom didn't move.

And DC Cornty had gone.

'Come on, Jim,' said Byrd. 'Cornty is down there some-where.'

Byrd went first, taking the steps quickly, sliding his hand down the blue neon railing. Leonard followed, with Timms and Grearer behind. Approaching the bottom it was clear that Brad hadn't moved. When Byrd got closer, the torch light illuminated the blood on the floor under Brad, the pool growing quickly.

They stepped over him and came to a set of double doors.

Byrd pushed down the handle and entered into a well-lit corridor that was twenty or so metres in length, but barely more than a metre wide. The floor was covered in a worn blue carpet that had seen better days and off-white walls, no doubt faded in time along with the rest of the place. There were doors on either side, roughly two metres apart; the last door on the right was the only one open, telling Byrd there was a chance Cornty had gone through there.

'Phil?' Byrd shouted. 'Phil. Please speak to me.'

No response.

Byrd, Leonard, and Timms moved on. Grearer had hung back to see to Brad, but it was evident, by his lack of pulse and pool of blood around his still body, he was dead. He called dispatch, asking for back up and medical attention.

Byrd approached the door on the right and shone the torch inside. He could see a wall on the left, indicating the space inside wasn't very big, unless it was another corridor.

'Phil? If you're in here, we're coming in. Talk to me.'

Byrd waited for a response, and when he didn't get one, turned and nodded to Leonard and Timms. They returned the nod, signalling they were ready. Byrd stepped in front of the door and kicked it fully open, the door swinging off its hinges and crashed into a wall. Byrd shone the torch inside. It was a small closet, roughly a metre wide, going back two metres at the most, filled with old cleaning equipment that hadn't been used in a long time, almost hidden under a mass of spider webs.

'Shit,' muttered Byrd.

Behind them, a little further up, a door opened quickly. They all turned and stared.

Cornty dashed out of it and ran towards the stairs, knocking Timms over, who was off balanced down on his knee. Timms fell back, cracking the back of his head against the wall.

'Fucker!' Leonard screamed, turning, and setting off after him. Timms followed and Byrd trailed. When it came to sprinting, Leonard was the man.

Byrd pulled his phone from his pocket and called Weaver. If Cornty made it up the stairs and through the room, there would only be Weaver blocking his path before he got out.

'Come on... pick up!' Byrd shouted into the ringing phone.

88

Tuesday Afternoon
Lingfield Point, Darlington

'Amy… can you hear me?'

'See… for ca… nat…' Weaver crackled.

Byrd sighed, pulled the phone from his ear to see the signal. It was on one bar. He bent down to Grearer, who was holding the back of his head. 'You okay, Donny?'

Grearer nodded.

'Amy, if you can hear me, go outside, shut the door, and put the crowbar across,' Byrd shouted into the phone. 'He's coming now!'

Timms was just ahead, a flight up. Leonard was out of sight, presumably through the room on his way to the exit.

'Who… hu fort…'

'Lock the door, Amy!' Byrd shouted clearly.

'Door?' There was a crackle.

'Yes. Yes. Lock the door.'

'Okay…' she said finally.

Byrd ended the call and helped Grearer to his feet, checking he was okay. He said he was so Byrd left him, taking the stairs two by two, propelling himself up with the aid of the blue-neon covered handrail.

He stepped into the room with the computer and through the door they'd first come through, out into the long corridor. He took a left and dashed towards the exit door.

No one was there.

The door was wide open.

When he stepped outside, he heard a commotion to the right: Leonard and Timms were on top of Cornty, wrestling with him, trying to keep him still while Timms attempted to put the cuffs on him, then after a struggle, managed to click them in place.

Leonard punched him for good measure, sending Cornty into a moment of dizziness.

To Byrd's left, just near the door, Weaver was on the floor, holding her head.

'Jesus, Amy.' He lowered to one knee, took hold of her. There was a cut to her forehead. 'What happened?'

'Fucker kicked the door open, hit me in the head.'

Byrd looked closer, noticed the cut starting to swell. 'Back up is coming.' He stood up, raced over to Cornty who was handcuffed on the grass on his front, bent down and grabbed his face, squeezing his cheeks so hard, his nails dug into his skin.

Cornty winced in pain, glaring up at him in defiance.

'You're going away for a very long time. Piece of shit.'

It wasn't long before the sirens were heard and back up arrived. An ambulance pulled up. Two paramedics saw to the cut on Weaver's forehead and then checked on Grearer, who'd suffered a cut to the back of his head when he'd been pushed into the wall at the bottom of the stairs.

They had Sarah McKay on a trolley inside the ambulance, hooked her up with fluids and an IV line to build her strength back up. It was obvious she'd been deprived of a decent intake of food and was hours away from dying. If she survived until the game on Friday, she'd have been lucky.

DCI Fuller came down to see the mess. As usual, he was less than impressed, and didn't mind showing it either.

'What a fucking shit show...' his final words were before getting back into his Jaguar F-Pace and speeding off, kicking up the gravel.

Byrd couldn't blame him. Fuller had been inside to see the computer where Cornty and Brad had used to run the games, then went down the stairs and through a door on the right, leading to the cold, concrete room where they found Sarah McKay asleep on a duvet covered in urine and faeces. The smell was atrocious.

Fuller was pissed off because there was only one left, meaning three of the missing four women had no doubt been killed. Byrd looked at it as a positive. They'd saved one of them and in the process, stopped whatever Cornty and Brad had planned for the future games. They'd let Mac inside later this afternoon to analyse the computers to see what more information he could extract.

What had bothered Fuller the most was the room next to where they found Sarah. Roughly twenty feet by twenty. In the centre of it was a wooden chair with ankle straps fitted to the legs and wrists straps fitted to the arms. To the side of it were drawers and a cupboard full of items that Stockdale had described were used in the games.

Fuller was right, Byrd had to admit. It was a shit show.

But the shit show was over. That's the way Byrd saw it.

After he watched Fuller disappear around the building, he went over to the ambulance and asked one of the paramedics how Sarah McKay was.

'Very weak,' the man in his late thirties said. 'But she'll live. You've saved her life. You should take credit for that, Detective.'

Byrd nodded appreciatively, and moved away, then checked in on his team, who were sitting on the grass over to the right, the afternoon sun beating down on their tired faces.

'Listen up, guys.' Leonard, Weaver, Timms, and Grearer looked up at him. 'You should be proud of yourselves today. I'm proud to have you on my team.'

89

Tuesday Afternoon
Lingfield Point, Darlington

Byrd arrived back at the station a little after three. The sun was still bright in the cloudless blue sky, and it was still hot. Probably the hottest part of the day. Byrd had put his thin black jacket on the passenger seat but even in his t-shirt, was sweating profusely. He tiredly pulled the key out the ignition and sighed heavily. He watched an elderly couple walking on the path beyond the perimeter.

He smiled, thinking about the future. About Claire. The idea of them at that age walking along, holding hands, after forty-plus years of a happy marriage. The thought faded away when he opened the door and sluggishly got out.

Leonard, Timms, and Grearer had gone back in Leonard's Insignia and were already back at the station. DC Phil Cornty had been taken away by additional units that arrived after they got the cuffs on him.

Weaver had been taken to the hospital for the cut on her forehead, so he mentally noted to check up on her very soon.

The senior forensic officers, Emily Hope and Jacob Tallow had looked inside the building, especially down in the room they found Sarah McKay. As she went missing with Lisa Felon, Lorraine Eckles, and Theresa Jackson, they needed to know from obtaining the DNA samples, they'd been there. They had proof that the body parts that had fallen from the blue Volkswagen van on the A66 had been Lorraine Eckles, but they needed to know if the others suffered the same fate. They'd assumed so, but assumptions weren't to be made without evidence to back it up. They'd need to speak with Sarah when she was well enough.

Byrd went through the sliding doors into reception. If he thought outside was hot, he had no idea he'd walked into a sauna.

'You okay, Max?' asked Lisa, the receptionist behind the desk.

Byrd gave a weary wave, and an equally tired nod before he went through the door and continued down the corridor into the office.

The round of clapping almost took him by surprise.

His eyes widened, unsure what was happening.

Fuller was standing at the end of the aisle, near the door to his office, clapping hard. Several others were also clapping, Leonard, Grearer, and Timms included. At first, he thought it was sarcasm, but by their looks of sincerity, and of course Fuller's too, it was genuine.

Byrd nodded at his peers in thanks. When he was close enough Fuller extended a solid hand.

'Well done, Max. We nailed the sonofabitch.'

Byrd shook his hand, lost for words.

'Come into my office, please,' said Fuller, placing a hand on his back, guiding him in. Byrd did and took a seat in front of his desk. Fuller closed the door, made his way around to his side, then sat down. The air inside was a blessing. Air-conditioned and bloody lovely.

Byrd didn't know what this was about. The last time he'd spoken with him, Fuller had stormed off.

'Max... I'm sorry how I went on before. It was unprofessional. A lot of how I felt was clouded by what I'd have to say to Barry Eckles.' He leaned and winced. 'You know how he can be sometimes.'

Byrd did.

'Although two of our own had proved to be on the different side of the law, it's because of you, Orion, and our team that this is finished.'

Fuller saw the doubt on Byrd's face.

'What is it?'

'We haven't found Linda,' replied Byrd. 'She was helping him.'

Fuller considered that for a moment, almost as if he'd put that into the back of his mind. 'No, that's true. We haven't. But there are no more online games and there's no more Mackenzie Dilton. So, for that, Max Byrd, I thank you for carrying out your role and doing it the best you possibly could.'

'Have you heard from Orion?'

Fuller nodded. 'I have. Fortunately, his leg – well, his knee – is only badly bruised. It isn't broken. They've strapped it. He's coming out today.'

Byrd raised his brows. 'That's good. That's really good.'

'How are you doing, Max?'

'Tired. It's been a tough one for all of us.'

Fuller agreed with a nod and smile.

'I was going to ask about Sarah McKay – have you heard from the hospital?'

Again, Fuller nodded. 'Yes. Just put the phone down before you arrived. She's sleeping. They've fixed her up with medicine and fluids, so hopefully, she'll be in a better state to talk soon.' Fuller stood up, extended his hand. 'Once again, Max. I'm proud to call you one of my DIs.'

Byrd shook it, thanked him, and left the office slowly as if his body was almost shutting down.

'Have some rest,' Fuller said through the open door.

'See you tomorrow, boss.'

On his way home, Byrd phoned Tanzy, who'd told him a similar story to what Fuller had, about the injury to his knee not being as severe as it felt hours earlier. Tanzy, although he wasn't meant to and should go straight home, told Byrd he'd pop over with some flowers for Claire to make sure she's okay and to say hi.

Byrd thanked him and ended the call as he pulled up outside his house.

Claire's friend's car was still there. They were probably on the sofa, resting up. He was glad her pills were working and equally glad she had company to cure her boredom. He couldn't wait to see her and tell her about his day. Usually, the last thing he'd want to do is sit with her, watching some crappy American show about people with less talent than a blade of grass, but tonight it's all he wanted to do. After the day he'd had, he wanted to sit, doing nothing and look at her and the little baby growing inside of her belly.

He unlocked the door and stepped inside.

'Hello?' he said, hanging his jacket on the hook to his right, then flicked off his shoes and put them in a rack near the bottom of the stairs. There was a sweet smell lingering somewhere, but Byrd couldn't place it. It was a mixture between perfume and baking, so instantly, the thought of homemade cakes or scones waiting for him on the kitchen worktop caused a rumble in his stomach.

'Hello?' he said, entering the living room.

The television was on. One of the American shows she loved to watch. Everything was in its place, apart from Claire.

And her friend.

On the small table in the middle of the room, were two glasses, half-empty, and beside them, two plates, one with a half-eaten scone on.

'Claire?' he said louder this time.

No response.

He frowned, wondering where they were. She was probably somewhere around the house showing her friend something. Another project for him, no doubt. She had, over the past couple of days, mentioned a list of things she wanted to do before baby Alan arrived. It was only natural, Byrd realised after reading up on pregnant women wanting to change things. Nesting, it was called.

He stepped out of the room, took a left and headed for the kitchen.

The unusual thing was there was no noise anywhere. Unless they were in the garden, lapping up the sun. The doctor had told her to rest, and sunbathing wasn't exactly an exhausting task. He might join them, lap up the rest of the day's sun which would still be warm.

As soon as he entered the kitchen he noticed the back door to his left was wide open. The cool breeze trickling in brushed his forearms where he'd rolled up his sleeves.

Then he stopped dead and glared at the floor near the back door.

'What the fuck?' he whispered, seeing all the blood.

C. J. Grayson

90

Tuesday Late Afternoon
Low Coniscliffe, Darlington

Slowly, he padded across the tiled floor over to the back door. The pool of blood was thick, roughly two feet in diameter, meaning there was a lot of it.

'Claire?' Byrd shouted.

He leaped down into the garden and glared around. There were two empty sun loungers in the middle of the grass, with a folded magazine on one of them and an empty glass beside the other.

'Claire!'

He went along the outside wall of the kitchen and looked around the back. There was no one there. If her friend's car was still here, that meant she was still here.

But where the fuck were they?

He dashed back into the kitchen, noticed something red on the floor, over to the left, in front of the door leading to the garage.

More blood.

'Claire?' he repeated. And still, no response. He went over to the blood. There wasn't as much as there was near the back door but looking closer, it seemed to lead towards the garage door. He leaned in, grabbed the handle, and very slowly opened it, not knowing what to expect.

'Jesus…' he said, then gasped.

In the middle of the garage floor was a woman, her eyes wide, staring up at the ceiling. It wasn't Claire. Regardless of that, Byrd panicked when he saw the enormous slit across her throat and the blood oozing from it. He jumped down, frantically looked around, but there was no sign of Claire.

'Claire!' he screamed.

He leapt back into the kitchen, took a left, and ran into the hallway. He checked the dining room. Empty. Then he darted upstairs, screaming her name over and over until he reached the landing. All of the doors were open apart from his bedroom, which was fully shut.

He dashed to his bedroom and opened the door.

Claire was tied to the chair, facing the door. Duct tape was wrapped around her ankles and over her mouth. She mumbled something but it was nothing more than a desperate moan.

'God...' Byrd said, stepping inside with his arms out to help her.

Then he froze when she came into view, stopping beside Claire, holding a bloody knife by her side.

'Welcome home, Max,' Linda Fallows said coldly.

91

Tuesday Late Afternoon
Low Coniscliffe, Darlington

Byrd couldn't speak, staring at Fallows, then at Claire, absorbing the fear in her terrified eyes.

'Linda... I don't understand.'

Fallows smiled. 'I didn't think you would, Max.'

He went to take a step forward but she lowered the knife to Claire's stomach, the tip of the blade touching her skin.

'I wouldn't do that if I was you...'

Byrd threw his palms up in surrender and suddenly stopped. 'Okay. Okay.' He took several deep breaths. 'I don't understand this, Linda. Talk to me...'

She sighed heavily, keeping the knife at her stomach, knowing Byrd wouldn't dare breathe near Claire, let alone try to save her.

'Mackenzie Dilton was like a son to me. Because of you, he's dead, Max.'

Byrd frowned and shook his head. 'What happened to Dilton was his own fault, and his fault alone. He's the one who broke the glass and fell through it. He killed himself.'

'He did not!' she screamed, startling both Claire and Byrd.

The whole house fell silent.

'Okay...' Byrd said, doing his best to remain calm. 'Please explain. Go on,' he added, nodding at her. The longer she spoke, the more time he had to come up with a plan.

'Like I said, he was like a son to me. When I was a criminal psychologist, I had the job of getting into his mind, learning why he'd done the things he'd done. I got to know him...' Byrd nodded, waiting for her to go on. 'He's very special, Max.'

After there was a lengthy pause, Byrd said, 'He killed people seven years ago, Linda. The last word I'd use to describe Mackenzie Dilton is special.'

Claire's eyed widened for a second, telling Byrd not to piss her off anymore.

Byrd gave her a slow nod, decided to say nothing more.

Fallows started laughing. Byrd wondered what was so hilarious. 'You – you think that was Mackenzie who killed them people seven years ago?' She tilted her head to one side. 'Well, you would do. After all... that's what I told you, wasn't it? Oh God... this was so easy, Max. How could I just walk into your department like that?'

Byrd felt an anger build up inside but didn't show her words were getting to him.

'I killed them people, Max. I did. They deserved all they got. They'd mistreated people all their lives and even killing them was not enough. I took Dilton under my wing after months of getting into his head. Yes, he'd violently attacked a man in Essex one night and had been enrolled on a program with me, so he wasn't exactly an angel, but once I knew him, Max, I realised he was a shy, young man, who didn't respond to the world like everyone else did. I blame his upbringing. It was awful. It's not what a child should go through – don't worry, I'm not getting into it. Let's just say his first attack was him expressing himself. During the time I got to know him, I realised there was more he had to give, otherwise he'd go crazy. So what better way to do it than to get back at people who really deserved it. You see, I know he wrote you and Orion a letter, saying he found this website online and he blah blah blah... the truth is, is that *I* found the website. And I contacted Dilton. I asked him if he wanted to unleash some of that frustration I knew he had deep down in him.'

'So killing people is the answer?' asked Byrd, shaking his head.

She nodded. 'If they deserve it, yes. This website was horrible. The things they did to victims on there is something I don't want to even think about. And to make money doing it – it's utter madness.'

'How did you find the website?'

'Someone – a contact – had sent me a link. I checked it out. I actually, to find out what it was about, joined up and paid the fee. After witnessing what happened as a watcher I knew I couldn't let this go on. You see, when getting to know Dilton, I realised he was a whiz kid on a computer. He did things beyond my comprehension. Codes. Algorithms. Jesus, Max. You name it. I told him about it, so he joined up. He had the skills to locate the players using their IP addresses, and well… you know what happened after that.'

'So,' said Byrd, 'what happens now?'

'Well, now I kill your wife, and the baby growing inside of her. Then maybe you'll feel like I'm feeling right now.'

Byrd looked at Claire. Tears ran down her cheeks.

There was no way he could let that happen, but he didn't know what to do. In all his years in the police, he'd never come up with this dilemma. If he tried to save her, Fallows would put the knife into Claire's stomach and kill their unborn son and her too.

He took a deep breath.

Fallows was still leaning over Claire with the tip of the knife at her stomach. Byrd calculated Linda's face was inches from Claire's. He looked at the tape around her mouth, hands, and feet. There was a loop of tape around her middle, holding her to the chair.

Maybe Claire could move a little, maybe just enough.

Byrd looked directly into Claire's eyes and nodded slightly.

Claire's eyes narrowed, not quite understanding, then it clicked. He needed her to do something to distract her. It was the only way out of this.

As Byrd raised his hands in surrender, Claire rocked to the side and gave her best headbutt into the side of Fallow's face, knocking her off balance a little. Byrd darted forward and wrapped his arms around Fallows, not thinking about the knife, and knocked her over the bed, onto the floor near the wardrobe with a thud. The knife flew from her hand and landed on the carpet. He punched her three times as hard as he could in the face, the second one popping her nose, the third one knocking her unconscious.

He jumped up, unwrapped the duct tape from Claire and held her for a long time while she cried.

After the police had come to arrest Fallows, it wasn't long before the house was filled with people. The forensic officers checked the house, particularly the kitchen and garage. The undertakers collected the body from the garage, and finally, the paramedics checked over Claire to make sure the baby was okay. Byrd and Claire grabbed some overnight things and left the house in the X5, checking into the nearest Premier Inn as she needed to get away from there.

Claire had explained that there'd been a knock at the door, and her friend had opened it to allow Fallows in, saying she was a colleague of Byrd's and was looking for him. Claire had asked her if she wanted a coffee so her friend had gone into the kitchen to make her one. Linda had followed her and killed her. She then came back with the bloody knife, demanding her to go upstairs.

Byrd counted his blessings.

He was a single moment away from losing everything.

Once Claire was settled in the hot bath filled with bubbles, Byrd answered his ringing phone and stepped into the bedroom for privacy. It was Fuller, who'd heard what had happened. Byrd briefed him and told him he was taking a few days off and that if Fuller wanted his report doing right there and then, he was retiring.

Fuller told him to take a few days off and come back when he was ready to.

'Look after your wife, Max. Family is the most important thing in the world. It's taken the last few years for me to realise that myself.'

'Speak soon,' Byrd said, and hung up, then threw his phone on the bed.

He went into the bathroom and sat down on the closed toilet seat and looked at Claire. Her eyes were teary, thin lines of mascara running down both sides of her face.

In the bath, the tip of her stretched stomach was just above the waterline. Byrd leaned forward, put a palm on it. Claire smiled and placed both her wet soapy hands on top of his.

'Everything is going to be alright, Alan,' Byrd said, then leaned over and kissed her forehead. He returned to the bedroom and yawned. What a day it had been. One he wouldn't forget for a long time.

His phone pinged with a text message. He picked it up. It was from Tanzy.

Heard what happened, Max. Hope you're both okay! Love you both very much. There's never a dull day in this fucking town.

92

Wednesday Morning
Police Station

Although Byrd had taken a few well-deserved days off to look after Claire, Tanzy, even with his bruised knee, had made it in to work just after nine. He'd dropped the kids off at school, which he seldom had the chance to do, then headed straight over, parking next to Fuller's Jaguar F-Pace.

He stepped out, and stretched, looking up at the sun. There wasn't a cloud in the sky. Today was going to be a beautiful day.

He passed Lisa in reception and smiled, then used his key card to get through the next sliding doors. Down the corridor, before he reached the office, he saw DC Leonard walking towards him. There was a skip in his step and a smile on his face.

'Morning, James.'

'Morning, sir. How's the knee?'

They stopped.

'Getting there. A little bruise won't stop me.'

Leonard smiled wider.

'What are you so happy about?' Tanzy asked, curious about Leonard's grin.

'We're getting a dog,' he said. 'A cross between an Alsatian and something else, I'm not sure. She's found a place online. Place in Romania. Dog shelter type place. Getting her at the weekend.'

'You already have a dog?'

Leonard nodded. 'We do. But she needs some company.'

Tanzy nodded this time, then narrowed his eyes. 'By 'she', who do you mean?'

'I think you know, boss.'

Tanzy would be lying if he said he hadn't noticed that Weaver and Leonard were close. They had been for a little while; it was obvious to see.

'Are you ready for this morning – did you get my text?'

'I did. I was coming to speak to you about it.'

They chatted a little while longer and come up with a plan, then parted ways, Leonard went to the canteen and Tanzy went into the office. His colleagues nodded in his direction, confirming they'd received his text message earlier and understood what was happening.

Yesterday, after they'd arrested Fallows and Cornty, they'd brought them back to the station to interview them both individually. It was interesting, to say the least.

Tanzy went in to see Fuller, who was sitting behind his desk, just coming off a phone call. They discussed the plan and Fuller gave him the go-ahead. He stood up, made his way through the office, out the other side, down the corridor towards IT. Mac didn't know the plan yet.

Tanzy knocked on the door.

'Come in,' Mac said.

Tanzy opened the door and stepped inside. Even though the window was open, the hot air coming in didn't help cool the room. The fan to the right of his desk didn't seem to be doing much, apart from circulating the hot air. 'Morning, Mac.'

Mac turned on his desk chair and smiled, lines of sweat trailing down his temples. 'Morning, boss. What do I owe the pleasure?'

'I've realised I hadn't updated you on what happened yesterday and the plan for today?'

His eyebrows furrowed.

Tanzy moved over to the desk and pulled out the spare chair, then sunk into it. 'About Dilton, Linda Fallows, and DC Phillip Cornty.'

'I heard about the arrests.'

'What did you hear?' Tanzy leaned forward a touch and tapped the desk with his right hand.

He turned further towards him, watching Tanzy's hand. 'That Detective Cornty had been arrested. He was the man responsible for the online website I tried to access for you.'

Tanzy nodded twice. 'What of Fallows?'

'That she was working with Mackenzie Dilton all along... she helped him.'

'Good. So the only thing I need to tell you is about the plan today,' Tanzy said.

He nodded, waiting, his hands hovering over his keyboard.

'Well, after speaking with Cornty yesterday, we made some discoveries. Let's just say I was surprised by this.' He smiled and leaned back. 'You see, I wondered how he had come up with the website. How a Detective Constable, who works for the police, came up with a website so intricate that *you* couldn't get in to. I couldn't fathom it out. You've got on to sites like that in the past. You're our number one man.'

'I know. But you were there. You saw me try. The website, had these—'

Tanzy raised a palm. 'Bear with me here...'

Mac fell silent, nodding.

'So if our lead IT guy couldn't get on to a site that a detective constable created, who by the way, had no genius IT training, let alone the ability to build firewalls so complex, they were unbreakable... it got me thinking.'

'About?'

'That someone must have helped him set it up. They must have. Someone with vast experience and expertise in the field.'

'Like whom?' Mac shook his head. 'Whoever it was, they were very talented. Whatever firewall they'd installed, trust me, was uncrackable. You saw it yourself.'

'I did, you're right. You know Denny from the Met?'

Mac nodded. Donald Dennett, aka Denny, had worked with Mac on several occasions in the past. If there was something Mac wasn't sure on, he'd ask Denny. The Metropolitan Police didn't mind as they helped each other out.

'What about Denny?'

'I got in touch with him. Sent him over the link.'

Mac frowned. 'Did he crack it?'

'He struggled to, but he got there in the end. You wouldn't believe it. The website had been set up on the dark web. That's why you couldn't get in. The original website was a front for the whole thing. Think of it like an onion. Attheend.com was only the outer layer.'

Mac nodded, intrigued. 'That makes sense.'

'The players and watchers paid via Bitcoin too. It was a genius idea. Almost untraceable…'

Mac widened his eyes, looked down at his desk in amazement, then smiled. 'That's a very clever way of doing it.'

Tanzy agreed with a wider grin. 'But… they didn't cover their tracks fully.'

Mac focused back on him. 'How do you mean?'

'IP address.'

'The IP address kept jumping all the time. Even I couldn't track it. What did he find?'

'Denny told me all about that. He told me if there's a trail, even something minute, there's a possibility it can be found.'

Mac waited. 'What was the IP address?'

Tanzy clapped his hands twice.

Mac frowned.

The door opened to the right, and DC Leonard walked in holding a closed laptop, followed by PC Weaver and PC Andrews. Leonard placed the laptop down on the desk.

'The IP address was located to that specific laptop,' said Tanzy.

Mac stared at it, said nothing.

'The only reason you'—Tanzy raised both hands to physically show inverted commas with his fingers—'couldn't crack the website, is because you're the one who set it up for him. You knew exactly how to get in because you designed it.'

Mac fell into a lengthy silence, looked away from the laptop he recognised as his own, and focused on the monitors in front of him. He didn't speak for nearly thirty seconds. The longest thirty seconds of his life.

Tanzy pulled a set of handcuffs from his pocket, threw them on top of the laptop. 'Put them on, Mac.'

'I – I…' He looked away and sighed.

'Now, Mac.'

He grabbed the cuffs and did as Tanzy asked, then Weaver and Leonard walked him out of the room.

Tanzy sighed heavily, leaned back in the chair, and closed his eyes.

93

Two months later,
Darlington Memorial Hospital

Claire held tightly onto Byrd's hand, her nails digging into his skin, sending waves of pain through his body, but he couldn't stop it now. Couldn't interrupt what was happening.

The head was visible, Byrd could see as he leaned over. A full head of black hair, just like his.

'I can see him, I can see him,' Byrd shouted excitedly, looking back at her red, sweaty face.

'Just breathe,' said one of the midwives, a woman bordering on the age of sixty who'd been a midwife since she left school. 'Come on, Claire. We're nearly there. On your next one, you need to give it one last push and he'll be here. You've done brilliantly.'

When the baby came out, the midwives took little Alan over to check him out. In that time, which felt like an eternity, Claire looked over with wide, searching eyes, asking Byrd where they'd taken her baby. Once he was checked and given the okay, the midwife brought him back to them.

'Everything is okay. There you go.' She lowered him onto her bare chest. 'He's beautiful.'

Claire started crying. Byrd couldn't control himself, crying more than she was, his body heaving in the emotions that a parent could only endure during these life-changing moments. Byrd stroked his little head with a trembling finger, then stood up, kissing Claire's sweaty forehead.

'You did it, Claire. There he is. Baby Alan.'

A while after, once the chaos had subsided, Byrd told Claire he needed some air. Before he left through the door, Claire and Alan were both asleep, holding each other. He stood for a moment, absorbing the beauty of it, realising their lives would never be the same again.

He made his way down the corridor and left through the security door, then to the lifts, pressing the button to call the closest one. From the four lifts, the left one opened. He stepped inside and pressed 'G' for the ground floor. Once he was outside he took out his phone and paused, feeling sad it wasn't his mother or father he was ringing first to tell them about their new arrival.

He found the number he wanted and pressed CALL.

It rang three times, then it was answered. 'What's happening, Max? She must be close by now.'

'Congratulations, Ori,' Byrd said. 'You're an uncle to Alan Max Byrd, born twenty-past four, weighing in at 9 pounds 3 ounces.'

'Aww, I'm thrilled to bits for you, mate. Well done. How's Claire?'

'She did amazing, Ori. She really did.' Byrd wiped a tear from his eye.

'Well, send her my love. Send them both my love. I can't wait to see him.'

'Midwife said she's staying in overnight. Something with having a different blood type so they need to monitor him to make sure he's okay. Nothing ever simple is it?'

'Well, you know what they say, don't you?' Tanzy replied.

'What do they say, Ori?'

'That there's never a dull day in this town. And today my friend, is no exception.'

Epilogue

Linda Fallows was charged with being an accessory to murder and taken back to Essex. After the courts had viewed her case, the jury had given her a life sentence. At her age, she wouldn't see another day outside of prison.

DC Phillip Stockdale, because of his involvement with the online games, taking part and telling the hosts to kill and make their victims suffer, was given twelve years. He'd be out just after his fiftieth birthday.

DC Cornty, the man responsible for running the online games, taking money from the people who logged on, and killing three victims, was sentenced to life in prison. He also wouldn't see the light of day again, metaphorically speaking.

Mac, the IT wizard in DFU, admitted to helping Cornty set the website up, and got eight years for his sins. Although it was he who aided Cornty in his horrific acts, he physically didn't kill or harm anyone.

Tanzy, Pip, and the kids decided to move to a new house. They'd had enough of where they were living and decided to move into a detached house near a great Primary School. The location would be ideal for Jasmine and Eric to go there and then a nearby secondary school afterward. Tanzy had promised to build Eric a den for his bedroom, not that he needed reminding by Pip, who, on a weekly basis, had mentioned it.

Byrd and Claire had settled at home with baby Alan, who as it turned out, didn't like sleeping. Claire spent most nights awake with him whilst Byrd slept, so he was able to go to work the following day. Byrd loved being a dad and recently asked Claire what they did with all the time they used to have before he came along. Regardless, he wouldn't change it for the world. When Alan was three months old, he got his first tooth. Claire had taken the most perfect photo of him and put it on a large canvas for the living room.

In his little village of Low Coniscliffe, the person responsible for breaking into houses had finally been caught by a security system that one of Byrd's neighbours, Jerry, had installed. It turned out to be a man in his fifties called Paul, who, for some reason, had turned bitter and couldn't stand his neighbours being happy, so went out of his way to cause a stir. Byrd had enjoyed personally taking him to the station after seeing the CCTV footage Jerry had showed him.

DCI Fuller stepped down, admitting to the superintendent Barry Eckles that he'd had enough of Darlington, and wanted to move back to the West Midlands. Eckles asked Fuller who, from his experience, would he advise stepping up from the current workforce. Without question, Fuller told him he'd recommend either Byrd or Tanzy, and that he'd speak with them about it. If one of them decided to take on the role of DCI, it left a gap for someone to step into the role of the new DI. Eckles had also asked Fuller who he thought would be a good replacement for DS Stockdale. Without hesitation, Fuller had mentioned James Leonard.

Let's just say things were looking good for Darlington and Durham Constabulary.

Acknowledgements

I hope you enjoyed 'No One's Safe'. It took me roughly eight months from typing the first word to publishing it as a complete novel. During that time there were: three drafts, a final copy, a proofreader stage, and an ARC reader stage too.

A big thank you goes to my family and friends. Their support in my passion is a blessing. I really appreciate it and could not do it alone. From my experience, as many writers will know, it's very hard finding the time to write when you work full time and have a family, not to mention day-to-day living and life's curveballs, so a big thank you must go to them for their patience.

A special mention to several Facebook groups such as Crime Fiction Addict, Crime Book Club, UK Crime Book Club, Books on the Positive Side, and Book Mark, for their continued support. There are many great individuals in these groups, some of those who are fellow writers and, almost every one of them, avid readers. In one way or another, they have supported me, whether it be friendship, light entertainment, or book recommendations. I would recommend checking out their pages. They are always looking for new members to share their passions for reading and crime.

I have to be honest and say No One's Safe wouldn't have been published the way it was without the following people.

James Leonard (who enjoys reading Linwood Barclay and Blake Crouch) took the time to go over this and, with his knowledge and skills on police procedures, he guided me where I was blind and picked up on several parts which didn't quite fit together. It was his idea to update this novel with the use of Bitcoin and information regarding the dark web so credit to him for making it more current. Thank you Jim for your never-ending support with my writing, believing one day, I'll be any good! And of course, for our long friendship over all these years.

Shez Barker (an avid reader who enjoys Chris Carter and Barbara Copperthwaite) connected with me via social media and, after plenty of social interactions, I now consider her a good friend. She is very busy up in Inverness, being a nurse, which as we know in current times, is a very time-consuming and demanding role in our society. Using her spare time to proofread this is massively appreciated, picking up on some very valuable points which have sharpened this novel up. I want her to know I'm very grateful for that. As I've previously mentioned, her support stretches back before I published my debut novel and that's something I'll always remember. Thank you for occasionally checking up on me to make sure I haven't gone mad and to make time my myself, as she knows family life can get hectic.

Another special mention needs to go to my ARC reader group. I have learned a lot from these valuable readers; much of which, I would have missed. A special thanks to Mark Fearn, Dee Groocock, Amanda Oughton, Angela Lamb, Kathryn Defranc, Carol Drinkwater, Anne Mosedale, Terri Lewis, Vikki Bradley, Jim Ody, Janice Elmer, and Marion Harris. Without you guys, this novel would not be what it is.

My biggest thank you goes to my wife, Becky. An absolute gem who holds our family together like glue, letting me hide away and write while she keeps the children busy. Thank you for believing in me. Without you, I couldn't do this.

Some of you have read all of my books so far and have continually shown your support via my social media profiles (Facebook, Instagram, etc.) with your kind likes, generous shares, and valuable comments. If there's one thing I've learned so far, it's that one person can only do so much or take something so far. It's the people around him;

the team; the support. So my last thank you is to you, the reader. You make all of this possible.

Thank you.

About the Author

C. J. Grayson has self-published his fourth novel eight months after he released his third novel, Never Came Home. Writing will always be hard (if you write, you'll know what's involved), but it's a passion he's always loved and he'll continue to do it for as long as he can. He loves reading crime thrillers, watching supernatural / horror films, and drinking gallons of coffee.

In his earlier days, he did an apprenticeship in Pipefitting and worked in Engineering and Construction. He completed his HND in Mechanical Engineering and a Level 6 Diploma in Business Management.

He's aged 32, lives in Darlington, in the North East of England, with his wife, Becky, and their three boys, Cameron, Jackson, and Grayson. If you didn't know, his pseudonym is a combination of his children's names. He dedicates his writing to them in the hope it'll be something they can be proud of in the future.

His next book will be a stand-alone (or the first novel in a detective series – he hasn't decided yet) based in Manchester. There's a very good chance he'll return to Max and Orion to see how they're combatting the crime in Darlington.

If you can spare a few minutes and enjoyed this book, he'd really appreciate some feedback on Amazon and/or

Goodreads. Your thoughts and support are more valuable to him than you'll ever know. They keep him up till the early hours writing.

Keep up to date with his current work and updates regarding future novels through his website and following social profiles. You can also sign up to his Newsletter by going on www.cjgraysonauthor.com and filling in the very short form at the top of the page. You will get updates on progress, exclusive giveaways, and news before the rest of the world does, so feel free to sign up.

Website - www.cjgraysonauthor.com
FB - www.facebook.com/cjgraysonauthor/
IG - www.instagram.com/cjgrayson_writer/
Twitter - www.twitter.com/CJGrayson4

Thank you.